THE LAST TIARA

A Novel

THE LAST TIARA

A Novel

M. J. ROSE

The Last Tiara
By M.J. Rose

Copyright 2021 M.J. Rose
ISBN: 978-1-952457-09-8

Published by Blue Box Press, an imprint of Evil Eye Concepts, Incorporated

Dedication

To my father, 100 years young and counting, for teaching by example how important it is to never give up, enjoy the work you do and love unconditionally.

"Every heart has its own skeletons."
— Leo Tolstoy, Anna Karenina

Author's Note

The tiara (magnified below) in this novel did indeed exist, and was catalogued, but has not been seen since this photo was taken in 1921-1922 and appeared in a 1925-26 catalog.

A selection of the 406 Romanov jewels featured in Russia's Treasure of Diamonds and Precious Stones by A.E. Fersman, 1925-26.

Foreword

"Isobelle, listen," she whispers. "It's time. I need to tell you about my last evening on this Earth and the days and nights leading up to it. Honor must be paid. Justice must be done."

She watches her daughter shift in her sleep, not knowing if she can hear her, but Sophia continues, nonetheless.

"I was standing on the corner when I saw him. Was it possible it really was him? With the snow falling so heavily, I couldn't be sure. Then he hunched up his shoulders the way I remembered, and I was certain. He always stood as if he was uncomfortable.

"I shivered. From the cold. Or the memory. Or perhaps both. Just like that, while standing on the corner of Madison Avenue, I was suddenly catapulted back in time to St. Petersburg more than twenty-five years before, to the last time I saw him. Over two decades had passed. Lifetimes lived. Loves lost. Treachery and death stood between us. And there he was.

"After all that I had endured and dealt with and survived, how was it possible that we were one crosswalk away from each other? And in the snow? As if nature herself was playing a game with us."

For this last year, Sophia has missed touching her daughter's hair, kissing her cheek. Although she has no corporeal presence, she reaches out and tries to smooth down Isobelle's ebony waves. Nothing happens. She tries harder. A single curl settles. Sophia sighs, feeling a deep satisfaction, and continues.

"He didn't see me. Even though he stood right across from our house. Even though he was staring at our building. Even though he had to be headed my way, looking for me. I've told you so many times, I never believed in coincidences. After all those years, he could not just happen to be there.

"I stepped off the curb to cross to him, so preoccupied with keeping my eyes on him that I didn't see the car. Or because of the swirling snow, the car didn't see me. I heard a screech. I felt a sudden jolt. Then pain. Everything was suddenly quiet. Like those winter nights in Russia when it seemed the snow muffled every sound in the whole world, and all I could hear was my own breath…and your father's.

"As I lay there on the pavement, I realized with an urgency as terrible as the pain that I should have told you our story long before. Instead of waiting for a time when I felt strong enough to face those memories. I shouldn't have kept them buried in that secret city deep inside of me. But sharing them would have meant suffering it all over again. The longing. The guilt. And greatest of all, the loss.

"So, I left you with a mystery. And I fear, not enough clues to help you solve it. My story is one of Mother Russia and its demise. Of the war and the tsar and tsarina and their daughters and their fortunes. Of the holy men and the psychics and the Bolsheviks and their revolution that came and wiped out everything we knew. Of starving and stealing. Of pity, pathos, and desperation. The story of your heritage and your influences—all the things I could never bring myself to share with you before because it is such a tale of sorrow. And my darling Isobelle, I wanted you to have only sunshine and joy. And because, even in New York, far away from the onion domes and frozen Neva and the terror, here in this land of freedom and hope, my fear controlled me.

"I wish you could have known your father. You are so like him. Your aristocratic features, your height, your jet-black hair and storm cloud gray eyes. They all come from him. Even without his influence, you've inherited so much from him—your curiosity, your willingness to meet a challenge head on. The way you remain determined despite your fears, even to the point of being stubborn. Most of all, I see him in the way you believe there is always a solution. Nothing ever broke your father, and I hope nothing will ever break you.

"Isobelle, can you hear any of this? It's important. It's time. You need to know that once your father risked his life to provide an insurance policy to protect us. But instead left us with a curse responsible for our separation and death. First his. Then mine. And now, you are about to discover it, and you will have to deal with it. What will you think, you curious darling? You determined soul.

"I should have answered your questions when you asked them instead of brushing them off with a wave of my hand and a curt caution that we can never go back, so why do you need to know?

"I was so wrong, my darling Isobelle. You did need to know. And now, you need to find out why this thing mattered so much. Why so many years later, the truth about it is worth hunting down. Why your father begged me to never let it leave my possession. Why something that was once thought to be so valuable proved to be nothing but glass, so easily broken. Like our dreams."

Chapter 1

Isobelle Moon
New York City
November 1948

Walking home from 57th Street and Fifth Avenue at the end of the workday the night before Thanksgiving, there's a sense of anticipation on the crowded streets. People are rushing home, excited about the upcoming holiday. I wish I felt that way. Instead, I'm dreading the elaborate dinner at my Aunt Lana's house, where there will be one less place-setting at her table.

Reaching 78th Street and Madison, I cross at the light and stop at Gentile's, where my mother bought our groceries for years. Through the window, I see all the last-minute shoppers buzzing inside and decide not to venture in. The wait will be too long for the few items I thought I'd buy for dinner—fixings for a salad and an omelet. But Sal, one of the salesclerks, has noticed me. He waves, holds up an apple, and motions for me to come in. Despite the crush of people, I can't ignore the gesture. Since I was a little girl, Sal has never failed to give me an apple whenever my mother brought me in with her when she came to shop.

Gentile's opened the same year she and my Aunt Lana bought the brownstone just a few blocks up. That the grocery store delivered seemed the height of luxury to the two young women who'd escaped from Bolshevik Russia and opened a furniture and art restoration business in Manhattan.

I hurry in, take the proffered fruit, give Sal a quick kiss on the cheek to thank him, and then wish him and his family a happy holiday.

"You're spending it with your aunt and uncle and the rest of the family, yes?" he asks in that way people do when they're worried you are going to be alone.

"I am."

"Good. That's what your mama would want."

I hold up my hand in parting, suddenly not trusting my voice. Sal's kindness has reduced me to tears. It's been a year since my mother died, and I thought the worst part of the grief was over. But for the last week, I seem to have regressed. I've been having dreams about her every night. And it's always the same.

I'm someplace I've never actually been, but my mother once described to me—the Alexander Palace in Tsarskoe Seloe in Russia, where she spent time as a youngster. I'm on the mainland, looking across a pond at my mother, who is stranded on the shore of the Children's Island. Because of the fog, I can't see her clearly. She's trying to tell me something, but the same fog muffles her voice. A man, who I think must be my father, waits with me. If I just turn to my left, I could see his face. Instead, I walk toward the rowboat on the shore. My father can wait, I need to row across the pond and get my mother and find out what she is trying to tell me. I start to walk toward the boat, but at that point, the dream always ends.

I wake up frustrated and sad. And the feeling lingers while I get dressed and have my coffee and toast.

I've been thinking the upcoming holidays are what's making me miss her with renewed vigor and prompted the dream. Thanksgiving and Christmas were major occasions for my mother and Aunt Lana. The first, a celebration of the country they'd adopted, the second filled with memories of families and friends they'd left behind. Our hall closet has boxes filled with decorations and menus my mother painted by hand. We made an event out of pulling them out at the start of the season, and together we'd turn the apartment into a wonderland of wintry ornaments and frills. My mother loved tradition and created one that makes me ache to think about.

Going around the table at Thanksgiving, my mother would ask each of us to list three things we were grateful for that year—my mother going last. Her third item was always the same. She'd look at me, blow me a kiss and say she was grateful most of all for her little *zaja*—the only Russian word she used—her little bunny.

I reach the crosswalk at 84th Street just as the light turns red. While I wait, I glance at our building. A short flight of stairs leads to the first-floor portico, and an iron railing surmounts exterior Doric pilasters and square columns. The most interesting architectural feature is the irregular fenestration of the façade. The bay windows have stained glass transoms in emerald green, lavender and royal blue colors. That configuration is repeated directly above it on the second floor. The single windows on the remaining upper floors are all topped with elaborate leaf moldings. A Greek Key band decoration extends across the front and side of the building.

After spending the last three years in Tennessee in a prefabricated house in a newly manufactured city, I have a renewed appreciation for our turn-of-the-century red cast brownstone. Erected between 1890 and 1892 by a building developer named Robert B. Lynd, it was designed by the noted architect John Duncan, who was also the designer of Grant's Tomb and the Grand Army Plaza in Brooklyn. In 1899, its owner, Alice Grace Holloway, hired the architect Albert Fredrick D'Oench to make some modest alterations to the interior. It must have been a successful effort since they married and lived there together until 1914.

As usual by this time of day, the first-floor workshop lights are off. But I'm still not used to seeing the second floor where we live being dark. My mother would have been home by now, sipping a glass of wine, listening to the radio and reading a mystery. The lights are on in Aunt Lana's third-floor apartment. I'm sure she's baking in preparation for tomorrow's feast. Aunt Lana cooked, and my mother was in charge of bringing the wine since she was a mediocre cook—mostly out of impatience. A trait I've inherited, just as I've inherited the job of bringing the wine tomorrow.

The lights are also on in Lana's son's fourth-floor apartment, where he lives with his family. My mother and aunt always hoped Michael, who is two years older than me, and I would wind up as a couple, but we're more like siblings. Competitive siblings at that. Michael is an architect as well, at his own firm. Both of us were inspired by his father, Uncle Paul, and studied at his alma mater, Cooper Union.

The light changes. I cross the street, walk up the stairs, and put my key in the lock and turn. I push open the front door, enter the vestibule, and inhale the subtle aroma of varnish, lemony furniture polish, wax, turpentine and paint—the scent of the restoration business. The perfume that has welcomed me home for as long as I can remember.

I climb the flight of well-worn marble stairs and let myself into our apartment. Even though it's mine now, I still think of it as *ours*. Probably because I haven't moved a pillow or vase since I moved back in.

I hang my coat, hat, and pocketbook on the fanciful cast iron hall tree made to look like graceful tree limbs and leaves and walk into my mother's homage to English cottages and gardens. Everything flowery appealed to her, from the perfume she wore to the lilac and leaf Limoges dinnerware, to the wisteria-patterned curtains. Each room is a mix of four Victorian colors as the style dictates—in our case, lavender, deep pink, leaf green, and forget-me-not blue. Cozy and inviting, the apartment is filled with chintz-covered overstuffed couches and chairs, fabulous bric-a-brac she collected over the years, and needlepoint pillows. She loved mixing patterns that shouldn't have worked together but always did.

I grew up living with all this visual clutter, which might explain part of the reason my style runs to Bauhaus modern. My plan is to bring the apartment into the mid-century with a single color—a cooled down pale celadon green—more glass, some chrome, sleeker furniture and nary a pillow in sight. I yearn for uncluttered versus this crowded mishmash my mother created, regardless of how perfectly it all came together and how charming it looks.

I haven't done anything to it yet. Not because I've wanted to keep it as a shrine, but because it's taken me a while to figure out how I want to redecorate and what modifications I want to make without destroying the architectural integrity of the original building.

In my bedroom, I change into work clothes and then head for the kitchen. Before I tackle the first job I've set for myself, I slice up and plate the apple Sal gifted me, and add some cheese and crackers to go with it. I pour a glass of wine, turn the radio on to the news, and sit at the table with what I suspect will wind up being the sum total of my supper. I have some of Aunt Lana's soup in the refrigerator if I get hungry later. Worried about me, knowing I don't take the time to cook, mothering me the best she can, Aunt Lana keeps my larder stocked. It helps her deal with the loss of her best friend and business partner, the *sister of her soul* as she says, reminding me that I'm not the only one my mother left behind.

It has been a long and strange year filled with great loss and seismic change, and I haven't minded any of my aunt's mothering. Twelve months ago, I was living in Oak Ridge, Tennessee, where I'd been since graduating from architecture school in 1943. At ten o'clock on the night of December 9th, my aunt called. In a voice punctuated by sobs, she told me that my mother had been hit by a car while crossing Madison Avenue on her way home. The doctors had done what they could, but she'd died within two hours of reaching the hospital.

I returned to New York the following day. After the funeral, I stayed for the rest of the week and then—still in shock I realize now—returned to Tennessee and my job. I am a junior architect for the prestigious firm Skidmore, Owings & Merrill.

In 1942, construction had begun in three different locations across the United States to build fully functional, highly secret cities from scratch in order to facilitate the making of the first nuclear bomb. The architectural firm of W. C. Kruger was chosen for Los Alamos, G. Albin Pehrson for Hanford, and SOM for Oak Ridge.

Now that the Manhattan Project was over, each firm was charged with transforming the secret cities into livable ones.

Other than my friend Charlotte, who'd started out with me but left after a few months, I was the only female architect on the Oak Ridge site. There are only two full-fledged female architects employed by our firm. The other, Natalie Griffin de Blois, a few years my senior, spent the war years in the New York office.

We *architectresses*, as we are sometimes referred to—and often with derision—are an anomaly in our male-dominated profession. There have only been a handful of women architects in the history of our field, all of whom I can name. Hell, at most universities that offer architecture programs, females weren't allowed to matriculate until 1942—and that was only a result of male enrollment dropping during the war.

A side benefit for the corporations that hire us is that we are paid less than our male counterparts. We know it, but we don't complain. Architecture is a chummy men's club, and to be allowed entrance is a feat in itself. We know we are expected to quit when we get married and have our babies, perhaps to return in middle age when our chickens have left the roost, or not. But in the meantime, our bosses can get twice as much out of us as most men. We know we are tolerated. We accept the attitudes and patronizing that often greets our ambition all because we are so passionate about design and building. Other than Julia Morgan, credited with being a winner in a man's world and a true anomaly, we have had few real heroes. So few of our sex have gained any prominence in the field at all.

But that's what I dream of, and have since I was just

nine years old, and Uncle Paul took Michael and me to his construction site. We went up an elevator 1250 feet to the roof of the almost-completed structure. We stood in the clouds and looked out at New York City spread out below us.

To my young mind, Uncle Paul's skyscraper as I called it—but more famously known as the Empire State Building—was the most amazing thing I'd ever seen. And I finally understood exactly what it was my uncle did for a living. Turning away from the view, I looked up at him and told him that when I grew up, I wanted to be just like him and build the next tallest building in the world.

I remember how he smiled and put his hand on my shoulder.

"I promise if that's still what you want to do when it's time for you to go to college, I'll move heaven and Earth..."—he gestured to the city below us—"I'll move all of this to help you. There's nothing that competes with the satisfaction of putting your imagination to use and creating something beautiful and worthwhile. Just promise me if anyone tries to tell you can't do it, you'll look them straight in the eye and say, *'Watch me'* and never give up."

Until that day, I was the kid at school the others teased for being so shy. I was the one so bad at sports that no one ever wanted me on their team. I wasn't popular. They made fun of me for not having a dad. And in every situation, confronted with conflict, I always backed off and let them all defeat me. But that afternoon, I began to change. I had found a desire stronger than my insecurities. Standing on that roof, I'd had a glimpse of another world.

I might not be beautiful or witty or charming or sexy, but I have as good a sense of design as any man I've worked alongside and am as obsessed with the art and science of architecture as any of them are.

That I have not been taken as seriously as my male counterparts, that I am on a different trajectory when it comes to promotions and held to higher standards than they are, has exhausted and depressed me when I've allowed myself to think about it. So I've made it my business not to. For the most part.

I inherited my father's idealism—which allowed me to dream about a career—and my mother's determination—which made me stick with it no matter how hard it was.

But back at Oak Ridge, after my mother's death, I lost my way. Modifying our prefab buildings didn't require much thinking. Unchallenged creatively, I was left with too much time to think. To miss my mother. To worry that my career was stagnating the longer I spent doing work by rote in Tennessee. And so, in October, when Frank Williams asked me if I would be willing to return to New York, I jumped at the chance. The firm had been engaged to build corporate headquarters for Clarion, one of the top magazine publishers. The clients—a husband and wife—had specifically asked if there were any women on the team. The majority of their magazines cater to women, and their staff is predominately female. They believed it was important to have female representation on SOM's part.

I said yes. And now that I'm back and settled in at work, I plan to finally do some much-needed renovation on our apartment this winter before we break ground on the Connecticut site this spring.

Done with my snack, I put the dish into the sink, pour some more wine and, bringing the glass with me, head for my mother's bedroom. I've chosen the hardest task first. Once I tackle her private sanctuary, the other rooms will be easy. It's not that I want to wipe the house of her memory, but I need to make the apartment mine, not keep it as a tribute to her.

My plan is to turn her bedroom into a library/office, repaint and redecorate the foyer, living room and dining room. I also want to freshen up my room, which hasn't changed since I was in high school. The kitchen and the two bathrooms are fine as is.

I stand in the middle of my mother's bedroom, sip the wine, and look around. The cabbage rose-patterned wallpaper is faded. The French style, nineteenth-century armoire and matching bed, all treated with pale pink and white antique washes, have some nicks. All they'll need for me to sell them is a few touchups—something easy for me to do since I used to work in the shop during summer breaks from school.

There are five Victorian birdcages, painted maroon and hanging from fern-colored velvet-wrapped chains over the windows that face east. Inside each cage is a small bejeweled bird that my mother picked up from some street fair long ago. She washed them with white vinegar twice a year so when they picked up the morning sun, they glowed. I called them Tiffany birds, after the grand jewelry store that my mother and I loved to visit. I don't think I can bear to sell these, but I can hang them in the workshop.

The light, gauzy petal pink curtains that pool in delicate swirls on the floor on either side of the windows will have to go, as will the wall-to-wall ivy leaf-patterned carpeting that finishes off the room and gives you the sense that you are in a garden, even in winter.

It is a beautiful bedroom, and I love it. But it is my mother's. Done in her style. And mine is wholly different. And so, the first order of business is to strip off the wallpaper. To accomplish that, I will need to move the furniture to the middle of the room. Since my mother was fairly obsessed with cleanliness, the heavy furniture—bed, armoire and vanity—are on rolling casters so I can move them on my own with minimum effort.

As I push the bed away from the wall, an aroma faintly scents the air—*Une Belle Rose* created by L'Etoile perfumers, who date back to the 1780s. My mother had told me once that my father bought it for her on the black market during the revolution. She never used another perfume, and it was as much a part of her as her ever-present necklace of miniature enamel eggs. Seven my father had given her—one for each year they knew each other—and the one from her parents, in honor of her working as a nurse during the First World War. Other than that necklace, her only other jewelry was a plain Bulova gold watch on a black leather strap. My mother was as simple and modest in her personal style as she was boisterous and extravagant when it came to home décor.

I glance over at the vanity with its big round mirror. Yes, there is her bottle of *Une Belle Rose*. Almost empty. In my memory, I summon a picture of my mother sitting on the dusty rose velvet bench, preparing for the day—rolling up her auburn hair, applying just a touch of rouge to her cheeks, and then pressing her fingers to the perfume bottle, tipping it over and then lightly touching her wrists and then the nape of her neck so that even her hair carried the rose scent.

I bite the inside of my cheek to stop myself from slipping into sentimental tears. I'm too emotional. As a little girl, I was often teased for crying when criticized. While I haven't gotten any tougher, I have become an expert at hiding my feelings. Except from my mother, who could always see right through me.

But now is not the time to give in. I have a job to do. Falling victim to the memories every object here holds will only slow me down. And my time is limited. Once February arrives, I'm going to be doing so much traveling to the Connecticut site, I won't have a lot of these long nights. I know it would go faster to hire someone to help, but I feel like doing it alone is a rite of passage I need to honor.

I move the bed a few feet farther into the center of the room. Standing, hands on hips, I inspect the wall I'm going to attack first. There is a distinct change in color where the headboard protected the wallpaper from the sunlight. The hidden roses are surprisingly vibrant. I'm shocked at just how much brighter they are, and how much attention they call to themselves.

I approach and run my hand over their deep red hues and feel an irregularity about eighteen inches wide and just as long.

I tap on it gently. It sounds hollow. My bedroom is on the other side of this wall. I need to remove the paper to see what's there. I start to work at a corner, carefully pulling. I've been at it for a minute or so when I realize it doesn't matter. I am going to be stripping all the wallpaper off anyway. With a firm grasp, I jerk at the panel. The paper rips—the noise a violent punctuation to the action.

I let it fall to the floor in a curl.

There *is* a niche in the wall. Wedged between the beams, the nook is roughed out in plaster. And tucked inside is a rounded leather box about eight or nine inches long and five inches high. It's so dusty I can't tell its color or condition.

How long has this box been hidden away here? Was the cubbyhole from before my mother's time, or did she create it herself?

Reaching in, I take out the box. It doesn't weigh much. Behind it is a manila envelope. I place the box on the bed, remove the envelope, and take both items into the kitchen, where I set them on the table.

Grabbing a dish towel, I wipe the box clean. I'm careful not to dislodge the clasp affixed to the top. I peer at it. Embossed on its leather covering are words in Cyrillic, which I can't read.

"We are American," Mom would say to me whenever I asked her to teach me Russian.

"But all of my ancestors are—"

"Dead, Isobelle. All of your ancestors are dead, and I have nothing of theirs to give you. You'll never meet them. Never need to talk to them. America is our present and our future. The past needs to stay there. There are people we know, your Aunt Lana and I, who have wound up buried alive by their memories. That will not happen to you."

She and my Aunt Lana and many of their Russian friends had worked hard to minimize their accents and made an effort to speak to each other in English. We ate upstairs a lot with my aunt, uncle, and Michael. Whenever the meal was the hearty Russian fare the women had grown up eating, my mother would often descend into a dark mood. It seemed she wanted to wipe out every reminder of Russia that she could—except for her necklace. There were so many stories I didn't know. Tales I yearned to hear.

Despite my curiosity, I decide to open the manila envelope before working on the box's stuck clasp. I slip open the back with my fingernail. Inside are two cream-colored, heavy stock envelopes. The size that might enclose a personal note. They are not addressed and have no postage.

On the back is a name and address, engraved and printed in black ink.

Alford Reed
6 East 57th St
6th Floor
New York, New York

I open the first envelope and pull out the folded letter inside.

May 16, 1930
Dear Mrs. Moon,
This is a receipt for 4 diamonds ranging in size from .2 carats to one carat and 8 large paste sapphires approx. 20 carats each. $1500.
Respectfully,
Alford Reed

The next letter, also from Mr. Reed, is dated approximately two months later and is for ten diamonds of similar sizes, and the total is for $3750.

I don't realize I am holding my breath until I expel it. These two receipts total more than $5000. During the Depression, that was a serious sum of money. I do the math—I was eight years old in 1930. That was the year my mother and aunt bought this building. They'd been renting here since 1923 from the owners who lived abroad. It was an ideal brownstone for them. My aunt took the top two floors for her family. My mother and I lived on the second floor. The first floor was the workshop. And the storefront on Madison Avenue, with its own entrance, housed Bespoke Art & Antiques, where they sold the old, ruined pieces of furniture and paintings they had bought for next to nothing and restored to their former glory.

No eight-year-old wonders how her mother can afford to buy anything. But I do remember my mother once mentioning how lucky she and my aunt had been that the building had come up for sale during the Depression when everything was so much cheaper. Had she sold whatever had been in the leather box in order to finance the purchase? And if so, why had she kept the case? And not just kept it—but hidden it.

Damn you, I want to shout at her. Why not just tell me what happened in Russia? Why keep it all a secret? I knew. She'd repeated it hundreds of times whenever I questioned her refusal to share an entire part of her life with me.

She was worried the weight of the memories would bury her alive.

And now I had found one of those memories. A fragment of her past. Maybe it would reveal some of the things she'd refused to.

I get a knife from a drawer and gently work the box's hinge, careful not to damage it. After a few moments, I feel it give. I lift the lid, not expecting to find anything at all. The inside is lined in cream-colored silk, and sitting in a half-circle depression is a piece of open-work metal.

I'm not sure what I'm looking at. Lifting it out, I turn it one way and then the other. I run my finger over the lacework of what appears to be silver and feel tiny metal points sticking up. One is sharp enough to scratch my skin, and a tiny drop of blood beads on the surface. I put my finger into my mouth. I realize the points must be prongs, pried up to remove stones, but no one bothered to push them back down.

I don't understand. Why did my mother keep this skeleton once she sold the diamonds it held? What good was the silver frame? Why did it mean so much to her that she'd kept this remnant? And if it had meant so much, why had she sold it at all?

Chapter 2

Sofiya Petrovitch
Petrograd
April 1915

Sofiya entered the Winter Palace through the Ambassadors'
entrance, accompanied by two other young women. Once
inside the Jordan Hall, she spied the head of the Sisters of
Mercy nursing unit waiting patiently for them.

"I am Nadezhda Filosofova. Welcome to the Tsarevich
Alexei Nikolayevich Hospital, housed in the former
staterooms of the Winter Palace," the matron said and then
blushed. She was obviously nervous.

Sofiya stole a look at her companions, and they shared a
smile. Certainly, of all the nurses Matron welcomed, none
needed less explanation for where they were, but the women
were polite and said nothing.

"If you'll follow me to the Jordan staircase, so named
for—" Flustered, Matron stopped herself and apologized.

"I'm sorry, Your Imperial Highnesses...of course you know where you are and more than I do about the history of the Palace..."

Grand Duchess Olga Nikolaevna, at nineteen the elder of the two grand duchesses, spoke for her sister, Tatiana, aged seventeen, and their childhood friend Sofiya, who was also nineteen. "It's quite all right, Matron. We know you're just doing your job."

The chief nurse relaxed visibly. "On all the landings on this and other staircases are various areas you'll need to learn." She pointed. "Over there is the staff dining room, the head physician's room, a reception room, the nurses' station, laboratory, and X-ray room. Now, if you'll come this way."

The women followed Matron up the ornate eighteenth-century white marble staircase. As they ascended, she noticed the walls were painted white, the moldings all gilded, and tall gray granite columns still stood like sentries. The richly detailed painting of gods at Olympus looked down on them as they always had.

None of the royal residence's grandeur was gone despite its transformation into a hospital. The gilt decorations, crystal sconces, and chandeliers still glittered. The structure of the building and its décor remained intact. But nothing else was the same. Instead of expensive perfumes, the smell of antiseptic permeated the air. Instead of servants bustling about, there were doctors and nurses. Instead of lofty silence was the hum of activity. The sense of calm had been replaced by urgency.

"We know the building as a palace, not an infirmary, so it is very helpful of you to show us around," Olga said kindly.

Matron bobbed her head. "Thank you for saying so, Your Imperial Highness."

"Maybe you could just call me Olga and my sister Tatiana and our dear friend Sofiya. We don't want any special treatment or to attract any attention. The wounded men deserve all the attention."

All the duchesses had been raised to be respectful, but Olga was the most compassionate. Of course, like her siblings, she was spoiled. And she had a terrible temper and was prone to moodiness, but she was bright and straightforward and generous to a fault. She was the sister Sofiya was closest to in both age and friendship. They both loved to read and keep up with the news and gossip. Olga confided about all her various amours and crushes to Sofiya, who had yet to meet anyone she even wanted to flirt with. But Olga insisted she'd find someone soon.

Sofiya's mother, who tutored the duchesses in painting, had warned her daughter about being raised alongside the royal children. Yes, she might spend every school day with the sisters, eat the same food and drink the same water as they did. They might learn all the same lessons. But Sofiya would never be a Romanov. She would never have the privileges the royals did. She needed to keep her expectations in check and behave accordingly. Always remember she was only part of the imperial household for as long as her mother was kept on as a tutor.

Mama didn't want Sofiya to get used to the life inside the Alexander Palace and forget her place. But Olga had once told her that being the tsar's daughter meant she had so few friends and often felt so isolated by her status, which meant she treasured Sofiya all the more.

"I want to warn you that because of the caliber of the doctors here, we get the toughest cases. You need to be prepared for what is to come."

As if anyone could really prepare them for what was to

come, Sofiya thought. Since the war had broken out, there was no telling what would become of any of them. Who could have imagined that the two women beside her would ever have taken off their lovely silk dresses and pearls to don these white cotton nursing uniforms and headdresses that made them all look like nuns? Sofiya knew the wimples and veils were necessary for sanitary reasons, but she hated the feel of the starched fabric cutting into her skin.

Until now, Olga and Tatiana, along with their mother the tsarina, had been working in the local hospital infirmary set up at the Catherine Palace in Tsarskoe Selo. But as part of their efforts to support all the soldiers, they would be working for a time at the larger hospital here in St. Petersburg.

Sofiya, who had reservations about nursing, was very apprehensive about what she was about to see, hear, and do. For the last few months, she'd been volunteering in her own way at the Propaganda Department, where she created posters the government used to raise morale. But Olga was having a difficult time. The stress of caring for the soldiers had affected her. She thought perhaps with Sofiya by her side, she could better cope with her responsibilities. So at Olga's request, Sofiya had agreed to try out nursing for her friend's sake.

The tour continued through the revamped part of the palace from the Nevsky Suite, running between the Fieldmarshals' Hall and the Malachite Room, and the Alexander and Picket Halls. They toured the medical storeroom in the Military Gallery, Fieldmarshals' Hall which had been turned into a dressing station, the Memorial Hall of Peter the Great, which was now reserved for doctors on duty, and the Nicholas Hall Galleries, where hospital attendants were accommodated.

As they exited the last gallery, two men carrying a stretcher passed the women without giving them a second look. Never guessing, Sofiya thought, that the nurses were grand duchesses. But all three women had noticed the young soldier on the stretcher with dried blood on his face and neck, moaning out in pain.

"Where are they taking him?" Tatiana asked.

"To the surgery," Matron said. She stopped then in the stately Armorial Hall and pointed to the room beyond the door. "As I mentioned, we see the most severe cases here. We deal with tragic situations and, despite our best efforts, not every soldier pulls through. So I do want to warn you that you're going to see things that are hard to take."

Olga reached out and gave Sofiya's hand a squeeze. She wasn't sure if the grand duchess was trying to get courage from Sofiya or give it. But when she spoke, Olga sounded every bit the composed royal. "These men are fighting and dying for us. It's our duty to work for them now."

As much as Sofiya loved her friend and cherished their relationship, she was becoming more and more sorry she'd agreed to join Olga and her sister by the minute. She didn't want to be there. Didn't want this to be *her* duty. She already hated the stench and the sights. And the sounds went right through her. She wanted to put her hands over her ears and run from the operating theater's anteroom. She hadn't been raised to feel a responsibility to her countrymen. She wasn't trained to hide her emotions. To be stoic and to brace herself. She didn't even want to go back to the propaganda department and paint those ugly posters. Sofiya yearned to return to her apprenticeship with Professor Sokolov, the head of restoration at the Hermitage. But everyone, even he, had told her the needs of the soldiers came first for now.

The matron looked at Tatiana. "You are ready as well?"

The second oldest daughter of the tsar and tsarina held her head high. "Of course," she said.

Matron turned to Sofiya. "And you?"

No words came. Olga, who was still holding her hand, gave it another squeeze.

Sofiya nodded at Matron. "I am."

"This way then," said the head nurse.

The surgery was brutal, the stench—as if the sewers had backed up—was awful. Sofiya began to retch and put her hand up to her mouth and ushered the girls out.

Once they were back in the hall, Matron, who'd of course noticed Sofiya's reaction, explained the smell was from gangrene and rotting flesh, which the surgeons were cutting away.

"Unfortunately, we have to handle a lot of infections and amputations due to the conditions at the front. Unless there is an emergency, you won't be assigned to work inside the surgery. That's for the professional nurses who had much more extensive training. You will be working in the ballroom."

Matron escorted them to the next stop on her tour. The young women hardly needed her hand gesture to suggest the way.

For the last twelve years, the Romanovs had mostly lived at the Alexander Palace in Tsarskoe Selo, less than half an hour from St. Petersburg, while the Winter Palace had been used for ceremonies and celebrations. Olga, Tatiana, and Sofiya had attended enough of these events to know many of the building's secrets. One of their favorites was in the ballroom. Hidden in an artfully concealed panel in an alcove was a narrow staircase that allowed servants access to the downstairs kitchen without having to walk the full length of the grand reception room. When they were young, the girls loved to disappear from sight, sneak downstairs, steal sweets, and create all kinds of mischief.

Sofiya wished she might use that staircase again after spending her first five minutes in the ballroom. It was worse than the surgery. But not because of the smell.

In the operating room, there had been two procedures in progress. Two men whose lives hung in the balance. But here, under the enormous crystal chandeliers, were rows upon rows of iron hospital beds filled with more than one hundred and fifty severely wounded soldiers.

The Winter Palace had been the former home of the royal family of Russia since the time of Catherine the Great. She wouldn't recognize it any longer, Sofiya thought. The hospital, created to treat the overflow of injured, sick and dying soldiers, was a study in contrasts of Russia's glorious past and its horrible present.

On Sofiya's last visit to this grand ballroom, she had worn a pale blue silk gown, white gloves, and a sparkling tiara. The room had been scented with perfume and flowers. An officer named Vladimir Menshchikov had twirled her around the dance floor to the strains of music played by the finest orchestra in Russia.

Now she was wearing a nurse's uniform with a red cross on the arm, smelling antiseptics and body odors and listening to the cries and moans of soldiers, many of whom would surely never dance again.

Matron continued educating the young women. "Only the best doctors and the most highly trained nurses attend the soldiers here in Tsarevich Alexei Nikolayevich hospital— which you probably know even better than I do, the tsar had named for his heir.

"Our staff includes thirty-five doctors, the majority of whom are surgeons, fifty Sisters of Charity nurses, one hundred and twenty Red Cross nurses, and about three dozen administrative staff..."

As Matron continued talking, the two orderlies carrying the stretcher the women had seen earlier came their way again. Sofiya couldn't help but glance at the young soldier. His face was no longer contorted in pain. His mouth was relaxed into an almost smile. His eyes, those frightened eyes, were now closed.

"I thought they were taking him to surgery," Sofiya said, suddenly desperate to know that this stranger was going to be all right.

"They didn't get there in time, it seems. He's passed on," the matron said softly.

Sofiya had never stood so close to death before. She felt the room spin. Much the same as it had when she'd been here at her last ball. But for an altogether different reason.

Chapter 3

Isobelle Moon
New York City
November 1948

Cradling the leather box, I leave our apartment, walk up one flight of stairs, and knock on my aunt's door.

"Come in, come in." She smiles. "I'm cooking pies for tomorrow, keep me company."

"As if I couldn't smell them," I say.

She hurries back to the kitchen before I've even crossed the threshold. I don't think she's noticed I am holding anything. I shut the door and join her in the fragrant kitchen. This is what I've always thought a home was supposed to smell like.

"I'm so glad you came up. I needed an excuse to stop and make some tea," she says and puts the kettle on.

Still holding the leather case, I sit at the worn wooden

table where she's cooked so many meals for all of us. Where she and my mother sat over cups of tea and confided and planned out their business and their lives together. Where Michael and I concocted adventures. Where Aunt Lana comforted and consoled all of us at one time or another.

My aunt is fifty-nine years old. Unlike my mother, who was reserved, controlled and never overdid anything, Aunt Lana is a bold-looking woman who wears too much costume jewelry, too much makeup, and whose hair is dyed too red. She has been known to drink vodka in excess at family celebrations and eat too much of the food she loves to cook. But she is the most generous and lovable person I've ever met. She believes in magic, reads tarot cards, and visits fortune-tellers religiously but has never visited a church since she left St. Petersburg in 1919.

Like my mother, she took an American name close to her own Russian moniker of Svetlana, but I've never heard anyone ever use it. Aunt Lana's uncle, Filatov Roman Sokolov, had been my mother's mentor and head of restoration at the Hermitage. He helped both women immigrate to America, and both Michael's and my middle names are Romana to honor him.

Aunt Lana is also a restorer, but her specialty is furniture, while my mother's was painting. The two of them set up their business in 1923, eight months after my mother arrived in America when I was five months old.

"Aunt Lana, I have something to show you," I say just as the kettle starts to sing.

"One minute, darling," she says and attends to the tea. Nothing stops her from making that sweet tea when it's what she has her heart set on.

I sit quietly, watching the ritual of her spooning the loose tea into the pot, wetting it first, then pouring in the rest of the water. As it steeps, she puts glasses into two of her best antique *podstakanniks*, traditional metal tea glass holders with a handle. With serious attention to the ritual, she pours in the tea and then adds a teaspoon of sugar to each glass. Carrying both, she puts them on the table and finally looks at what I've brought to show her.

"I found this…" I say, watching her face, expecting her to recognize it. Hoping she will.

"I don't know what that is, Isobelle."

I feel deflated.

"Are you sure?" I push it across the table to her.

She wipes her hands on her apron and only then takes the case from me. She inspects the peeling label. Lifts her glasses from around her neck, puts them on and reads.

"It says *Property of the Provisional Government* and then there is a long number." She glances at me. "Where did you get this?"

"Look inside."

She opens the case. The kitchen's overhead light illuminates the silver skeleton. I can tell she's confused.

"Isobelle, what is this? And where did you find it?"

"You really don't know?"

"If I did, darling, I would tell you."

I explain and add that from the receipts that were with it, my mother sold the stones.

"Mama never told you she had this?"

"No, never. For how close we became, we were merely acquaintances growing up. And then once your mother arrived in the States, she was…well, you know better than anyone what she was like. She never wanted to talk about the past. I know everything about her life here down to where she bought her stockings, but I never even saw a picture of your father. Sophia kept secrets from me too." Lana sighs and shakes her head. Tears fill her eyes. *She misses my mother as much as I do*, I think, not for the first time.

"I thought she talked more about her old life in Russia with you since you were friends."

"No. Believe me, I pressed at first, but she always shut down when I did. So eventually, I stopped." Aunt Lana picks up the silver tiara frame, runs a finger over the edge and then, leaning over, puts it on me, pushing the ends of the band through my hair. Leaning back, she looks at me with her head cocked, then reaches out and tilts the tiara to the right a bit.

In the darkened window behind my aunt, I see my reflection. I move my head, and the tiara seems to wink at me. I don't like the sight. It's not a beautiful object, not anymore. Now it's just a remnant of another era, another life.

Removing it, I hold the tiara in my hands and put my pinkie through one hole after another as I try to reason it all out.

"Where did you get the money to buy this building?" I ask my aunt.

"We had about half in savings, so we sold some things to make up the difference. The Depression had hit the owners of this building hard, and they needed to liquidate as many of their assets as they could."

"It still must have cost a lot."

"Then, yes, but not when you think about it now. In the 1920s, the average price for a brownstone like this was fifteen dollars per square foot. During the Depression, that fell to five dollars or less if the owners were desperate. Your mother and I were so proud of ourselves that we negotiated the asking price from $15,000 down to $12,000. Looking back, we probably could have pushed them lower. But we didn't know better."

"What did you sell?"

"Three Rembrandt drawings my uncle had given me that I smuggled out of Russia when I left. And your mother sold some jewelry that had belonged to her grandmother."

I feel a surge of excitement. "Was this my grandmother's tiara?"

"I suppose so. I certainly never saw your mother wear any jewelry other than that enamel egg necklace."

"She never specifically told you what she sold? You never asked?"

"Darling, I honestly don't remember if I did or didn't. We were both so excited and nervous about whether or not we could afford to buy the building. All that mattered was between her jewelry and my drawings and our savings we had what we needed."

"But you must have been curious."

"Isobelle, you know your mother. One knew not to be curious when it came to Sophia's past. We couldn't have been closer, but I learned early on that she shared what she wanted to about her life in Russia, and I respected that. Many of us who came over were traumatized in one way or another by what we'd lived through. Memories could be precious or painful. I never pushed when your mother held back information."

"So you have no idea if what she sold really did belong to her grandmother, or if she just told you that?" I ask, even though I know I've exhausted my aunt's knowledge on the subject.

"I wish I could tell you I do, but I don't."

"I wish you could too."

I put the silver frame back in its case.

"How about I give you a slice of that pie I have cooling?

I'm hungry, and knowing you, you barely ate anything for dinner."

I stay for a while, eating the delicious pecan pie with my aunt, listening to her tell me stories about her Uncle Roman. I grew up starving for these reminiscences, always a little angry at my mother that I'd have to go upstairs to Aunt Lana to get my fill.

Once we're done, I kiss her goodnight and then, clutching the box to my chest, go back downstairs, silently cursing my mother, who left absolutely no record of her past. Since her death, I've gone through all of her files and papers. She left no diaries, hardly any letters, certainly nothing from her life in Russia or anything related to it.

It's not until hours later, when I'm lying in bed, running through the events of the evening, that it occurs to me that maybe the jeweler who bought the stones might know the story behind the tiara. Perhaps he was the sort who only purchased pieces if he knew their provenance. With what I knew about art and antiques, if he was ethical, he'd insist on knowing something. Except would Alford Reed remember a transaction that had occurred eighteen years ago? Was he even still in business? Or even still alive?

Chapter 4

Sofiya Petrovitch
Petrograd
May 1915

Sofiya's days in the hospital took their toll. All she did was roll bandages, fetch meal trays, and take orders from the experienced nurses. She hated how helpless she felt. Even worse was how upsetting it was to witness all the pain. Olga felt the same way. Only Tatiana seemed suited to the tasks and the atmosphere.

But even as much as Sofiya disliked it, she kept at it. If the royal duchesses could endure the hospital work, so could she. Each night when she returned home, with the stench of the infirmary in her clothes and hair, she took a long bath. So long sometimes that her fingertips and toes puckered and became prunish. Her mother often came to the door and insisted that Sofiya get out of the tub.

This night, after she toweled herself dry, she thought she could still detect the smells of the day on her skin, so she dabbed on some of her mother's French perfume—a blend of jasmine, carnation and cinnamon. Then she wiped the steam clouds off the mirror, stared at her image, and tried to will herself into being stronger.

Why she was so afraid of what she saw in the infirmary? Why couldn't she be braver for the men who fought for her and her family and friends? Why could the soldiers endure such hardships and pain and suffering, and she could barely tolerate walking among them?

There were no answers in the mirror. But as she stared, she felt herself separate her consciousness from her body as if she was standing outside of herself. It was such an odd sensation that for a few minutes, she remained immobile. It felt freeing. As if she'd just been shown a trick. Or maybe the answer. This was how she needed to be in the hospital. Removed from her body, standing outside it, watching but not feeling.

She watched herself make a smile, just the corners of her mouth turning up. And with that action, she was back in her skin.

Had she just done something like the hypnosis Rasputin purportedly used on the tsarevich, a hemophilic who suffered brutal, life-threatening episodic internal bleeds?

Sofiya had first seen Rasputin at the Alexander Palace in April of 1906 when he stood at the foot of Alexei's bed and, through what he called prayer, calmed the heir, alleviated some of his worst pain as he stopped his internal bleeding. She couldn't believe that the tsarina would put the life of the young tsarevich in the hands of a mad monk who looked like a peasant and smelled like a barnyard animal.

Sofiya's mother, Fedora, used to travel to Tsareskoe Selo five times a week to tutor the girls in art. And since the tsarina had invited her to bring her daughter to study with the girls, Sofiya accompanied her every day. But not until Rasputin became part of the Romanov retinue had she seen her mother worry about Sofiya's safety.

Fedora, who had been raised in Southampton in the Church of England, found the Russian Orthodox religion and all of its mysticism disturbing. Sofiya was certain her parents would never have married if her father had been devout. But he was an atheist, having seen too much poverty and suffering to believe in a benevolent God. If there was such a being, her father would often say, he would not be this cruel.

Sofiya was startled that first time she saw Rasputin. The Romanovs had talked about the man with the pale gray eyes as if he was a saint. Which was what he was to them—soothing and able to stop the tsarevich's bleeds and pain when no one else could. But Sofiya thought he was repulsive-looking with his unkempt beard, bushy eyebrows and long, filthy hair.

She'd heard the rumors that he was a sexual satyr having an affair with the tsarina and abusing the grand duchesses. Sofiya didn't believe it. Yes, Olga and the rest of the family might be in awe of the man, but the duchess laughed at the gossip. And besides, no one who spent any time with Nicolas and Alexandra could imagine that the tsarina would ever allow that filthy man near her pearls and silk. She was devoted to him for one reason—he alone seemed to be able to help Alexei when his hemophilia kept him bedridden and in agony.

Olga explained to Sofiya that Rasputin hypnotized Alexei in order to help him relax so deeply that it alleviated his pain. That calm then helped stop the bleeding. Alexei always turned the corner when the mystic visited. Sometimes, Rasputin could even work his magic over the telephone. Apparently, the sound of his voice, intoning instructions, was enough to set the process in motion.

Sofiya didn't understand much about mysticism or the occult. Her parents scoffed at the irrational beliefs. But the tsarina and half of Russia were highly influenced by many things they couldn't understand. Often at the dinner table, Sofiya's parents discussed why that was. Living in such extreme poverty, the peasants had little to hope for. But the onion-domed churches, designed to bring heaven down to Earth, elevated them and provided beauty. Through flickering candlelight, ribbons of incense wafted up to gold-leafed ceilings. Frescoes of holy figures glittered with jewel-like colors. Chanting and choral music interspersed throughout the complicated service added to the otherworldly respite from the day-to-day drudgery the church provided. The whole religious experience offered—for a little while, at least—hope to those who, in so many ways, had given up.

Despite her parents' admonitions to stay away from Rasputin, Sofiya was fascinated by him, and Olga indulged her friend's curiosity. One winter afternoon, when they walked in, the staretz, who seemed to be in a trance, knelt as if in prayer at the young prince's bedside. Alexei appeared to be in one as well. The two girls were invisible to both the healer and his patient. The incident made Sofiya even more curious.

A few weeks later, they both hid in a closet and watched Rasputin hypnotize the prince. Afterwards, Olga convinced Sofiya to let her practice on her. The young duchess used the ruby cross she wore on a gold chain to try and mesmerize her friend. She failed. Then she told Sofiya it was her turn to try. Sofiya was scared. What if she harmed her friend in some way?

And now, in the bathroom in her own home, staring into the mirror after the bath, Sofiya realized that she had utilized one of Rasputin's tricks and hypnotized herself a little. She knew she wasn't doing well at the hospital. The matron, Nadezhda Filosofova, had chastised her just the week before when Sofiya had requested a different assignment than the post-operative room.

"You are the only nurse who asks for special treatment. Not even their imperial highnesses ask for different assignments."

Now for the sake of the men in their beds, for the sake of Olga and Tatiana and the royal family, for the sake of Russia, she tried to use what she could of Rasputin's method so she could be of more value at the hospital, not just rolling bandages and clearing meal trays, but helping with the patients.

The next morning, upon entering the great hall, she approached the matron and told her she was ready to do more. The matron looked skeptical but directed Sofiya to the pre-op room.

"We have six surgeries this morning. All amputees and needing secondary surgery to repair the butchering they got on the front. And we're down a nurse."

Just thinking about the stench of those kinds of wounds made Sofiya gag. Yesterday, she would have begged for any other assignment, but she'd worked on her weaknesses and she was ready.

Sofiya walked down the hall and entered the pre-operation room. There were six beds, lined up in the order they were to be taken in.

She approached the nurse. "I'm here to help, what do you need?"

The nurse looked up from the syringe she was

preparing.

"I can handle the pre-operation patients. If you can take over in there"—she pointed to the recovery room—"then I don't have to run back and forth."

There was only one patient in recovery. As it was early in the morning, the doctors had only done that one surgery so far. Sofiya approached the gurney. The man on it was clearly still under the anesthesia he'd been given. His arm was in a sling, and his hand was heavily bandaged. She looked at his chart and saw that his name was Victor Drozdov.

Once the room was full, she'd have to go from patient to patient, checking on them as they recovered, watching for signs of distress and administering pain medicine if needed. But for now, with only one patient, she could focus all her attention on him.

She pulled up a chair and sat beside his bed. She could tell from the outline of his body under the sheet that he was tall and slender. His curly dark brown hair was damp with sweat, and she brushed it back. Where her fingers touched his skin, he was warm.

The patient reminded her of an eighteenth-century painting in the Hermitage entitled *Andromeda's Return* by Jean-Baptiste Regnault that Sofiya often stopped to look at in the museum. It had been the first canvas she'd worked on during her apprenticeship and she'd fallen in love with its young, naked hero as she filled in an area on Perseus' arm where the paint had cracked off.

Now a man who looked so very much like him lay before her, and he also had a damaged arm.

Sofiya ruminated on the coincidence, which she felt certain was no coincidence at all. With the naïve confidence of youth, she believed there was a kind of grand plan, a design to her life. And that it was portentous that the first painting she'd restored was of a Greek god whose arm had been damaged.

It had to mean something that she had specifically been chosen to take care of this man. She just wasn't sure what. Or at least not yet.

Sofiya spent the morning alone with Victor Drozdov. No other patients were wheeled in despite Matron saying it would be a busy morning. During these hours she sat with him, she waited to see signs of either distress or consciousness. There were none. She watched his sleeping face, imagined who he was, what he liked, where he had grown up, what had happened to him. She held his free hand and talked to him.

"You're going to get well now. And if you are in pain when you wake up, the wonderful doctors here will be able to help you with that. This is now the finest hospital in all of Russia for your injury. Not surprising since it was the finest palace in all of Russia. Did you know that you're in the Winter Palace? This room we are in is a portioned-off section of a receiving room. They left the chandeliers up. And it's strange to see all the medical beds, surgical equipment, soldiers in hospital gowns and nurses in nun's clothing under these great crystal chandeliers that once shone down on tsars and tsarinas, princes and princesses, dukes and duchesses, kings and queens and all kinds of nobility for so many centuries. Now there is no pomp but rather a great tireless effort to saving men's lives. A fine use for this place, the Grand Duchess Olga says. She and her sister Tatiana are nurses here as well. Few of the soldiers realize the tsar's daughters are nursing them. But we all have to do our part. You are all giving so much more than we even have to give."

He still hadn't moved.

"Victor Drozdov?"

No reaction.

"I like your name. It's strong. Names say a lot about a person, don't you think? I always wondered if we grow into our names, or if our names help form who we become. For instance, if you have a very common and popular name, are you less inspired to be someone creative and independent? If you have an uncommon and startling name, are you moved to live up to it and become someone who is an artist or writer?

"I suppose I should tell you my name. I am Sofiya Petrovitch. Not very unusual but not a name you hear every day either. I'm nineteen years old. My mother is a fine artist who has been tutoring the grand duchesses in painting for the last eleven years. That's how I've spent so much time with them. My father is the Keeper of the Paintings in the Hermitage. I worked there as well until I came here to be a nurse. My mother spent most summers in the Cotswolds in the English countryside where her grandmother lived. I speak English and French as well."

Sofiya prattled on. Victor didn't respond.

"Maybe if I tell you part of a secret and then stop, you'll be so intrigued that you'll wake up so you can hear the rest? Do you think that will work?"

He didn't answer.

"The secret is about my career. Not something that you'd expect a woman to do. Not a painter or sculptor or printmaker or engraver, but it is related to the arts.

"Are you curious?"

She waited for any response. Still, there was none.

"I am an apprentice restorer. I know how to mimic the style of many of the grand masters. I work at the Hermitage under the auspices of Filatov Roman Sokolov, who is a master restorer. There isn't another woman in all of Russia studying to do this job. Some of my friends, artists I studied with at the academy, find it strange that I am satisfied restoring works as opposed to creating new ones. But it is my passion."

She watched his face, hoping there would be some reaction. What else could she tell him?

"You look quite a lot like the main figure in a painting I restored. Do you know the story of Perseus and Andromeda? He had winged sandals and could fly. On one of his flights over the coast of Ethiopia, he noticed a figure chained to a rock and descended to see if he could help. Andromeda told him that she was the daughter of the country's king, Cepheus, who had chained her to the rock as a sacrifice to Poseidon. After hearing the story, Perseus became determined to save and then wed her. Brave hero that he was, Perseus persevered and, unlike many of the gods, remained faithful to his Andromeda. They had a child who eventually inherited the whole kingdom."

Victor Drozdov did not wake up at any point during the retelling of the myth. Or later that morning.

Sofiya was asked to stay on in the post-operative room for the rest of the day and tend to the patients that came out of surgery. In between checking on them for any signs of trouble as they came out of anesthesia and following up on their pain level, she kept returning to Victor's cot to see if there had been any change with him. He remained unresponsive, even as all the other men recovered and were taken one by one back to the main ward where the night nurse could tend to them.

Before Sofiya left for the day, she stopped to check on her Perseus one last time. Victor Drozdov was still asleep.

Or to be more precise, she thought, still unconscious. Pulling up a chair, she sat beside him. It was time to leave, but she was afraid to go. What if he woke up suddenly and didn't know where he was? From the chart, he had never been told about the fingers he had lost. He'd remained unconscious since he was found at the front.

Sofiya knew that the head surgeon, A. K. Valter, who had operated on the men that morning, would be making the rounds before he left to check on the soldiers whose lives he'd held in his hands. And so, she waited in order to speak with him.

The doctor came around at 7:00 p.m., long after Sofiya knew her mother expected her home. When he arrived, he nodded to Sofiya. It was a small staff. Plus, being friends with the grand duchesses, she was more visible than the other Sisters of Mercy.

"How is he, nurse?"

"He hasn't woken up."

Dr. Valter nodded and then proceeded to check on his patient's surgical site and vital signs.

"How long can he last like this?" Sofiya asked.

"There's no telling."

"But he will wake up, won't he?"

"Is he someone you know?"

She shook her head.

"It's easy to form attachments to the patients," he said kindly. "But it's not wise. They are here for a little time only and then get shipped back to the front or to their families. You have to build an iron case around your heart."

"What will happen to him if he doesn't wake up? Will he stay here at the Palace?"

"No, once his condition is stabilized, and the infection that the amputation caused is cured, we'll send him to a sanatorium in the Crimea."

"And then?"

The doctor shrugged. "You should go home, Sofiya Petrovitch. Have dinner and be with your family. Let us worry about Victor Drozdov. He's in very good hands here."

She didn't want to leave but was being dismissed and, as a lowly Sister of Mercy volunteer, she was not in a position to argue with the doctor.

The next morning, she discovered that Victor had been moved to the far corner of the main ward. Whenever she had a break, she pulled up a chair and talked to him. She didn't have enough to say, so after a while, she found a newspaper and read to him. During her training, she'd been informed that after recovering from a serious head injury, many patients reported having heard friends and loved ones and staff talking to them even while unconscious.

Every morning after that, on her way to the hospital, she stopped at the kiosk and bought a newspaper. She'd never been someone very interested in the news. But her father and her grandfather and Professor Sokolov all were. She thought it mattered more to men—this business of war and politics—and not knowing anything about Victor, she guessed he too might be interested in such things. Maybe, she thought, some story might stir something in him and wake him up. She feared that Victor would be sent to the sanatorium in the Crimea and didn't want that to happen. She'd formed a silent, secret bond with him. Maybe, she admitted to herself, she was even a little in love with him. Though how could she be since she didn't know anything about him? She didn't even know the sound of his voice.

On the fifth day, when she arrived in the morning, Victor Drozdov's bed was empty. Sofiya stood there, her hand on the fresh pillowcase, running her fingers back and forth over the cool cotton.

She knew what empty beds meant in the hospital. Too many men came back from the war with infections and wounds that not even the finest doctors could fix. They weren't like the Niena tin soldiers her cousin played with that her uncle had bought in the store at the river embankment. When one of those was damaged, you just straightened out the limb or got some paint and filled in a scratch or glued back a detached hand.

But there *were* possibilities other than the one she didn't want to contemplate.

Perhaps they'd just taken Victor Drozdov back into surgery. Or he'd recovered overnight, and they'd moved him to another ward. Or the time had come for the sanatorium, and they had taken him earlier this morning.

Deep in her stomach, the anxious coil of dread started to unwind. For Sofiya, nervousness was always just waiting for a trigger. She had been born on a Wednesday and true to the nursery rhyme, Wednesday's child is full of woe. Sofiya's mother often called her *moy malen'kiy bespokoynik*, my little worrier, and then would play a game with her to calm her.

"What's the worst that will happen?" she'd ask about whatever it was troubling Sofiya—a friend's reaction to something she'd said, a test she was sure she had failed in school, a snowstorm that would ruin party plans.

She'd list the worst things that could happen for that particular situation, and mother and daughter would discuss each and figure out a solution if in fact that particular worst thing *did* happen. Only when it was the idea of one of her parents dying did the game fail to bring about its desired end.

Sofiya hadn't had any direct experience with a close family member or friend dying, so her childhood preoccupation was not only disturbing but also baffling. Her parents and grandparents, aunts and uncles, were of good peasant stock and rarely got sick despite the cold winter temperatures and the sometimes-filthy conditions in the city.

"I suppose I let you read too much. You are personalizing the tragedies found in books," her mother said one day. And then, seeing the expression of horror on Sofiya's face at the idea that she'd curtail her reading, she smiled. "Don't worry, I won't stop you from going to the top shelves for the grown-up books, but you have to understand that a writer's job is to make their story as dramatic as possible. Yes, stories are recreations of real life, but no one lives one lifetime with all the tragedy that a Russian writer can cram into a novel."

Sofiya wasn't sure how long she stood at Victor Drozdov's empty bed, playing her mother's what-if game. The worst that could happen would be if they took him to a sanatorium...but they might have a cure there. So that wouldn't be too terrible. She could find him and go visit him. Or the worst could be that he might be back in surgery...but the doctors here were excellent. They would cut out the new infection if that's what it was, and he would recuperate.

"I'm sorry to have to tell you this, nurse, but Victor Drozdov passed away during the night."

She turned in the direction of the voice. A soldier sitting up in a bed in the row behind her was speaking to her.

"Are you sure?" she asked.

"Yes."

She didn't so much sit down on the edge of the bed as she crumpled onto it. Her eyes blurred with tears.

"I'm sorry," the soldier said tenderly. After a moment, he continued. "I'm sure that he heard you," the soldier said. "And that your being here every day eased his suffering."

"How are you sure?" Her voice was harsh.

"Because I too have been recovering here, and even when I was unconscious, I had a sense of what was going on around me. The sounds, the voices—yours, even. It was reassuring. And I'm certain it was a great comfort to our comrade."

She picked up the pillow and hugged it to her chest, crying into the fabric. Sofiya supposed it was irrational to be so upset. All the nurses had been warned about forming attachments with the soldiers under their care. They'd been lectured on how to keep their distance even as they tended to the men and soothed them.

"I've been listening to you read and talk to him these last few days," the soldier said. "I've come to look forward to your visits. Perhaps you would be willing to read the news to me?"

Chapter 5

Isobelle Moon
New York City
November 1948

At 8:50 a.m., the bus stops at 59th and Fifth Avenue, and I disembark, tighten the belt on my camel hair coat, turn up the collar and head left. I have galoshes on over my black step-ins because of the last vestiges of the Thanksgiving snowfall that dusted the city. I'm wearing brown trousers and a camel-colored cashmere sweater underneath my coat. It isn't the fashion anymore. Sure, women took to pants during the war. But since? They've gone back to dresses—fit and flare, especially. But I don't have a good figure for dresses. I'm too small-breasted and too high-waisted. And I just don't feel comfortable with the doll-like femininity. Katherine Hepburn and Greta Garbo are my screen heroes. Women who don't play the same game as everyone else. I'm not glamorous—anything but—and I don't expect to ever attract the kind of man who wants a femme fatale, or even anyone close. But there is another reason for my plain and somewhat mannish clothing. I'm working in a man's field, and I stand out enough for being a woman. I've already been compromised and taken advantage of, clueless as to how to stand up for myself. The last thing I want is for another incident like the one I endured in Oak Ridge.

I navigate the slush and the crowd of people hurrying to work and head to the corner of 57th, where I cross. A few hundred feet east of the avenue is Number 1 East 57th, which houses the offices of Skidmore, Owings & Merrill. This morning, before I go in, I stop and look across the street at Number 6 East 57th—the address on the receipt from Alford Reed Jewelers. I count up six floors and stare at the shop's windows. Is the answer to my mystery there? As much as I want to rush over now, I refrain. My plan is to pay them a visit during my lunch hour.

I spend the morning drafting a set of plans for the magazine headquarter's lobby and cafeteria, which I didn't get to finish before the holiday. And then at a half hour before noon, Frank Williams calls me into his office. On his desk are at least a dozen blueprints and three different cups of coffee, which are his tell that he's under pressure. It happens, but not often.

"This is the worst time for Ted to be on vacation..." he starts.

I feel my skin goose bump hearing Ted Forester's name. Having him on his honeymoon has been a relief, and I've enjoyed some time working directly with Frank these last few days as I did back at Oak Ridge. I'm still a junior architect, but in the time I've been back in New York, I've been on Ted's team. Frank, who has six architects working under him, is Ted's boss.

"We need to alter all of these drawings for a 4:30 meeting," Frank continues. "The Fields have had a change of heart about the façade, so I've come up with an alternative, but you know how hard it is to get them to read blueprints. You need to do one of those great elevations you're so good at. I know it's going to be tight to get it done on time. You don't have any lunch plans, do you?"

As disappointed as I am, I put off my excursion to the jewelers. I've never said no to my mentor. If it weren't for Mr. Williams, I would never have gotten a job with SOM.

In addition to his heavy workload at the firm, Frank Williams teaches a senior-level design class at Cooper Union, which I took while I was there. Just a few weeks before I graduated, he told me he was recruiting graduates for an important war project and described a cryptic but fascinating job. I'd be moving out of the city and working on a secret project in Tennessee. The pay was good, and I knew how amazing the opportunity was. SOM was one of the leading architectural firms in the United States. Almost no one was offered a job there fresh out of school.

When I told my mother about the offer, despite my enthusiasm, she refused to agree to my moving away for a job I couldn't even describe. When I told Mr. Williams why I was turning his offer down, he offered to come to our house and chat with my mother.

She agreed to at least talk to him. She'd barely poured him a cup of coffee before inundating him with a barrage of questions.

"Isobelle can't even explain what she will be doing in Tennessee. What is this job exactly? Living on a site in the middle of nowhere? A city that doesn't even exist? All my daughter keeps telling me is what a great opportunity it is."

"The job itself is easy to describe. We have over three

hundred architects, engineers and staff working at Oak Ridge, building a town from scratch. We are in need of more architectural assistants. I know living on-site is fairly unusual, but so is this project. It involves a highly confidential war effort. In fact, few of the people who work at the site are aware of what exactly they are working on or what the factories surrounding the town produce. But you have to trust me, it's all critically important."

"And exactly why should I trust you?" my mother asked.

I wasn't surprised—she trusted almost no one other than my Aunt Lana, Uncle Paul, and me. She'd told me once in her typically obtuse way, that she'd learned the hard way that people do what they have to in order to get what they want. She'd seen families treat each other like strangers—stealing ration cards, food, treasures, even turning each other in for infractions in order to survive in Russia during the revolution. She'd witnessed such acts of horror during the food and housing shortages that she refused to give me any details.

Mr. Williams laughed. "You know, Mrs. Moon, now that you put it that way, there's very little reason you should trust me. I have two daughters who are only eight and ten, but I can just imagine how I'd feel if I were sitting where you are."

Mama nodded. She appreciated the honesty, I knew that much.

"Maybe it would help to tell you that Isobelle won't be alone at Oak Ridge or without friends," he continued. "I've offered similar positions to two of her classmates who have accepted."

That did nothing to sway her. "Be that as it may, I don't know about a clandestine project."

Even though she kept so much of herself secreted away, my mother's experiences in Bolshevik Russia had made her suspicious of the government and anything that sounded hidden or subversive.

"Mama," I tried, "it's normal in times of war for a country to keep certain things secret."

She often gave me that look that was usually accompanied by the same sentence: "I saw what I saw. I know better than you do."

But in front of Mr. Williams, there were no words, just the glance.

"Where will she live? Alone in a strange place with *who* watching out for her? Don't tell me about her friends, what about adults?" my mother asked with an attitude suggesting that she had found the next problem.

"Isobelle will be living in the women's dormitory." He opened his briefcase and pulled out a sheaf of photos then handed her one picture after another. "Here's a photo of the outside. Here's the lobby. Here's a picture of a room similar to hers. She would have a roommate—Charlotte Vorhees also from Cooper Union. And here are some shots of some of the buildings SOM has already built...a hospital, churches of all denominations... Here is a restaurant, and another, and a movie theater, a concert hall, a library..."

He had come to the end of the stack. My mother handed them back to him.

"Of course, it's not New York City," Mr. Williams continued, "but it is a fully functioning small town. But most importantly, it is an exciting opportunity we are extending to only the most talented students from this year's graduating class."

"Except you can't tell me what exactly the opportunity is."

"Mrs. Moon, I know you want more complete answers. I can't provide them in full. But as a father to two precious daughters, I am telling you that this is truly an amazing chance for a young woman like Isobelle to get her start in her chosen field. That opportunity is not covert—she'll be working with some of the best architects in the country. Doing something that has to our knowledge never been done before—helping to build an entirely self-contained and functioning city for at least fifty thousand people. And when the war is over, she will of course be offered a position with Skidmore, Owings & Merrill in New York. Or Chicago if she prefers."

"New York," my mother said as if this was the sticking point.

Mr. Williams nodded. "New York."

I thought that meant she'd agreed I could go, but as it turned out, she still insisted that I reject the offer. We fought about the opportunity for the next few days, right up until the night before the deadline Mr. Williams had given us for my answer.

"But you picked up and left St. Petersburg all by yourself when you were only a few years older than I am now," I argued over dinner that night.

"I had no choice. I was saving your life."

"And now, I am cementing my career. This is such an important job, Mama. We've talked about how hard it is to try to get ahead as a woman in a man's field. Architecture is all men. It always has been. The war is giving a few of us a chance. And everyone says it will get just as bad once the war is over. We started with five women architecture students at Cooper Union. All but two of us dropped out."

"There are jobs here at home."

"Not at Skidmore, Owings & Merrill. It's like the

Hermitage, Mama. You didn't work at a second-rate museum. You had the opportunity to apprentice at the finest museum in all of Russia. One of the best in the world. Why can't I have the same chance?"

"It's dangerous to go work for the government."

"You worry too much."

My mother let out a deep sigh. The fact was, I was just as concerned and cautious as she was, maybe more so.

"I know you want to take this job, but I just can't agree."

I was over twenty-one. I didn't need her permission, but leaving home—leaving her—for the first time in my life was a big step. I wanted her blessing. I looked at her across the table from me, her expression set in stone.

"Mama, you've been so brave. Never taken the easy way out. And whether you like it or not—whether you meant to or not—that's what you've taught me. Now you want me to be someone who cowers in the corner and never takes chances? What changed?"

That was what it took. She agreed that I could go. To do otherwise would have made a mockery of everything she had fought so hard and made so many sacrifices for.

Mama saw me off at Grand Central Station two weeks later. As other passengers boarded and the train hissed, my mother kissed me and handed me the box lunch she'd packed for me—two cheese sandwiches, a small bottle of milk, two apples and some of my Aunt Lana's homemade chocolate chip cookies.

An hour later when I unwrapped the first sandwich, I found a note under the wax paper.

Your father would be so proud of you, Isobelle. Almost as proud as I am.

Your mama

Tennessee was as far away from New York City as I'd ever been—both emotionally and physically. At first, I was homesick, even with my friends Charlotte Vorhees and Stan Benjamin there, but that didn't last long. It was exhilarating to be a working architect—even an assistant—and involved with such an enormous and crucial project. Building a city from scratch involves everything from laying out the streets to figuring out how many movie theaters are needed for the population of workers and their families. When SOM had started construction in 1942, they'd expected only about twenty-five thousand people. By the time we arrived a year later the number had grown to fifty thousand. By 1945 over seventy-five thousand people were living in the Tennessee valley.

The most curious aspect of being at Oak Ridge was that none of us quite knew what we were doing there. Yes, we were building residences, stores, leisure activity places and civic buildings and factories—all the structures any town would need. But why? What was being built in the factories that were clearly the heart of this *ready-in-an-instant* town as we'd taken to calling it in the drafting room? We had all walked into our boss' office and had a conversation halt because of our presence, or caught paperwork being turned over when we came to close to seeing it.

Stan, Charlotte, and I never ceased wondering and speculating what was going on. And since we spent most of our free time together, we had endless theories. Charlotte and I were roommates. Though Stan lived in the men's dormitory, the three of us were inseparable. We spent all day, every day in the drafting room together. We took our meals together and went to the movies together. The Cooper Union Three, we were dubbed. We made friends with other associates and assistants, but we were closer to one another than anyone else.

Stan and Charlotte were especially determined to discover what was going on at the site and what was being built in the factories. Though I too was curious, the effort required to find out seemed too risky. There were billboards and signage everywhere at Oak Ridge, warning us to protect the secrecy of the town's mission. The most duplicated had an illustration of the *see no evil, hear no evil, speak no evil* monkey with the legend:

What you see here
What you do here
What you hear here
When you leave here
Let it stay here.

Another popular one showed Uncle Sam issuing a warning:

Loose talk helps our enemy, so let's keep our traps shut.

But what was being hidden? What were we doing that our government didn't want anyone to know about? After we'd been at Oak Ridge for three months, Stan, who was even more obsessed about the secrets than Charlotte, decided to do something about it. At dinner, he laid out his plan.

"We need to hide somewhere in the SOM office while it is being locked up for the night, then sneak out when everyone leaves," he said.

"I am not spying on our bosses," I said, already not liking the sound of it.

"I think we should let Stan finish," Charlotte said. "I think it sounds a little bit exciting."

"Exciting?" I wasn't surprised by her reaction. Charlotte was always more adventurous than I was.

"It wouldn't hurt for you to take at least one foot out of

your comfort zone and not always do what is expected of you."

It wasn't the first time she'd pushed me. I always took her challenges, but this time seemed different. Really dangerous in a new way.

I started to protest, but Stan stopped me.

"Enough, Izzie, hear me out. If you don't want to join in, then we'll investigate without you. I'm not suggesting you get all dressed up with feathers and fake pearls, undress and turn into a Mata Hari-type spy here."

We all laughed at his exaggerated description, and then he explained.

"We'll hide out until everyone leaves and then hunt around and try to dig up blueprints or papers that might shed light on the factories. Surely, there are specs and requirements that will give us some clues."

I begged off. Charlotte agreed to join him. But on the appointed day, she was sick in bed with the sore throat that was going around, and Stan asked me to fill in for her, tempting me with how satisfying it would be if we actually knew what the hell we were doing in the middle of nowhere, building a full-fledged city. I tried to get him to just postpone the mission, but he said it had to be that night because he'd found out the security team was changing their rotation, and it would take too long to learn their new schedule. I'd been fighting my curiosity all along anyway, and I agreed.

We hid in the drafting studio's walk-in supply closet, which was always kept locked, which meant the night guard never opened it. Since it could be locked from the inside or the outside, it was an ideal place to wait while security did their evening rounds.

At eight o'clock, the guards left the architecture offices and moved on to the engineering offices. Stan said they usually left the building at 8:30, so we waited till 8:45 and then came out. Stan had learned where Mr. Williams kept an extra set of keys to the file cabinets and retrieved them. He opened the first, and we started going through the blueprints, looking for any kind of clue.

We'd been reading plans, to no avail, for about a half an hour when the door to the studio opened, and Mr. Williams walked in. He looked astonished to see us.

"What are the two of you doing here after-hours?"

Stan answered quickly, *too* quickly. "I misfiled some drawings and wanted to retrieve them. Isobelle was helping."

"How did you get in?"

"We never left. We were both working late."

Stan wasn't a good liar.

Mr. Williams took the drawings out of Stan's hands and, in a voice literally quavering with anger, told us to go and that he wanted to see us at 9:00 a.m. the next morning.

I didn't sleep at all. Charlotte tried to calm me down in between sneezes, but nothing she said mitigated my worries that I would lose my job the next day.

At the appointed hour, both Stan and I were waiting outside Mr. Williams' office. At 9:15, he opened the door and called Stan inside. I could barely contain my nerves while I waited. Had I really worked so hard to get to this point, only to risk it all out of curiosity?

After about twenty minutes, the door opened, and Stan exited. His face was white, but as he walked by, he gave me a little half-smile.

"Isobelle, you can come in."

My legs shook as I walked the few yards from where I sat into Mr. Williams' office.

"Take a seat," he said.

I did.

He gave me a searching look as if he was looking for some answer on my face.

"Stan told me that this mission was all his idea. And I believe him. But at the same time, you went along with it, didn't you?"

"I did." My voice was barely audible, even to me.

"Why?"

"We just wanted to know what's going on. It's all such a mystery."

"For a good reason. If our enemies were to figure out what is going on here…if they were to accomplish our goals first…it would be a disaster for the world. That is all any of us need to know." He stopped speaking.

Was he waiting for me to say something? I was so scared I was about to lose my job. I couldn't think of anything to say.

"You need to think really hard about whether or not you can be satisfied with not knowing. Of living with the mystery. If you can't, then I'm going to suggest you be sent back to New York."

I imagined taking the train back home. Explaining to my mother that I had failed here. Failed at the one thing she had tried to teach me—to be patient with secrets. To accept them. Allow them to just be.

"Do you think you can deal with your insatiable curiosity?" he asked.

"I want to." It was a totally honest answer. "I really do. It's just very difficult to work this hard and not know what we are working toward."

"You are working toward building a town that is fully functional and has everything that the other people who work here need. That's not a secret, correct?"

I nodded.

"Beyond that, well, I'm not sure you know this, but even I don't know the details of what is being made in the factories here at Oak Ridge. No one does except those who are in charge. So I can empathize with how you feel. But I have also been charged with making sure that our employees adhere to the rules. So, based on what Stan has told me, and the quality of your work and otherwise exemplary attitude, I'm willing to give you another chance if you think you can control your inquisitiveness. Do you think you can?"

Could I? I at least owed Mr. Williams honesty. I thought about my mother and all the secrets she'd kept from me about her life. How the more she didn't tell me, the more I wanted to know. She said I tortured her with questions and had sometimes frustrated her to the point of having to send me to my room when I was younger. I'd never learned to stop asking. But I had learned how to live with not knowing. If I could do it at home...

"Yes, I can."

"Okay then," he said and sighed a little as if he were relieved to have this over with. He handed me a sheaf of drawings.

"Can you give these to Ted? There are notations indicating my changes."

"I will. And, Mr. Williams, thank you. Really. I won't let anything happen again."

He nodded. "See that you don't. Your mother would have my hide. Now get to work."

My hands shook as I walked out of his office and down to the drafting room. As soon as I opened the door, Ted's eyes locked on me and followed me as I walked in. He had always been flirtatious with me, but now I wasn't sure if he was giving me that same sort of attention, or if he was merely curious about why I had shown up late to work, and why Stan hadn't shown up at all.

This secret city we were building had created a den of suspicions amongst everyone, not just the Cooper Union Three. There was a pervasive feeling of intrigue all around that was both unsettling and arousing.

I handed Ted the sheaf of blueprints. Taking them from me, he gave me one of his sparkling smiles. He was one of those good-looking men who is just a bit too slick, or did I only realize that now in retrospect? He was at least six-foot-three with strong shoulders and long legs. Somehow, his dirty blond hair always fell just right over his forehead, framing his truly blue eyes. He had that habit of looking directly at you, making you feel as if he was concentrating on you and only you. And then there was the scar on his right cheekbone, never explained, that gave his face an unexpected roughness.

I walked away from Ted and toward my station. Everyone was there already. Only two drafting tables were empty. Mine and Stan's. He didn't come back for the rest of the day. And he wasn't in the dining room at dinnertime, waiting for Charlotte and me when we arrived. After we finished eating, she and I went to his room. His things were gone. But there was a letter for me propped on his desk.

Dear Isobelle,

I'm sorry for getting you into hot water with Mr. Williams. I thought he was going to fire me, but that's not exactly what happened. I lost my job here, but Mr. Williams offered me an entry-level position in the New York office.

He's a good egg. Said he understands how hard it is to live in the middle of a secret and that it's not for everybody. Or anybody, really. I'll be on probation for a while, but I can live with that. And I'll be waiting for you when you get back to Gotham. Say goodbye to Charlotte and the rest of the gang for me. And if you figure out what the hell you're all doing there, send me a message by carrier pigeon because as the signs all say, Loose Lips *and all that.*

Stan

Stan and Charlotte and I had speculated endlessly about what was going on at Oak Ridge. We knew it had something to do with the war effort. We knew it was dangerous. We knew it was something no one wanted our enemies to know. We'd guessed it had to be a weapon of sorts.

We learned we were right when in August of 1945, the United States dropped atomic bombs on Hiroshima and Nagasaki in Japan, instantly killing more than one hundred and fifty thousand people. Yes, Japan surrendered several days later. Yes, the war was over. But for me and tens of thousands of others who'd been at Oak Ridge and Los Alamos and Hanford, it was a very bittersweet victory.

How to absorb the fact that we'd taken part in the making of such destruction? How to process the idea that children and their mothers and fathers had died in the conflagration? And that, in some small way, we had contributed to the making of the deadliest weapon ever created?

My nightmares started that month. I suffer from them still. I've talked to other people who were at Oak Ridge with me and who work at SOM now. We're all still haunted. We'd done the job that SOM and our country asked of us. We knew it was time to move on. But how? How did you file something like that away?

The experience taught me a lot about myself. Secrets were my nemesis. I was drawn to them, preoccupied by them, obsessed with them. I'd thought when I decided to stay on at Oak Ridge that I'd accepted there were things I'd never know. I thought when my mother died, I'd resolved myself to the fact that she'd never tell me the things about her life and mine that I wanted to know.

In the case of Oak Ridge, the bomb that dropped made me realize that it's not always a positive thing when you learn about the secret that has been kept from you. But that doesn't mean it is in my power to give up searching for the secrets to my mother's treasure. I didn't make it to Alford Reed's jewelry shop today. But I'm going tomorrow with my only and very last clue.

Chapter 6

Sofiya Petrovitch
Petrograd
May 1915

That morning, she read to the soldier whose bed was behind Victor Drozdov's. They didn't converse after he'd told her the news. She didn't ask his name, inspect his chart or try to find out what was wrong with him. She didn't want to know. But reading to him was good. It forced her to focus on something other than how she felt.

She read the soldier an article about a ballet opening at the Mariinsky theater. And then read him an article about the changes the critics were seeing in art across Europe as painters responded to the World War.

The soldier lay on his bed, listening intently. No one who came back from the front was in excellent health. The conditions were dire. His right foot had a large bandage around it, but other than that, he appeared in decent health and a few years older than Sofiya. His cool, gray eyes were open and focused on her. Twice she noticed them go to her necklace. A chain with a small white guilloche enamel Easter egg with a tiny ruby cross had been a gift from her father and mother when she decided to sign up to help the soldiers as a nurse. The stones sometimes caught the light and sent reflections onto the wall.

Next, she read him a review of the poet Vladimir Vladimirovich Mayakovsky's latest work, *Backbone Flute*. Like with her Perseus, she avoided reading articles about the war but focused on the arts and culture. And when she finished, he asked for more. She scoured the paper and found a review of a new performance of *Swan Lake*. She had just started to read when Matron requested Sofiya make her way to the post-operative room.

The soldier thanked her solemnly. Unlike so many of the men she had come into contact with, he didn't want to chat, and yet at the same time, he didn't seem broken or depressed or defeated. There was an unusual calm about him. A quiet dignity, she thought, despite his condition, in spite of his bandage and rumpled bedclothes.

She didn't promise to come back at the end of the day. He didn't ask her to. But she asked him if he needed anything before she left.

"Yes, a glass of water if you please."

She took him the drink, wished him a good afternoon and walked off. On her way out, she stopped at Victor Drozdov's bed where she'd left the pillow crumpled and wet with tears in the middle of the cot. She removed the pillowcase, went to the closet where the linens were kept, got another, and replaced it. Finished, she walked toward the doorway, then hesitated and turned back to look at the empty bed once more.

The soldier she'd just been reading to was watching her, a sad smile on his face.

It had become her routine to visit the ward when she arrived in the morning and before she left at the end of the day. And so, without thinking, her feet took her back that night. Almost as if she'd forgotten, she was shocked anew to see Victor Drozdov's bed empty. Sometimes, beds were filled immediately. Other times, a day or two passed before a new patient took the other's place. She wondered if anyone but she would remember the man who had occupied it for the two weeks before his passing. Adjusting her view, she looked beyond the bed and saw the man who she'd read to that morning watching her intently, curiously.

She walked over to him. "Do you need something?" Sofiya asked.

"Well, I have been wondering all day if the critic liked the ending of the new production of *Swan Lake* that you were in the midst of reading."

She laughed, and he joined her. She saw a special light in his eyes. It pleased her that for him, and she supposed for her as well, there could be a moment of gaiety amid of all the sadness that surrounded them.

"I don't know your name," she said to him, suddenly wanting to know more about him.

"I don't even know my name."

"What do you mean?" she asked.

"Do you have time to hear my story?" He gestured to the grand clock on the marble mantel of the enormous fireplace. An ornate ormolu clock left behind when all the other elaborate furniture and *objets d'art* had been removed from this section of the palace to make way for the hospital.

"Yes, I'm off duty now. Nowhere I need to be."

"No husband waiting at home?"

"I'm only nineteen. I go home to my parents, but I'm often delayed here, and they don't worry if I'm a bit late."

"All right then. I'll tell you my strange story. My name is a mystery. So is all of my life before ten days ago. All I know about any time before that is what the doctors have told me. I was fighting in the offensives in the Carpathian Mountains. Apparently, I suffered a skull injury and was found wandering in the freezing cold. For how long we don't know for sure, but the doctor thinks no longer than a day. The officer who found me took me to the field hospital where they discovered I had developed frostbite on two of my toes on my right foot. They're gone now."

"You're very matter-of-fact about it," Sofiya said.

He gestured to all the beds around them. "Two toes, Nurse Petrovitch. Other men have lost arms, legs, their eyesight, parts of their faces, noses, jaws. Many don't make it out alive. Two toes was a small sacrifice."

It said a lot about him that he could rationalize his loss that way. She believed he meant it, and she was drawn to him for it. There were so many terrible wounds and losses inflicted by this war. He was very compassionate to acknowledge it and put his own troubles in perspective. She saw more tragedy each day than she could comprehend, and it was a relief for her to talk to someone who she didn't have to console. She'd only been working at the hospital for a few weeks, but like Olga, it was taking a toll on her. Tatiana, on the other hand, was thriving in her role. Sofiya's parents had said they weren't sure how much longer either of the two young women could withstand the emotional weight of processing what they were dealing with and that maybe it was time to think about giving up nursing per se and start contributing to the war effort in a different way. Sofiya was beginning to think they might be right, but when she and Olga talked about it, they always came to the same conclusion—how could they give up caring for the men who hadn't given up?

"Do you remember being found? Or do your memories start at the field hospital?"

"I remember the soldier who found me. That's the first memory I have, of him helping me up and talking to me. And how damn cold I was."

Sofiya had learned a bit about skull injuries and amnesia during her month at the hospital. Some patients never recovered all their memories. Others recovered except for memories about the incident that incapacitated them. Most were difficult patients. Understandably so, angry and frustrated and scared. And lonely. The different losses of memory were affected by where the injury had occurred. She was prepared for this soldier to turn morose or angry or sullen at any time, but at the moment he just seemed in need of company.

"Have I lost you?" he asked.

"I'm sorry. I was just thinking how brave you are that you aren't feeling sorry for yourself."

"Where would that get me?"

"But you can't control your emotions like that. You can't be that rational about how you feel."

"Why not?"

His question took her aback. "Because…"

"It's all about making a decision. I decide how to approach an issue or problem or reaction and then I do what I've decided."

"Just like that?"

He thought for a moment. "No. Not just like that. It takes effort."

"Maybe you could teach me how to do it. I seem to be a victim of my emotions."

"I'd be more than happy to. We can make an exchange. You can read to me—maybe a novel instead of the newspaper—and I can teach you to think less emotionally."

"I'd like that. What kind of novel?"

"I always loved Chekhov. He is the least depressing of the greats," he said, and then his eyes lit up and his whole face broke into a grin. "Well, look at that, Nurse Petrovitch. I just had my very first memory. I remembered that I loved Chekhov."

"Now that we have to celebrate," she said, feeling his joy. "Do you remember which of his novels you like the best?"

He cocked his head. Thought. "I almost just remembered. And then it disappeared again."

She nodded. "You can't get frustrated. That's how it comes back for some men. I've seen it before. Those fleeting memories are good for you, even if you can't grasp them."

"So the doctor says."

She wanted to get his mind off his failure to remember the title of the book. She gestured to his bandaged foot. "So that's healing well?"

"Now. But it wasn't. Shortly after the surgery at the field hospital, an infection set in. They pumped me full of medication and sent me here. Four days ago, they operated on me again and removed the remaining dead tissue around the primary site to prevent any more infection. But they can't do anything about my memory except wait."

"But you remembered your favorite author, that's a very good sign."

"I hope so."

"It is—" She broke off. "What do they call you?"

"Well, that's the second problem. I didn't have the prerequisite wooden identification phial in my uniform pocket. They say a lot of soldiers put matches in those phials and run the risk of not being identified if anything happens to them. My predicament wasn't due to my stupidity, though. My uniform was in tatters. The pocket was ripped off. All they know from the insignia on the collar is that I'm a captain. I can't very well go parading down the streets of St. Petersburg seeing if anyone recognizes me."

"But you know you live in St. Petersburg? Petrograd, I should say. I still can't get used to the name change."

He was staring at her.

"What is it?"

"This brain condition really is so mysterious and confounding. Actually, no. I didn't know that I lived here at all. I have no memory of a house or a family or a street or a route to work. But the way I phrased it makes it clear that, yes, I must have. Before the war, I must have lived here or else I wouldn't have phrased it just so."

"I agree. The doctors have described that to us in lectures about the process. One of the best cures for amnesiacs is to get them talking so they give themselves clues. Especially with family members. But that's the conundrum. If we don't know enough about the soldiers, and they don't know anything about themselves, we can't find the family members. So now that I'm here, you can talk to me, and we'll find the clues."

"Am I to be Victor Drozdov's replacement?" His tone was a bit sarcastic.

"If you like," Sofiya answered hesitantly.

"Actually, I would. Around here, everyone's got their own troubles."

"Then I'd be happy to stay for a while longer until your

dinner comes around. I can keep reading the paper or we can just talk. Maybe we'll figure out something in addition to the fact that you lived in this city. But I need to figure out what to call you other than Captain."

"I think of myself as Carpathian—named after the mountain range where the new me came to life."

They talked for another half hour until the orderlies brought dinner.

"I'll see you tomorrow," Sofiya said once he was settled with his tray.

She was gifted with a smile from Carpathian that kept her warm on the walk home. They hadn't uncovered any additional memories, but Carpathian had seemed pleased that he had remembered where he was from and who his favorite author was and that was something. Sofiya had been so disconsolate every night when she'd left her Perseus at the hospital. It was a welcome change to leave that night with some hope.

The next morning, she held her breath when she entered the ward, worried that Carpathian would be gone. But no, she remonstrated herself. He was well, he was healing. He wasn't sick with fever and infection.

She was rewarded with a welcome hello as she pulled up a chair and sat down beside Carpathian to read to him from the book of Chekhov stories she'd taken from her parents' library. She'd seen *The Cherry Orchard, The Seagull,* and *Uncle Vanya,* of course, but she'd never read any of the stories. When she pulled the book off the shelf, her father had been happy that she'd chosen it. Like many, he considered Chekhov the master of the form and told her he was looking forward to discussing them with her after she'd read them.

"Wait a bit before you start, would you?" Carpathian put his hand over the open pages.

The sight of his hand on her book sent a shiver through her. His hand was large, but graceful. He'd rested it there with a dancer's flourish, and for a moment, she thought he had put it on her thighs. That it thrilled her was a shock. Had she ever had such a specifically erotic thought before? Olga was always flirting with soldiers and talking about how attractive she found this one or that one. While Sofiya had had infatuations before, she'd never experienced a sexual surge like the one Carpathian's hand had just caused.

"Yes, I can wait. Of course. What is it?"

"Maybe we could chat a little. Tell me what you did last night when you left here."

"I went home—"

"Which is where?"

"An apartment on Zamyatin Pereulok Street."

"And who was home?"

"My father and mother."

"No brothers and sisters?"

"No, it's just me."

"And what happened when you got home?"

"My parents were waiting for me to have dinner."

"I'm sorry, that was my fault."

"They understood. In fact, they were very interested in what I told them about you."

"You told them about me?"

He seemed pleased.

"Well, I had stayed late to talk to you. They were very interested in how we stumbled onto the fact of where you lived."

"As was I. I thought about that all night. How very natural it was to just say it without fighting to find it. And then?"

"We had dinner."

"What did you eat? Our dinner here, as you saw, was filling enough but hardly a gourmet meal."

"We had roasted chicken with potatoes and carrots."

"That sounds delicious."

"Do you like chicken?"

Seemingly without much thought, he nodded and smiled broadly. Until then, Sofiya had thought Carpathian's looks were fairly ordinary. Especially compared to her now-lost Perseus. Still recovering from his ordeal in the mountains, Carpathian was emaciated. His lips were chapped. His light brown hair was too long and badly needed a trim. His eyes were his best feature—an unusually light shade of gray—the color of an early-morning fog.

At art school, Sofiya had studied facial expressions. While there are many variations, her professor believed there were sixty basic expressions based on photos taken by the nineteenth-century neurologist Duchenne de Boulogne, who made a study of the mechanics of how facial muscles moved. Including how they contracted into a smile. While researching, he had resorted to some gruesome methods, such as attaching electrodes to a person's face to shock them into responding. So painful was the procedure that Duchenne had no choice but to try his experiments on the recently severed heads of revolutionaries. Finally, in a Paris hospital, he came across a man who was immune to facial sensitivity and agreed to be the doctor's test subject.

Sofiya studied the mechanics of Carpathian's smile. It involved only two muscles. The zygomatic major cheek muscle tugged at the corners of his mouth. And then what made his smile so particular to him was that the orbicularis oculi, which surrounds the eye, lifted up his cheeks. The effect was twinkling eyes. Not every smile reached the eyes, but those that did were always the most intense and intimate.

And that was the kind that transformed Carpathian's face and enchanted Sofiya.

"I do like chicken. We've had it here in the hospital. But I just remembered something else that I like to eat. I didn't know it five minutes ago. Pirozhki and Shchi."

The meat pies and cabbage soup he mentioned were two of Sofiya's father's favorites as well. Her mother had told her how when they were first married and didn't have enough money to hire a cook, she did her best to make Russian food. But she wasn't a particularly good cook, and her upbringing in England hadn't prepared her at all for Slavic cuisine. Every meal, she said, turned out a disaster. The first thing she did when Sofiya's father was promoted at the museum wasn't to buy jewelry or a new coat, but to hire a woman to come in and cook. Eventually, Sofiya's paternal grandmother stepped in and gave her daughter-in-law some much-needed lessons. Now Fedora was more than competent at preparing basic Russian dishes.

"I am extremely thankful to you for talking to me once again. The doctors said it could take many weeks, months probably, for us to know if the area of my brain where memories are stored will heal. So it's very heartening to have any memory come back…even if all I ever recover are these little bites."

He looked down at his hands for a moment, and Sofiya noticed his mouth lowering at the corners just a touch. From her drawing class studies, from the other soldiers, from the streets, from her own family and friends, she knew this expression as well. Carpathian had become melancholic, which was more than understandable.

"I'm only an average cook but can make both of those dishes for you. Would you like that? I am off tomorrow but can bring them in on Monday. What would you like for dessert?"

"Really? You would do that?" He reminded Sofiya of her little cousin when surprised with a special treat.

"It would be my pleasure."

"Can you make *vatrushka*?"

Sofiya had never quite mastered the pastry dessert with the sweetened cottage cheese center, but she could try. She always mixed it up well enough and it always tasted right but when she made the sweet yeast bread dough circle, it never came out as a true circle and looked lopsided. Her father would tease her that she was not baking at all but experimenting with modernistic art.

"Do you like raisins or bits of dried fruit mixed in with the cheese?" she asked.

"Raisins. Are you really going to cook for me?"

"I am. It seems that if you can remember what you like to eat, the least I can do is try to make it for you."

"There are some other things I remember that I like," he said with a different kind of smile playing in his eyes.

Sofiya felt a blush creep up her cheek. Was he flirting with her? She'd had so little experience with boys because her mother and father were so strict. They often warned her about loose women who didn't wait until marriage to indulge in pleasures and reminded her about Aunt Maria, her father's sister. In whispered tones, they'd bemoan Maria's fate. After she found herself pregnant with a married man's child, Maria had been forced to marry a much older and unpleasant widower who agreed to accept her child as his own in exchange for a wife who would take care of him. At the end of the warning, Sofiya's father would always add: "And she never became the artist our family believed she had the potential for."

"What are those things you remember?" she asked

Carpathian, flirting back, feeling brazen. But wonderful.

"I liked the way your perfume scented the air when you came in every morning to read to Victor Drozdov."

There in the middle of the ward. With so much horror and sadness and pain all around them, with every terrible thing Carpathian had been through—the loss of part of his foot and his memory—this tall string bean of a man *was* flirting with her—and she was enjoying it more than she ever imagined she would.

"When you came to say goodnight to Victor Drozdov, I liked how one of your curls always escaped from under your headdress by the end of the day."

The mention of Victor's name saddened her. She must have given herself away with her expression.

"Did you know Victor Drozdov before he was brought in? You seemed so attached to him," Carpathian asked.

"No, not at all, but he…" She broke off.

"Yes?"

"It's sort of silly," she said and told him about the Perseus painting.

"Ah, you're the kind of girl who looks for signs and portents. Are you a mystic or a romantic?"

She shrugged. "I'm not sure I can say I'm either."

"Well, you're not purely a realist."

"Is that what you are?"

He laughed. "I, my dear, can only guess at what I am. But I think I'm an idealist. I am trying to piece it all together. When you read the news, I pay attention to my reactions and have discovered quite a bit about myself. I am very opinionated. I am not religious. And I lean more toward the ideas of the intelligentsia than the proletariat. By that I don't mean that I'm not sympathetic to the plight of the peasant, but at the same time, I don't believe we should do away with the tsar and the monarchy altogether. I want reform but not revolution." He spoke the last words softly. "Not an altogether popular opinion among many of the men here."

"My parents believe much of what you do as well, Captain."

"No, no, please call me Carpathian. I like to hear you say it."

She was blushing again.

"Would you like me to wheel you out into the gardens during my lunch break?" Sofiya said. "I could ask Matron and come back for you if she agrees."

He said he would, and Sofiya returned three hours later after helping in the recovery room all morning.

"It feels good to be outside," Carpathian said as she wheeled him down the stone path into the small private garden that the tsarina had created in an inner courtyard. It had a fountain, flower beds and several shade trees as well as evergreens all laid out in a formal pattern. Sofiya preferred the forests at the Alexander Palace in Tsarskoe Selo.

"The jostling doesn't bother you?" Sofiya asked.

"I barely feel it. It's the breeze that I'm focused on."

That was him, she thought. She could learn a lot from this soldier who ignored the wheelchair bumping on the garden path in favor of the cool spring breeze washing over him.

"Maybe by next week I'll be able to walk alongside of you with crutches, and then a week after that, I should be able to wheel you down this walkway. Not that you'd need it, but I'd like to repay the favor of giving you a ride."

Sofiya laughed. "Now that would be something. A patient wheeling a nurse around."

They walked between two pine trees and down the path until they came to an arbor covered with wisteria. Beneath it was a bench.

"This garden," Sofiya said. "Sometimes I rush my lunch and come outside and sit here and read during my lunch hour."

"What are you reading?"

"E.M. Forster's *A Room with a View*."

"An English book?" he asked.

"My mother's aunt sends them over."

"And you read in English as well as speak it. That's impressive."

"My mother thought it was important for me to speak her native language."

"Are you an avid reader of novels?"

"I am. My mother too. She's as much a romantic as I am."

"What's the most romantic thing that's ever happened to you?" Carpathian asked.

"I'm afraid nothing yet."

Carpathian shifted to look at her.

"Ah just wait, Nurse Petrovitch, just wait. I have the sense that your life is going to be one of great romance."

"I thought you said you weren't a mystic?" she asked.

"I lied. Isn't every Russian part mystic?" He laughed.

"I brought a surprise," she said. Reaching into the basket on the back of the wheelchair, she pulled out two oranges and handed him one.

"A real surprise, how did you get oranges?"

There were so many food shortages, oranges were rarer than diamonds.

"They have been cross-breeding hardy versions of oranges, lemons and mandarins in the Sochi region. I have a friend who brings me treats now and then."

"How lucky am I?" he said as he began to peel his piece

of fruit.

Her eyes filled with tears. Yes, the oranges were a treat, but Carpathian's gratefulness overwhelmed her. She'd never met anyone like him.

He handed her the orange he'd peeled, exchanged it with hers and began to strip that one of its outer skin.

Sofiya pulled out an orange section, put it between her teeth and bit down. The juice spilled out and down her chin.

"Oh no, what a mess," she said, laughing.

She reached into her pocket and pulled out a handkerchief. She was about to touch it to her mouth when Carpathian reached out with his forefinger, wiped away the drop of juice and then licked it off his finger.

Sofiya felt a slow burn deep inside of her. She was at a loss for what to say or do. This feeling was even more intense than when he had touched the book on her lap. He'd moved past the moment, though, and was eating his orange and talking about how hard it was in a time of war to keep up with things like gardens but that he was glad the Winter Palace garden was still being tended to.

"The head gardener is too old to go to war. Or to do much work. So many of us nurses volunteer a few hours a week to help him. It's important, not just for the patients' morale, but for us who work here too."

After they finished the fruit, Sofiya cleaned up the peels, and then walked behind the chair, ready to wheel Carpathian back, but he caught her hand and held it.

"Not just yet."

"Is something wrong?" she asked.

"No, I'm just not ready to leave. Being out here is a godsend. I had no idea. Out here I can forget…" He smiled ruefully. "Odd that I want to forget anything when I can't remember anything, but out here I don't have to think about all that. True, I have no past and that's torture, but in there I have no future either. Out here I can just be in the present."

Sofiya checked her pocket watch. She had a bit more time before she had to be back on duty, so she indulged him and sat back down under the wisteria arbor and took in deep sniffs of the peppery-sweet flowers.

"I'm glad you like it here. This has always been my favorite spot in all the garden."

"Why this spot exactly?" he asked.

"Because of the scent of the wisteria."

"The way they fall is exquisite too. I saw a wisteria stained glass lamp once that I thought was quite astonishing," he said.

"You did, where?"

Carpathian's eyes took on an eerie expression Sofiya recognized. She knew he was searching an invisible landscape looking for a clue, a memory, any thread to grab on to.

"Sofiya, I don't know."

It was as close to pity as she had seen him come.

"I've seen some Tiffany glass," she said brightly to diffuse the moment. "At Tsarskoe Selo at the Alexander Palace."

"And what was my Sister of Mercy doing at the tsar's palace?"

Sofiya told him about her mother being the tutor to the duchesses and described taking classes with them at Alexander Palace, how few outside friends they had and how close she and Olga were.

"There's so much fantastic artwork at the Palace. Including the tsarina's collection of Tiffany. Two lamps, a very elaborate silver repoussé vase on her dressing table and a whole desk set."

"Tiffany silver…" He was thinking again, she could tell. "You know, I've seen Tiffany silver, too. I can picture the items. An elaborate swan water pitcher."

"Maybe you were at the Alexander Palace too."

He shrugged his shoulders. "I could have been anywhere. I could have been anyone. Who would you like me to be?" he said in earnest and leaned forward toward her, pleading in his eyes.

"Just who you are."

"No, really, Sofiya. Since I can be anyone in the whole world, who should I be? What would please you the most? I'm no one, don't you see? A soldier without a name. I have twelve days of memory. A cabinet of images in my mind that are attached to no one and no place. You and this hospital and these grounds are all I am, and it's not enough. So let's make me someone. Someone you can fall in love with." He reached out and fingered an errant curl. "We're outside, and you're not nursing. Can you take that headpiece off? I want to see your hair."

She did as he asked and shook her hair loose. Most women kept their hair long and wore it up. But a few months before Sofiya had seen Anna Pavola as she left the ballet after a performance and noticed her chin-length bob. Sofiya had her curly hair cut in the same style. It was shocking to her mother and the grand duchesses that she'd done it, but then Tatiana followed suit.

Before she could react, Carpathian reached out and buried his fingers in her hair and then pulled her forward and kissed her. She had never been kissed by a man before. Only furtively by boys with sweaty palms, stealing a moment, experimenting. Those kisses had been titillating for all their audaciousness. But this was the kind of kiss Sofiya had read about in books and seen once or twice in the park or on the street between passionate couples embracing. This was the kind of kiss that she had seen at the cinema and that she and Olga had longed for.

Carpathian held Sofiya's face between his hands and kissed her for a long time in the garden. She was, at first, overwhelmed. So many sensations. So much newness. Feelings on her lips, her cheeks, inside of her, deep in her center. An overflow of feelings, and then she started to float on the sensations. Got drunk on the scent of the wisteria and the cool breeze and the occasional birdsong, all while this man's lips pressed against hers and opened up her world to a thrill she had only guessed at. Her skin was on fire. Her mouth knew somehow to press forward and open.

And then she had a thought that broke through—that this was her first long kiss and she was eternally grateful that it was so wonderful—and she knew that she wanted to remember it forever and began to commit it to memory even as she remained under its spell.

The kiss lasted for a few moments—how long? A minute? Two? Really a lifetime because it changed her forever. Altered her center. Opened her to knowledge she'd never had. Suddenly, she understood lust. She *wanted* someone. She'd never even imagined what it would feel like. And now it suffused her whole being. She wanted to hold him and be held by him. She wanted him to put his arms around her and hold her tightly to him, and she wanted his hands in other places.

"I hope I didn't shock you," he said when he finally ended the kiss for a breath. "But you don't seem shocked."

"No, not shocked... I'm..." She stopped and searched for a word to describe what she was feeling. A single word? She needed a whole vocabulary.

"Sofiya?"

"I suppose I'm surprised."

"Pleasantly, I hope.'"

"Yes, yes. You know…" she offered, not sure why she had decided to tell him. "That was my very first real kiss."

"I had no idea. You managed it like an expert." He laughed.

"I think I'll remember it forever."

She cringed. So lost in the moment, she'd forgotten not to say things like that. He was a man who couldn't find his memories. Certainly, she shouldn't be talking about remembering.

"As will I, Sofiya. It was a kiss for the ages. I'm certain the most astonishing kiss of my life. So special in fact that I think we should celebrate it with another. And maybe you could come sit in my lap so neither of us have to lean over quite so far."

She was shy going to him. Sitting in his lap was quite forward. But she did want to be closer to him. To stay closer to him. And so, she went. And their second kiss was even better than the first because there wasn't the awkwardness of not being sure that time.

"You know," he said when they pulled apart, "for me too it was the first time. Since I don't have a past anymore, you and your kisses and your very touch, each is the very first one."

Chapter 7

Isobelle Moon
New York City
November 1948

"Miss Moon?"

I've been reading a two-month-old issue of *Town & Country* magazine and look up at the first sound of the honey-deep voice.

"I'm sorry, I was with a client." A tall, elegant man wearing a white smock over black slacks walks toward me.

"Mr. Reed?"

He has high cheekbones, an aquiline nose, and black wavy hair without a thread of gray. I'm confused. The contract in my mother's vault was dated more than eighteen years ago. Jules Reed is certainly no more than thirty or thirty-five at the eldest. In 1930, he would have been no more than seventeen.

"Yes," he says and extends his hand.

We shake. His skin is warm and the grip assured. When he smiles, his expression is more welcoming than I'd expect from someone so urbane. His almost-black eyes are—I try to think of how to describe them and settle on watchful.

"Are you looking for something in particular, or to have something made?"

"I'm sorry, I'm not here to buy anything. I was hoping you might be able to help me research a receipt from your firm."

"Let's go into my office, then, and I'll see what I can do."

His voice makes me think of molten gold. He even moves the way melting metal would—in a strangely languorous fashion as if time doesn't matter.

"It's this way." Mr. Reed gestures to the right, and I follow him out of the showroom with its glass cases filled with innovative and glittering gold and platinum baubles.

Like the outer room, the walls and furnishings of his office are caramel-colored with rich walnut, burl and ebony wood furniture and paneling.

There's a sleek modernity to the décor, though the man sitting on the other side of the desk is more classical in appearance. Mr. Reed has the look of an artist who doesn't quite belong to any specific time period. It's those eyes that take in everything. And there's something in his expression that you usually see in someone much older. It's in the way he moves so gracefully. And how his hair, longer than is fashionable, defiantly curls over his collar. He could be a Renaissance sculptor who just stepped out of his studio. Or an Edwardian painter. He clasps his hands together and rests them in the middle of his desk, the fingers so expressive, they seem to speak a language all their own.

I notice that on the ring finger of his right hand is a

battered-looking signet ring with a worn insignia. It appears to be vines, curling around letters. But I can't make them out. Is it a thorny stem curving around a flower? Realizing I'm staring, I look away and up at his face.

I'm struck again by the familiarity. He has a scar on his cheekbone beneath his left eye, a thin ribbon paler than his already-pale skin. I'm sure I've not only noticed it before but thought the same thing about it. And this isn't the first time I've been aware of how there is a hint of pine green in his almost-black dark eyes. As sure as I am that I've seen him before, I'm equally sure we don't know each other.

Mr. Reed is looking at me with what seems to be the same curiosity.

"I'm sorry for staring," I say. "You look so familiar, except I don't think we've met, have we?"

"I'm so glad you said something." He laughs, and the sound is like a deep sonorous bell. The green flecks flash in his eyes. "I didn't want to be rude and stare, but you look familiar as well. And I agree, we haven't met. I'm absolutely sure I'd remember if we had."

Is there a suggestion in his tone, or do I just want there to be? Which is the last thing I should think. This man is far out of my league with all his sophistication and *savoir faire*.

"Well, we'll figure it out," he says. "Can I see the receipt?"

I'm not particularly good at reading people—I'm much better with blueprints—but his abrupt shift in conversation alerts me. Something just made him uncomfortable. I want to say, scared. But he doesn't strike me as the kind of man who is ever afraid.

I open my bag and retrieve the envelope I took from the hiding place in my mother's room. Extracting the two receipts, I hand them to him.

He takes them, reads each one twice. Then looks up.

"Is Sophia Moon your mother? You wouldn't have been old enough back then to have sold my grandfather anything but homemade brownies from a school fair."

"Yes, my mother. Is Alford Reed your grandfather?"

Mr. Reed nods. "Yes, I'm Jules Reed. And before you say anything, yes, I know, a jeweler named Jules. My mother has a perverse sense of humor."

"I wasn't going to say anything."

"But you were thinking it." He smiles.

"Well…"

He laughs. "How can I help you?"

"Well, if it was your grandfather my mother dealt with, can I talk to him?"

"I'm afraid not. He's not with us."

"Oh, I am sorry. I shouldn't have assumed. My mother isn't either and I—"

"No," he interrupts. "I just meant he's not here in the store. He's—" Jules Reed clears his throat. "Well, it's refreshing to meet someone who doesn't read the gossip columns. My grandfather is actually currently residing in Sing Prison."

I have no idea how to react. But it appears Mr. Reed is used to that from how he handles my surprise. He doesn't hesitate at all.

"It's not the easiest thing in the world to deal with, but he's healthy and handling it as well as can be expected. But you didn't come here to discuss my grandfather's incarceration."

His eyes shift back toward the receipt in his hand. Then he looks back at me.

"So how can I help you with these?"

"I'm trying to find out more about the two sales. More

specifically about the stones. I think I have the piece they were taken from and was hoping Mr. Reed might know more about it."

He looks confused, and I feel like I'm babbling. But all my frustration with my mother's secrecy, all my anger that she left me so abruptly and with so many questions, is bubbling to the surface. "I'm sorry. I've found a piece of jewelry that belonged to my mother. It's no longer intact. All the stones from it are missing. The receipts were with it. Altogether, it's presented quite a puzzle. I was hoping your grandfather might help me figure it out."

"Figure out what exactly?"

"I guess I was hoping that he saw the piece. Got its history. That he must have wanted to know more about the provenance before he bought the stones. I was thinking he could tell me what my mother told him."

There's so much more I'm not saying. That I *can't* say to a stranger. How do you tell someone that you are desperate to find out about your mother, about what she never shared with you? And even more, find out why she never shared it.

Almost as if he can hear my thoughts, he says, "It's not at all unusual for people to search for answers about their ancestry through objects inherited after a loved one has passed."

I turn away from him as I feel the first sting of tears. What on earth is wrong with me? I've come to terms with my mother's death. I've had my year of mourning. I'd been living on my own for more than five years when she died. As much as I grieved, I was used to our separation. So what about finding a tiara in a vault has rendered me so emotional?

I get up and walk to the window and look out across 57th Street to distract and compose myself. The view surprises me.

"This is crazy. I can see my office from here."

"The building where you work? Which one?"

"Not just the building. The actual office. Right there."

Mr. Reed gets up and joins me at the window. I catch a faint whiff of his cologne and take it in. It's dark and moody with hints of spice and vanilla that sparkle, the way the green flecks in his eyes do.

"Those windows directly opposite at 5 East 57th," I say.

"Wait a minute. You work in the drafting room at Skidmore?"

"I do. I'm an architect."

"So that's why you look so familiar," he says. "I stand here quite often and catch sight of all of you. You're the late-nighter, aren't you?"

"What?"

"I have names for each of you. There's coffee boy—he's the redhead who always has a cup of coffee with him. Then there's pacer—the short guy who constantly walks back and forth. There's the chewer—"

I turn away from the window to face Mr. Reed. "Harrison, who always has a pencil in his mouth."

"You're catching on."

"And I'm the late-nighter because I stay after everyone else?"

"Yes, why is that? Are you that ambitious?" He smiles in sympathy, not like it's an accusation. And he leans forward just a little as if he is actually interested in my answer.

"I am." There's more I want to say but I don't know this man at all. It wouldn't be appropriate.

"There aren't many women in that office, I've noticed."

"You have?" I'm not sure how to take that.

"I'm not some ogler, I just happened to notice."

"Yes, well, architecture isn't all that welcoming to women."

"And yet, there you are."

I shrug. "It's not something I spend much time thinking about if I can help it." Which of course is a lie, yet I continue on. "Nothing is easy for anyone. My mother escaped from Russia by herself when she was six months pregnant, leaving everything and everyone she knew behind. She had to start over once she arrived. Compared to that, my situation isn't the least bit challenging."

We're still standing by the window, facing each other. It's strangely easy to talk to this man and I'm not sure why.

"Let's sit," he says, and it sounds like an invitation for more. Or is that my imagination?

I follow him back to the desk, and we sit opposite each other. The piece of furniture seems bigger than it was before. As if it's putting distance between us. I look down, examining the desktop. I didn't pay much attention before, but now I focus on a box of Crayola crayons next to a sketchpad. Mr. Reed sees me looking at them.

"Not a very highly sophisticated way to sketch out a design," he says. "My grandfather uses them—used them when he did preliminary sketches. You can't get caught up in the details that way and can focus on the overall structure. He's very architectural with his designs."

"I noticed that when I came in and looked at the pieces in the cases. So do you use them too?"

"I do. He taught me pretty much everything I know. The good and the bad."

I'm not sure, but I think I see a grimace. Mr. Reed continues, "He got me started examining stones when I was only seven years old. He'd pull out a new purchase, and we'd sit and look at it and inspect all its tables and colorations and then talk about different ways to set it. When we came up with an idea that he thought had merit, we'd both open our own box of crayons, pick out the color that best matched the stone and sketch out the idea. There were boxes of crayons all over his apartment. The artful gouache drawings most jewelers create weren't for Grandfather. Some people said he was too avant-garde to do it the way anyone else did anyway. But it wasn't that. He wasn't a trained artist and he found brushes and delicate work beyond him. He could hide his lack of drawing skills behind the brash sketches. I've had more training and can do a gouache Van Cleef and Arpels would be proud of, but I prefer the crayons too. I love the simplicity and joy of using less nuanced tools."

I glance at a line of drawings laid out on a shelf behind the desk. A series of brooches that remind me of fireworks. The bursts of blue, red and yellow are simple and almost primitive, like a Matisse painting. They are powerful and beautiful and have a spontaneity and excitement that I imagine a more detailed study in washes wouldn't.

"Are those your designs?" I ask.

He nods.

I wanted them to be his and am irrationally happy that Jules Reed is truly talented and creative. "I'd love to see the pieces when they are made."

"Then I'd be more than happy to show them to you." He smiles and holds my gaze for a moment too long. "So back to the piece of jewelry you found that you think the stones were taken from. Can you describe it?"

I don't answer right away. Is there a reason not to tell him? I can't think of one. I tell him that what I found is a tiara.

"Is it from Russia?" Mr. Reed asks.

"I don't know, but the case it is in is from Russia."

"What is it made of?"

"The tiara? I think it's silver."

He nods. "If it is from Russia and predates the revolution, it probably is. They used gold in many of the tiaras, with a silver overlay."

I nod.

"What is it you wanted to know from my grandfather? If he recognized it? Where it was from?"

"Yes, and if my mother told him how she got it. If there are any stories attached to it. My father was a jeweler who worked for a company called Carl Fabergé and—"

"Your father worked for Fabergé?" Mr. Reed sounds genuinely surprised.

I nod, reach under the top sweater of my twinset, and pull out my necklace to hold it up.

"My father made all but one of these enamel eggs. I'm afraid some of them are a bit battered. My mother wore it every single day that I can remember."

"May I see?"

I lift it over my head and hand it to Mr. Reed, who takes it from me and places it on a velvet tray. I am struck by how gentle he is with it. Treating it with more care than I ever have.

Reaching under the neck of his smock much the way I just did to bring out my necklace, he pulls out a leather cord. On the end is a gold oval object about an inch wide and an inch thick. He flips it open and separates it into two parts. Mr. Reed slips his index finger into the opening of the top half and brings the rest of the contraption up to his right eye. Then, holding the necklace in his other hand, he begins to examine each of the eggs.

"What are you doing?" I ask.

"This is a loupe with a ten-times magnification so I can

see the details and markings on each of the charms more clearly. Would you like to see?"

I say I would, and he hands me the tool. I notice the engraving on the top. It's a complicated design, worn and battered, but I think I see the letters *MS* wrapped with a thorny stem. Or maybe it's a rose wrapped with its own stem. Either way, I'm fairly certain it's the same insignia as on his ring. But if it is initials, his aren't MS. Neither are his grandfather's. So whose is it?

Mr. Reed sees me studying the engraving and a tiny frown creases his otherwise smooth forehead.

I return to the loupe and fiddle with it but can't figure out how to use it.

"Let me show you," he says.

Is it my imagination, or is his voice gruffer than it was before?

He takes it back. "Hold it like this. Don't keep your left eye closed. Keep both open and move the egg up and down until it's in focus."

He hands it back, and I follow his example.

"Okay, now look at the link attached to the egg. Do you see the markings on it?"

I nod.

"The largest one is a *K* with a Cyrillic letter after it. Do you see that?"

"Yes."

"That's Fabergé's mark. Now look for a small rectangle pressed into the gold with the initials *SZ* inside of it. Do you see that?"

"I do."

"That's the individual jeweler's mark. If your father made these, that would be his mark. It's *SZ*."

"Then it's not my father; his initials would have been

CM. His first name was Carpathian and his last name was something unpronounceable with an *M*. My mother changed it to Moon."

"Then someone else made these eggs."

"Can I examine the others and see if his initials are on any of them?"

"Of course." He smiles. "It is yours."

He waits patiently while I examine each one.

"This one, the white one with the red cross, has a different mark. But it's not a *CM* either," I say.

I hand the necklace and the loupe back to Mr. Reed, who looks at what I found.

"*H.W.* That's Henrik Wigström. One of the better-known workmasters at Fabergé." Mr. Reed takes the loupe away from his eye, closes it and slips it back inside his smock, patting it to make sure it's once again hidden away.

"This is a wonderful necklace, Miss Moon." Mr. Reed returns the piece to me, and I put it back on. "The House of Fabergé has a legendary legacy. My grandfather has been buying their pieces for years from emigres. I've heard bits and pieces, and I'm fascinated. What stories you must have heard."

"Actually, none. I never knew my father. He died in a Siberian prison, probably in 1922 or 1923."

"I'm so sorry."

Even though we've just met, Mr. Reed emotes empathy. His experiences with tragedy must be profound. He almost seems more moved by this fact than I have ever been. I never actually lost my father since I never had him. Not knowing him, I've only been able to long for him in the abstract. To miss the idea of him, not the actuality.

There's something in Mr. Reed's eyes. A look my mother used to get when I'd ask too many questions about her past. I change the subject.

"You said your grandfather has been buying from emigres for a long time. That's probably how my mother came to find him."

"I would imagine, yes."

"So would you still have records of this sale?"

He re-reads the receipt. "More than this? Probably not. Typically, this is all we'd record—a description of the transaction. In this case, diamonds of various small sizes and paste sapphires. The prices look fair for the time."

"And you don't think your grandfather might have kept any other information?" I am so frustrated. I want to know what I found. Why my mother held on to the empty frame. Why she hid it. All this man is doing is confirming that his grandfather paid market value.

Mr. Reed gives me a sympathetic smile. "I know I'm not giving you much. I'd be happy to pull the records and double-check. They're in storage, and it will take a day or two."

"Thank you. That really would be so helpful."

"Give me your number. Once I've retrieved the papers, I'll ring you and we can make an appointment."

As I wait for the elevator outside his office, I imagine that my mother once stood here with her tiara in its case, its stones removed and a check in her pocketbook. How did she feel having stripped her treasure? What did the tiara mean to her? Where did it come from?

In the elevator, I push the button to the lobby with much more force than necessary.

You came here. You stood right here. You met this man's grandfather and sat in that office and talked to him and watched as he pried the stones out of what must have been your prized possession. You did all those things, and I know nothing about any of them. I know nothing about who you were other than an art restorer and my mother.

I'm angry at her. I didn't think I still was, but I am. I was often upset with her when I was growing up. She could be obtuse and silent and unsympathetic to what I needed. But I was never as angry at her when she was alive as I am now that she's dead, having left me with the biggest unanswered question of all—who was she before she was my mother?

Chapter 8

Sofiya Petrovitch
Petrograd
May 1915

Carpathian smiled at Sofiya conspiratorially when she stopped by the day after their garden excursion.

"I have a little jaunt prepared for us after work today. So come as soon as you can. We're going to go exploring."

Sofiya shook her head. "It's strictly forbidden for any of the staff or patients to venture beyond the confines of rooms designated as part of the hospital. The rest of the Winter Palace is out of bounds."

"I don't care about the rules anymore. What can they do to me? Throw me out of the army? I'm no good to them now anyway. And you? They need you more than you need them."

The day moved slowly for Sofiya, the sense of

anticipation weighing on every moment. What was he planning? Finally, it was five o'clock in the evening, and her shift was over. She made her way back to the ward and found Carpathian waiting, ready, sitting in his wheelchair.

"Would you care to take me for a spin in the garden?" he asked, showing off a little and making sure that the men who shared that section of the room heard him. When he was the most upset about his memory loss, she learned that he became almost cheery.

Sofiya wheeled him out of the ward and into the hallway.

"Are we really going to the garden?" she asked.

"No, turn left at the end of the corridor," he said.

She did as he asked.

"Now down this hallway, the last door on the right. Go through there," he instructed.

As she wheeled him, she recounted bits of trivia about the palace, partly to entertain him but also to distract herself from her nerves. "The tsar used to keep cows on the palace roof so there was always fresh milk and cream for the family. And there were dozens of rooms set aside for specific tasks: one for flower arranging, one for repainting furniture, even one just for pie making."

"How did you find all this out?"

"I took history lessons with the duchesses. There are 1,500 rooms, 1,786 doors and 1,945 windows in the palace."

"Well, I've found one of those rooms for us to make ours."

Carpathian directed her through several empty staterooms and corridors.

"Isn't there any security in here?"

"Usually, yes, but I had some cigarettes that I gifted to the guard to take a little break."

Finally, they came to a paneled room of no particular note.

Carpathian pointed. "There," he said.

Sofiya looked into what, by all appearances, seemed an ordinary corner of the room. "There?" she asked.

"There," he said.

Once they arrived, he pointed to the waist-high molding.

"See that wreath motif. You want the last wreath before the corner. Twist it."

She did as she was told. With a loud creak, the wall itself opened, revealing a secret passage.

"Excellent. It's not much farther."

"It's so dark."

"No fear." He turned on a light switch. A small chandelier cast soft light into a hallway. At the end, a doorway promised a destination. They proceeded to the door, which she opened to reveal a small room—the size of a bedroom in a modest home. The walls were lined with shelves, filled with various bottles, rock formations, scientific paraphernalia and rows of leather-bound books, some that looked quite old. There was a couch in the other corner, with pillows and a blanket as if whoever used this room might need to stay overnight.

"What is this place?"

"I think it might be some kind of alchemist's lair."

They took some books off the shelf and found treatises on magic and the occult.

"There have always been rumors that rulers had courtiers who dabbled in magic."

"Including our own tsarina. Do you think Rasputin has ever come to this room?"

Carpathian sniffed the air. "No, he's far too filthy. I

smell a woman's perfume."

Sofiya sniffed as well. "I wonder whose room this was. There's such a sense of..." She hesitated, not sure how to describe what she felt here. The secret room felt forbidden. As did being with this exciting, mysterious soldier. She looked across at Carpathian.

"Have you been here before?"

"Yes, last night."

"How did you hear about it?"

"I don't actually have any idea." For a moment, an expression of pain crossed his face. Sofiya knew this look. At first, she thought he was experiencing phantom pain which some patients who had amputations experienced. But she'd learned that this was the ache of him almost remembering something that he couldn't pull out of the ether.

"But," Carpathian continued, "when I saw the molding, I just knew...a remnant of information from some other life?"

"But how did you get here—to this room—to this part of the palace? Did someone wheel you here?"

"Ah, yes, that. Let me show you."

He put his hands on the wheels of the chair and maneuvered it himself, rolling toward her. "My arm is healed enough that I can wheel myself now. I was up most of last night exploring."

"And now we're here."

"And so we are. Our own room. We can come here and be by ourselves."

Sofiya sat down on the couch. Carpathian hoisted himself out of the chair to sit next to her.

She cringed, watching him.

"Does my foot disgust you? Do you think me maimed?"

"No. Hardly. Two toes? Why would you think that?"

"From the expression on your face watching me get up."

"I was worried about how fast you were moving. I don't want you to impede your healing by stressing the site. But that you would think I was disgusted makes me wonder if you are disgusted with your injury."

He shook his head. "No, not disgusted. But I am worried about how other people will react to my deformity. I don't want anyone's pity."

"The people who love you won't pity you, they will be thankful you're alive. The rest...they won't even notice."

"People will notice that I'm walking with a cane."

"There's every chance you won't need any walking aid once the wound totally heals and you practice balance exercises with the physical therapy team. But if you do wind up needing a cane, knowing you, you'll get a fabulous one." She smiled. "I can see you with an ebony cane with a carving of a peacock on its head—the symbol for rebirth. No one will think you have an infirmity but rather that you have style. You'll look dapper and important."

"As I do whatever it is that I do," he said in the rueful voice she'd come to recognize. "Sweep the streets...drive a troika... Very dapper to do those jobs with an ebony cane."

He was not self-pitying, though he sometimes defaulted to sarcasm when he became frustrated about his memory loss. Sofiya wished he'd just break down. She could have comforted him then. But she didn't know how to help him when he wouldn't talk to her about how much his memory loss bothered him.

As she often did—too often according to her mother—Sofiya began to play with the chain around her neck. Carpathian leaned over and took it from her hand.

As he did, she examined him, marveling at how much

he moved her, how much she wanted to help him, how much she felt when she was with him.

Olga and Tatiana and some of the other nurses often teased Sofiya about having a special friend. But the duchesses shouldn't talk since neither of them were ever without one special friend or another. Carpathian was the first for Sofiya. She was worried about how much longer he would be at the Winter Palace hospital. And without him knowing where he lived or who his family was, where would they send him once they released him? A typical stay in the hospital was thirty to forty days. He'd already been there for ten. His memory was still frozen. Occasionally, he would remember something else that he liked but nothing that gave him any indication as to who he had been other than a soldier.

He knew he had lived in St. Petersburg. What a few of his favorite foods were. He discovered he favored music and theater and reading. He was well versed in ballet. But he still didn't know anything about his family. His occupation. Who his friends were. Or lovers. He didn't know if he'd traveled beyond where the war had sent him, or if he'd ever had any illnesses. Was he a good person? Had he saved money, or was he a spendthrift? He especially wanted to know if he'd accomplished anything. That mattered to him more than almost anything else.

Carpathian was watching Sofiya play with the chain. "That little egg is quite beautiful." He sounded thoughtful. "Everyone needs to have some beauty in their lives," he said. "I can't remember my mother's face or my father's name, but I can remember what stirs me. Paintings, sculpture, music. I still know these things elevate our lives. Without being able to look upon them, listen to them, we are just existing."

"That's why the Hermitage is so important, isn't it?" Sofiya asked. "Why inexpensive seats and standing room at our theaters and concert halls are necessary for a healthy society. Why artists are so important."

"Yes, a great symphony or ballet...a grand painting...these are the things that matter. They still matter to me even though I don't know who I sat next to when I saw *Swan Lake* or studied a Rembrandt. I think one of the things that bothers me the most about not remembering is I don't know if I have any talent. If I was a creator or an observer."

She could tell the idea of not being a creator was difficult for him to imagine.

"Not everyone can be an artist," she said, trying to be consoling.

"I am not afraid to find out that I'm an accountant in a business office because there isn't anything wrong with any job. But with the way I feel about creativity, I hope I'm someone who contributes to the artistic world in some way."

"I'm sure that you are," she told him. "The way you speak about art, the way you notice colors and shapes and the beauty around us...you have to be."

He looked off. "I spoke to the doctor this morning. He said that there is no guarantee that I will ever remember everything."

"But didn't he also say there is every reason that in time, everything will come back?"

Carpathian reached for the chain that Sofiya was still playing with. He turned the charm this way and that with his head tilted like a child discovering a new toy.

"Your trinket is familiar to me." He let it fall back on her breast. "Have you ever looked at the link? Is a maker's mark engraved there?"

"I never looked." She was surprised he'd ask such a thing. Why would that interest him? But she lifted the egg and examined it. And, indeed, she found a mark.

"Yes, it's an—"

"Don't tell me. Is it *H.W.* in an oval?"

"Yes, how did you know?" Sofiya stared at the mark she'd never noticed but he'd guessed was there.

Deep furrows lined Carpathian's brow. "I'm not sure...but I know who H. W. is. It's Henrik Wigström, a Finnish jeweler who is a workmaster at the House of Fabergé."

"That is where my parents bought me this gift, but how could you know that?"

Watching his face, Sofiya saw one of the most remarkable sights she'd ever witnessed. Carpathian's whole face changed. His eyes came alive in a way they hadn't before. His countenance lightened. He looked at least five years younger.

"You must be my lucky talisman, Sofiya Petrovitch. I know more than what city I come from and some of the food I like to eat, I now know what I did before I was a soldier. I'm a goldsmith." He took her hands in his, his face alight with his discovery. "And I work for the man who made your egg. I am a jeweler at the House of Fabergé." He shook his head in wonder, looking at her with awe. "You know, you might just give me back my life."

Chapter 9

Isobelle Moon
New York City
December 1948

Every day now when I go into work, I'm conscious of not staring out the window. I visited Mr. Reed three days ago, and I haven't heard from him yet. I have no idea if he is indeed looking for the paperwork I wanted to see, or if he was just placating me and has no intention of helping.

And so, I am avoiding looking across the street for fear I'll appear anxious, or worse, that I'm interested in him. I know better than to dream when it comes to men.

My mother had an optimist's mind but a pessimist's heart. She wanted me to have every opportunity, to reach for every goal when it came to my career, but at the same time was determined to prepare me for reality when it came to romance.

She wanted me to have complete self-confidence but also no illusions about myself. "So you never wind up as heartbroken as I did," she said.

As a result, as a designer, I have always believed I could aim as high as a skyscraper. But not as a woman. I'm no beauty. Not feminine. My mother used to call me gamine. I look younger than my years. My face is angular, not soft. My hair is thick but a simple nut-brown color. I wear glasses. My breasts are small, and my hips are narrow. My eyes are not an exotic blue or a stunning green but a strange gray. And the way I dress—slacks and blouses, sweaters and bathrobe style coats—isn't seductive. I've tried to dress more provocatively in the past, but I look silly in lower-cut necklines without the cleavage to do them justice. And the fit and flare dresses that show off a woman's curves don't help me much since I have none. The men I notice never seem to notice me. But I've learned that outside the boyfriend arena, those tomboy looks help. Both at Cooper Union with my professors, and at SOM with my bosses, I am treated more seriously. For the most part.

When I was a teenager, I was jealous of how other girls looked and complained about how they were maturing and I wasn't. Nothing angered my mother more. But try as I might, no matter how much she tried to convince me otherwise, no matter how many movie stars who didn't fit the mold she pointed out, my mother couldn't make me feel differently about my appearance.

So I had been ripe to be used by Ted Forester back at Oak Ridge after Stan was sent back to New York. But that will never happen to me again. I've stopped dreaming about ever having a man moon over my eyes or write poetry about my curls. I avoid putting myself in positions to be hurt by any man's lack of romantic attention. Or letting any man know that I find him attractive. I don't want to know the feeling isn't reciprocated.

That's why I'm avoiding the window. Except that's a problem. It's not that easy, since my desk is right in front of it and I'm used to leaning on the sill and looking out when my eyes get tired from too many hours of drafting. It's a respite to spend a few minutes watching the street below, the activity in the buildings across the street, or clouds or storms moving across the sky.

But I've managed not to look directly across the way once since Tuesday. Little did I think that anyone would notice that.

"Is there something out there you don't want to see?" Stan asks me.

"What do you mean?"

"Come on, Izzie, you take window breaks the way other people take coffee breaks and for the last couple of days, you've looked everywhere but out the window."

He knows me too well. Even during the years we spent apart while I was still in Oak Ridge and he was here, we kept up a constant correspondence—albeit a highly censored one since the government redacted half of every letter I wrote.

Stan's career had benefited from leaving Oak Ridge. He hadn't committed a crime but had simply been too curious about what was going on there. So the New York office, which had been depleted by war with most of the architects either off fighting or in Oak Ridge, welcomed him back. Stan was F4 because of being slightly deaf in one ear. It wasn't anything you'd ever notice, but it made him ineligible to serve. Returning to New York, having given the war effort a valiant try, he'd risen rapidly.

While I am a junior at SOM, he is already a full-fledged architect. We're both on Ted Forester's team, working on the Connecticut magazine headquarters, but Stan has more seniority. In all honestly, that irks me. It's my suggestions and solutions that are chosen more than anyone in the group. My problem is bigger than seniority, though. It's Ted. It's not just what happened at Oak Ridge. Our affair only lasted two months and that was during my first year there, which is now three years ago. It's that Ted is dumping his problems on me to solve and not letting the head of the department know. I don't think anyone realizes how much of his work I'm doing. The one time I brought it up to Ted, I received a shoulder squeeze and a reminder of how I'm "invaluable to the team" and that "the team is what matters." I wanted to throw up. But all I did was nod, thank him, and go back to my desk.

I'm wary of going to Mr. Williams or higher, to the chief architect, Mr. Bunshaft. I'm a realist, thanks to my mother. I know I'm lucky to have this job. With all the men back from the war who want their old jobs back, filing a complaint would be too much of a risk. And I worry they wouldn't believe me. I've seen it happen before. Women who complain too much are considered troublemakers or too sensitive.

I'd known from the day I first told my mother I was serious about attending architecture school and pursuing my childhood dream that it was going to be a hard-won battle. Architecture has never been kind to women. The few well-known females in the field either entered through interior design, like Eileen Gray, or married architects and came to prominence as a team. Or worse, suffered like Marion Mahoney Griffin, who we all know is the real talent behind the Prairie-style drawings that Frank Lloyd Wright has never given her credit for. Julia Morgan stands almost alone and is my hero. She never took no for an answer, never married, and last I heard, is seventy-six and still working on William Randolph Hearst's Castle and San Simeon Ranch. She was the first woman to be admitted to the architecture program at Paris' L'École Nationale Supérieure des Beaux-Arts in 1897 and the first woman architect to be licensed in California.

Despite all my frustrations, the fact is, I *am* working at Skidmore, Owings & Merrill and there are opportunities afforded me here that I wouldn't get at a smaller, less prestigious firm. I try not to let my dissatisfaction get in the way of the work I'm doing. My goal is to forge on without complaint. Yet it seems the more I try not to think about it, the more agitated I become.

"So aren't you going to tell me why you are avoiding the window?" Stan asks. He gives me one of his boyish grins. He's my age but he looks younger. He's thin and wiry with reddish curly hair and freckles. He's always dating someone new and always worries that I'm working too hard and ruining my chances of having a social life.

"I'm not avoiding it," I say, and prove it by turning right around and looking out. Of course, this is the exact moment that Mr. Reed is in the process of opening his window. Seeing me, he lifts his hand in greeting. Perfect.

"Who's that?" Stan asks.

"A jeweler who works across the way," I answer casually.

"And you know him?"

"I've met him, yes."

"How? Are you seeing him?"

"No." I laugh. "I'm not dating anyone and have no intention of dating anyone for the time being. I am concentrating on work, and in my spare time, trying to get started with renovating my mom's apartment."

"You sound so strident about not dating."

I shrug, not interested in explaining, but my friend is nothing if not persistent.

"Izzie, what happened to you at Oak Ridge after I left?" Stan asks with a sweetness in his voice that makes me want to share the story. But I haven't told anyone.

"You know what happened. We built a city to house the scientists and factory workers and their families and support systems so that our government could be first in creating a bomb that annihilated hundreds of thousands of people. What do you think happened at Oak Ridge?"

He's quiet for a minute.

"I'm not talking about the work. I know all about that. *Now.*" He's joking, but then looks down sadly, knowing his worst suspicions were confirmed. "And I know about the shock of learning about what we did there and the scars. We've talked about that."

He is quiet for another minute, and I wonder if he is thinking about how close he came to bearing the same burdens as those of us who stayed. I don't question that we had to end the war, but I can't help but question the way we did it considering the horrific deaths that so many hundreds of thousands of innocents endured. I shudder involuntarily—which I always do whenever I think about it. I've become obsessed with the bombs built by the scientists at Los Alamos, Oak Ridge, and Hanford. Scientists who lived and worked in the houses that I helped design. Went to restaurants, movies, bowling alleys, and libraries that I and the other SOM architects helped create. I've read everything I could find about how the bombs worked, about the terrible destruction they wrought. I close my eyes and see the photographs printed of the women and children running for their lives. The mushroom cloud. The aftereffects. The gross destruction. The sheer horror.

"I don't want to pry, Izzie. But I know something happened to you. Yes, the larger ethical issue of what went on at Oak Ridge changed you to some extent. I understand that. But it's more than that. The girl I knew at Cooper Union, my best friend for five years, isn't the one sitting here now. And it's more than the obvious, so don't tell me about the tragedies of war, or what happened to Charlotte. You know she's married to her high school sweetheart and expecting a baby now?"

I nod.

"And it's not just losing your mom. You've changed in some other way."

"You've changed too," I say, which is not at all an answer and annoys him.

"Yes, I acknowledge that. We've all changed. And hopefully learned a lot. Don't play games with me. Tell me what happened, Izzie. I know there's something else and it's eating at you... Listen, do you want to get out of here and go get a drink? We can go to the Oak Room."

He knows I love the clubby bar at the Plaza Hotel a block away on Fifth and 59th Street. We've gone twice since I've been back in town. Both times, his treat. But I'm not in the mood for more questions. And Stan can be as much of a pit bull as I am when he wants answers.

I shrug. "I would but I have to get these drawings done tonight."

"Well, if you ever want to talk about it..." he says, sounding a bit insulted and then goes back to his desk and prepares to leave.

He's got his coat on when the phone rings, but he answers it.

"Yes, she is, hold on a second." He turns to me. "Izzie,

it's for you."

I walk over to the phone and take it from him. He waves and walks out, leaving me alone in the studio.

"Hello?"

"Miss Moon, this is Jules Reed. I wanted you to know that I've found the papers. I'm not prying, but I can see you're still in your office. If you'd like to come over after you are done with your work, I can take you through them."

"That would be great. I have another forty-five minutes to an hour of work though. Is that a problem?" I am both excited and scared. And I don't know why. I'm after information, I remind myself. Whatever story the receipts tell, they will just give me information about the past. A past that has no bearing on my present or my future.

"Not at all. I have a lot of paperwork I can do," he says, and I hear a click.

In order to walk back to my desk, I have to face the window. And so, I see that Mr. Reed is standing there, watching me. The telephone still in his hand. I wish I could see his face, but he's too far away for that.

Chapter 10

Sofiya Petrovitch
Petrograd
May 1915

The following day Sofiya asked for permission to leave the hospital at lunch. It was a formality, of course. She was working as a volunteer without pay. Once the matron gave her approval, Sofiya left. She walked from the Winter Palace to 24 Bolshaya Morskaya, which took less than fifteen minutes. It was late spring and wonderful weather. Despite the war and the sad news that was a constant, the trees were all in leaf and the flowers in bloom. Thank goodness, Sofiya thought, that nature ignored the news. They all needed the lift of spring.

Reaching her destination, Sofiya stood outside the five-story building. It was a smart-looking edifice but didn't begin to suggest the untold riches inside.

Two women were being waited on by a salesclerk, but otherwise the shop was quiet.

She stepped deeper into the interior and was about to start looking around at the merchandise glittering in the wooden cases when a salesclerk approached.

"May I help you?" he asked.

She looked up at the elderly man. There were so few young men working in the shops, restaurants, theaters, or utilities—they were all off at war. Their jobs had been taken over by women and elderly or wounded men.

"Yes, I'm trying to…would it be possible to speak to the manager about jewelers who have worked here in the last few years? I want to find out if someone specific was employed here."

"Certainly, if you'll have a seat."

A few minutes later, another man, clearly over fifty, came out from the back and over to her.

"Good afternoon, I'm Emil Kostrov. May I help?"

"Yes, good afternoon. I am Sofiya Petrovitch, a nurse at the Winter Palace hospital. We have a soldier patient with us who has lost his memory. He noticed this"—she held up her egg charm—"which my parents bought for me here. It sparked something in his memory. We think he might have been a goldsmith. Perhaps even here…or maybe at another jeweler. But since he recognized the hallmark on my egg, I thought your establishment would be a good place to begin. I wonder if you might know if he worked here."

"Of course, I'd be happy to help you…any way I can, that is. So many of our workforce has gone off to war. Almost all of our younger staff. And, sadly, we've lost quite a few of them. What is his name?"

"Well, that's the problem. He doesn't know his name."

"Ah. That will make it more difficult now, won't it?"

"Yes. I have a drawing I've sketched of him."

"Excellent."

Sofiya pulled the drawing out of her purse and showed it to the manager.

"Well, now...this man is so terribly thin, isn't he?" He continued studying her drawing. She didn't think it did Carpathian justice. It didn't capture the sparkle in his eyes or the depth of his interest in the things they talked about. Sofiya thought him so handsome, but the drawing depicted an exhausted soldier.

"I don't recognize him. No, he doesn't seem at all familiar. But then I have only been here in the Petrograd store for the last ten months. I came here from our Moscow shop. So, if this soldier left for the front before I arrived, I wouldn't know him. Maybe we should take it to the workshop and see if anyone there recognizes him."

Sofiya didn't allow herself to lose hope yet. She followed Emil Kostrov past the glass cabinets and showcases, trying to get a look at as many of the beautiful objects and jewels as she could and still keep up.

"Few concerns are operating at full capacity anymore...what with the war on...we have so few jewelers here but let's see..."

He opened the door to a large room that was flooded with light. There were more empty stations than there were with men working at them.

A man in his sixties sat at the first station. He was polishing a gold cross set with amethyst. The stones were so deep a purple they looked almost black until the jeweler moved the cross one way or the other and then the imperial hue flashed.

Emil Kostrov explained their mission. The jeweler

examined the drawing with his head tilted and then shrugged.

"He could be one of several men who were here." He turned around. "Dimitry?" he called.

A much younger man, perhaps in his thirties, looked up from his desk. He had a thick head of almost-black hair. His mouth was generous and his bone structure strong.

"Come look at this, see if you recognize this man. He might have worked here, but he's been wounded in the war and has no memory."

The man got up and walked over.

"Dimitry Zorin, this is Sofiya Petrovitch. And here is the drawing of the man she's trying to identify."

Sofiya watched Dimitry Zorin stare down at the drawing. She couldn't be sure, but she thought she saw a flicker of recognition in his eyes. But when he looked up and back at her, he shook his head.

"No, I'm sorry, but I can't help you. The problem is we had over five hundred men working here before war broke out. I didn't know all of them. And this man"—he gestured to the drawing—"he has that look that a soldier gets from too little food and too much battle. With that shorn hair, you can't see his curls"—he paused—"if he has curls. Or he might have straight hair. I've seen men I once knew like brothers and not recognized them when they returned from the front."

The older jeweler took the drawing back. "You know…it's just possible… Dimitry, do you think it could be Fyodor Minskoff?"

Dimitry Zorin nodded vehemently. "Yes, yes, I think it could. In fact, I'm almost certain."

The manager who had brought Sofiya up to the workshop clapped his hands. "This is wonderful. An identification. Please tell Fyodor Minskoff that when he is recuperated if he wants to come and talk to us about returning to work here, the door is open."

"Maybe we could show this to some of the other men?" Sofiya asked. Something about Dimitry's responses made her suspicious. He hadn't asked what color the soldier's hair or eyes were. Wouldn't you do that if you were really trying to reconcile a pencil drawing to a real person? And he'd mentioned curls as if he knew the short hair would curl when longer. Was that indicative of something?

"There's no need, really. I have no doubt that it's Fyodor," Dimitry insisted.

"That's good enough for me," Emil Kostrov said. Given his body language, Sofiya knew he was ready to escort her out. She had no choice but to follow him.

Back at the hospital, she went right to Carpathian to tell him about the excursion. He'd asked her to bring him some art supplies and paper the day before so he could draw a little. She found him sitting up in bed, a tray on his lap. On it was a sketchpad and a box of colored pencils. He showed her his drawing—a sketch of a fanciful necklace suggesting the wisteria vine that sheltered them during their excursions in the garden.

"I missed you at lunch," he said.

"I went to do some sleuthing on your behalf. I didn't want to tell you in case nothing came of it, but something did. I have information for you, about who you are."

He put down the pencil he was holding. "Yes?"

"I took that drawing I did of you to the Fabergé shop to see if anyone there might know who you are. Or if you worked with anyone there."

"And?"

"Have you ever heard the name Fyodor Minskoff?"

Carpathian looked up at the ceiling the way he did when he was searching for a shred of memory. Sofiya waited, watching him.

"Not that I can recall."

"Two of the jewelers there thought they recognized you and told me your name is Fyodor Minskoff."

Carpathian swiped his hand across the tray on his lap, throwing the pencils off. Some fell to the sheets, others onto the floor. Sofiya watched them land on the parquet design, their points breaking off, scattering tiny bits of colors across the dark expanse.

This rare display of anger was unusual.

"Carpathian?"

He didn't look at her but continued staring down at the random pattern of pencil points.

"They are like stones," he said so softly she had to lean in. "Like stones on a worktable waiting to be set."

She nodded, awed by the sound of wonder in his voice as he remembered an image he'd seen before at work. Maybe, Sofiya thought, what he needed was more visual memories. Perhaps that would help him.

She returned to the Fabergé shop the following day with her father's imported Kodak camera, which he often let her borrow for work at the museum. After explaining to the manager what she was hoping to accomplish, he led her upstairs so she could photograph the workshop and one of the workstations in detail.

Several of the men she'd met the day before were there, including Dimitry Zorin.

"Does Fyodor miss us that much that he wants photos of the place?" he asked with a charming smile.

"He doesn't remember his name. I thought maybe seeing pictures would help stimulate his memory."

"You're a very dedicated nurse," he said. "If anything ever happens to me again, I'd like you to take care of me."

"Again?" she asked.

"I broke my shoulder a few years ago. I was in the hospital for a while and can't imagine any of those nurses caring enough about me to help the way you are helping Fyodor."

"Carpathian," she corrected him.

"What does that godforsaken place have to do with Fyodor?"

"He took the name of the battleground where he was found."

"He was in the Carpathian Mountains in the Winter War?"

"He was."

Dimitry shook his head. "Poor bastard."

His hand crept up to his shoulder and massaged it.

"Did you hurt your arm in the war?"

"No. My arm is why I couldn't fight. In 1912, I was in a troika accident. One of the horses stepped on my shoulder in the mess."

"But your work?" Sofiya asked.

"I can move my hands and wrist, even my elbow. I just don't have the range required to move my whole arm, which is what kept me away from the army."

"You're lucky then."

"Safe, yes, but not lucky. I haven't been able to be much of a patriot from a jewelry shop. At least now that the government has given Fabergé orders to make munitions, I feel like I'm doing something. But it's still not like the men I know who went off to war. Not like Fyodor, or Vasily or Stephan or Sergei…" He broke off suddenly. "I'm keeping you from your work. I hope the photographs help."

Sofiya felt bad for Dimitry. His guilt over being unable to fight was clearly a burden he was having a difficult time carrying.

She finished photographing the workroom and some of the jewelers. On her way back to the hospital, she dropped off the film to be developed with her father's friend, a chemist and amateur photographer. She didn't tell Carpathian what she'd done. She'd wait until she had the photographs back.

Two days later, she picked them up from the chemist's shop on her way to work. Arriving at the hospital, as usual, she went to see Carpathian before she reported for duty. She walked into the large ballroom filled with cots and started toward his corner. After only a dozen steps, she could see that his bed was empty. Sofiya felt her heart race. She intoned her mother's calming words and reminded herself that there was nothing to worry about until there was something to worry about. That men were not in their beds for various reasons. Especially ones who had access to wheelchairs.

But what if he had gotten sick during the night? What if he had a new infection? What if something was wrong and he was back in surgery? Had they shipped him off without her knowing?

She and Carpathian had believed the doctors were going to keep him there until he was fully ambulatory. The best physical therapy doctors were on staff, so soldiers who'd had amputations typically had longer hospital stays than other patients.

Sofiya went running down the hall to try and find out what had happened. She went to the surgery first and grabbed the list of operations that had been performed in the last twelve hours. There was nothing for Patient #516—

the number Carpathian had been assigned since he had no name.

Despite the information, she checked in the recovery room, blocking her ears to the moans of the men coming out of anesthesia and feeling their pain, often for the first time.

No Carpathian. Where next? She headed for the administration office, hurrying down one hall and then another until finally arriving at her destination. She knocked, entered and asked the official in charge if they had moved out any patients overnight. She specifically did not reveal who she was searching for. The country's general mood, the rumors, secrets, and assassination attempts over the years, the way the tsarina was so careful about what she was overheard saying, the comments that Olga and Tatiana made about the very volatile political situation, all had made Sofiya quite cautious.

"No, there have been no transports in the last twenty-four hours," the head of admissions told her. "No patients have expired in the last twelve hours either. Why is it you want to know, Nurse Petrovitch?"

What should she say? Anything but the truth. "One of the patients on my rounds said he saw someone die during the night and is very disturbed. I didn't notice anyone missing and think it is probably a dream, but I told him I would make sure."

She walked back toward the ward. Carpathian could be anywhere. Since he could now wheel himself around, he might be exploring any number of places in the palace, even though it was strictly forbidden. Sofiya couldn't let what had happened with Victor Drozdov affect her.

So she reported for work and set about bringing the patients their morning medicines, Carpathian never far from her mind. She didn't have a break until lunchtime when she went to look for him again. Had he gone to his morning physical therapy session? She couldn't very well ask. Instead, she went out into the garden.

And there he was, sitting under the wisteria arbor. She was relieved. Like so many of her fellow nurses, she had allowed herself to get too involved, had been too swayed by the vulnerability of these brave, guileless, needy, grateful men. By the way they so appreciated even the most basic kindness. They were so vulnerable now despite their past bravery and needed the nurses so openly without guile.

Sofiya walked to him. When Carpathian saw her, he smiled.

"I looked for you this morning," she said. "Where were you?"

He leaned forward, whispering. "I was in our alchemical laboratory and made quite a discovery."

"What did you find?"

Carpathian looked around carefully, then leaned even closer. "In between the pages of some of the old books, I found what seem to be very sensitive documents. And that made me curious, so I kept looking. Let's go back in so I can show you."

He directed her down one hallway and then another. After taking a labyrinthine route, they reached a well-hidden room. Inside, he opened a cabinet revealing a complicated-looking encryption machine and a stack of papers. Sofiya took one of the letters and read the first few paragraphs.

"This seems like an innocent letter."

"Yes, one would expect them to read that way. I believe this is an encryption machine. This room could be a spy's lair."

She nodded. "We need to tell someone then," she said.

"But who? We don't know for sure what side this spy is on. What if by interfering, we disturb plans crucial to our winning the war?"

"But what if we could stop… I don't know… an attack… or even an assassination attempt? We've had so many already," Sofiya said. "We never should have been in here in the first place. What if this is something the tsar is behind? What if we're found out?"

"On the other hand, if we've discovered an enemy, we'd be heroes," he countered.

"But if there is a spy in our midst, he might retaliate. Your life would be in danger. How about if we send an anonymous letter to the hospital administrator?"

"I'm already anonymous, Sofiya. How much more anonymous can I be?"

That reminded her of what she had with her. "We'll have to think about what to do later. Right now, I have something for you."

She reached into her pocket and pulled out the recently developed photographs.

"These are for you, I thought they might help."

"What are they?"

"You tell me."

She handed them to him and was disappointed to see him look at the first, the second and then the third without any obvious flicker of recognition. But when he reached the fourth, he stopped.

He stared at it. Then pointed to an empty table in the corner of the room. "I think…" He was still staring, but now he was nodding. "This is the workshop at the House of Fabergé. And that is my workstation."

He looked at Sofiya with the satisfaction of a man who had won a foot race, broken a record, or climbed an impossible mountain.

"Right there?" she asked. "That one?"

He nodded again. "Yes, I'm sure. I don't know how I know, but I do."

"So you are a goldsmith?"

He looked up from the photograph and at her. "Thank you for this."

She smiled. "Do you know the names of any of the people in this picture?" She handed him a new photo in which several of the men she'd met had posed.

Carpathian scanned the faces.

"I've seen this man before." He pointed to the one she knew as Dimitry. "But I can't pull his name. I seem to have an easier time recognizing images and knowing things... rather than recognizing people or remembering names."

"His name is Dimitry Zorin."

Carpathian looked up at the ceiling. "No, that name doesn't mean anything to me."

Sofiya rattled off a few more of the names she'd heard, but none of them struck him as being familiar.

"But we've made a huge breakthrough. We know your name and that you worked at Fabergé before the war. You must be an excellent goldsmith. As you told me yourself, it's the finest jewelry store in all of Russia."

"Yes, the jeweler to the tsar," he said in a faraway voice.

"Maybe we should go there? You could meet with the workers. See if they remember you."

He didn't answer right away.

"What is it?" she asked.

He shook his head. "I don't know but I feel... I need to be sure."

"And you're not?"

"It seems unreal still."

"But you recognized your worktable."

"A worktable, Sofiya. I recognized a worktable."

She saw he was getting agitated and knew she couldn't press him. From working with other patients who had suffered memory loss, she knew that the recovery of memories and acceptance of them was complicated and often fraught with surprising emotional reactions. As it was time for Carpathian's physical therapy appointment, Sofiya walked with him, left him there and went back to the ward to attend to the other patients, but her mind remained with Carpathian and his discovery.

At the end of the day, she found him in the library, actively drawing, and looked over his shoulder.

"That's like the imperial Easter eggs the tsar gives to his mother and to the tsarina every year."

"Yes…" His voice sounded far away. "I can't remember anything at all if I try, but if I stop trying and just let my mind go, my hand seems to know what to draw on its own."

He looked away from the sketches and up at her. He took Sofiya's hand.

"You gave me this, Sofiya. I can finally see a light in a long, dark tunnel. And you are the one holding the candle."

Carpathian bundled up his art supplies and put them in the pocket on the side of his wheelchair.

"Can you spare some time, or do you need to go home for the evening?" he asked.

She said that she was free. Sofiya knew that his time in the hospital would be coming to an end in a week or so. He was fully healed physically and managing on crutches half the time. In physical therapy, he was quickly learning to balance himself and walk with just a cane. The doctors felt certain that, in time, he wouldn't even need that.

She didn't have to ask where they were going. She knew.

Even if it was a spy's enclave, it was the only place they could be alone. Once they were ensconced in their little room, Carpathian hoisted himself out of the chair and onto the settee with its jewel-colored cushions. Sofiya joined him. Carpathian gathered her to his chest and stroked her hair. She settled into his arms and looked up at him. He smiled his sweet smile, filled his eyes with her and then leaned down and kissed her. Usually, their embraces lasted for a long time, so Sofiya was surprised when Carpathian pulled away after the first kiss.

"I think I'm ready to go to Fabergé and meet the men I worked with. Or who I *think* I worked with. Maybe talk to them about getting my job back. I certainly won't be able to return to the front with this." He pointed to his foot. "If the doctor agrees on the outing, will you accompany me?"

"Yes, of course."

"Maybe one of the jewelers there will know me. Maybe even well enough to help me find my family. Of one thing I am certain, I'm not any Fyodor Minskoff. I *will* know my name when I hear it."

He was talking quickly, excited about the idea of discovering who he was.

"What is it, Sofiya?" he asked, noticing a frown settle on her face.

She was so naïve at nineteen, she didn't realize you didn't just blurt out your feelings.

"I want you to find out everything. But..."

She shrugged. How could she be thinking about herself now? How could she be worried that once he rediscovered who he was, there wouldn't be room for her?

"What is it?"

"Once you go back to work, everything will change."

"You mean with us?" he asked.

She nodded. Gently, he took her hand. "A lot of things will change. But not how I feel about you. You are my present; I have made all my memories with you. Once I am back at work, I am going to make you a piece of jewelry as a thank you. What would you like? A pair of sapphire earrings to bring out the blue of your eyes? Or a string of pearls that match your complexion?"

He touched each part of her as he named it, touching her earlobes first and then letting his thumbs trail across her cheek.

"Or maybe a diamond chain"—he drew a line around her neck—"with a disc hanging from it that has Carpathian on one side and Sofiya on the other so that we can never be parted."

He kissed her in that way he had of blocking out everything around her. Wrapping her up in his long arms and hiding her in his embrace as if to protect her from anything in the world beyond that room...from the doctors and nurses and pain and suffering and from the war that had stolen so much of his mind and from the city and the politics and the unrest and the ugliness. Hiding her away in their spy room where they could lie with each other and no one ever found them.

He unbuttoned Sofiya's blouse and slipped his hand inside, searching for and finding her breast. He cupped one and then the other. Her breath caught in her chest.

"Or maybe I'll make you a chainmail bib. Tiny gold links soldered together. Like armor, but you would wear it for me with nothing on underneath so I could get glimpses of this..." He bent his head down to kiss her. Teasing her nipple with his tongue. She breathed in his scent. A particular one that was his alone. Carpathian had a habit of picking pine needles off the trees in the garden and playing with them, crushing them in his fingers so he smelled of the outdoors. Of a forest. Of dark and green things. Of mystery.

Sofiya couldn't wait to get out of her clothes. She shrugged out of her blouse and unbuttoned Carpathian's shirt, and they pressed up against each other. She shivered.

"Cold?" he asked.

She shook her head. How to explain the exquisite sensation of his skin on hers? Of that first feeling of coming together. Of anticipation of what was yet to come and at the same time wanting to hold back and make it last. And last. And last.

"Maybe…" he said, encircling her waist with his hands and squeezing just enough to send sensations cascading through her, "I will make you a golden belt studded with rubies to wear around your waist. To show off your curves. To celebrate how perfectly you fit my hands."

His fingers slipped around and unbuttoned her skirt. She stood as quickly as she could. So did he, albeit gently. This was the first time she was totally naked in front of him. In front of any man. But she didn't even realize that until later. In that moment, it was just an urgent need.

The sight of Carpathian's naked body didn't shock her. Not in that way. What surprised her was how much she wanted to touch the long torso, the longer legs, the shoulders. To caress the soft skin inside his elbow, to hold on to the hard muscles in his arms, his calves.

He leaned toward the place where her legs met. "There's nothing I could make you as wonderful as this, though," he said as he touched his lips to her. She pressed back, thrusting out toward him, not even realizing what her body was doing, just needing to get closer to him. To get closer to the feelings waving inside her.

She shuddered.

"Do you like it?" he whispered.

"Yes."

"Like this?" He stroked her with his fingers.

"Yes," she said, barely able to get the word out.

"Or like this?" He teased her, squeezing harder.

She nodded her head.

He moved his hands up and around her waist and pulled her toward him and then lowered her down, slowly, until he met a barrier.

"Sofiya, is this your first time?"

She nodded, now a little afraid. She and her friends had talked. They all knew how it worked. Some said it could hurt and bleed when the man went inside you. Others said it was nothing more than a quick twinge. And if you had done a lot of horseback riding, like she did in the summers with the duchesses, that could make it so men had easy access without any discomfort.

"Are you afraid?"

"Not of you... I just don't want it to hurt."

"We can stop if it does," he volunteered. "I promise."

"All right."

"You know your first time...it will be my first time," he said softly.

"Really?"

"I don't remember any other woman. So yes, you are my first."

"But you do know what to do."

He laughed. "I do."

"So we can assume that…"

"Shh. We have to stop talking now because I can't bear having you sitting there like that."

He repositioned her onto her back and then very gently moved her legs apart and stroked her until she was writhing.

Only then, when she was wholly focused on sensation, did he slip inside.

There was a moment—but it was only a moment—when she felt a single bolt of pain. But then it was gone, and sensation filled her again. All new and unknown and amazing.

Chapter 11

Isobelle Moon
New York City
December 1948

"I'm sorry there's not more here," Mr. Reed says as he hands me two thin sheets of paper that rustle as I take them.

I glance down at the first, scrolling through it. Turn to the second and do the same.

"These are just carbon copies of the same receipts that my mother had."

"They do appear to be."

"Now I'll never know..." I say before I can stop myself.

"Never know what?"

"I'm sorry, Mr. Reed. It's just that it's another dead end and—"

He interrupts. "I wish you would call me Jules."

"Jules, then. And please, call me Isobelle."

"Not Izzie?" He smiles.

"Only my closest friend gets away with that," I say, chagrined he'd heard Stan earlier.

"Maybe at some point you'll grant me the honor."

I'm not at all sure I understand the intonation in his voice or the expression in his eyes. Before I can figure it out, he's speaking.

"Now what did you mean by another dead end?"

"I had this sense... I know it might sound irrational..." I can't believe that I am even telling him this. "That I had finally found the thread that would help me unravel..."

I haven't tried to articulate this before. Not even to Aunt Lana, and I'm struggling. "Let me start again. My mother's life before she came to America—well, she kept that from me. She was secretive about almost every part of it. When I found the tiara, I suppose I thought it would lead me to...lead me to answers about her past. And about mine."

"She never hinted anything to you about the tiara?"

I shake my head. "I didn't know she even had it."

"Do you think I could see the tiara? Inspect it? If it is Fabergé, we should be able to trace it and find out more about it and who made it and who it was sold to. The jewelry concern kept very detailed records of every piece they made. And when Carl Fabergé escaped to Finland, he took many of the records with him, so they survived. There are a lot of *ifs* here, I know, but it is possible there might be some real information we can glean for you if everything lines up."

He's giving me hope, and I feel a surge of gratefulness that is probably out of proportion with the offer. "Thank you, yes."

"You could bring it in tomorrow. We're open on Saturdays and—"

"I can show it to you now," I say. I don't want to wait any longer than I have to. "If you're free, you could come uptown. But it's getting late, isn't it? Your wife is probably waiting with dinner and—"

"No wife, no fiancée, not even a date tonight..." His usually warm voice chills. "So now is perfect. Let me just lock up."

I wait for him as he shuts the windows, checks that there are no errant pieces of jewelry left around, and shuffles some papers on his desk. Grabbing his hat, he puts it on. He looks rakish wearing the fedora. A little bit like Gregory Peck in *Gentleman's Agreement*. I have a little crush on Mr. Peck that started with the Alfred Hitchcock movie *Spellbound*. My mother and I both loved the movies and went to the theater every Saturday together. When I was at Oak Ridge, we got all the movies that appeared in New York. My mother and I would see the films in our own respective theaters and then go over them in delicious detail on the phone, critiquing the stories and the acting, the sets and locations, and of course the leading men and women. The movies, even more than the novels we read, were a bond between us. There was never her past to stumble over when we talked about them. Nothing she held back when she shared her thoughts. Sometimes, in her comments, I'd catch a glimpse of the young girl she must have been. Curious, intrigued, and romantic.

"All done," Jules says as he opens the door. "After you."

I walk out into the hallway. Behind me, Jules locks the door, and we walk toward the elevator together.

Down on the street, he turns east. "Should we get a cab on Madison?" he asks.

Something about this alarms me. "How do you know

which way we're going?" I ask.

"The receipts have your address on them."

I nod. "Of course."

During the short ride uptown, Jules asks me what kind of project I'm currently working on. It's small talk, which is all right. I don't know why I feel oddly disappointed that the conversation isn't more substantive. But we're strangers. What else would we talk about?

Upstairs, I show Jules to the living room.

"Would you like something? I can make some coffee or—" I point to the bar cart in the corner—a Japanese lacquer piece that my mother restored. "Or if you prefer a drink?"

"I wouldn't mind a scotch. Do you have ice?"

"Of course, I'll be right back."

I take the antique crystal bucket that my mother used for ice, carry it into the kitchen, and bring it back filled. Jules is standing by at the far end of the room, inspecting a black and gold lacquer desk. Another piece that my mother salvaged from the garbage heap.

"This is beautiful. Do you know its history?" Jules asks.

"My mother and aunt ran a restoration business and shop, here, in the building. My aunt still runs it. My mother was trained in restoring paintings and did decorative finishes. My aunt focused on the more traditional furniture restoration. Sometime in the 1930s, my mother became fascinated with the ancient art of lacquer and started studying with a Japanese master here in New York. Restoring small pieces of lacquer furniture and *objets d'art* became one of her specialties. I used to watch her work, applying one layer at a time and then putting the piece aside. Waiting till it dried for days before applying the next layer. Even a small box could take weeks. She once told me that the nine-thousand-year-old art appealed to her because it reminded her of *becoming*. How we, as adults, come to be who we are, one layer at a time. How those early layers are the core that shapes and informs us but then each additional layer adds to our whole selves."

"She sounds very special."

"She was."

"And judging by this, quite a master herself. I know a bit about lacquer since in addition to jewelry, we sell small objects and have a very good collection of lacquer boxes, incense burners, and screens. We once had a dog-shaped box sitting on a low table that was Edo period, late seventeenth to mid-eighteenth-century, that belonged to Marie Antoinette."

"Who bought that?" I'm a little in awe that he would sell a piece that important.

"No one. It was incumbent on us to return the box to the museum in France it had been stolen from."

I note the curious choice of words. "Incumbent on you?"

Jules picks up the silver tongs, puts two ice cubes into a glass, and then pours in an inch of scotch. He hands me the drink and then makes a second for himself. I can tell he's thinking about something.

"So the tiara?" he asks and then takes a sip of his drink.

I feel let down. He was going to tell me something else, I'm sure of it. But he changed his mind.

"Let me go and get it."

I leave Jules in the living room, retrieve the case from my bedroom, and return moments later.

I put the box down on the coffee table in front of Jules. The paper label that was originally affixed to the top of the case fell off at Aunt Lana's house and I've put it away. So he's just looking at the worn leather case. I don't imagine there are any clues there.

"May I open it?" Jules asks with his hands hovering just above the clasp.

"Of course."

But he doesn't open it right away. First, he runs his fingers over the worn leather top as if testing it, then around the sides as if he's getting to know it. I don't have any idea what he's trying to learn, but something about the way his fingers move on the smooth surface gives me shivers. He unhinges the latch. Then waits a moment. As if those seconds between knowing there is a treasure inside and seeing it for himself are to be savored. Even though I am fully cognizant of what's inside, anticipation grows within me, and when Jules finally does open the box, it's almost as if I'm seeing the tiara for the first time. The silver framework seems to soak up the lights in the room and gleams cold and hard against the cream-colored silk.

He focuses on the gold writing on the silk.

"Yes, this is a case from Carl Fabergé's St. Petersburg shop. I'd date it to approximately 1910 to 1915. Let's see what I can find on the piece itself."

From his pocket, Jules pulls out his loupe and places it on the table. He lifts the tiara out of its case, holds it, puts the loupe up to his eye, and begins his inspection. First the front of the piece.

He takes his time studying the swirls and turns. While he does, I sip my drink and study him. The way he holds the piece so carefully but with assurance is encouraging. And his intensity is inspiring. I sense that he's inspecting the tiara the same way I examine plans—blocking out everything around me, shutting out sounds and smells and noises and focusing so intently it's as if I'm entering the lines and shapes.

He turns the piece around and studies the back, finally stopping when he gets to the section where I saw markings. I hadn't been able to make them out with my household magnifying glass, but now I'm sure Jules can with his loupe.

He replaces the tiara in its silken curve, then collapses the loupe and drops it into his pocket.

"There are markings but only silver marks. Which is strange. Most if not all pieces at the time had maker's marks on them."

A surge of disappointment overwhelms me. "So we don't know if it is in fact Fabergé or not? We've hit another dead end?"

"I'm sorry," Jules says in a voice that truly sounds as if he is. "I do think it's Fabergé, but without markings, without dates, and without being able to see and evaluate the original stones, trying to find it in their old records is going to be difficult."

I take a swallow of the scotch.

"What I don't understand is why my mother hid it. Especially the way she hid it." I just shared something I had no intention of telling this man I hardly know.

"How did she hide it?"

Of course, he would have picked up on the provocative comment. Oh well, what does any of it matter anyway?

"Let me show you."

I usher him out of the living room and into my mother's bedroom. I've still got tarps covering the furniture to keep it protected from the dust and debris of stripping the walls. I haven't made any progress since the night I peeled off that one strip, so the hiding place is fairly obvious.

"It was here?" he asks, pointing.

"Yes, right in this alcove, which had been wallpapered over."

"And the case and the papers were in there? Nothing else?"

"Nope, nothing else."

Jules runs his fingers over the inside of the alcove the same way he did with the jewel case. As if he doesn't understand a thing until he feels it. As he moves his hand, the light gleams off his signet ring. I feel sure he sees my eyes on it, but he doesn't comment.

"Your mother left you quite a mystery, didn't she?"

I nod.

Jules steps back and takes in the whole room. "Any other mysteries here?"

"What do you mean?"

"Well, if she was secretive and clever enough to hide one thing, maybe she hid more."

"I hadn't thought of that."

"Who knows what you'll discover. Maybe there's a false back to the armoire? Or something taped under one of the drawers in that dresser."

"You're not joking, are you?"

"No."

"None of that even occurred to me."

"Well, I've been trained."

"What do you mean?"

He's looking at the alcove again as if there might be a message there we both overlooked. He turns back to me.

"Let's get back to the scotch before the ice all melts and dilutes it, and I'll tell you."

In the living room, he sits down on the couch. I sit in the chair catty-corner to him. He picks up the crystal tumbler. I like the way the heavy glass looks in his hand. As if it fits there. As he takes a sip, I pick up my glass and sip as well.

Jules looks from his glass to mine. Then looks back at the bar.

"None of the glasses match, do they?"

I laugh. "Among the other things my mother collected, she bought stray glasses—only the best—Baccarat, Tiffany, or Lalique—and stray china—also the best—only Limoges—but almost every one a different pattern. She loved finding the strays at antique shows and flea markets. 'No one seems to want them since they aren't part of a set anymore,' she told me once. 'But being displaced doesn't make any one of them less beautiful.'"

"As if she was talking about herself," Jules says. "She really was special, wasn't she?"

His insight brings a lump to my throat. I nod, not trusting my voice, take another sip of my drink and then return to the comment Jules made in the bedroom.

"So what did you mean that you are trained? Jewelers take classes on where to hide rare pieces?"

The corner of Jules' mouth lifts with the start of a smile. "Not all of them, no."

"But you have?"

"Yes, I've been trained to look for ciphers, enigmas, mysteries, and puzzles. To be on the lookout for that single odd fact that doesn't fit. Also, how to judge the stories people tell me to ascertain if they are lying, or if they're hiding certain facts. Telling me something about a piece that isn't fact even if they don't know it themselves."

"It sounds more like you're a detective than a jeweler."

He is looking at me as if he's trying to solve a very complicated math problem. I'm not especially good at reading people. I'm much better with blueprints. I can look at two-dimensional lines and see the whole building in three dimensions as if it's forming in my mind. I can envision how the negative and positive spaces will impact each other. How someone will move through the rooms. But I'm rarely able to look at someone's face and understand what they are feeling if they don't give me verbal clues. Except it seems to be different with Jules. For the second time, I'm certain that he's trying to figure out if he can tell me something.

I can't hold his gaze anymore, though; it's disconcerting. This whole evening is. I've brought this man into my house and showed him something that I didn't even know existed two weeks ago. I've broken my own rules about sharing any information at all about me or my life with people outside my family. My mother taught me that. And my time at Oak Ridge reinforced her lessons. You never truly know who someone is...what they want from you...what they will do to get it.

By her own admission, my mother was paranoid, having grown up and endured a brutal revolution that tore lives apart. That pitted children against parents. Teachers against students. Family members and friends and neighbors stole from each other for bits of food... soap... clothing... the barest of necessities.

At Oak Ridge, I dismissed every one of her lessons and wound up being played by someone I thought I knew. And here I was, letting down my guard again.

"I am a detective and a jeweler," Jules finally says.

"What do you mean?"

"It's not something that I share often..."

"But you are telling me? Why?" I shouldn't have asked him that. But I feel off balance. I want to hear his confession—because that's what it feels like he'll be making. At the same time, I want to understand the reasons he's offering it. And what are the ramifications of me hearing it? Because there are ramifications to everything. No one who accepts a confession ever gets away scot-free. Once someone tells you their secret, you have power over them. And that can cripple a relationship. A well-established one, or a brand new one.

Jules laughs. "You don't hold back, do you?"

"What can I say, this isn't the first time I've been told that."

He smiles. "I'm not surprised."

"I just don't like not knowing things."

"Fair enough. First the *why*. I'm telling you because I have a sense that you need the answers to this puzzle more than I need to keep this to myself. And that if I give you this information, it might give you some hope that one way or another we'll find your answers."

I am touched and want to tell him that. But all I say is, "That's really kind of you."

"And that's not something I hear a lot."

"Aren't you kind?"

He laughs. "I try to be of course, but...since the war..." He shrugs, not finishing his thought.

"You're unhappy, that gets in the way."

He looks surprised, then annoyed. "Why would you think I'm unhappy?"

"I'm sorry. I didn't mean to suggest anything or pry... I just...a feeling. I don't know where it came from. I apologize. Here you were being kind and I—"

"So we're back to me being kind," he jokes, clearly attempting to move the conversation back to more neutral territory.

"We seem to be."

"Well, I have an offer to make. Not out of kindness, but because at this point, I'm almost as curious as you are about this tiara and why it is inside a Fabergé box and who made it and where it comes from. I think we should take it to my grandfather and see if he remembers anything about the transaction that might tell us about the tiara's provenance and how your mother came to own it."

"I thought your grandfather was in prison."

"He is, but he can have visitors. Are you okay with visiting a prison?"

"I've never thought about it." Even if I'm not, I can't turn down the offer to speak with Jules' grandfather. "I'm fine with it. And I'd really appreciate that. Do you have to set it up or something? Do they need to check me out?"

"No need to check you out. Other than inspecting what you are bringing in. The tiara will pass muster. And no need to set it up. We just need to be there and processed by two o'clock. How does late tomorrow morning sound? Saturdays are usually when I go anyway."

"Then tomorrow is perfect."

"We can drive. I'll pick you up at ten. It's about an hour and a half to Ossining. Does that work?"

"Absolutely. Thank you."

"Don't thank me yet. This may be another dead end."

I nod, not wanting to anticipate the worst but fearing it.

"If it is, though, there's something else we can do," Jules says as if to buoy me.

"Yes?"

"What I was going to tell you before..." He hesitates.

So I was right. He picks up his glass, looks into it, judging what's left, then takes a sip of the drink. He continues holding on to the glass, shifting it from his right hand to his left and then back again. Suddenly, he looks up at me and begins speaking. Quickly.

"I am a junior member of a secret society of jewelers, curators, collectors, antique dealers, auction house owners, and the like. The organization goes back to the Renaissance, started by an Italian prince who was horrified by his father's looting practices."

Jules takes another sip of his drink, and from the way he looks down into the glass before he finishes explaining, I get the sense that this isn't something he talks about often or openly.

"We each take an oath that if an object comes across our desks that we believe to be stolen—be it coins, paintings, sculpture, jewels—we will do everything in our power to restore it to its rightful owners. And if one can't be found, we will put it into safekeeping until the time comes that we can return it."

I'm speechless. He continues.

"So if my grandfather doesn't remember anything helpful about the tiara, we can take it to the Midas Society."

"The Midas Society? That's what it's called?"

"Yes, after the man who was so greedy that when given his magical power, he destroyed his most beloved roses and then his precious daughter by turning even them into gold. Only when confronted with the dangerous and addictive power of avarice did he learn and then beg the gods to reverse the power."

For a few moments, we sit silently. Jules is watching me. I'm fully processing what he's told me. I have so many questions. "I just realized something. The Midas Society's initials are MS. That's the insignia around the flower on your ring and on the loupe you let me use. And the flower…is it a rose for Midas' lesson?"

Jules takes his last sip of scotch. "I saw you notice that. Yes. We all have one of these rings, which we are given during our initiation. The loupe was a gift from the head of the society."

"Have you returned many items yourself?"

"Four. That's why I am only a junior member. Five and I am fully inaugurated. But it's been over two years without anything crossing my path." He says it with frustration.

"Is two years a long time?"

"Not really, I'm just ambitious. And impatient."

"So you are sort of a modern-day Robin Hood?"

"I wouldn't say that." Jules puts his glass down. "He stole from the rich because he thought it was unjust for the poor to go without. We return what's been lost or stolen to their rightful owners. We're not making a philosophical statement, just righting a wrong." Jules smiles. Something in his posture and his expression seems lighter, less intense. "I haven't told anyone about all this in a very long time."

I'd guessed that, but I'm not sure I should say that. I want to ask him why he hasn't told anyone in a long time, but I feel like I've asked too many questions tonight.

"Well, thank you for telling me. It's all quite amazing. And honorable." And then I remember something. "You know, my mother told me about a similar promise she made when she was apprenticed to the master painting restorer at the Hermitage. I wonder if she'd ever heard of the society."

"She certainly might have. If she was a member, though, she would have had a ring like mine. Maybe her mentor was."

"Well, if she had a ring like that, she never wore it. And I didn't find it among her things. But that doesn't mean she didn't have it in Russia. Would you know if she was?"

"I wouldn't, but the office has membership records going back over five hundred years."

"Maybe my Aunt Lana knows…but I probably can't ask her since you said it's a secret society… Except…you just told me."

"While we are encouraged not to discuss the society or our work, members are free to tell people we intend to help that the Midas Society exists. But only those people. We are, however, sworn to secrecy about any of the objects currently in dispute and who our other members are."

I wonder if Jules' grandfather is a member, but based on what he just said, I can't ask. And that's all right. At this moment, it's not something I need to know.

He's looking at the painting on the wall opposite the couch. It is a medium-sized painting, cubist style of a couple flying over a small town. The man is wearing black pants and a blue shirt, and the woman has on a red blouse and a long black skirt. He is holding her around the waist as they soar. There's some damage to the lower right corner that you can't see unless you go up close.

"My mother always said that painting reminded her of what it was like falling in love with my father. Of literally being swept off her feet. Of feeling that she was floating in those early, heady days."

Jules gets up to examine it more closely and notices the red house has had its roof taken off, showing that beneath it is another painting done in a totally different style of a highly realistic flower garden.

"This painting looks like a Chagall, except what's in the corner."

"A customer brought it to my mother to have it restored. It had been bequeathed to him by an elderly relative. Despite a lot of damage, he believed it was a Chagall. As did my mother until she started working on it and discovered that underpainting, which was her first clue it was a fake. She did more research and found out it was indeed a forgery. When she told the customer, he refused to pay for the work she'd done and walked out without it. My mother left that corner of the underpainting showing so that that there'd never be any question about the painting's origins, and she hung it in a place of honor because of how it made her feel. She said it didn't matter who had made the copy. Whatever the artist's name, they knew what it was like to fall in love and how to transfer that emotion to canvas."

Jules remains in front of the painting for another moment, studying it. "I was married," he finally says.

"Yes?"

He keeps his back to me. "My wife betrayed me horribly during the war while I was overseas."

I put out my hand and tentatively touch his arm so softly I'm not sure I even make contact, but he turns to me. The story is in his eyes. I recognize the look from my mother. The history you don't want to talk about. The details you wish you could forget. The pain that never goes away, no matter how much time passes. I want to reach out and take his hand. To offer some kind of solace. The impulse surprises me.

"Yes, horrible. On so many levels. Horrible."

This time, for the first time in a long time, I know better than to ask any questions.

Chapter 12

Sofiya Petrovitch
Petrograd
June 1915

Sofiya and Carpathian's visit to Fabergé occurred a few afternoons later. She had received permission to take the soldier out since he was quite mobile and had given up the use of the wheelchair. He was now exclusively using his crutches. Sofiya hired a troika and gave him the shop's address.

They were quiet on the short drive there. Once they arrived, Sofiya helped Carpathian out of the vehicle. They stood on the sidewalk.

"Does it look familiar?" she asked.

He shook his head.

"No matter, let's go in."

They walked together up to the store's entrance. She opened the door for him, and Carpathian stepped inside. For a moment, he stood still, looking around. Not saying anything. And then he turned to her and gave her a slight nod. "I know this place. I do."

She smiled.

There were two customers in the showroom being helped by the manager Sofiya had met on her last visit. He noticed her and acknowledged her with a friendly nod. She saw him glance at Carpathian, but he didn't seem to recognize him at all. Then again, he had told Sofiya that he'd only been working at the Petrograd store for a short time.

As soon as he finished with his customers, the manager approached Sofiya and Carpathian. He greeted them and asked how he could help. Sofiya explained and asked if they could go up to the workroom.

He escorted them.

"Does anything in particular seem familiar?" Sofiya asked Carpathian.

"No. It's almost as if I am remembering a dream that remains vague."

That's what he said. But clearly, Carpathian's unconscious mind remembered much more. There was no hesitation as he walked side by side with the manager heading to the elevator, almost ahead of him rather than lagging behind the way one would do if he didn't know where he was going.

Carpathian remained silent in the elevator. He concentrated on the embellishments of the car. Sofiya watched him examine the complex patterns in the wooden inlay of the walls and floor.

When the door opened on the second floor, Carpathian got off first, and without hesitation headed in the correct direction even before the manager showed him the way. Sofiya didn't speak. Neither did the manager. They both walked a few steps behind Carpathian and watched as he opened the door to the workroom and then stood in the doorway, examining the sight before him. Then, Carpathian walked toward an empty desk beside a window and sat down without a word. He laid his hands on the flat wooden surface and remained motionless for a moment.

There were five or six other men in the workroom, jewelers who all stopped what they were doing to watch. No one said anything at first.

Carpathian remained sitting, still with his hands on the desk, when finally, a voice rang out.

"Sergei? Sergei? Is that you?"

A portly middle-aged man rushed over and knelt beside Carpathian's chair. He gripped both of Carpathian's hands and held them in his own. "It *is* you. Oh, my dear lord, it is you." His voice was thick with emotion.

Carpathian looked at the man for a long moment. And then he nodded, knowing. In a whisper, he uttered the man's name. "Henrik?"

Henrik Wigström nodded.

"What happened to you, Sergei?" He looked confused, sensing it seemed that the man he knew was not quite himself. "We heard...oh, we heard the worst news."

Sofiya stepped forward.

"He's had a brain injury..." she began. "But he is on his way to a full recovery. You do know him, then? You called him Sergei?"

"Of course, he is Sergei Zorin, one of my best workers."

Sofiya had been listening to Henrik Wigström but watching Carpathian—or as she now knew, Sergei. She saw him take in his own name. She saw it settle over him like a blanket on someone who is freezing. Something relaxed in him that had, until that moment, been tensed. And something inside Sofiya died.

"Sergei Zorin," she said out loud.

Carpathian turned to her.

"I will have to get used to not calling you Carpathian," she said.

"Not yet. The other name doesn't sound right coming from you."

Henrik Wigström ignored the conversation between the two lovers and pushed Carpathian for more information. "We heard about the battle and waited for news for weeks." He shook his head as if he was reliving those days.

Carpathian waited for the older man to continue, not taking his eyes off him. Not making a single movement, so riveted was he to the tale.

"Finally, they reported to your wife that you were missing and presumed dead. No one wanted to believe it. We held on, hoping and hoping…but then after so much time had passed and when no one had found you…" He had tears in his eyes.

Carpathian—Sergei—began to explain to the man he worked for what had happened to him. He'd seemed to skip right over the one word in the sentence that Sofiya had heard louder than all the others.

The man she'd fallen in love with, who seemed to have fallen in love with her, was married.

Sofiya was trying to process this fact when Dimitry Zorin came into the room. He must have heard what was going on and immediately made his way over to their corner. By that point, all work had ceased, and the jewelers who were present were all watching, listening raptly. All were moved by the return of one of their own, whom they'd thought dead. One had tears flowing down his cheeks. Only

Dimitry didn't look relieved. Or delighted. The expression on his face was dark. His brow was furrowed. He stared at Carpathian as if he was one of the enemy, suddenly transported from the front into the main workroom of the House of Fabergé.

Carpathian felt the man's intense stare and looked up and over at him. He frowned. There was something between these two men, and he had remembered it.

"Dimitry Zorin," he said.

"It's good to have you back, cousin," Dimitry Zorin said.

Cousin? Sofiya couldn't believe what she'd heard. This was the very man who had identified the drawing as being Fyodor Minskoff. He hadn't recognized his own cousin?

"Yes, yes," Henrik Wigström said. "You are coming back, aren't you? Is your hospital stay over? When can you return to work? We are doing less than we did before the war, of course, but there is still important work to do."

"The doctors are very satisfied with my recovery— except for my memory, of course. I'm in the final stages of my physical therapy and should be done within a week or two at the most."

"Irina Nikandrovna must have been so delighted to see you, to have you back. It is not easy for a young wife to have a husband go missing," Henrik said.

Carpathian appeared confused.

"Irina Nikandrovna?"

"She has been distraught," Dimitry said bitterly. As if what had happened to Carpathian was his own fault.

How, Sofiya wondered, did Dimitry know how Sergei's wife had fared? She didn't have to wonder long because Dimitry left them then and returned a few minutes later with a young woman by his side. From her jeweler's apron, it appeared she too worked there.

Irina Nikandrovna had light brown curls that framed a pixyish face. Her frilly white blouse showed off her creamy skin. Her bow-shaped lips, painted red, opened in surprise when she saw Carpathian. She looked shocked. Which made sense. But there was no happiness mixed in. No tears of relief. No expression of joy. Sofiya knew she was trying to find fault with this woman, but even so, Irina Nikandrovna did not seem at all pleased to see her husband.

Husband! The word ricocheted through Sofiya's mind. How had he not known he was married? Why had she not wondered? Here she was in love with this man who had a wife and perhaps children. She knew nothing of this Sergei Zorin. And now all she could think about was that she had helped him find the past that would force her to let him go. Carpathian would become, for Sofiya, another casualty of war. Another soldier who died in the hospital. A man who she could only hold on to in memory and try to take solace in the fact that she had helped him solve his mystery. That she had brought him back from one kind of death. Even if it was to die another kind herself.

She didn't want to listen to the things that Carpathian and Irina Nikandrovna said to each other. There was a bank of windows in the workshop at the far end, and she went to stand there and look out at the street and the passersby and the cloudy sky, which had been sunny when they arrived.

After ten minutes, Carpathian joined her. She felt him standing there beside her, but she didn't turn around. She didn't want him to see the tracks of tears on her cheeks. He touched her arm. It would have to be the last time she allowed him to touch her, she thought. He was a married man. They could not go back to their old ways. They could be lovers no more.

"Come, Sofiya, let's go back to the hospital."

She turned and walked out before him, letting him follow. She kept her head down and averted from him as they walked out into the street. After only a few moments, a troika pulled up. She got in and helped Carpathian. She didn't know what to say. She felt betrayed. Not by Carpathian but by this Sergei Zorin who had a job and a wife and a whole world waiting for him. But how could she blame him? So she stopped thinking about how she felt and focused on him. As a nurse, that was her job, wasn't it? And that's what she had to remember. This man was still her patient, even if her heart now had a deep fissure running through it.

"You must be exhausted…" she said finally in a voice that was as flattened as she felt. "And elated to learn who you are. Where you belong. To know you have a lovely wife and a home to go back to."

"I am very happy about my job. And I have to thank you for that. Once I saw the workshop, I felt as if I had come home. And then when I saw Henrik, I felt such a sense of respect. Of gratitude to him. I knew I had been his apprentice. I remembered him teaching me. I could even recollect a few of the pieces we worked on. Especially one egg. An imperial egg…The Tiara Egg it was called. For me to work on that, for him to trust me to that extent had been a monumental step for me. But I don't remember much more than that. Not the other people there. None of them were familiar. Only Henrik. Only my desk and the workshop."

He had still hadn't mentioned the one thing—the only thing that Sofiya was thinking about.

"What about Dimitry? He's your cousin. He didn't look familiar?"

"No. I don't have any memory of him." Carpathian's hands clenched into fists. "I can't stand this, Sofiya. There is only a big gaping hole where the other memories should be. Looking at those people who supposedly were my family...I felt nothing. Could remember nothing. I felt as if I was going mad."

Sofiya was prepared for these outbursts. All the patients who suffered brain injury and amnesia suffered them occasionally. They were always uncomfortable to witness. But with Carpathian, they disturbed her more profoundly because of how she felt about him. She desperately wanted to find the memories for him even if they separated them further so he wouldn't have to suffer like this. But she couldn't. No one could.

She took his hand in hers. His was so much larger. She stared at his left ring finger. Had he had a ring once? Had he lost it? Or left it home when he went to war?

"I don't remember Irina Nikandrovna at all, Sofiya. Not a shred of a memory. She is a total stranger to me."

Sofiya felt tears threatening again. She didn't know what to say.

"Sofiya? What are you thinking?" he asked.

"That I shouldn't be holding your hand."

"Yes, you should. Of course you should."

"No. You are a married man. Who will go back to your wife."

"I don't know her."

He sounded as distraught as Sofiya felt. Of course, he would have to go back to Irina Nikandrovna. Even if she hadn't seemed happy to have her husband back, Sofiya had seen the way she looked at him. She had knowledge of him. She had a history with him. They had married. They must have been in love. Sofiya decided to address the rest of her fears.

"Do you know if you have children?" she asked.

"I asked her. And thank God, no. Because then I would have no choice but to be bound to her."

"Sergei Zorin," Sofiya said, using his real name. "You *are* bound to her. As much as I wish it were not so. If it were me, if you had been married to me, I would want you back with or without your memory. You loved her once."

"But now I am in—"

"There is no *now*. Our weeks together were an intermission between your past and your future. *We* are a result of a medical anomaly. Your memories of Irina Nikandrovna will come back. Your love of her will come back."

She hated every word she was saying, but she also knew all of them were true. In time he would remember. And when he did, he would hate Sofiya if she had kept him from where he was supposed to be.

He leaned toward her and kissed her, but she pushed him away.

"You are married."

"Sergei Zorin is married. I am still Carpathian, who is in love with you. Don't do that, don't push me away again, Sofiya. When I am Sergei Zorin again, I will take on his responsibilities and his place in the world. But just for these last days at the hospital, while I am still there, be with me. Be with Carpathian. Give us this time. Make more memories with me. I may have to live off of them for a long time to come."

She couldn't help the sob that escaped. He reached for her and pulled her to him and buried her head against his chest. He held her so close she feared she wouldn't be able to breathe, but that thought brought relief. How much easier to die than to have to live without him. And she knew she would. The truth was you could live without anyone. She'd seen it over and over. As much as her grandmother wanted to die when her grandfather passed on. As much as she turned off the stoves and closed the bakery and sat alone in the dark, mourning him, she survived her grief. And after a time, she turned the lights and the oven back on. As much as Sofiya would want to love only Carpathian for the rest of her life, she knew she might not. And somehow, that was the saddest thing of all.

Carpathian leaned forward and told the driver to stop the carriage. There were still a few blocks before the Winter Palace.

"Come," he said to her. "Let's get out of here. It's almost dinnertime, and I want to eat in a restaurant with you. I want to pretend that this is our life. That we have meals together all the time. That this is normal for us."

"But the hospital—"

"It will still be there when we are done. I'll take the blame with Matron. Don't worry, it will be fine."

They crossed the street and entered the restaurant. It was one Sofiya knew, having been there with her parents for celebrations. Carpathian asked for a table, and they were shown to one in a corner. He ordered a bottle of French champagne and caviar and blinis, and when the waiter had brought it and poured the glasses, Carpathian held his up to Sofiya's for a toast.

Champagne is such a festive drink with the bubbles dancing in the glass. But there was nothing to celebrate. Sofiya didn't understand how she was going to sip the effervescent wine and pretend that she was happy. And then he made a toast.

"One day, you and I will come back here and raise our

glasses to our present. But today, we are raising our glasses to our future. Yours and mine. We will have one. I am as sure of it as I am that I am looking at your beautiful face. I don't understand everything yet. I certainly don't remember everything yet. But I know with every fiber of my being that I am in love with you and no one else. And no memory that surfaces will prove otherwise. You have to believe me. You will, won't you?"

"I will try," she said. It was the best she could do.

He clinked her glass with his. To her, it sounded like something breaking. She sipped, and the bubbles mocked the moment. How many days were left to them? How many hours? How many minutes? How to spend them? She couldn't bear it. She'd made the mistake that Olga and Tatiana and all the nurses spoke of. She'd believed she'd be different. That fate would have a different plan for her. She had been stupid and naïve. And soon, she would pay for it.

Back at the hospital an hour later, Carpathian kissed her goodnight outside. A long kiss that smelled of the lilacs blooming in the gardens. She stayed outside and watched him walk into the entrance, adroit on his crutches. Tomorrow or the next day, he'd move to a cane. And then their time would be up.

Sofiya didn't report to work that next day. She sent word that she had come down with a stomach illness. She stayed home and wrote Carpathian a letter. She wrote it over and over. Alone in the family apartment, she wrote it more than a dozen times. Sometimes, it was short. Other times, long and rambling. She tried to explain all the reasons she had for what she was going to do. And then wrote the letter one last time without bothering to explain.

In the end, it was just a paragraph.

I have loved knowing Carpathian. And I will be his forever. But you are Sergei Zorin now. And I can't be yours at all. You have a life to return to, and you are just days away from doing that. I think it best for me to let you return to that life clean. I free you from the promise you made to me last night. I wish you every happiness in your life. I will treasure the memory of our days together with joy.

The word joy was smudged with her tears, but she didn't write it over again.

Chapter 13

Isobelle Moon
New York City
December 1948

"Mr. Reed? You can go in now," the prison guard says.

"Thanks, Ike." Jules hands the guard one of the two boxes of donuts we'd stopped and bought from a bakery a mile or so away from the prison.

On the ride when I asked him about the frightful stories I'd heard about Sing, Jules told me about all the reforms the previous prison warden Lewis Lawes had instituted in the last twenty years, and what a difference they had made. There was a heavy emphasis on the prisoners playing sports, and in fact, once a year the New York Yankees visited to play an exhibition game against the inmates. There were also activities for the mind and soul, including a large birdhouse the prisoners could visit, a chapel, and a well-stocked library.

They could also choose from a large variety of classes. And the current warden was a big proponent of the most modern approaches to incarceration.

I'm not sure what I'd expected—the only impressions I had of prisons were from movies like *Castle on the Hudson*, *Girls in Chains*, *Jonny Apollo*, and others. I'd been obsessed with them for years, trying to imagine what my father had endured in Siberia during the last years of his life.

The guard inspects my package. Looking over the tiara, he whistles and turns to Jules.

"I'm not sure I can let you take this in."

"We need my grandfather to identify it. It's a tiara."

"Like a queen would wear?"

Jules nods.

"So what happened to all the pretty stones they usually have?"

"That's what we're hoping my grandfather can tell us."

The guard runs his fingers over it, checking for what, I'm not sure.

"I guess it's okay."

"Thanks, Ike, these are for you."

He gives him one of the boxes of donuts.

"Thank you, Mr. Reed," the guard says. "The boys and I appreciate you always thinking of us."

"No problem," Jules says. "I hope you had a good Thanksgiving with your wife and little boys."

"We did. And you as well."

Jules nods his thanks, and Ike opens the door for us. We go through, walking over the threshold that separates those who are free to come and go and those imprisoned in the penitentiary.

In the visiting room, a wave of sadness washes over me. Even the up-to-date facilities and innovations can't disguise what this place is. The barren walls and benches, the air that carries the stink of unwashed bodies, the whispers and furtive looks between prisoner and visitor tell the story, as do the tears in the wives' and girlfriends' and mothers' eyes and their expressions of hopelessness.

I can't help but think that surely this place, for all its hardship, pales in comparison to where my father was sent. He had no visitors. No baseball team. No boxes of donuts delivered by his grandson. No phone calls or letters—no news of home.

"Are you all right?" Jules asks.

Concern is clear in his eyes.

"I will be."

He guesses what is wrong. "Are you thinking about your father?"

"Yes."

He takes my hand and squeezes it. I'm surprised by the personal touch. And strangely soothed by it.

"Let's sit down." Jules leads me over to an empty table, and we take seats.

Another guard approaches.

"Hi, Mr. Reed. It'll be just a minute. Your grandfather asked to go back to his room and freshen up before coming to see you."

Jules nods and to me says, "These visits are important to him. I'm the only one who comes regularly. My mother stayed close to him, especially after my father, his only child, died, but she lives in France. There is Gina, his third wife, who probably would have stood by him, but my grandfather divorced her shortly before being arrested."

At this point, a door opposite us opens, and Jules watches as a dapper, well-groomed man in pressed slacks and a starched white shirt hurries over to us. The winning smile on his face belies the setting.

"Jules." He hugs his grandson. "It's so good to see you." He pulls away from the embrace and fixes his gaze on me. "And you've brought me some beauty to brighten up my day."

Jules laughs. "Grandfather, this is Isobelle Moon."

"*Enchanté*." Mr. Reed takes my hand then bows over it and kisses it. Straightening, he continues holding it and says, "No rings? Not even a bracelet. And this watch…" He shakes his head and looks at Jules. "Not a single bauble?" He looks back at me. "What kind of boyfriend is my grandson if he hasn't even gifted you with—"

Jules interrupts. "Grandfather, Miss Moon is here to talk to you. She's not…we're not seeing each other." He seems embarrassed.

Mr. Reed doesn't make it any easier on him. "Well now, that's a shame. If I were younger"—he chuckles—"and not spending time in this fine establishment, I'd be wooing you for certain."

I'd heard quite a few stories about Alford Reed on the way up to Ossining from the city, and now that I've met him, I understand the charm that Jules said endeared his clients to him. Among them, Katherine Hepburn, Marlene Dietrich, Greta Garbo, Merle Oberon, Laurence Olivier, and many more stars in Hollywood's firmament and New York City's society denizens.

Mr. Reed looks at Jules, examining his suit and then checks his cuffs. He smiles widely.

In the car, Jules had shown me his cufflinks. Two gold female hands, the fingers tipped with red enamel nail polish. Each hand formed a sign language letter—a *J* on the left, an *R* on the right. Jules said his grandfather had also created a line of brooches with the fingers spelling out signed letters as well. It seems Alford Reed lost some of his hearing in his thirties and had started wearing hearing aids. He'd become sensitive to the plight of the truly deaf and designed the sign language jewelry to help raise money for New York City's School for the Deaf. Little did he realize his clients would fall in love with the idea of wearing the letters. Secret lovers wore each other's initials without anyone knowing. Men wore cufflinks; women wore brooches. A husband would buy his wife a charm bracelet spelling out a whole word. Women would gift friends their initials. Jules said he wore them when he came to visit Grandfather to lift his spirits.

"My grandfather is facing a total of five years, if he doesn't get out early for good behavior, and yet he never shows me how terrible it is. In fact, he insists that being in jail is only a minor hardship. I don't believe him. I know Sing is a test prison for leniency and giving prisoners a different experience in the hopes it will reform them, but it is still prison. My loquacious, charming grandfather is in fact locked up even if he is allowed to keep a pet bird. And can wear his own clothes. And has a radio in his room. Even if he is allowed a steady stream of visitors, most of the people he was close to have abandoned him. And honestly, I can't blame them."

Mr. Reed lets go of my hand, pulls out his chair, and takes a seat. Jules and I follow suit.

"I've missed you, Jules," Mr. Reed says with a hint of a French accent. "And I have a little gift for you." He puts a package on the table. About the size of a book, wrapped in plain white paper. Then he turns to me. "I'm sorry I don't have a gift for you, Miss Moon, but I didn't know you were coming."

Jules takes it but doesn't open it yet. "You already have given me the most important present anyone ever could."

He turns to me. "I always knew I wanted to follow in Grandfather's footsteps, and on my tenth birthday, he gave me a full set of jewelers tools and a small jewelers table—just like his but smaller. And so, my lessons in making and designing jewelry began." He smiles at the memory. "I still use those tools."

Mr. Reed seems a bit overwhelmed by the sentiment and handles it by being gruff. "Enough with the memories, open your present, Jules." He points.

His grandson obeys and unwraps his gift. Inside is an arrow-shaped tie clip. It's neither gold nor silver but some kind of aluminum that has been beaten into a detailed pattern.

"It's stunning," I say, meaning it.

As jeweler to the stars, Mr. Reed has been one of the most visible and talked-about jewelers of the last twenty years. Jules told me he'd started out in the 1920s working for Tiffany's and then went out on his own. He had a sense of style and flair combined with a winning personality that garnered him both attention and fans. His first shop was in New York and was so successful that in the late '30s, he opened another in Beverly Hills, which immediately became popular with the film industry. In no time, Reed's pieces were making their way onto the silver screen because, as Marlene Detrick so famously decreed, only real jewels light up the screen.

"Where did you do this? How did you do this?" Jules asks his grandfather.

"They're letting me work in the shop. That's where we produce totalitarian things like license plates. I have to do my share of those, but I get some free time where I can use the equipment to make whatever I want."

"Other than weapons, I assume," Jules says.

Mr. Reed laughs, and there's an innocent joy in the sound that surprises me. It's far more childish than Jules' laugh and entirely incongruent to where we are.

"I made this too. I've been praying, Jules." He holds up a rosary made of small amber-colored wooden beads strung together in a loop with a darker one at the center and at the end of the pendant a stylized, simple but elegant wooden crucifix.

"Feel it," Mr. Reed says to Jules. "When I was carving them, I thought a lot about the Tahitian and South Sea pearls I used to deal with."

"The finish is fantastic. But a rosary, Grandfather? I thought you gave all that up. I haven't heard you utter the word *God* unless you were cursing."

"There's a very beautiful chapel here. Have I told you about it before? It's very peaceful, and I like to spend time there. At night, they offer classes on religion and Bible study. At first, I attended just for the look and feel of the place. But the more time I spend there...the more I've been thinking about my childhood in France and about my parents and their faith and why along the way it became all right for me to turn my back on this holy thing that is so much larger than us. I guess I like the idea of something magical and magisterial beyond us. I'm not sure that I'm in accordance with the concept of an all-powerful God...but when I meditate on the beads, I feel something. Do you remember the jade mala I made for Barbara Jeffries?"

"Yes," Jules says. He turns to me. "They were exquisite lavender jade beads with a silken tassel and a tiny Buddha that hung from it."

"She's been writing to me and encouraging me to learn to meditate while I am here. They have classes in that too."

I raise my eyebrows at the mention of the Fifth Avenue

society matron whose father was responsible for donating at least half of the impressionist paintings in the Metropolitan Museum.

Once more, Jules gives me the skinny: "Mrs. Jeffries visits our store often, ordering a new piece for herself or for one of her daughters. She always stays a while to have a cup of coffee and talk about what's new in the world of jewelry. She spends a lot of time 'over the counter' as you used to call it." He looks at his grandfather, who chuckles, and Jules turns back to me. "Many of Grandfather's clients enjoyed having coffee and biscuits or a glass of wine with him while discussing jewelry, art, gemology, design, and of course gossip. He's always referred to them as his 'over the counter' friends. And now quite a few of them have continued the custom with me, although I'm not nearly as witty or humorous. But I am trying to keep up with the gossip."

I laugh, as does Mr. Reed.

"I'm surprised to hear Mrs. Jeffries has been in touch, Grandfather. The last time I asked, you said you didn't expect any clients to stay in contact, social mores being what they are."

"I am just as surprised as you are. Mrs. Jeffries wrote first, and I answered. Then she wrote again. We went back and forth for a few letters. I thought I'd mentioned it to you. Then she surprised me with a visit since you were here last."

Jules turns to me again. "My grandfather is quite a Lothario and—"

"I am. I'm an incurable flirt," Mr. Reed interrupts Jules and says to me, "It is partly how I became successful. I'm not ashamed to say I know how to talk to a woman and make her feel that she's understood. I can appreciate what makes her unique, and I see that uniqueness as her beauty. Each person, be it a woman or man, is special in much the same way as every stone, be it a topaz, or an aquamarine, or emerald. It would do my grandson a world of good if he'd take after me a little and not give up over one doomed—"

"Enough." Now Jules interrupts his grandfather.

"But you are wasting the best years of your life."

"Well, Mrs. Jeffries is a lovely woman. I'm glad she is visiting," Jules says, clearly refusing to discuss anything else.

"And lonely. So many of our clients are lonely," Mr. Reed tells me. "The extreme wealth they possess separates them from the rest of us mere mortals. They can't trust who wants to be with them for themselves or who wants to be with them for their aura and stature and place in society."

"Lonely or not, the fact that she visits you and has you meditating sounds serious," Jules jokes.

Mr. Reed laughs. "I swore off serious a long time ago. You know that, Jules."

He looks at me. "I'm sorry, dear. You didn't come all the way here with Jules to listen to stories about my sad little life in prison. Tell me how I can help. If I can help."

I pull the leather box and papers out of my satchel and put them on the table. Mr. Reed reaches for the case and, much like Jules did when I gave it to him, feels the leather as if gleaning information from its quality.

"Whatever is it?" he asks.

When I open the box to reveal the tiara, I can tell that Mr. Reed is surprised by what he's looking at. Even though I don't know him, I'm convinced that he not only remembers it but is disturbed by it. He makes no effort to lift it out of the case. I pass him the receipts and explain the reason for my visit.

He does not interrupt me. He waits until I have finished speaking, and then he picks up the receipts. At first, it seems like he is reading them, but as I watch I realize his eyes are not moving. He's simply staring at the top sheet as if he's seeing a film play out there.

"Do you remember this transaction?" I ask.

He doesn't answer but puts the paperwork down and picks up the tiara. Holding it gently, carefully, acknowledging how precious it is to me by his touch, he looks at it for at least thirty seconds without saying anything.

"I do remember this piece," he finally offers and then glances from the frame to me. "Your mother owned it, you say?"

"Yes."

He nods. "I remember your mother." It appears he's thinking about something, is about to speak, then changes his mind.

"Did my mother tell you anything about it?"

"A bit. But before she said a word, I could tell from the workmanship how valuable it had once been."

"What do you mean *once*?" Jules asks.

Mr. Reed glances over to his grandson. Every other time he's talked to him, he's looked him right in the eyes, directly. This time, he only gives him a quick side look and then he's looking at the tiara again.

"The diamonds were of excellent quality. But not particularly large, hence they were not worth that much. The sapphires were paste. Very good paste, but glass, nonetheless. As I told your mother, I believed they would have been real when the piece was made because the quality of the tiara suggested it was made by Fabergé or another top-level jeweler. And they did not use paste. If they were still intact, matched sapphires of that size would have been very important stones and worth quite a lot of money."

"Worth how much?" I ask.

"It's hard to say without having seen them," Mr. Reed

says.

"Your best guess?"

"At the time your mother brought me the tiara, if they were real, I'd say many tens of thousands of dollars, if not more."

"But they weren't real," Jules says in a slightly odd tone of voice that I can't quite interpret.

Mr. Reed doesn't respond. Which makes sense. It wasn't a question. But Jules is staring at his grandfather as if awaiting a response.

"Your mother was shocked when I told her the sapphires were paste. And angry. But that isn't unusual. Most clients who discover that something they believed to be of great value isn't are devastated."

"Did my mother tell you where she got the tiara?"

He takes a moment to think. "No. Or if she did, I don't remember. The transaction was over eighteen years ago. Hundreds of customers ago. I have been buying from Russian emigres for a very long time, Isobelle. All the stories have melded into the other. So even if she did, I don't remember any details."

"There's nothing you remember? I don't know how she got it. Or why she hid it... I don't know anything..." I hear my voice crack and stop speaking. I'm frustrated. To have found a clue to the past and still wind up at a dead end is hard to accept.

"You know, there is one thing." Mr. Reed is looking past Jules and me, over our heads, at the window and the patch of gray sky visible there. "I doubt it will help you figure anything out, though."

I glance at Jules, who is staring at his grandfather with narrowed eyes. As if he's angry at him. But why would that be?

"That's all right," I say. "What is it?"

"I offered to buy the whole piece from her. Even though the stones were paste, I thought the tiara itself was a lovely thing. I told your mother it was a shame to break it up and that I might get her a better price if I could sell it as a tiara. But she said she couldn't part with it."

"Did she tell you why?"

He nods. "She did. She said something about needing to keep it so she could hold on to her memories. That wasn't an unusual sentiment among the emigres I bought from. Most of them came to America with very little. Jewelry was small enough for them to manage to keep with them. So these items became imbued with values beyond their actual worth."

I sigh. This is nothing to go on. Mr. Reed must have read my frustration in my reaction.

"I am so sorry," Mr. Reed says.

"I'm sure you are," Jules says with an edge in his voice that takes me out of my misery and makes me focus on the undercurrent running between the two men and wonder if it's something I should be paying more attention to.

Chapter 14

Sofiya Petrovitch
Petrograd
June 1915

Sofiya wrote two other notes and sent them to the hospital as well. One to Matron saying she had a bad sore throat and would probably be at home for a few days. The other to Olga, explaining a little of what had happened and asking her to call and let her know when Carpathian was released from the hospital.

Two days later, Olga did call, and in a sympathetic voice told Sofiya he had gone. And that he had left a note for her.

"Rip it up, please. Don't ever give it to me," she told her. "We have no chance. Nothing he says can matter."

Olga said she would and didn't mention the note to Sofiya when they met the next day at the hospital to take their lunch together. Sofiya thanked Olga for also arranging

Sofiya's new assignment at the other end of the hospital so she wouldn't even have to pass by the ward where Carpathian had been in recovery. Where they had met. Where she had read to him and sat with him and where they had grown to know each other and then care for each other far, far too much.

"How can I thank you for that thoughtfulness?" Sofiya asked Olga.

The grand duchess shook her head. "Don't thank me. It was just one comment to the matron." She put some of her chicken on her fork. Then left it sitting on her plate. "These soldiers that we meet are breaking our hearts, aren't they?"

Sofiya agreed.

"And our souls," Olga said. "I don't think I can keep on working here like this, and Mama agrees. I think this is my last week on the ward. I'm sorry to have brought you here and now leave you."

"I don't blame you for leaving. Surely there's something else you can do to help the effort that doesn't require you to witness so much grief and pain every single day."

Olga wasn't the only one whose mother was worried about her working at the hospital. The next week at dinner, Sofiya's mother said she and her father thought it was time she took a break from the hospital.

"It's been brave of you. But you are taking it to heart too much. You have lost weight. Your cheeks are sunken in. You seem listless and so sad all the time."

Sofiya shook her head. She had to be at the hospital, in case—in case what? In case Carpathian came back to find her? But he wouldn't. He was with his wife. He was back at his job. His life was continuing the way it was meant to. And hers, she thought, had stopped. But still...what if he did come back?

"I'm not ready to go back to work. I want to be at the hospital. I need to be there."

"No, you need to be anywhere *but* there," her father said, joining the discussion. "I've talked to Filatov Roman Sokolov, and he needs you back in the restoration department. With this war continuing, he has no one to help him. All the men are gone, and you are his only female apprentice. Our country needs its heritage cared for as much as its soldiers."

Sofiya pushed back her chair from the table so they couldn't see that she had started to cry. She wouldn't do what they were asking. She would go back to the hospital and stay there. She had to be there.

Her mother knocked on her door a few minutes later.

Sofiya didn't respond, but her mother came in anyway. She sat on the edge of the bed. "Darling Sofiya, I know what is going on with you. I know how you feel. But you are a strong girl. You will get over this man. You will find someone else. You have to let go of this obsession and go back to work. You are destined to do great things. You are like your sign, Capricorn, a goat. Do you know how a goat climbs up the mountain against all obstacles? That's you, my darling. You have your own mountain to conquer, and you can't allow yourself to be slowed down by anyone. I know this man touched your heart, but you can't let him stop it cold."

Sofiya didn't leave right away. She went back for a week, but her mother was right. Like Olga, she needed a break. She went back to work at her beloved Hermitage with the paintings that needed her. Faced with obstacles and problems she could solve and feel some satisfaction from. Spending each day under Filatov Roman Sokolov's tutelage, learning more and more.

The events of the world outside the Hermitage only got more serious and confusing. The war raged on, the soldiers kept dying, and the political situation in Russia became more complicated and conflicted. The factions who wanted to oust the tsar and the imperial family were growing. There had been uprisings for the last seventeen years, but the war had made everything worse. There was significantly more famine and more poverty. The gap between the wealthy and the poor was greater than ever before. Citizens sensed the unrest and reacted badly. Hoarding, becoming bitter and suspicious. It was an ugly time. Summer swiftly turned to fall, then winter. The cold, bitter air had the metallic scent of snow and strife and change. Sofiya, like so many of her countrymen, was afraid.

Sofiya saw Olga less often since neither of them were at the Winter Palace hospital anymore, and her work at the Hermitage took up so much of her time. But whenever she had a day off, she'd accompany her mother to her job at the Alexander Palace, where Olga and the rest of the family were in residence. There, she could spend the day with her dear friend, who was still suffering from nerves from her time at the hospital. The doctors were treating her, but their efforts weren't helping much.

By May, the rumors of a revolution increased. Olga confided in Sofiya that her father was always behind closed doors with his ministers and when he finally emerged his eyes were full of worry. For the first time in her life, Olga said she was afraid for him. For all of them.

On Sofiya's birthday, Olga invited her to a lovely luncheon she set up in the pavilion on the Children's Island which was an iceboat ride across a canal from the west wing of the Alexander Palace. The tiny island had a full-size, four-room playhouse originally built for the children of the first

Tsar Nicholas in 1830 but was a favorite of Olga and her sisters and brother.

For an hour, they made an effort to be the way they used to be. Gossiping and laughing and trying to forget the outside world for just a little while. When the meal ended, Olga handed Sofiya a beautifully wrapped package.

"This is for you. None of us know what is going to happen, but Papa fears the worst. We're not going to be staying here much longer, he says. He won't tell us where we are going, but from the way he's talking, I'm not sure when I'll see you next. Or what is going to happen to all of us. To any of us. So I want you to have something of mine that you can use if you ever need it. I wish I could do more. I wish I could keep us all safe, but at least I can give you this."

Sofiya opened the box to find a tiara. A delicate, beautiful thing that looked like lace crocheted with diamond thread. Intricate swirls formed a dozen loops and inside each one was a teardrop-shaped sapphire. She'd seen many of the family jewels, of course, and not just at the balls she'd attended as a guest of the imperial family or at state occasions. When they were younger, Alexandria had let the girls play dress-up with her clothes, costumes, and jewels.

This modest tiara, or diadem to be more precise, was one that Olga had been given just the year before.

"I think you should have this one because the stones are the exact color of your eyes."

"I don't know what to say," she said to Olga. "Isn't this the diadem your father gave you for your last birthday?"

"Yes, but I have so many things, and I want you to have one that is special."

She took Sofiya's hands in hers. She had tears in her eyes. "The times ahead are going to be very hard for us. I was sworn to secrecy not to tell you this, but I can't keep this from you. You can't tell anyone. Not your parents or anyone at the Hermitage. Do I have your word?"

Sofiya was afraid—Olga had never been this distraught before—but of course she promised.

"My father is going to abdicate soon, and we will be going into exile. He's taken care of things and made preparations so we will be fine, but the world as we all know it is going to change. We have to try and stay in touch. Please? I have so few friends outside of my sisters, and you have been so dear to me for so long. And your wonderful mama—to all of us. I only wish you could come with us."

Olga clasped Sofiya to her, and both girls wept.

Chapter 15

Isobelle Moon
New York City
December 1948

I stand and stretch and then arch my back, feeling the muscles relax. I raise and lower my shoulders, trying to get the kinks out. I've been drafting for the last two hours. The air in the room is stale and stuffy from the forced heat. My fingers are stiff. Ted has yet another challenge and is giving me the rest of the day to solve it.

It seems Mr. Williams rejected Ted's third try at the inner courtyard for feasibility and for cost. And he wasn't crazy about the aesthetics either. As Ted has done so many times before, instead of making the effort, he just gives up and turns to me and lays out the assignment.

"I'm relying on your strength here—solving the problems in someone else's design. No one is as adept at that as you are, Isobelle," he said in a tone of voice that doesn't invite argument.

I wanted to argue, nonetheless. I don't agree that it's my strength. It's simply that since school, that's what I've mostly been handed. When I have had the chance to work entirely on my own, like at Cooper Union, I was always lauded for my creativity. But I haven't been given any opportunities since to do any designing from scratch. After all this time, I'm simply an extra pair of hands.

I stretch out those hands.

For the hundredth time, I think about my mother preparing me for these moments. How I argued with her, telling her it wouldn't be this way. Society had moved on, I'd insisted. Women were being treated more equally. I wouldn't be treated differently because I was a woman. She'd shake her head and tell me she hoped I was right but at the same time, I needed to be prepared for it not being that way.

Ted walks out and leaves me alone with Stan.

"It's a good sign that he relies on you, Izzie. It's not just a compliment that he depends on you so much, but it bodes well for a promotion."

Stan doesn't know about the affair and my subsequent humiliation and I'm not yet ready to tell him. I can feel he's waiting for some response from me.

"I hope you're right about the promotion," I say, hoping I've put an end to the conversation. I don't want to discuss Ted with Stan. He can be too perceptive sometimes.

I need some air. But before I march over and open the window, I peer across the street into Jules' office. It's dark and empty. I'm safe. Twice in the last few days, he's caught me at the window and waved. I've returned the gesture, but turn away, mortified every time, hoping he doesn't think I'm trying to catch sight of him.

Opening the window, I lean on the ledge. A biting wind blows in and ruffles the papers on the drafting tables. It's too cold to be standing here in my sweater, but the freezing air is better than the stuffy radiator's belching heat.

I'm watching the street below when I see a light flicker

and look up to see Jules entering his office, someone following just behind him.

I should back up before Jules notices me, but I can't. I'm riveted by the man who is with Jules, who takes the seat across the desk from him.

I've seen him before, this man. How can this be?

It was yesterday morning, when I first walked up to the bus stop. There were at least eight people waiting; I was perusing the *New York Times* when a movement caught my eye. A little boy, who couldn't have been more than five years old, was riding his tricycle toward the group of us, his mother running behind him, shouting out for him to slow down.

For some reason, the little boy sped up instead of slowing down, heading directly toward an older man. At the last minute, the man leaned over, put his arms on the handlebar and stopped the little boy's trajectory.

The boy's mother finally reached our group. Out of breath and upset, she began apologizing profusely to the man. He interrupted, telling her not to be concerned, that he hadn't been hurt. He was a bit curt and impatient with her. She persisted with more apologies. He repeated that he was not hurt with even more impatience, as if he was bothered by her concern.

I was riveted to the conversation. Not only because of his attitude but also because his accent was so familiar.

Even though my mother never spoke Russian to me, and hardly ever to Aunt Lana, she never rid herself of her distinctive accent. This man had the same accent.

At that point, the bus arrived. The doors opened. The waiting group shifted with all of us moving into an informal line and we began to board. Once I had stepped up and deposited my token, I walked toward the middle of the bus where there were still several empty seats. I took one by the window.

The doors hissed shut, and the driver started up the bus. I was looking out the window and saw that the man with the Russian accent was still standing by the curb. He seemed to be watching me. I couldn't be sure because the bus had pulled out and we were moving. As we drove off, I twisted in my seat so I could catch a last glimpse of him. He was walking away in the opposite direction. Heading north on Fifth Avenue. He'd been waiting for a downtown bus. So why was he walking uptown? The more I thought about it, I realized there could be a dozen reasons. The boy *had* hurt his leg, and the man was going home. Except he wasn't walking with a limp. Okay, he'd changed his mind about the bus and was walking to the corner to hail a taxi. But he could have done that from the bus stop as well.

Why was I wondering at all? Because I don't hear many New Yorkers with thick Russian accents? Because, as if I needed a prompt, it had made me miss my mama afresh? Because he had been looking at me, so intensely, it had seemed.

And now there he is. Across this very street. Sitting in Jules Reed's office. Of course, it was a coincidence. What else could it be? Both Jules and his grandfather had told me that Alford Reed Jewelers had always done a lot of business with Russian emigres, going back to the 1920s. Certainly that's all this is—a Russian emigre visiting a jeweler he'd heard about from friends—trying to sell a family heirloom.

I stand off to the side and watch the two men for the next few minutes while they talk. When the Russian leans across the desk and offers Jules his hand, Jules shakes it. Then both men stand, and Jules escorts him out of his office. The odd thing is the man has a slight limp now. But he didn't have one after the little boy rode into his leg. Had the child hurt him after all, but it hadn't presented until later? I suppose it is possible.

I go back to my desk and try to work. But I'm too distracted. Even though there was nothing about what happened at the bus stop or just now in Jules' office to make me think this is connected to me, I am certain it must. How can it not?

The phone rings on Ted's desk.

The only one left in the office, I get up and answer it.

"Isobelle, it's Jules."

Hearing his deep voice, I feel a frisson of excitement.

I turn and face the window and see him standing there holding the phone. He raises his hand in greeting. I do the same.

"I just had a visitor and think you might want to hear what he had to say. Would you like to get a bite to eat, and I'll fill you in?"

I don't hesitate. "Sure."

"Good, I'll meet you downstairs in your lobby in, say, fifteen minutes?"

I go to the ladies' to brush my hair and freshen up. I apply lipstick and a little bit of rouge. The color on my cheeks helps me look a little less pale. I brush my hair. I'm not certain what I'm more excited about. That Jules might have new information for me. Or that he has asked me out to dinner.

Except, I tell myself, this isn't a date. He's not asking because he's interested in me. It's simply that it's late and he's hungry and he has information for me. He's just combining the two.

I reach into my purse and find the tiny silver perfume bottle from Tiffany's that my mother gave me on my sixteenth birthday. I dab L'Etoile's La Lune perfume on my wrists and then the back of my neck. The perfume was also a gift from my mother. She said it was practically made for me given its name. The scent contains only night-blooming flowers—jasmine, tuberose and moonflowers. It smells how I wish I looked, if that makes sense. Mysterious and glamorous, like Gene Tierney in *Laura*.

I purse my lips, suck in my cheeks to exaggerate my cheekbones and pose, trying for a look I have never been able to pull off. I'll never be a siren. Never be sultry.

I hear my mother sigh that way she always did when she caught me in moments like this and say, "You have a style that is all your own, sweetheart. Why don't you see that?"

Jules is waiting for me when I come downstairs. He gestures outside where snow is now falling.

"It just started. We're only going a few blocks. You okay to walk? I don't think we can find a cab now anyway."

"Yes, I'll be okay."

As we walk outside, he takes my arm and says, "It's slippery."

I wish he hadn't explained. I was hoping he'd taken my arm because he wanted to be a little closer to me. Except he wouldn't. A man like Jules—

"Your hair is getting wet," he says, interrupting my thoughts as we cross Park Avenue.

Is he saying that because he's worried I'll look like a mess by the time we get to the restaurant? He must be used to much more stylish women accompanying him to dinner, I think. Then I square my shoulders and recall my mother's admonition that I'm wrong about men.

"They don't all want cookie-cutter looks and a curvaceous figure. They don't all want lollipop voices and fawning fans. Unique is beautiful. Smart is beautiful. One day your prince will come," she'd say and add, "He'll divide his crown down the middle and give you half and you'll know he's the right guy."

We've only walked a few blocks when we reach our destination, Café Nicholson on Third Avenue and 58th Street. Of course, I'd read about the restaurant in the society columns. The likes of Tennessee Williams, Gore Vidal, and Truman Capote had adopted it as their new favorite canteen. The menu, I'd read, was just one meal a day, presided over by a chef who was getting raves, a Southern woman named Edna Lewis.

I read that the owner, Johnny Nicholson, also owns an antique store, and as soon as we step inside, the décor reminds me of how my mother decorated. Eclectic and unusual. My mother was forever buying ruined paintings or damaged *objets d'art* she loved. I worried no one else would find them as appealing as she did after she restored them. But she didn't. "If no one else wants it, I'll keep it," she'd say. And then remind me that beauty is always in the eye of the beholder. Sometimes, I thought she was just trying to prove to me, over and over, that being liked or looking like everyone else was not a goal worth pursuing.

The restaurant is filled with strange and exotic paintings, a mix of potted palms, marble nineteenth-century nudes on pedestals, and odd vases and mirrors.

An impeccably dressed man with black eyes, beautiful golden skin, and a parrot on his shoulder greets us. Jules introduces me to Johnny Nicholson and his bird, Lolita.

As the proprietor shows us to our table, I pick out a few famous faces in the crowd.

Once we're seated and Nicholson walks away, I tell Jules that I'm impressed he's a regular at one of New York's hotspots.

Jules shrugs. "Don't be. It's just a restaurant. And I tip well."

"You don't enjoy it here, then? Being at the swankiest eatery with all the swankiest people?"

"I'm really not much for socializing, and I certainly don't care about being seen at the right parties or places. That's my grandfather's style. I'm happier spending the evening with a sandwich at my desk in the studio, designing. But with Grandfather away, I have to do my part and keep Reeds in the columns."

"I'm sure he appreciates your effort."

Jules is about to say something when the waiter approaches. We order cocktails, a Dubonnet for me and a dry martini for him. But just as the waiter is about to leave, I change my order and ask for the same as Jules. A martini sounds a little dangerous and more sophisticated and fits so much better with the décor and well-dressed crowd.

The waiter returns carrying a tray with two martini glasses with a single olive on a toothpick in each and two cocktail shakers. He makes a great show of rattling the mixture and then dramatically pouring out the drinks with a flourish.

Once he's gone, Jules lifts his frosty glass to mine. "To solving your mystery," he toasts.

I clink my glass with his but use a bit too much force and some of the drink sloshes over the side. Why did I think I could pull off a martini glass? Of course, I'm mortified. And not just by that. I'm not dressed right for this restaurant. The women here are coiffed, their hair flipping up in perfect curls, or rolls, or twisted into tight chignons. Their dresses are silk or velvet with sweetheart necklines or bare shoulders despite the winter weather. They're wearing pearls and diamond rings. I'm wearing one of my two everyday uniforms—either a white shirt and black gabardine trousers or a neutral-colored sweater set paired with black wool trousers. Today with a nod to the temperature I have on a black twinset and the woolen pants. And my hair is a mess of curls, disheveled from the snow, clearly not coiffed. As for jewelry, I have no pearls. Just my mother's necklace tucked inside my sweater. And I couldn't even toast properly. But Jules didn't seem to notice. He's taken a sip and is now stirring the olive around in the liquid.

"So," I say, attempting to recover gracefully. "Your visitor?"

"Yes. He didn't have an appointment. He told me my grandfather had called him and left a message to come see him. It took me a while, but I finally figured out that the man's housekeeper, who had taken the message, must not have gotten all the information right—so the man had come to the office instead of the prison. When I asked him if I could help him, he said only if I had the information about the tiara that he was looking for."

"The tiara?"

Jules nodded. "I was just as shocked as you look."

"He specifically asked about the tiara?"

"Yes."

"And he spoke with a heavy Russian accent?"

"Yes, how do you know?"

"I'll tell you in a minute. What did you say?"

"I asked him what tiara he was talking about, but he insisted he would only talk to my grandfather."

"Did you find out anything else?"

"I tried, but no. Even though prisoners can't usually get calls after five in the afternoon, I called my grandfather and told the operator it was very important. She said unless it was a matter of life and death, she couldn't break the rules.

That's when I called you. Now tell me how you knew the man has a Russian accent?"

I explain about the bus stop and then seeing that same man through the window.

Jules frowns. I feel a shiver crawl down my back.

"It can't be a coincidence that he was only a block from your house and then came to talk to my grandfather about a tiara."

"No, it can't. Who do you think he is? What do you think he wants?"

"I have no idea. He could be a historian doing research or a museum curator looking for some items for a show. It could be anything. I was going to go up and see my grandfather tomorrow anyway so I'll see what I can find out."

I take a sip of my martini for courage. "Do you mind if I come with you? I may have questions after we hear his explanation."

Jules laughs. "Oh, no doubt you will have questions. Of course, you can come. I'd welcome the company."

I wonder if he means me specifically, or if any company would do. Before I can spend much time trying to figure it out, the waiter arrives to tell us about the dinner special. Tonight is roast chicken and potatoes with a vegetable medley. Jules orders a bottle of white wine to go with it.

The food is delicious, and Jules regales me with entertaining stories over dinner. He tells me about his indoctrination into the world of sales and without any self–aggrandizement, about all the mistakes and missteps he's made in dealing with his grandfather's oh-so-famous clients.

"You're so honest about all the messes you've made," I say.

"You say that as if it's unusual."

"Where I work, everyone is jockeying for position and building themselves up at each other's expense. I'm not very good at it."

"Doesn't sound like a great environment."

"It's not. Especially for me."

"What do you mean?"

"Skidmore, Owings & Merrill is a very progressive firm when it comes to women architects. They have two. Me and Natalie Griffin de Blois. She is a lead designer currently doing the Terrace Plaza Hotel in Cincinnati. I can't tell you how rare that is in our profession."

"So what's the problem?"

"It's not working out as well for me. Natalie was in the New York office during the war. Short-staffed with so many male architects either off at war or at Oak Ridge working on building the secret city—"

"You were at Oak Ridge?" he asks.

I nod.

"That's fascinating, I've read about it…we all have, but what a unique and intense opportunity."

"Intense being the operative word."

"I'm sorry that I interrupted. You were telling me about Natalie here in New York?"

"Yes, she had a lot of opportunities to show what she could do. And she had a boss in New York who wanted her to rise to the top. Meanwhile, I was at Oak Ridge, where there were fewer opportunities. First, because there was already a stable of talented male architects on the project. Second, because by the time I got there, all the styles for the buildings had been set. We were just building more of the same. There weren't many chances for me to put my creativity on display. I couldn't shine. And now that I'm back, my new boss has no interest in me, other than to do the same tasks I've been doing for the last five years."

"He's holding you back?"

"You could say that."

"Isn't he happy with your work?"

I didn't answer right away—I was lost in thought—some people would look at my situation now as a great opportunity, but behind the scenes it's awkward and complicated because of my past relationship with Ted. Now that he's my direct boss, I have to go to him to negotiate for advancement, and I feel uneasy about it. He's taking advantage of me and I believe intentionally holding me back and benefiting from it.

"Isobelle? Is he unhappy with your work?" Jules asks his question a different way.

"Quite the opposite. He's too happy with it. He has me solve all the tough problems he doesn't want to be bothered with or can't figure out and won't give me any of the credit. If he did, I'd get promoted sooner rather than later. I'd be working on my own projects, not fixing his."

"You must be furious."

"I should be…"

"But?"

"I guess I have a hard time getting angry. Intellectually, I know that's what I should be feeling but—"

I'm interrupted by the waiter. We've finished with our dinner and the waiter arrives to remove our plates and then offers us dessert, which tonight he informs us is red velvet cake. We both say yes to the cake and ask for coffee. Then Jules gets right back to where we left off. I wish he hadn't.

"Can we not talk about this?" I ask.

"Why?"

"I'm embarrassed I can't just stand up to him and demand to be treated differently. That I'm *not* angry. But I'm not. I'm so lucky to even be working there. What if I said something and it backfired, and I was let go?"

The dessert arrives.

"I hate that you think it's luck," Jules says with passion as the waiter puts the plates down. "You don't get as far as you have with luck. Why are you downplaying your talent?"

I don't say anything. I'm incredibly uncomfortable with his reaction.

I watch him realize I'm not responding. He moves back a little in his seat. A fraction of an inch farther away from me.

"You're right. This is none of my business."

Now I feel worse. He sounds disappointed. With me? Or himself?

The energy at the table has changed, and it's my fault. But that's what I do, isn't it? Push people away so I don't have to talk about how I feel. I'm not sure how to maneuver the conversation now that I've upended it.

"I'm sorry," I say.

"No, I was out of line."

He takes a bite of his dessert and then leans across the table to tell me that a very well-known film director, Meryn Leroy, who is Reed's client, has just been seated.

For the rest of our meal, we have a spirited conversation about what turns out to be our similar taste in movies. Both of us are addicted to films directed by Alfred Hitchcock. My favorite is *Rebecca*, his is *Notorious*. Neither of us like swashbucklers like *The Sea Hawk* or *The Mark of Zorro*. We both like dark mysteries like *Laura* and are partial to romantic movies like *His Girl Friday* and *The Philadelphia Story*, but neither of us like slapstick nor care much for musicals.

We end the meal in a much better frame of mind, and Jules pays the check. When we step through the door and walk outside, we are greeted by snow blowing so furiously it's hard to see more than a few yards in front of us. There is only whiteness and the sound of the wind. No city sounds at all—no car wheels or horns. I peer into the street where there is hardly any traffic.

"It's a blizzard," I shout over the storm.

"It certainly is," Jules says as he takes my arm and gently pulls me back into the shelter of the restaurant's vestibule.

"I doubt I can get a cab for you."

"The busses must be running, though. I can catch the Third Avenue bus up to 83rd."

He looks at me as if I'm crazy.

"I wouldn't let you even attempt that. What if something were to happen to you? I'd never forgive myself."

"I don't see that I have any choice. Besides, it's just snow."

"Isobelle, you said it yourself, it's a blizzard. Listen, I live two blocks away. You can sit it out for a while there." The way he's said it, it's not a question. He looks down at my shoes. "Thank goodness you are wearing sensible shoes and not silly high heels. Now button up your coat. And do you have a scarf?"

I nod and pull it out of my pocket.

"Wrap it around your nose and mouth like this." He shows me. "It's freezing out there."

Once we're suitably bound up in wool, Jules opens the door and we venture out again. He takes my arm and we set off.

He was right. It's tough going. The wind pushes against us. The snow isn't soft and kind but hard, biting, and unrelenting. It's a nasty storm. Only Jules' arm linked with mine makes me feel safe.

The short walk seems to take a very long time, and

we're both out of breath by the time we reach his apartment at 14 Sutton Place South on the corner of 56th Street. We're just across the street from the East River and the wind is worse here. The doorman pushes against the storm to let us, and a lot of snow, inside.

"Good evening, Mr. Reed, ma'am. It sure is ugly out there. Glad you made it home safe and sound."

Jules thanks him. For a few moments, we stand there, stamp our feet, and try to dislodge the mess from our shoes.

An elevator man, like the doorman, greets Jules by name. Inside the wood-paneled cabin, Jules and the uniformed man discuss the storm and then we're at the fifteenth floor.

Inside apartment 15E, Jules turns the lights on, illuminating a glossy dark green foyer. We take off our coats, now damp from melting snow, our scarves, and our boots. I notice the parquet and herringbone floors and moldings that from the looks of them are all original and date back to the early 1920s. Beyond the entryway is a living room large enough to accommodate two sofas and a wall of casement windows, beyond which I can see the city's twinkling lights.

"Welcome," he says. "It's small but serves my needs."

"It's like a jewel," I say and mean it. Every inch of the apartment is lush. The walls are deep emerald green and highly lacquered. There are silver-framed drawings—two in the entryway, several more inside. They are pencil drawings, and from where I am standing, some look like Matisse, others like Picasso, Braque, and Leger. I want to go up and check, but it would be too rude.

The comfortable-looking couches are upholstered in mohair velvet sapphire blue with green and black cushions. The side tables and coffee table are etched opalescent glass circles, sitting on black lacquer bases. The lamps and chandeliers are also opalescent glass and chrome. I almost gasp when I see the lacquer screen in the corner of the room. The molded glass panels show palm fronds in high relief. All this glass looks to me to be French from the early 1930s, and I recognize they are Lalique or Sabino. Both have that distinct look of milky shininess with a bluish tinge and internal golden reflections.

Jules is pointing down a hallway, telling me the bathroom and bedroom are that way and that the kitchen is to our right.

"Would you like some coffee or some tea?" he asks.

"Anything as long as it's warm," I say. "I feel like I'll be cold for the rest of my life."

He laughs, and I follow him into a room that has been transformed into a combination kitchen and library with a windowed dining nook. He sets about making coffee. There are two more of the silver-framed drawings here. Both appear to be Salvador Dali. I ask about the décor and the artwork.

"My grandfather was born and raised in the South of France. Even when he moved to America, he kept a residence there and spent vacations and summers by the sea. He introduced my mother to the area when she and my father married and then when they divorced, she moved there. She still designs jewelry and has a small gallery in a town called St. Paul de Vence. The area has been a haven for artists since the First World War, and my mother knows them all and has been collaborating with them for years. She also collects their art, and I'm lucky that she's generous. She's given me a drawing or painting or piece of pottery every year for my birthday since I was thirteen. I can show you some more once we warm up."

"What a coincidence that our mothers were…" His is

still alive, I think to myself, and amend my comment, "Are both in the arts."

"My grandfather is a great Agatha Christie fan, and he had this quote from one of her books framed. It hangs behind his desk in his office. *I've often noticed that when coincidences start happening they go on happening in the most extraordinary way. I dare say it's some natural law that we haven't discovered.*'"

"Do you believe that?" I ask.

The coffee is done, and Jules pours it and then takes out a bottle of Irish whiskey. "I think we need something extra to take the chill off, okay with you?"

I've already had a martini and wine. I probably should say no, but I don't.

"I don't have any cream," he adds, "or I'd try to impress you with the full range of my culinary skills."

"You cook?" I ask.

"I do."

"Well, I don't. Not at all. So I'm impressed even without the cream."

He takes both coffees and I follow him into the living room where we sit on opposite ends of the couch. We're facing the southern exposure windows and the snow is still falling heavily. Lights from the nearby buildings give the scene an amber glow, transforming it into a sepia postcard.

Jules gets up and turns on the radio. Dick Haymes is singing *Little White Lies*. It's been a popular song all year, and since I always have the radio on when I'm drafting, I know the words by heart.

> *If this room was burning*
> *I wouldn't even notice*
> *'Cause you've been taking up my mind*
> *With your little white lies, little white lies*

It's a slow, jazzy, romantic song and, given the hour and the drinks and the man sitting across from me, it makes me self-conscious. I sip the coffee. And then sip it again, right away.

Next up is Doris Day singing *It's Magic,* and I burst out laughing. It's partly the drink but mostly the absurdity of this whole scene. Jules and I are acquaintances. Without any romantic interest. At least on his part. On mine it's pointless for me to even imagine such a thing, I'm so out of his league.

You sigh, a song begins
You speak and I hear violins
It's magic...

"What's so funny?" Jules asks, smiling.

I'm trying to think of how to answer without embarrassing myself when the song dies before it's ended and at the same moment all the lights go out.

"Look," Jules says, pointing to the window.

The entire city has disappeared. Snow is still falling, but beyond it, there's nothing.

For a few minutes, we both stare.

"The whole city is dark," he says. "It must be a major electrical outage from the storm." I hear Jules get up. "Sit tight. I'll be right back."

"Not a problem. I wouldn't dream of moving."

In less than a minute, he's returned with light—a silver candelabra with eight candles, all burning. Their glow illuminates his face, giving him a mysterious look that only makes him even more attractive.

"Don't tell my mother about this. It's blasphemous."

Confused, I study what he's holding and then realize it's

a menorah. Aunt Lana is Jewish, and I've participated in her Chanukah ceremonies for as long as I can remember.

"You're Jewish?" I blurt out.

"You're surprised?"

"Yes, your grandfather's rosary?"

"He converted. He fell deathly ill when he was still a young man, living in Paris, apprenticing at Chaumet. He was rushed to a Catholic hospital, not expected to survive, but he did. In the process, he had some emotional epiphany. Or so he claims. Ultimately, I think it was a business decision. Similar to him shortening our family name from Reisschmidt. My mother is very much Jewish, and I was bar mitzvahed, though I think of myself as an atheist now. Since the war…" He stops talking and sets the menorah down on the coffee table.

He walks over to the window and peers out into the black city. "I really can't see a thing. What a storm to have knocked out the electricity."

I join him.

"We had to build backup electrical systems at Oak Ridge to make sure the factories never lost power. I would think New York City would have similar systems."

"I would too."

I'm very aware of standing so close to him and want to distance myself, but at the same time I don't want to be obvious about it. I'm certain he's not in the slightest bit uncomfortable or thinking about me the same way. I feel like I have a crush on him. And I don't get crushes. My last was Steve Gardner in high school. I hated all that yearning and wishing and wanting so much that I decided I was never going to allow myself that indulgence again. And I haven't. I've dated men who made an effort to woo me. But fancying someone who has not expressed any interest? No, I've avoided that trap. Even with Ted.

Except now, I seem to be unable to stop myself.

"I need to go home," I say too suddenly. "I assume the elevator's not working but there are stairs, aren't there? Every building has a fire staircase." I walk toward the front door where Jules has hung our coats.

He reaches my side and puts his hand on my shoulder.

"Isobelle, I wasn't going to let you out in a blizzard with streetlights on. I'm certainly not going to let you attempt to go home in a blizzard without any lights at all. You have to stay here. I'll give you the bedroom, and I'll take the couch. I've fallen asleep many nights reading there, it's quite comfortable."

"I couldn't put you out of your bedroom."

"It's not up for discussion. And the room has a lock, so as much as I might enjoy it, you don't have to worry about me visiting during the night."

Of course, I assume he's joking, but there's a light in his eyes that confuses me. I remind myself that I'm a bit tipsy from being exhausted and overwhelmed added to the drinks at dinner and the whiskey in my coffee. This light is probably just a reflection from the candle and the comment must be him being polite.

Jules escorts me to his bedroom—which is painted dark blue with white molding, dark curtains and white bedding. He shows me where the bathroom is and gives me—from the smell of them—a freshly laundered pair of pajamas. He says he'll use the bathroom first and then this whole end of the apartment will be mine.

I sit on the edge of the bed. My head is spinning. I'll just lie down until he's out of the bathroom, I think as I sink back against the pillows.

Chapter 16

Sofiya Petrovitch
Petrograd
December 1917

Eighteen months had passed. Sofiya missed Olga. The friends wrote each other often but hadn't seen each other in many months. Sometimes at night, like this one, when she missed her the most, she would take out the tiara that her friend had gifted her. She'd put it on and pretend she was at the palace at a ball, dancing with a handsome soldier. But on this night, she wondered if she'd ever go anywhere grand enough to wear it ever again—wondered if there would ever be another ball in Russia. If there would ever be a time to dress up in silk and satin and lace and be twirled by her dance partner across the ballroom in the Winter Palace.

She couldn't imagine that those days would ever return. Idly, she flicked one of the sapphires and realized the stone was loose. That was dangerous. She knew anything that had belonged to the imperial family had to be of the very best quality. Each of the stones must be worth a fortune. She needed to have it fixed. And of course, it had to be repaired by the jewelers who had created it in the first place. The House of Fabergé. But dare she walk into the shop?

Surely, Carpathian had forgotten about her by now. Besides, taking the tiara to Fabergé's wouldn't require her stepping foot in the workshop. Of course not. She wouldn't see Carpathian. There was no chance of it. If he'd even gone back to work there. She had no idea. Perhaps he'd stayed in the army—and been given a desk job. Yes, most probably. Even though the war was over, the country had a robust military that needed smart men more than a jewelry store needed another jeweler when there was no royalty to cross its doors anymore.

The streets were covered in snow the following day. They glistened as she walked from her apartment to the famous jewelry store. She opened the door and walked in. It was even more quiet than she had remembered. The jewels still glittered and shone but in a lost and lonely way. As if the pieces were waiting, like they all were, for a happier time when they would adorn beautiful women who had parties to go to and—

"Can I help you?" The salesman approached.

He wasn't anyone Sofiya had seen before, and she was relieved. After she explained about her repair, she handed him the case. He unwrapped it carefully and studied it.

"I'll go and get the jeweler who made this. It should be a simple repair."

"You know exactly who made it?"

"Of course. His mark is right here," he said and then left her.

She hadn't ever looked at the marks. Which jeweler was it? The man Carpathian worked for? Another one of the workmasters?

"Can I help you?" She turned to the male voice.

It was Dimitry Zorin. The man who had looked at her drawing of Carpathian and failed to identify his cousin the first time she'd been there. The same man who'd looked unhappy when she'd brought Carpathian here. There was no recognition on his face now. Clearly, he didn't remember ever having met her.

"No, I'm being helped, thank you."

He nodded and proceeded to put what he was holding inside one of the glass showcases and then left and walked to the rear of the store and disappeared behind the door to the workshop.

It had shaken Sofiya to see him. He'd been no friend to Carpathian. When he'd seen him that first day, he'd looked at him as if he was an unwelcome ghost, not a beloved cousin home from the war in need of support.

"Here we are, miss…" The manager had returned. "The master wasn't available, but his assistant can help you."

She knew before she even turned. She sensed him being there. As if her whole being was attuned to his presence. Something in her shifted. Her instinct was to run. But they had the most precious thing she owned. She couldn't leave it there. Except she didn't want to turn around. Didn't want to see Carpathian. Didn't want to see him whole and healed and back to his work and his world and his wife. For all she knew, he had a child by now. Enough time had passed and—

"I looked at the tiara and there are three loose stones altogether. It would only take a few days to repair it. Would that be all right?"

Sofiya turned. She had to answer him. And as she did, she saw his face change. At first, it was relaxed, and then he recognized her. There was a countertop between them. A gulf of more than eighteen months. And a mosaic of memories of fourteen short days when she'd lived an entire life that had left her wholly different—awake to what love could be, wounded and grief-stricken having lost it, and bereft knowing no one had come close to moving her the way Carpathian had and no one ever might. The truth was she barely gave anyone a chance. It was too dangerous to open up to anyone again when they could be taken from her in an instant.

"I wanted to find you," Carpathian said. "But I didn't know your last name. I sent you a letter at the hospital, but they sent it back telling me you didn't work there anymore."

"Why? Why did you write me?"

The manager returned to the showroom. Carpathian resumed explaining the repair to Sofiya. The manager fussed with something in a case and then retreated.

"I need to see you," Carpathian said. "Please. The café on the corner. At six this evening. Please, Sofiya. I—"

The manager returned yet again.

"Is everything in order, Sergei Zorin?"

"Yes, I was just telling our client that the repair would take no longer than a week."

"All right then, let me give you a receipt," the manager said to Sofiya and then turned to Carpathian. "Thank you, Sergei Zorin," he said, dismissing him.

Sofiya did not go to the café at the appointed hour. She couldn't. But she waited across the street and watched Carpathian walk toward it. He was obviously healthy again. Still too thin, but he'd lost the hospital pallor. Not only was he not using a cane, but he barely limped. If she hadn't been looking for that slight hesitation in his step, she wouldn't have seen it at all.

The rest of that week passed slowly. St. Petersburg, or Petrograd, as she was supposed to call it, was in the throes of getting accustomed to the newest political regime. The food shortages had worsened and become seriously grave, and everyone was feeling the effects of it. Sofiya and her parents were lucky that even though her mother had such strong ties to the Romanov family, her father's position with the Hermitage protected them to some degree.

The government, which was in the process of stripping so many of the upper classes of their entitlement, understood the value of the country's cultural heritage. The leaders of the new regime spoke big philosophical words decrying the royals for their greed, Sofiya's father said at dinner one night, but these new leaders were no different. They were just as self-serving. They were eating fine. Living in the luxurious houses that they had conscripted from the nobility. They claimed that they needed to safeguard and protect the treasures that belonged to the country so if the time came that they needed money, they would have them to sell. And so the keepers of the paintings, sculpture, the cameo collection, the furniture and the clocks all kept their jobs, as did their staffs. As a member of that working group, Sofiya had remained in her restoration job. Unlike so many, she went to work every day in a beautiful place where she could walk among artful and inspiring *objets d'art* and could spend her days concentrating on infinitesimal repairs that restored these great works to their full glory. She found both joy and a relief in disappearing into a pastoral scene from Holland in the 1600s or spending the day with an old woman in a Rembrandt or standing in a ballroom with Fragonard. Even if at the end of the day, on her walk home she had to reenter the strange and violent world of tsar-less Russia, she had her oasis of calm to look forward to the next day.

Sofiya wrote to Olga religiously and received letters back telling her about the Romanovs' lives in Tobolsk. What struck her over and over as she read her mother the letters over cups of tea was how the imperial family was living with more hardships than the Petrovitches were. And how surprising it was that Olga made it sound as if the family had come to terms with their treatment and terrible circumstances. They were, she wrote, thankful to be alive and all together.

At the end of the week, as much as she was loath to return to the House of Fabergé to pick up her tiara, Sofiya made her way there. The manager asked her to wait a moment and said he would fetch it. But it wasn't he who returned with it. As she had feared, and even hoped a little, Carpathian did.

He and Sofiya were alone in the shop. She knew from talking to her parents and friends that so many of the elegant stores were suffering, but the cases were even more empty today than they had been the week before. The despair hanging over the illustrious showroom was palpable.

"I had to make some adjustments to the tiara," Carpathian said as he opened the case to show her. But she barely looked. She just wanted to take it and leave, walk away, not hear his voice or smell his scent or be reminded of how he would hold her face between his hands when he kissed her or how he liked to bury his head in her neck and inhale her perfume or how he playfully gnawed on her shoulder when they made love and how that inflamed her— of all strange things—the way nothing else did.

"Thank you," she said, feeling her cheeks flush. She glanced at his hands resting on the countertop, remembering how they felt cupping her breasts.

She shut the case. "How much do I owe you?"

"Don't you want to look at—?"

"No, thank you. I have to be going and would like to pay and—"

"You didn't come to the café," he said in a whisper even though no one was around. She felt the intimacy of his voice in that timbre deep inside her.

"There was no point."

"Why?"

"I told you in my letter. You are married. And for all I know, you have a child."

"I have a wife in name only. She had a lover during the war. And they had a son. And she is living outside of the city now with her parents. We have nothing to do with each other. I wanted to explain all of this to you."

"Yet you are still married, though?"

"Yes."

"Why?"

"Her lover—who is my traitor of a cousin—you met him—Dimitry Zorin—is also married. With children. What a snake he is. We've been in competition since we were boys, and he's always hated me. Always tried to cause trouble for me. And why? Who knows? He's a year younger, so I got things first. Because I was older and taller and so better at games? I do not know. But he's tried to outdo me. And with me at the front, he thought he found a way. I'm disgusted. But at the same time…" Carpathian shrugged. "He's welcome to her. The only problem is Dimitry can't leave his family because of the damn rations. They need his cards. If he left her, they wouldn't have enough to subscribe. For the sake of those children, I have chosen not to pursue a divorce for now. But you have to understand, she's not part of my life, Sofiya."

"Regardless, you are still a married man."

He threw up his hands. "Why does that matter if it is in name only?"

Because a married man cannot marry you, and if you stay with him then you are a mistress, and a mistress has no rights, Sofiya wanted to say. She knew all about her own mother's upbringing. Sofiya's grandmother was the mistress of a well-respected banker in London. He set her up in a lovely house and gave her generous gifts and when she got pregnant provided for the child as well. She added a Mrs. to the front of her name and said she was a widow. She sent her daughter to a fine school where she studied art until she turned fourteen. Then her lover died. And while Sofiya's grandmother owned her house and the jewels and everything else he'd given her over the years, she had no allowance from him anymore. After selling everything but a few pieces of jewelry she couldn't bear to part with for sentimental reasons, she returned to St. Petersburg with her teenage daughter and moved in with her family. Now truly a widow. For a year, she grieved. As a mistress, she had been forbidden from being at her lover's side at his deathbed. She was unwelcome at his funeral and burial. When she visited his grave for the last time, she could not linger or leave flowers.

No, Sofiya could not bear to risk traveling down the path her grandmother had tread. She knew the elderly woman, always in black, always bereft, never really recovered from the love she lost because she'd never really had it as her own in the first place.

"Thank you for repairing my tiara," Sofiya said as she picked up the package.

Carpathian reached out and put his hand on her arm as

if to stop her.

"Please, don't...we need to talk. We need to be together... we need—"

Sofiya didn't trust herself to speak. She shook her head as she tried to pull away. Carpathian didn't let go.

She looked at him, into his warm eyes, trying to tell him without words that this was hard enough, begging him to not make it any harder.

And because he knew her so well, for all the reasons they did belong together, she thought, even though they never would be together again, he withdrew his hand.

Leaving the House of Fabergé, clutching her package to her chest, trying not to cry, Sofiya turned right to head home. She had walked less than a quarter of a block when someone shoved her hard into a doorway and tried to grab what she was holding.

Crime in the streets had increased since the tsar had abdicated, and chaos reigned. Between the beggars, the swindlers, and the starving, there was no resemblance now to the St. Petersburg of even four years ago. Citizens, afraid for their lives, all looked the other way when there was an altercation on the street. It was too easy to be labeled a troublemaker and put on a watch list. The police also ignored minor incidents. They were too busy spying on dissidents and filling the jails with them.

With all of her strength, Sofiya held on to the package, her last gift from Olga and the memories of times that were gone now. She started to scream out for help. And when she found the man's arm up near her mouth trying to silence her, she bit into his skin. He screamed and jerked his hand away. Taking advantage of his shock, she pushed him away and started to run. But all too quickly he was running after her. He was fast, and in a matter of seconds had reached her and grabbed for her. He had a fistful of her hair and had pulled her backwards when she felt a last tug and then a release. She turned.

Carpathian had the hooligan by the neck. He spun him around and punched him in the stomach. The thief doubled over and went down. He lay on the sidewalk clutching his midsection, moaning. Carpathian kicked him. The man groaned.

"Are you all right, Sofiya?" Carpathian asked as he put his arm around her.

She took off her glove and touched the spot on her head where the thief had pulled her hair and her fingers came away bright red with blood.

"The bastard hurt you," Carpathian said in a hoarse whisper. "Come, let me take you back to the shop and clean you up."

She didn't protest. Still in shock, she couldn't stop feeling the thief's hands on her. Couldn't stop smelling his terrible garlic breath or the sensation of his greasy hair when it had brushed her face, or the horrible taste of his blood.

She started to shake.

"It's all right now. You are with me, you are safe. I promise," he said trying to soothe her.

"Why did he pick me?"

"This man has been hanging around the shop and waiting for clients to come out so that he can accost them and steal their purchases. He's smart enough to pick the House of Fabergé rather than the pharmacist shop around the corner. This is the third time it has happened this week. We have been talking about hiring a private security guard, which now I think we have no choice but to do. You left so quickly I didn't have time to warn you. And you didn't let me wrap the package, so it was there for anyone to see that you were carrying a package from the House of Fabergé, which everyone knows sells priceless goods. That's why I took off after you."

He brought Sofiya upstairs to the workshop and sat her down. First, he brought her a shot glass of vodka from Carl Fabergé's office, which he made her drink down in one gulp. And then he retrieved a first aid kit.

"That's more like a doctor's bag," she said, surprised by the array of medicines, bandages, and other supplies.

"We have quite a few accidents in the workshop. We must be prepared for all kinds of situations."

Carpathian stood above her and very gently parted her hair. Using a square of cotton, he swabbed her injury with disinfectant.

Sofiya jumped a little.

"Does it hurt?"

"It stings. You could have warned me."

"You're a nurse, I assumed you knew."

He swabbed again, and again she winced.

"I'm sorry to be hurting you," he said.

In so many ways, she wanted to say. Instead she said, "No, it's all right. You need to do that."

"So we've reversed positions," he said as he put the cotton pad down and picked up a tube of the same ointment they used at the hospital.

"What do you mean?"

"You're the patient, and I'm the nurse. I only hope I can take care of you half as well as you took care of me."

Sofiya's shoulder ached. The wound on her head throbbed. She must have twisted her ankle too because that also hurt. But it was when she looked down and saw she was still clutching the tiara case to her chest that she finally started to cry.

"If you are in that much pain maybe we should go to the hospital," Carpathian said.

"No, that's not necessary. I was just thinking of how horrible it would have been if I had lost Olga's tiara."

Carpathian got down on his knees in front of her and took her in his arms, holding her quietly, letting her cry. And she did. She sobbed on his shoulder, letting her tears soak into his shirt, thinking that this was their final meeting, their last embrace. They'd never see each other again. She wished Carpathian would just pick her up and take her to their secret spy room and they could spend the rest of their lives hidden there, loving each other instead of what she knew had to happen. She had to get up and go home and never see this man again.

He held her and rubbed her back and whispered to her that he could keep her safe and that he loved her and that he would never let her go until she started to believe him and stopped crying. Then he kissed the tracks of tears on her cheeks.

"Please, Sofiya. We must see each other. What does it matter that some woman and I were once married? My memories of my time with her that have come back are nothing like the memories you and I made. We never had a marriage forged in love. Irina was the daughter of the man I was apprenticed to at the time. He was a father to me and so when he told me he wanted me to marry his daughter so I could be his true son-in-law, I agreed. I know now he wanted the marriage because she was willful and wild, and he was afraid of what would happen to her if he didn't marry her off quickly. And that's exactly what did happen to her once I went off to war. Marriage can't be a payment of thanks to a man who has opened his world to you. And marriage doesn't work like a prison to keep someone from their true nature. It shouldn't ever be a convenient solution to a father's problems with his daughter. So what does it matter that she and her son have my last name? The tsar abdicated the throne. I abdicated my marriage. She is the past—a past I barely remember. You and I are the present. And please God, the future."

Sofiya didn't say anything. Her head throbbed. Her ankle hurt. Her wrists burned where the thief had grabbed them.

Carpathian left for a minute and came back with another shot glass and the bottle of vodka. He poured some for himself and more for her. They sat side by side on the worn couch sipping the strong liquor and talking. He asked her what she was doing now, and as she started to tell him about the restoration work, all the sadness she'd endured during the months they had spent apart disappeared. So did her resolve to stay away from him.

"Come, let me walk you home," he said once she was calm and relaxed again.

She didn't argue. She leaned on him, and he took her arm and they left the House of Fabergé and walked into the street where the first snow of the season was falling, turning Petrograd into the St. Petersburg of her childhood—a sparkling, magical city on the channel where everything had seemed possible.

Chapter 17

Isobelle Moon
New York City
December 1948

I awake the morning after the blizzard with a pounding headache. Opening my eyes, I realize with a start that I'm not home, and then the whole night comes back to me. Up to a point. I don't remember going to sleep. I'm under a coverlet, which I pull down and check—yes, I'm still dressed. Thinking about the entire evening, I feel a twinge of disappointment knowing that I don't even tempt him. But then again, why would I, given the kind of people he mixes with? The rich and famous, the glamorous stars and starlets. A working girl in trousers and a sweater set without pearls or fancy high heels or any décolletage showing.

In the bathroom, I thankfully find a bottle of aspirin and take two. There's a stack of fresh towels on the sink with a note on top that says:

Isobelle - the water gets very hot in the shower, so be careful.

Putting some toothpaste on my finger, I use it as an ersatz toothbrush. And then step into the shower. The water does get quite hot, but I'm careful. I spend longer than usual under the stream, letting it wash away the fog I'm in while the aspirin starts to work.

Wrapped in one of the large fluffy towels, I dry my hair. Without my curling iron, it's going to dry all wavy. I look around and find Jules' hairbrush. At least I can try to make sure it's not any messier than it has to be. As it is without my mascara, rouge and lipstick, without any perfume, wearing yesterday's slept-in clothes, I know I look far from my best. I shouldn't care. But I do.

Jules has been making breakfast, and he greets me with a plate of eggs and toast with sausage. "I got started when I heard the shower go on."

"Thank you so much. I feel terrible you're going to all this trouble for a stowaway."

He smiles, then makes a plate for himself, and once he's done, joins me at the table.

"You look wonderful with your hair like that," he says.

I must look awful for him to say that, and now I wish I hadn't washed it at all.

"I mean it," he says, reading the expression of disbelief on my face.

"Thank you again," I say as I feel a warmth rising to my cheeks and hope I'm not blushing.

"Sleep okay?" he asks.

"Yes, but I don't actually remember going to bed."

"Well, you didn't really. You sat down on the edge of the bed. I turned around to draw the shades and when I'd turned back, you'd curled up and were fast asleep. So I covered you. I didn't think we had that much to drink."

I nod. "Maybe not for you but...tell that to my headache."

"Do you need some aspirin?"

"Found it in the medicine cabinet."

"Eating will help," he says.

Over breakfast he tells me that the roads are already starting to clear, and we should be able to start out for Ossining to see his grandfather after we eat.

Jules and I are sitting across from Mr. Reed by 11:30 a.m. Jules wastes no time in describing his visit from the Russian.

"Why did he go see *you*?" Mr. Reed asks.

"He said you called and told him to come," Jules says.

"I gave the woman who answered his phone the address here and a phone number."

"Well, she didn't give it to him, but that's beside the point. Who is he and why is he asking about the tiara and why did you call him in the first place?"

Mr. Reed looks at me. Then back at his grandson. He looks chagrined.

"Maybe I shouldn't have."

"Too late now, Grandfather. We both need to hear your explanation."

"He came to our offices having found me through another Russian who had sold me some pieces. He said he too was a jeweler and was searching for a tiara which he described in detail. I vaguely remembered it. He wanted to know if I'd bought it. I told him that I had seen such a piece, yes, but that no, the owner hadn't been willing sell it."

"So what he described was my mother's tiara?"

"Yes. He asked for the owner's name, but I would never give out a client's name." Mr. Reed says this as if it was one of the Ten Commandments. "He did offer me the name of the woman who he believed owned it—I think it was something like Petrovitch—but that wasn't your mother's name. Before he left, he gave me his name and phone number and begged me to contact him if I ever heard from the tiara's owner again. The whole visit, he was visibly upset. He told me he'd been very close to the owner and her child and was desperate to find them, and the tiara was the only clue he had to help him. After meeting you, I remembered him and thought he might be your father. That's why I called him."

"My father is dead. He died in Siberia in the early 1930s. I never met him," I say.

"I am sorry," Mr. Reed says softly.

"When exactly did this man first come to see you?" Jules asks.

"About a year and a half ago."

"How close to the break-in?" Jules continues.

"About a month before."

"What break-in?" I ask.

"Well, we call it a break-in, but it wasn't really," Jules says. "Nothing was taken as it turns out. Which was very odd. The cleaning crew was bribed into letting a man into our offices after-hours. All he did, apparently, was search through our files for about fifteen minutes before the head of the crew called me. And I called the police. But the intruder was gone by the time they arrived."

His grandfather says, "We believe it was an irate husband who wanted to find out if his wife sold something he'd given her. As well-known as I am for purchasing estate pieces, I also have a reputation among women planning to leave their husbands. I help them dispose of their jewels confidentially and often make copies in paste—or glass—

giving the women a nest egg to start a new life."

"You have a reputation all right," Jules says under his breath.

I look at him, trying to read his expression, not understanding the sarcasm, but nothing on his face gives me a hint as to the meaning of the comment.

"Were any papers taken?" I ask both of them.

Mr. Reed responds. "We have records going back over forty years in the office. There's no way we could have figured that out."

"The police didn't find the man, I'm assuming?"

"They didn't really have any reason to investigate. Nothing was taken, and he didn't break in. He knocked on the door," Mr. Reed says.

"Could it be the same man?" I ask.

"The cleaning crew gave a description of the man to the police..." Jules says. "If I remember correctly, it was pretty damn vague. Medium height, average build. But then again, it was winter, and he wore a bulky coat. He had on a hat and wore glasses. The police were frustrated by how unspecific it was...except..."

"Yes?" I say.

"He had an accent. Grandfather, do you remember?"

"Yes, the head of the cleaning crew said he spoke with a slight French accent."

"It's possible the crew confused the two accents, isn't it?" I look from one of them to the other.

Jules nods. "Of course."

"Did the crew mention if the man had a limp?" I turned back to Mr. Reed.

"No. And I wouldn't have asked," he said. "There was no reason for me to have connected the visitor to the file incident."

Jules looks at his grandfather with surprise. "You remember that the Russian limped?"

"Yes. Are you really surprised?"

I was confused, and Jules saw it on my face.

"Because Grandfather has a slight hearing impairment, he's more sensitive to other forms of disability, even very minor ones."

"Like a limp," I say.

Jules nods.

"I wish I knew what was going on," I say with a sense of despair. "Why didn't my mother tell me about the tiara? Did she expect me to find it? Why was it hidden? Why has this Russian been looking for it—for what, almost two years? And who is he? And are my mother and I the woman and child he mentioned?"

"I can clear one thing up for you," Mr. Reed says.

"Yes?"

"I believe the tiara was once part of the Russian imperial jewels. And that is why, if this man is not related to you, he lied to me. He must be looking for it."

"Wait, are you saying my mother stole it?" I'm incensed.

"No. No. I do not think that for a moment. I only said I believe it was stolen."

"And how do you know it was once part of the Russian imperial jewels?" Jules asks.

"I saw a photograph of it in a catalog of Russian jewels that my friend George Kunz had."

"Who is George Kunz?" I think the name sounds familiar but am not sure why.

"The foremost gemologist in the United States and most of the world. He worked for Tiffany's & Company until he died in 1932. After I met your mother, I went to George and told him about the tiara. I was determined to find out more about it and convince your mother to sell it to me."

"And you saw it in a book?" I ask.

"A rare book he had, privately published that—"

"Time's up."

We all turn to look at the guard who'd just interrupted.

"Seriously? Time's up this very minute?" Jules says.

The guard nods. "Yes."

I look at Mr. Reed. "Will you tell me more about the book and photo if I come back?"

"Yes. I'll be like Scheherazade. But with the genders reversed."

"My mother once started to read me the story of Scheherazade. She got almost to the end but couldn't finish it. It made her cry."

"Do you know why?" Jules asks.

"She wouldn't tell me." I shake my head. "I can't believe I just remembered that."

The guard clears his throat. Everyone at the prison likes Mr. Reed and always gives him a little leeway, but Sing is strict about visiting hours.

After we say our goodbyes, we leave and walk to the car. Jules and I are quiet until we're on the road.

"It seems your mother kept a lot of information from you," Jules says.

"I wonder which one of us she was protecting. Her from her past. Or me from her past."

"That's quite a question."

"Just another in a long list of them." I lean back and shut my eyes.

"What are you doing for the rest of the day?" he asks.

"I was going to go home and work on the renovation."

"Would you like some help?"

"You want to roll up your sleeves and tear off wallpaper?"

"Sure. After I see my grandfather...I don't like going home right away."

When we pull up to my apartment, Jules parks. We get out and take a few steps toward the building.

"Instead of getting right to it, what about if we go to lunch first?" Jules suggests.

I agree. We get back in the car. I don't ask where he is taking me and am surprised when about fifteen minutes later, he parks on 48th Street between Fifth and Sixth Avenues.

"Rockefeller Center?" I ask.

"Yes, we're going to The Promenade Café that looks out on the skating rink. Is that okay? It always cheers me up," he says. "My grandfather always used to bring me here on Saturdays after he closed the office. He only worked half-days. We'd have lunch and then skate. I still come just about every Saturday."

Jules is surprisingly sentimental, and it makes me smile. When he asks why I'm smiling, instead of telling him and embarrassing myself, I tell him I have my own happy memory of this place.

"My mother and I used to come here, too," I say.

"I don't want to make the day more difficult—rather the opposite."

"No, the memories here are good ones. Like you and your grandfather, my mother and I came here often on weekends for lunch and then to skate. She always drew a crowd. Growing up in Russia, during those long winters, skating was how most young people got around. She was incredible on the ice. I'd once asked her if my father skated too, and she told me that she'd never skated with him."

"Did you ask her why she didn't?" Jules asks.

"I'm not sure. If she said, I've forgotten...except I can't believe I'd forget. I memorized everything she ever told me about him."

We've arrived downstairs at the café. Jules greets the maître d' by name, and he shows us to a window table.

Once we're seated, Jules suggests we could do with a drink to cheer us both up and orders champagne.

"Let's toast to something," he says once the waiter has filled two coupes.

I nod.

"How about to making new memories?"

"Perfect," I say and reach out with my glass to clink his. And then we both sip. "I do want to make new memories. Here in New York. In my apartment. With new friends." I worry for a moment if he is going to take that the wrong way, but if he does, his reaction doesn't suggest it.

"But you can't focus on the present until you understand the past?"

I sigh. "That pretty much sums it up."

"Well, that's what we have to do then," he says.

"How?" I ask.

"I'm not sure, but I promise you I'm going to work on it."

Our repartee lightens my whole mood. Until I start to think about preparing myself for disappointment... That I can't allow myself to enjoy his company this much. But what harm is there really in allowing myself the pleasure? As long as I don't exaggerate what his attention means, that is.

Halfway through our meal, I look up and out at the rink. Across from it, on the other side, I think I see the mysterious Russian.

"Jules, look. I think that's him." I point, but just as I do, a family with three children position themselves at the railing for a photograph, and when they move, the man is no longer there.

"Maybe it was just someone who looked like him," Jules suggests when he sees how shaken I am.

"I really thought it was him. What are the chances that he'd just be here? Do you think he could be following me?"

"This is one of New York's top tourist attractions and winter weekend activities. If it was him, then it is possible he could just be here," Jules offers, trying to reassure me.

"Have another sip of your champagne. And don't worry. We'll figure all this out. I promise."

I want so badly to believe him that I do as he suggests. As the bubbles burst on my tongue, I force myself to let go of my worry.

After we are finished eating, Jules asks if I want to go skating.

"I haven't been in so long," I demur. I've embarrassed myself in front of him so many times already it seems, I don't want to get out on the ice and fall.

"Muscle memory. You never forget."

We rent skates, put them on, and step out on the ice where it's crowded and daunting. All around us skaters are enjoying the Christmas music and seasonal spirit. I am a little lost in memories at first, until Jules takes my arm.

There are moments that you know you will remember for always. When there is a shift in the atmosphere. When you see with more clarity. Feel with a keener depth. Yes, I'd been aware of how attractive Jules was before that exact moment. I had thought about not wanting to look silly or foolish in front of him. I had realized I was too plain for someone like him. But there is something in the gesture when he takes my arm on the rink that makes me turn and look at him, really look at him. And that's when I see it, in his eyes, something I hadn't noticed before. A familiar longing. The look of someone who has been lost and is also trying to find their way. Of someone who is a bit broken inside. All feelings I know. Have lived with every day for a long time. I haven't seen these things before and now that I am, I want to help him mend and become whole again.

A memory surfaces. Of my mother fixing broken vases. She'd taken several classes when she came to America. One was in the Japanese art of Kintsukuroi, which translates to golden repair. It is an ancient art of repairing broken vases, bowls, mugs—any kind of pottery—but which she extended to furniture, with a lacquer mixed with powdered gold, silver, or platinum. The cracks in the item become threads of gold or silver. Instead of the object being ruined it becomes a unique work of art. Sometimes even more beautiful than before.

Jules and I skate to the strains of Tchaikovsky's *Nutcracker Suite*. Both in step with the music. And with each other. We are so in synch that I feel as if we are even breathing to the same beat. I want to hold these minutes tightly. Freeze them in the spray from the ice so that I can take them out later and experience them all over again. And pretend again, as I am now, that I *am* the kind of girl for Jules. That he yearns to cup my face and pull me toward him and kiss me. And keep kissing me. And that all that is holding him back is finding the exact right moment.

But he doesn't find the moment. We continue skating, looping the rink, dancing on the ice. That's what my mother called it. For a second in my peripheral vision, I imagine seeing my mother there with us, turning the way she did to skate backwards. It was her favorite thing to do. "*So I can see where I've been*," she would say. And then she'd spin around and face forward. "*And now look forward and imagine where I'm going.*"

"What do you think happens to people when they die?" I ask, breaking the silence of the last few minutes.

"That's a serious thought. You're supposed to be having fun."

"But I am."

"Having so much fun you're thinking about death. You're a very unique girl, Isobelle Moon."

Does he say it like that's a good or bad thing? I have to stop thinking like that. This isn't a date. I'm not a potential romantic interest to Jules. I'm the daughter of his grandfather's client who has shown up with a mystery he's intrigued by because of his extracurricular involvement in the Midas Society.

"Asking serious questions like that is a very Russian thing to do," I quip.

He laughs. "Yes, I've read Dostoyevsky too. I know all about the Russian soul. So to your question, I happen to have a theory about what happens. My grandfather and I used to talk about it a lot after my father died. He told me that when people die, they become stars in the Milky Way, and they come out and check in on us at night while we sleep. When I was missing him too much, Grandfather would take me onto the roof of our house. We'd bring pillows and blankets and lie there and look up at the stars. 'When you see a shooting star,' he'd say, 'that's your father letting you know he's right there, shining for you.'"

"That's lovely," I say, feeling the sting of tears.

"And very comforting for a little boy of eight who has lost his dad to a vicious illness."

"I'm sure it was a comfort to your grandfather as well, after losing his son."

We skate on for a few moments.

"My grandfather also said that once the person you love knows that you are not lonely for him or her anymore, once they know you're all right, they can move on."

"Move on?"

"My grandfather is a great believer in reincarnation."

I nod. "Are you as well?"

"I suppose. It's not inconsistent with being an atheist, and it sure beats believing we just disappear forever after this life. When I think of all the men we lost in the war…it would be unbearable to think of them as just gone. But if they have another chance…if they can come back, then there's something to hold on to."

"A waste of souls," I say.

"What's that?"

"Something my mother once said about the First World War… It haunted me all through the second. And since my mother died as well."

"I hate that you're so lonely, Isobelle." Jules says it as a fact. He doesn't ask if indeed I am, he simply seems to know it. "What happened to you? It's more than your mother dying, isn't it?"

I'm surprised by the insight. I am lonely and have been since before my mother died. Since before the end of the war. Since what happened at Oak Ridge…but how to explain it to Jules. My silence goes on a beat too long.

"Sorry, it's totally the wrong time and place for that question. And probably inappropriate no matter where we might be," Jules says. "We should be enjoying ourselves. Come on, let's try something a little daring here. You're better than you think," he says as he faces me, takes both of my hands in his, and skates backwards. I go with the movement, a little unsure of myself, but let him lead. And when he's found us a little bit of space, he twirls me around, and suddenly I'm dancing, and the music is wonderful, and my skates are moving just right, and I start to laugh. Jules does too. I feel suddenly light. Different. I can't quite figure out what the emotion is. And then I realize that I feel happy. And try as I might, I just can't even remember the last time I've felt like this.

"Thank you," I tell him a few minutes later when we're back arm in arm, circling the rink.

"For what?"

"For bringing me here. For suggesting we skate. For the story about the stars."

"I like you, Isobelle Moon. I like seeing you happy and enjoying yourself."

"I was just thinking that I haven't been even half this happy in a long time."

Jules skates me over to the side of the rink and stops. He puts his hands on my shoulders and turns me so that I'm facing him again. His cheeks are red, and his eyes are bright. His hair has fallen over his forehead, and I want so badly to reach up and put the wave back into place.

"Would it be all right with you if I kissed you?" he asks.

"Why?" I blurt out.

He laughs. "Well, no one has ever asked me that before. But I'd be pleased to answer. Because we're here, and the war is over, and the past doesn't have to be a noose around our necks. Because from what you've said and what I've guessed, no one has kissed you in a while. And I haven't kissed anyone in a while. And I think we're good for each other."

All I can do is nod. But that is enough. Jules leans down and presses his lips to mine, and his arms go around me, and I'm engulfed. My whole body responds to the touch, and as much as I don't want to feel this much from just this one kiss, I can't hold back. His kiss is kind and sweet.

I forget where we are and that there are people skating by. I forget that I'm not glamorous or beautiful. That I take my job so seriously that I usually stay at the office five out of five nights. That I'd rather go to the museum than a party. I forget everything but the feeling that I have been lost and am now found.

The kiss doesn't last long, but when we pull apart, I'm breathless. And so is Jules. He smiles at me with a broad grin, and his green eyes seem electric.

"I have an idea," he says.

I think he is going to say something about us. About the kiss. About what is going to come next. But what he says shows how much he has come to understand me and what I need and what he can offer that no one else can.

"I think I know how we can find out about the tiara's provenance. Can you get a day off work?"

And with that, I think I might have just fallen in love.

Chapter 18

Sofiya Petrovitch
Petrograd
December 1917

Sofiya and Carpathian returned to the apartment. She hadn't expected either of her parents to be there—and they weren't. At this hour, her father would still be at his desk at the Hermitage, and her mother would be teaching the art class she gave at the university. Carpathian had her sit in the parlor, asked where the kitchen was, and told her to rest while he made tea. She started to protest, but he insisted. After a few minutes, he brought out a tray. He'd chosen her favorite *podstakanniks* from the cabinet—nickel silver with turquoise enameling. He'd also found a tin of tea biscuits— there were only four left—her mother had and arranged them on a plate.

Sofiya watched him spoon sugar into her glass and stopped him as he was about to add a second helping. Due to the rationing, this might be her family's last jar of sugar for a long time.

"Just one," she said.

"You need it sweeter than you think, you've had a shock."

"Just a little then." Sofiya had never even come close to being attacked before. Her parents had taught her how to look out for herself—they wanted her to be self-sufficient—but she'd never been in a situation where she'd felt threatened.

"I can't stop thinking how close I came to losing the—" And then she looked around, beginning to feel frantic.

"Carpathian, where is…what happened to my tiara?"

"It's in the safe at the shop. I couldn't help you and carry the package. So I put it away for the time being. We'll retrieve it on Monday when we're open again."

"You locked it up?"

"Yes. So there's no need to worry. The House of Fabergé stores millions of rubles' worth of jewels and objects. And there are guards around the clock. The entire shop would have to be at risk for anything to happen to your tiara."

They sat and sipped their tea. Sofiya didn't say much but every few moments glanced over at the man sitting opposite her. He was there, in her parents' apartment. This man whom she had tried to forget for the last long year and a half. And now that he was here, she didn't know what to say to him. Despite all the conversations she'd had with him in her head…all the stories she'd imagined telling him…all the letters she'd written him and then ripped up… Despite all of it, she couldn't think of a single thing to say that didn't sound embarrassing or maudlin or childish.

"I don't know if I can stop thinking of you as

Carpathian," she blurted out. "I've tried to use your given name."

"Don't let it trouble you, I prefer you call me Carpathian. That's who I am, really. I've never regained all of my memories from before the battle. And except when I am sitting at my workstation making jewelry, I've never quite felt as if the life I am living is actually *my* life."

"There were other soldiers at the hospital who said similar things."

He ran his finger around the rim of the glass, and she remembered how he used to do that to her lips in the garden or in their secret room. She shivered.

"You're still in shock. Where can I find a sweater for you?"

"No, sit. I'm fine, I can use this." She pulled over a crocheted throw that lay across the back of the couch and arranged it over her shoulders.

"When I was a child," he said, "I had a favorite book about a woodcutter who lived in a forest who was so lonely that one day he carved a little boy out of the trunk of an oak tree. That night, the child came to life and became the woodcutter's son. He lived with him and helped him, and they were both very happy for a long time. But after a time, the little boy asked his father for a playmate. So the woodcutter carved another little boy, who also came to life. But this wood-child didn't have as pure a heart. One night, he set his older brother on fire. Except there was a wind blowing, and one of the burning embers blew back into his own face. The older boy threw a pail of water on his younger, evil brother first and then attended to himself. He saved himself, but large parts of his face and arms were charred. The woodcutter offered to clean up the wounds so that they wouldn't be a constant reminder of his brother's jealousy, but the older boy said no. That it was important to remember the bad things as well as the good, so that you never forget how easy it is to take things for granted.

"It was a complicated story. But I loved it and set about learning every part of it. I read the book over and over, studying each illustration and the captions underneath. Until eventually I could recite the words by heart and didn't need to look at the book at all.

"It's been that way with my memory. I have studied every face and the story of who they are and how they related to me. And I've learned the tale of who Sergei Zorin was and what he did. But there are certain feelings that should be attached to many of those people that have never surfaced which makes me wonder if they were ever there in the first place. For instance, I have come to love both of my parents again. And my sister. And I'm living with them here in the city in the apartment I grew up in, which helps my memory. But I can't find any emotion for my wife. Or for my cousin, Dimitry. I have visited the top neurosurgeon in the city to try and learn why this is and discover if there is anything I can do about it. What he told me is that he believes there must be bad memories there that I don't want to remember."

She took Carpathian's hand. "That's what they told us at the hospital. That the brain and how it works is a mystery."

"A mystery is the perfect word. I wish I could explain what it is like to have your own mind be a mystery to you. There was an Easter egg that Henrik and I worked on before I went off to war. The Tiara Egg, it was called—" Carpathian nodded. "Which is quite a coincidence since it is a tiara that's brought you back to me."

"I'm not back to you," she protested.

"Forgive me. I should have said a tiara that might have

brought you back to me." He smiled.

All she did was nod. She was afraid to do more.

"What happened to the egg?"

"It was hidden away, intended as a nest egg." He smiled sadly at his pun. "As much as none of us wanted to believe we were coming to the end of an era, there were those who knew the revolution was upon us and made provisions."

"That's wise. It seems that those dark days have descended."

"Not even the darkest, I fear."

She took a sip of her now lukewarm tea. She and her parents discussed the state of their homeland every night and she didn't want to spend what precious time she had with Carpathian talking about it as well.

"What is the mystery in the Tiara egg?" she asked. Everyone knew the imperial eggs made by the House of Fabergé for the royal family had secrets inside.

"Have you seen any of the imperial eggs?" he asked.

"Yes, at the Alexander Palace. The tsarina let Olga show them to me."

Sofiya knew the Clover Leaf egg opened to reveal enamel portraits of all four grand duchesses, the Alexander Palace egg opened to reveal a gold and enamel miniature of the entire palace, and the Orange Tree egg had a singing songbird that emerged from within the nephrite leaves. Her favorite, the Lily of the Valley egg, had portraits of the royal family set in diamond-encrusted frames inside of it.

"Relearning my life has been like those eggs. I see the outside without knowing there is a surprise inside. And when I open it sometimes, what is inside is a revelation and other times a nightmare."

"What do you mean?"

"My wife began having an affair with Dimitry Zorin

while I was training for the army. I discovered it on my first trip home for compassionate leave when my grandfather died. A full year before I was wounded."

"How terrible. What did you do?"

"I attended my grandfather's funeral and then went back to the front."

"You didn't say anything to your wife? To Dimitry?"

"No. And the damndest thing is that I don't remember why. Just one other thing I can't remember among a thousand more. But apparently, for some reason, I didn't confront either of them. I just went back to fight for Mother Russia," he said bitterly.

"Maybe you were just too upset with your grandfather's death to want to deal with it."

"Of course, that's possible. But I just don't know. Besides, it doesn't matter anymore. There are so many of these fragments that elude me. I think that's part of the reason I like you calling me Carpathian. I know every one of *his* thoughts. Nothing that has happened to him since he first opened his eyes at the hospital is lost to me. I remember every moment of my life as this man who only had one name, a first name given to him by a winsome angel in a nurse's uniform."

She was silent. One of the first rules of restoration she'd learned, one of the most important rules, is patience. You are dealing with priceless masterpieces that have various kinds of damage. To rush is to risk. But if you have patience, the painting begins to speak to you. It shows you what was there before based on another portion of the canvas or a fragment beneath a film of filth. There's no blueprint to go by. You have your instincts and your training and that is all. You just have to wait. And this conversation was like that. She had to wait and be patient. He'd told her so much and so little all at once. Both had equal meaning.

"I don't know what is going to happen to any of us, Sofiya. The world as we know it is changing by the hour. But for as many of those hours as we have, I want them to be with you."

He pulled her toward him. She knew she should protest because no matter what, in all of the things he'd told her so far, he still hadn't said that he was divorced. Which meant he was a married man with a child—even if it wasn't technically his child. It still had his name.

But on the other hand, he was right. What did they have ahead of them to count on? Where was Olga? Where was Tatiana? The tsarina? Where was the family Sofiya had grown up with and her mother had taught? Who was in charge of the government? Did they know what they were doing? Her grandparents and cousin were living in the country on a plot of land that used to be a vacation getaway and now was a modest farm. Her parents still could put food on the table, but for how long? They had jobs, but for how long? They still were the only people living in their apartment, but for how long? The provisional government had taken over everything. No one was allowed to own anything anymore. If you had an empty room in your flat, the government could foist a stranger on you to live there. Stoves had been turned off and many people cooked on a kerosene primus. The stink of linseed oil permeated the city mixed in with the stench of unwashed bodies. Even good milled soap was impossible to buy except on the black market where most things could be had for outrageous sums of money or ridiculous trades. A gold wedding ring for a bottle of vodka. A chandelier for enough ham to make one meal.

And in the midst of all that poverty and change and

terror and chaos was this man holding out a hand and offering her an oasis in the madness. At the Alexander Palace her favorite place had been the Children's Island. A secret city just for them where they ruled. Where they dreamed. And now she was being offered another one.

Sofiya took his hand and brought it to her face and kissed it. His fingers moved to cup her face the way she loved so much, and he held it for a moment, looking at her, smiling at last. And then he leaned forward and kissed her. Sofiya heard the familiar sounds of gunshots ringing out in the street and a voice shouting. But she ignored them as he picked her up and asked her which way to her bedroom.

Chapter 19

Isobelle Moon
New York City
December 1948

On Monday morning, Jules meets me at the train station, and we board the Marylander to Washington D.C. Everything is first class, and the trip itself is an adventure. There's a library on board, sleeping cars for those who are traveling overnight, and the famed Martha Washington-series dining cars with glass chandeliers and colonial-style furnishings. The menu includes Chesapeake Bay specialties, and when lunchtime comes, we both order oysters and crab cakes served with cornmeal muffins, all presented on Dresden china.

After we return to our seats and the train continues speeding down the Eastern Seaboard, Jules opens his briefcase. Inside, in addition to papers and pens, are two books. One is a battered copy of *The History of the Russian Revolution* by Leon Trotsky, and the other is *The Big Clock* by Kenneth Fearing. He takes out the history tome. I've also brought a book, a mystery, *Laura* by Vera Caspary. We read for an hour or so.

Jules eventually puts down his book and asks if I'd like some coffee, and we return to the dining car where we order and start a long conversation about our reading habits.

He asks if *Laura* is as good a book as it was a movie.

"Better. Caspary is one of my favorite writers. Her plot twists are always a surprise, and her characters really complex. There's nothing overly flowery or romantic about her dialog, and I appreciate that. Along with Du Maurier, I think she's my favorite writer."

"I'll have to try her if you like her that much."

"What's yours about?" I ask him.

"The Trotsky?" he smiles.

"No, I'm all too familiar with that one. Why are you reading it?"

"Because of your tiara. I'm a little rusty on the revolution, and if your piece was stolen and smuggled out of Russia during those years, I want to be able to place it in context in case we have to return it."

"It was my mother's. She didn't steal it."

"I know you believe that, but we're going to have to prove its provenance if in fact—"

"Jules, the tiara was my mother's. She was not a thief."

"I am not saying she was, but someone else might have stolen it and given it to her. She might never have known."

I'm angry at the implication and frustrated. Feeling the sting of tears, I turn from him and stare out of the window at the snow-covered scenery rushing by, trying to control myself.

"I'm sorry I've upset you," he says.

I shrug. A pathetic response, I know, but I'm feeling overwhelmed.

Jules keeps apologizing. "I'm getting way ahead of myself. We don't even know if it's authentic. Or important. Please, don't be upset," he says with real earnestness.

I turn away from the window, back to Jules. There's kindness in his eyes. And a half-smile that makes him so attractive. I want more of him than his help, and it makes the tears come faster. He takes his handkerchief out of his pocket and hands it to me.

"I'm mortified that I've made you cry."

"It's not your fault...just that my mother...all this secrecy...I don't know so much more than I do know. My hunt for answers is making me miss her all over again. Miss her and be mad at her for leaving me with this mess." I wipe away the tears and take a deep breath. "I'm sorry, too. You are right. As sure as I am of my mother's ethics, I don't have any proof of ownership."

"And I should be more sensitive. Of course this is an emotional minefield for you. Let's just get where we are going and find out what we can learn and figure out each step as we reach it, okay?"

I nod.

"Would you like something else? More coffee? A glass of brandy?"

"Nothing. I'll be fine, thanks."

Jules puts his hand on top of mine, and I feel little sparks of lightning shoot up my arm and down my back. How can such a tiny touch affect me so much? I've thought about the kiss at the skating rink a dozen times—no, more— what did it mean? A moment out of time? A sympathy kiss? Something else?

"I know how hard it is not to know the truth and blindly go looking for it with no idea of what you will find. I think you are doing a great job," he says.

His fingers are burning into my skin. I want to lean down and kiss the top of his hand. To inhale his scent—that combination of clean skin and the opulent woodsy fragrance with its hint of leather. I want to burrow my face in his neck and keep smelling him forever. But I don't do any of those things because I remember my last mistake with a man. I didn't see the truth of his attention. I wonder if it came from not having had a father. From not learning the subtle shifts in a man's face when he goes from caring to using. From seeing you to seeing an opportunity.

We return to our seats. We still have another hour to go before we reach Washington. Jules puts away the history book and pulls out the novel.

"What is your book about?" I ask.

"A mystery in which a man escapes from himself," Jules says, with a little bit of a resigned sigh that makes me want to ask him if that resonates with him. But I don't want to pry. This is a delicate balance. The man is helping me with such an important quest. If I make it all too personal, I could push him away. And I don't want to do that for so many reasons.

"I've always loved reading a wide variety of fiction, but since the war I hardly read anything besides mysteries," he says. "I used to buy everything reviewed in the *New Yorker*. But during the war I started craving books where good triumphed over evil. And I still do. As much as I appreciate Fitzgerald and John O'Hara and Sinclair Lewis, I only want to read books that offer puzzles that capture my imagination and challenge my problem-solving ability. That's all that seems to satisfy me. I've stopped wanting to deal with bleak, doomed characters going through existential crises. I'm having a hard enough time living through one."

"I think a lot of us feel that way. And still do," I say. "I tortured the librarian at Oak Ridge until she had purchased everything Agatha Christie ever wrote and a promise she'd get in every new one as soon as it was released."

"There is something very reassuring about having Poirot on the case, isn't there?"

I agree.

"My love of mystery novels and my work with the Midas Society dovetail as well," he says.

He hasn't talked much about that, and I'm curious. "When did you first—were you recruited? Is that how it works?"

"Yes, you have to be recruited. And I was at eighteen. I had been fascinated with treasure hunting since I was a kid because of Harold Carter and his discovery of King Tut's tomb. It was in the news all the time during my childhood. There was even a huge revival in Egyptian jewelry that my mother was at the forefront of. She used to design for my grandfather before she moved to France, which is how my parents met. Did I tell you that before? Anyway, the idea that the jewels Carter found had been hidden deep inside those pyramids for so many thousands of years, protected and left intact, became my obsession. I was ever after fascinated with hidden or stolen objects and jewels. As soon as I heard about the society, I knew I wanted to be a part of the history of people who find lost things. When I first read Christie, I found my hero in Poirot. I still think of him whenever I undertake a search. I hope that I follow the trajectory of a stolen or lost object with the same finesse as Christie's detective."

"Who recruited you? How did they find you? Or did

you find them?"

"I'm afraid I can't tell you that. I can only talk about myself as a member."

"Sorry, you did mention that. Does your family know you're part of it? Your mother? Grandfather?"

He nods.

"What about your father?"

Jules' eyes focus beyond me and out the window. I can almost see a curtain drawn. The green irises become clouded, like the ocean in a storm. I've touched on something that he doesn't want to talk about. I can't tell if it's sadness or anger that changes the whole physiognomy of his face. And then he takes a breath—as if the inhalation is part of some ritual—and he looks at me with his old face back. The sudden flare-up of emotional angst gone.

"We're almost there," he says, completely sidestepping my question. And I know much better than to ask it again.

We exit the train terminal at 2:30 p.m. and take a taxi to the U.S. General Services Administration Building, which takes up the whole block at Eighteenth and F Streets. The neo-classical limestone building spreads low and long with windows on at least fifty percent of its façade. I stop walking to really look and examine its lines.

"This is a good design for getting the maximum amount of light for the many architects, draftsmen, pressmen, and scientists working in the building," I say. "Even if it is a little stubby."

"You know about this building?"

"I didn't before, but I looked it up yesterday once you told me we were coming here."

"So shall we?" He gestures to the way forward.

We walk up to the entrance, but just before going in, I notice the giant eagle sculpture above the door.

"I read about this too. It was carved by Ernest C. Bairstow, a decorative sculptor who did a lot of work around D.C. He designed the outside of the Lincoln Memorial. If we have time, do you think we can walk around to the other side of this building and look at his ornamental work on the F Street entrance before we leave? There are iron and glass marquees overhanging the entrance and steps I really want to see."

"Of course, you do." He laughs.

"Are you making fun of me?"

"Not at all. Are you always so curious?" Jules asks.

He's asking about more than my interest in architectural form and function.

"Yes. And sometimes to my detriment," I confess.

"Maybe, but don't ever change. It's one of the things that makes you so intriguing. And admirable."

I feel a blush creeping into my cheeks.

"You're the same way about treasure hunts, aren't you?" I ask. "Just us being here is proof of that."

He smiles. "Yes, and maybe that's why you feel like such a kindred spirit."

It's the kind of comment I've daydreamed about. That one day I'd meet someone who would find my questions endearing and not annoying. I shake my head without realizing it.

"What is it? Did I say something wrong?" he asks.

I can't tell him that I'm chastising myself for letting my imagination run away with me.

"You didn't say anything wrong."

He frowns. "I doubt it was nothing, but that's all right. It's very easy to ask questions but sometimes very difficult to answer them. Let's just go in."

I'm still thinking about what Jules said as we make our

way inside and upstairs to the Gemological Institute Library. Jules gives our names to a receptionist and after a few minutes a very tall middle-aged woman wearing tweed comes out, introduces herself as Rose Rezot, chief librarian, and greets us warmly.

Jules had called ahead, explaining what he was looking for, and she had assured him what he was searching for would be here if it was anywhere.

"Just this way," Miss Rezot says while showing us into a room filled with stacks snaking back and forth.

"Over here is where we store George Kunz's library," she says, pointing out a particular section. "The USGS acquired the Kunz Collection in 1933 for one dollar from Mr. Kunz's daughter. You do know Mr. Kunz's history, correct?"

Jules says, "We do."

"Well then, let me get right to it for you. I know you don't have any idea about the title of the book you are looking for. Or any kind of description except that it was old and contains photographs. More than half of Mr. Kunz's books are illustrated. Altogether there are over 1,575 books and pamphlets that Mr. Kunz amassed in his lifetime. We do have them all fully classified and cataloged. They include many rare books and articles on gemology, gems and minerals. There are also numerous books about the folklore of gemstones, lapidary arts, as well as archival gem trade records, which are used to research the provenance of named stones and pieces. According to the family stipulations, in addition to the items being listed in our general catalog, we made and now keep a separate catalog file of the items comprising the collection which will probably be of great help to you." She points to the card catalog. Then she takes one book off the shelf at random and opens it to the frontispiece, where there is a cream and ink bookplate. "We put one of these bookplates in each item to identify it as part of the collection." She explains the numbering system that they employ in addition to Dewey Decimal. "And finally, if you have any questions, I'm just down that hallway, first door on the left."

Our quest seems even more daunting after hearing Miss Rezot's description, so Jules and I waste no time in getting to work. We decide which subjects to take—I'm going to search for books cataloged in the Russia or Russian jewelry category. Jules is going to search royal jewels and imperial jewels and Aleksandr Fersman—the Russian gemologist who wrote the catalogs that Jules' grandfather said Kunz had shown him.

"I found it," Jules says after we've only been looking for about twenty minutes.

I stop what I am doing to read the cards he's pulled that describe a four-book set, entitled *Russia's Treasure of Diamonds and Precious Stones*, published in 1925 by The People's Commissariat of Finances, in French, Russian, English, and German.

There is a newspaper article cut out and clipped to the back of the card. We both read it. In essence it explains that the government's motive in creating lavish monographs was to both attract wealthy foreign buyers and also to show the world there was still Russian treasure in the country. The monographs were to quell the rumors that after the 1917 revolution, the Romanov crown jewels, valued at an estimated five hundred million dollars, had disappeared through theft and vandalism.

The article went on to say that many treasures were snuck out of the country. Wealthy citizens as well as members of the royal family had flooded the market with diamonds and other precious gems. So many that for a time the value of diamonds dropped. A common method of hiding the gems was to sew them into the hems or seams or waistbands of clothing. Or cover them with fabric and use them as buttons. There are rumors the wife and daughters of the tsar had so many diamonds sewn into their corsets that the soldiers' bullets ricocheted off them.

The article makes me wonder how my mother managed to smuggle the tiara out of Russia. Was she frightened? Had she been in danger? And did sneaking it out suggest that she, even in a small way, was a criminal?

Jules goes to collect the books based on their call numbers, but it turns out that none of the volumes are shelved where they should be. Leaving me with the books I'm looking through, he goes off to inform Miss Rezot and to see if she can help him. When he returns, he says she's going to look for them.

Meanwhile, I have found several books that might hold some clues since they are about Russian jewels. Page after page, I study the photos, but there are no images of my mother's tiara.

We're still looking when Miss Rezot arrives to tell us that she hasn't found the Fersman volumes yet. "I'll keep looking, but library hours are over. I'd let you stay, but this is a government building that gets locked up at 5:15 p.m. exactly."

"But we haven't found anything yet," I say to Jules, hearing the whine in my voice that used to make my mother shake her head and say my name not as an embrace but rather as a sharp admonishment.

Jules smiles at the whine. He gives me one of his half-smiles, and his eyes twinkle, as if he finds my childish disappointment cute.

"How about we come back tomorrow?" he says to Miss Rezot.

"Perfect. We open at 9:00 a.m. I will have all four volumes waiting for you both."

I don't say anything until we are outside on the steps.

"But we were going to take the 7:00 p.m. train back tonight."

"Well, now we aren't. You can call into work in the morning and say you got stuck here, can't you?"

"I don't really have a choice, do I?"

He hears the anxiety in my voice.

"Will you get into trouble?"

I can't bear the thought of having to call Ted, but Mr. Williams is always in a half hour earlier. I'll call him at 8:30 tomorrow and let him know instead.

"I think I can manage."

"Good. Now what do we do about my boss—he's going to be furious," he jokes.

"You'll have to come up with a good excuse."

"No problem. I already have one."

I don't say anything.

"Want to hear?"

"Sure."

"I'm helping a dear friend."

There's something about the word *friend* that bothers me. I should be delighted that he didn't say client. Instead, I feel suddenly deflated. But why? What do I think I am to him? For what seems like the hundredth time since I first met this man, I remind myself that he doesn't see me the way I wish he did. One kiss on the skating rink does not mean anything. I'm stargazing again. I hear my mother's laughter and her words.

"*What else should I expect from Isobelle Moon?*" she'd say and then remind me that yes, it's important to dream, but it's more important to keep your feet planted firmly on the ground. To know where you stand so you can't be blindsided. She never said any more than that, but I knew a phrase was missing. Blindsided like *she* was. Thinking that everything was going to be fine and then having her husband imprisoned. Never getting to say goodbye. Never seeing him again. My mother's past made her suspicious. It kept her always a little afraid of taking too many chances. Yes, she'd taken a huge chance in coming to America, but she had a baby to protect, and she knew she had Lana and a job waiting for her here. Once she arrived, though, her decisions were always the safest ones.

"So where are we going?" I ask Jules as we walk toward the corner where there's a taxi stand. He opens the car door for me, and I scoot in. He follows.

"I know a great hotel," he says and gives the driver the address. Then he sits back in the seat and turns to me. "I stayed here a lot during the war and know the manager. Let's see if he can get us some rooms at the inn."

Less than ten minutes later, we pull up in front of the Hay Adams. We get out, but before we enter the lobby, Jules stops me, putting his hand on my arm. I feel a surge of heat radiate out from the spot. Every damn time he touches me it's like this. But I'm good at acting like nothing is wrong. My mother taught me that, too. She said she learned it living among people who would turn you in for a potato. You should never give anything away about how you are feeling until you are sure what you are dealing with. Hold everything tight inside. People use your weaknesses.

"Look." Jules turns to the left and points across the street at a park where the White House sits on the other side of the greenery—majestic in the encroaching twilight.

The hotel manager does in fact remember Jules, who explains our unexpected layover. The hotelier tells us he has two rooms and would be happy to supply sundries and that the restaurant is, of course, open for dinner, or we can call down for room service. Which is what I assume we will do, each in our own room—spending the evening apart. The manager calls for a bellman to take us up.

We get out on the fourth floor, Jules walking with me and behind the bellman, who leads us to room 422. He opens the door with the key, turns on the lights, and shows me around, explaining how the heat works and where the radio is.

The bellman goes back out into the hall. Jules follows then stops at the door, holding it open.

"Why don't you freshen up, and I'll meet you downstairs at 6:30? I'll take you to my favorite restaurant for dinner and maybe we'll take a walk after on the Mall over to the Lincoln Memorial and the Washington Monument. I've always thought they are at their best at night."

I told him on the train that I've never been to our capitol.

"As long as you aren't too cold," he adds.

I want to tell him that I'd bear the cold to take the walk with him, but I don't of course and swallow the thought.

"I'll be fine, but you really don't have to entertain me."

He reaches out and brushes a stray curl off my forehead. "I know I don't. I want to spend the evening with you, Isobelle Moon, all right?"

"Why?"

"Let's say I'm just as interested in seeing where this leads as you are."

He leaves me at my door wondering if he means the mystery of the tiara or if he's feeling what I'm feeling, too.

No. I shake my head. I'm stargazing again. But as I take off my coat and shoes and then sit in the big armchair by the window, I'm still feeling his touch on my forehead.

It's a ten-minute walk from the hotel across Lafayette Square to Tabards Inn at 1475 Pennsylvania Avenue, a small, lovely, and comfortable restaurant. We're seated without waiting—Jules mentions he called ahead. The waiter brings menus and a plate of celery, carrots, and olives. Jules asks if I'd like a martini—since that's what he's having—and I say I do.

We look at the menus, and we order when the waiter returns with our cocktails.

"Tomato soup with rice and Lobster Newburg," I say.

Jules closes his menu. "And I'll have the onion soup and the lobster as well."

Once the waiter is gone, Jules lifts his drink to toast. "To solving mysteries," he says.

Jules' eyes stay on me as he puts the glass to his lips. I feel the look as much as I see it. His neck is long, and his Adam's apple moves as he swallows. I realize I'm staring. I look away and take a sip of my icy cold drink and try to think of something to say. As much to fill the silence as to distract myself from where my mind keeps going.

"You said you were here in D. C. often during the war. What were you doing?" I ask.

"It's actually a secret, I can't tell you."

"Seriously?"

"Why do you find that so surprising? You lived through the same kind of secrecy yourself."

"I suppose what I find surprising is that I told you what I did, and you aren't telling me."

"But what you did is no longer a secret. Everyone is now aware of what went on at Oak Ridge and Los Alamos.

What my unit did still hasn't been made public."

"I'd ask you why, except that's probably part of the secret. But really, no one has talked about it? There haven't been any leaks or any rumors?"

"Not that I've heard about. We weren't even supposed to tell our families."

"No one can keep a secret forever," I say, except I'm thinking that my mother did seem to do just that. "Did you tell anyone in your family? Not your mother? Your grandfather?"

"Not even my ex-wife." There's the chill in his voice I heard the second time I went to his office. And that hollow look in his eyes.

"Were you together long?"

"No, actually not long at all."

I'm curious what happened, but I have no idea how to ask. So I remain quiet, hoping he'll continue. I can still remember the feel of his touch on my forehead from earlier.

He picks up a stalk of celery and snaps it in half. But he doesn't eat either half. Instead, he places them down on his bread and butter plate and stares at them for a moment.

"She was an actress. I just never realized how good an actress she was."

"What do you mean?"

"It doesn't matter. It's all in the past now."

"And since then?"

"You mean has there been anyone since her?"

I nod, a bit astonished by my audacity at asking.

"Did you ever read Ernest Hemmingway's *A Farewell to Arms*?"

I nod.

"There's a section…" Jules looks past me into the darkened recesses of the restaurant. "'Often a man wishes to be alone and a girl wishes to be alone too…'" he recites. "'And if they love each other they are jealous of that in each other, but I can truly say we never felt that. We could feel alone when we were together, alone against the others. But we were never lonely and never afraid when we were together.'"

Jules' gaze returns back to me. "I'm afraid I'm a bit of a romantic. I read that book when I was seventeen, and it had a profound effect on me in many ways. One of them was that one day I'd find someone who I felt that way about. It became a test for me. I was a loner, am a loner, and that kind of being together made sense to me. After years of never finding it with anyone, I relaxed my standards and then Lily happened. Since then I've gone back to looking for the impossible girl it *will* be that way with. I know better than to settle now." He tries for a lighthearted smile, but what's in his eyes belies his effort.

Jules knows profound loneliness.

"I know the way loneliness can separate you from other people," I say. "How it makes you feel as if everyone is in on the secret, but you are on the outside. That they can all be light and gay and of the moment. And you are right there with them but separate and distant. Almost as if you are always standing back a bit and watching—wondering how everyone else has such an easy time joining in. Except for you."

Jules is looking at me as if he wants to say something but isn't sure he should. During the silence, the waiter brings our appetizers.

While we are eating our soup, Jules starts telling me about his wartime secret without any preamble as to why he's changed his mind.

"During the war, I was part of the 23rd Headquarters

Special Troop soldier unit. We were referred to as the Ghost Army. Our job was to impersonate other allied army units in order to deceive our enemies. Using our skills, we created deceptions and disseminated false information. Basically, it was camouflage to trick the enemy. Sometimes we called ourselves a traveling roadshow because it really was a kind of circus. Everything we did was faked, fudged, and phonied up, from inflatable tanks to our completely false transmissions. I don't have the exact count, but we created more than twenty battlefield deceptions. We impersonated generals, built mock headquarters, and set up phantom troops. We got so good that in less than five hours we could create entire scenes complete with dummy airfields, tank formations, and motor pools. We even had fake laundry we could hang out to make our phony troop bivouacs look authentic."

"It sounds crazy. And crazy dangerous."

"Oh, it was. We were a group of about a thousand guys almost all under thirty putting on a show. They recruited a lot of us from art schools in New York or Philly. And from ad agencies. Places that encouraged creative thinking. There were painters, illustrators, sculptors, radio and sound guys. We used every kind of trickery at our disposal to provide decoys. Our uniforms were even full of fake patches because we had to pretend to be other units so enemy spies wouldn't figure out what we were doing."

"I don't even know what to say. What was that like—all that pretending?"

"It was exhilarating, plain and simple. We were lauded and rewarded even if no one outside our unit and those very high up knew what we were doing."

The waiter removes our soup. Our drinks are finished. Jules orders a bottle of Sancerre wine.

"So many of us spent the war keeping secrets," I say. "It was a lot to ask of us all."

"But for a good and just cause."

"That's the patriotic answer."

"Is there another one?" he asks.

"Sometimes I lie in bed at night and think about the people who are dead because of this war. All the people whose lives have been ruined. Every soldier was a child once. Every civilian who was killed in a raid had parents who once held him or her. Even our enemies had families. Did that general have a child? Did that spy have a wife who had no idea what he was doing? I'm haunted by knowing that the plans I drew housed the scientists who worked in secret, figuring out how to create the most powerful bomb that the world has ever known. How they sat in a living room that we gave dimensions to, ate in a kitchen that had a table by the east window not the west window because we decided that. And how then they would leave that kitchen and walk down streets that we decided should curve here and run straight there...and walk into their lab which we decided should have these kinds of doors and windows not those...and sit down at a desk that we chose, and then go to work on their formulas of annihilation. Have you seen the photos of Hiroshima? Or Nagasaki?"

Jules reaches out, takes my hand, and holds it. I'm thrown. The conversation we're having is serious, and the electric touch is out of place. Shocks go up my arm, and I feel a lurch inside me.

"We can't make our nightmares go away forever," he says. "But for me, now, three years later, I shake them much faster when I wake up than I did two years ago. And even faster than I did one year ago."

He is still holding my hand. And I want him to. But is

he feeling any of the same things I am? Or is he just being kind?

I nod. "I know what you mean. When I first lost my mother, the missing was so absorbing, it was who I was. Then one day I realized I had gone a whole morning without thinking about her. And then a whole day. And now when I do think about her, it still hurts, but for less time. Sometimes I can even think of her and remember something wonderful without tearing up. Like when you took me skating."

"You're living with it, instead of not living because of it," he says.

Our food arrives. And with it a new request from Jules.

"I've told you the biggest secret I have," he says in a slightly teasing voice. "Now I need to extract one from you so we're equal."

I wonder for a moment if he is flirting and then force myself to stop imagining anything is going on here other than Jules Reed wanting to discover what he can about the bejeweled mystery of my tiara.

"We're already equal. I told you about Oak Ridge."

"But even you admitted that's not a secret anymore. So you have to share something else."

I take a bite of my lobster. It's creamy, delicious, and decadent.

"This is wonderful," I say.

He's taken a bite as well. "It is, but don't change the subject."

"All right. When I was at Oak Ridge I got played. And the end result was that I inadvertently exposed my best friend, who it turns out was selling secrets about the factory."

"To our enemies?"

I shook my head. "No, to an American journalist. She

was using the money to help her family. Her father had died early in the war, and her mother…"

Tears are filling my eyes.

"I'm sorry. You don't have to talk about it, I shouldn't have pushed."

"I've gone this far. I want to finish. I haven't told anyone…except of course for the man involved. I didn't realize that he was just using me. I thought it was real. That part doesn't matter now. What does is that Charlotte was arrested and put on trial. She was found guilty and spent months in prison. And if I hadn't been so naïve, that never would have happened."

"Oh, Isobelle, I'm sorry." Jules' voice is comforting. He reaches into his jacket and pulls out his handkerchief and gives it to me. I have one in my bag but take his. As I blot my tears, I realize it smells of him.

"Are you okay?" he asks.

"Yes? No? I'm embarrassed and still feel terribly guilty. And stupid." I choke out a laugh. "Charlotte is out, but her career is over. She won't talk to me, of course. And I don't blame her. Honestly, she doesn't know the half of it. And I still have to deal with Ted…he's my boss, if you can believe it. Which is why it's so hard for me to put it all behind me and move on. Besides, I have a habit of dwelling on things. My mother used to remind me that while we will always carry our past with us, we don't have to wear it like a noose."

"She was right. So why are you doing it?"

"Charlotte went to prison."

"Because of what *she* did, though."

"But if it wasn't for me, no one would have found out."

"That she was breaking the law?"

"Yes, but…" I shrug. "You don't understand."

"I do. I do more than you can possibly know."

"What do you mean?"

"The reason my grandfather is in prison... I'm the one who found out what he was doing, and I told someone just like you did. Someone I trusted. It never occurred to me...I didn't think in a million years that my mother would turn in her own father-in-law. But she did. She said he had broken the law. But I have to live with the knowledge that if I hadn't told her, my grandfather wouldn't be in Sing."

"You did the right thing," I say.

"So it seems to someone looking at it objectively," he says. "That's the trick. Don't look at what happened through your own eyes, feel it with your own feelings. Force yourself to view it with some perspective."

"And how good have you been at doing that?"

Jules bursts out laughing. "I'm a total failure."

For the moment, I laugh with him and forget that I have admitted that I had a relationship with the man I work for.

"What's the part of all of it that you can't let go of?" Jules asks after the waiter takes away our plates.

"I know what Charlotte was doing was wrong. But she wasn't using me or hurting me. She was doing what she did on her own. Ted still claims he was genuinely interested in me. He says he didn't know anything about Charlotte before we got together. But how can I ever know that I wasn't being played from the beginning so that he could do his good deed?"

I focus my eyes on my martini glass for a second, trying to gather my thoughts. "That's the part I *can* let go of...I think," I add, then continue. "Ted wasn't only an architect. He was spying for the government. He came back to my room with me one night and apparently saw something on Charlotte's desk that made him suspicious. I didn't make the connection at the time. But after that, he would often suggest we go back to my place if Charlotte wasn't there, even though he had an apartment of his own in town.

"He finally convinced me to help him trap her by leaving some fake plans in our room. If they got out, it would implicate Charlotte."

I am remembering how Ted promised not to tell anyone about my involvement, to protect me, which was actually a good thing, since if word got out about our affair it would be damaging to me at work, not him. As far as I know, to this day, Charlotte has no idea of my involvement, and no one at SOM knows that Ted and I were ever together. But that protection has obviously come at a price. Plus, it's brought Ted undeserved glory.

"And you agreed?" Jules prompts.

"Yes, I agreed. I guess I still felt so bad about that original snooping with Stan and trying to figure out what we were doing when we were expressly told not to. I was so eager to serve my country that I believed helping was the right thing to do—if my friend was leaking information, it could compromise the security of the nation during a time of war.

"Looking back, it was probably my stubborn curiosity that got the better of me again. But then when Charlotte was actually arrested and imprisoned—not just stopped and reprimanded—I was devastated."

"Of course, you were," Jules says in a kind, sympathetic voice. "And still are, aren't you? And so remorseful that you've sentenced yourself to a kind of emotional prison that you can't seem to get yourself out of."

His insight makes me uncomfortable. I feel laid bare.

"What happened then with you and Ted?" Jules asks.

"After the arrest, he left Oak Ridge a hero, came back to

New York, married his fiancée, and got a big, fat promotion. And now…well, now he still has me working for him. Not in the field of espionage, mind you, but let's just say my work is helping him reach his bonus requirements for the year."

"What? That's outrageous. You have to do something about this. Isn't there anyone you can talk to?"

"Ted is a senior partner. I am a junior architect. I already went to Mr. Williams and asked to be reassigned. He asked why. Seemed he couldn't imagine anyone not wanting to work for Ted, who is his protégé."

"But you told him? About the work you're doing that Ted is claiming as his own?"

"I didn't think he'd ask and when he did, I got nervous, so I lied. Frank Williams is my mentor. He was my professor at Cooper Union. Without him, I never would have gotten a foot in the door at SOM, much less a job. His opinion and respect mean the world to me. The fact is, I didn't think he'd believe me if I told him the truth, and the thought of that was unbearable. So I said I wanted to work with different architects to develop my style. He said he'd talk to Ted and see how he felt about losing me. And from there it all got worse."

"How?"

I don't know why I am telling Jules this whole sordid story, but it's too late now.

"Ted confronted me and accused me of starting to build a case against him. He assured me that if I pursued getting out of his group, he'd go straight to Mr. Bunshaft and tell him I had tried to seduce him at Oak Ridge in an effort to get a promotion. Ted swore to me that he would make much more trouble for me than I could make for him. 'Who is he going to believe? You, Isobelle? You, who's saying I used a junior architect's ideas? Or me saying you're a woman who is so desperate to make it in a man's business that she'd——?'"

I didn't finish. I couldn't repeat what he'd said, not because I was being a prude but because I felt so stupid.

"You don't have to tell me," Jules says.

"You basically know it all now. And no one else does. Well, except for Ted."

"Sometimes, it helps to talk about it. I hope this time it did."

He lets go of my hand, and my skin feels suddenly cold. The waiter arrives with the dessert menu, but I can't stop thinking about what I've just confessed. What must Jules think of me now? I probably shouldn't have told him, but I've been so unhappy with this weighing on me.

After dinner, as promised, Jules and I head for the Mall. On the way there, we're quiet. When we arrive, and I see the monuments all lit up with a dark wintry sky behind them, I agree it is magnificent. We start at the Lincoln Memorial. Its spotlights and shadows, the emptiness of the walkways, the cloudy sky all combine to give the statue not just an imposing grandeur but a slightly haunting aspect. Walking from the front to back and around, we come to a stop and stand, small and inconsequential, in front of the sculpture and read the words written on the marble walls.

Despite how beautiful the memorial is, as eloquent and important as the words are, I feel sad. True to form, Jules senses that something's not right and asks me what's wrong. His question unnerves me. How does he have such an easy time reading me? Does it mean we have a special bond? Or am I as bad at reading people as he is good at it and he's just this intuitive with everyone?

"Isobelle, what is it?" he asks again.

"We're in awe of these ideals. All these great and lofty beliefs. But when it comes down to it, most of us are just greedy. Very few of us really care who we destroy in the process of getting what we want. I look at this beauty and all I can think about is that at Oak Ridge we built a whole city in order to build a bomb in order to destroy a city. Hundreds of thousands of people who just happened to be living there and not here were killed or had their lives destroyed. I think it's the arbitrariness of those ruined lives that I can't quite shake."

"But that arbitrariness can be amazing too, though. If your mother hadn't decided to sell the stones in the tiara then you wouldn't have come looking for my grandfather and I wouldn't have met you. And there's more to the chain we don't even know yet," Jules says as he takes my arm and leads me down the steps and toward the reflecting pool, luminescent and shimmering. Beyond it the Washington Monument, beams of light from its pinnacle illuminating the darkness, looms in the distance.

I shiver. Not because of the Mall's beauty or the cold, but because of Jules' comment. My mother and I used to talk about this, too. She was fascinated with how lives can change after one tiny moment that didn't even seem consequential at the time, but in retrospect altered the trajectory of life. Like the way she met my father in the hospital in St. Petersburg, all because another patient who she had been reading to had died. And yet she didn't believe in either fate or predestination.

I ask Jules if he does.

"I'm not sure about that. I don't like to think that our lives are mapped out already and we're just walking along a path that's already been chosen."

A bird flies overhead, and its wings catch the moonlight. I watch it soar up and toward the marble obelisk.

"Do you believe in fate?" he asks.

"My mother, who had survived so much, whose life had taken so many turns she never expected, used to tell me that fate is sometimes easier to see in retrospect. We take a million steps, but it is only the one that leads to a change that we recognize as being fateful."

We've reached the end of the pool.

"Look back," Jules says. He turns as do I. Far in the distance is the Lincoln Memorial. No longer towering over us, but a glowing reminder of the power of the President's impact.

He leads me to a bench at the base of the needle, and we sit.

"Was your mother also always practical?"

"Yes. She said my father was the dreamer, so she had to be the one who faced reality. As much as she loved him, I think she hoped I wouldn't be too much like him because it was his optimistic impracticality she said that had, in the end, led to his death."

"What do you mean?" Jules asks.

"My mother said that my father wound up in prison and ultimately died because of his schemes and ideas."

"What schemes?"

"Good question. All she said was that my father had sacrificed himself for us and been incarcerated for it. She was never more specific than that. When I'd push, she'd just shut down. I have always believed she never forgave him for dying."

"What a terrible thing," Jules says.

"I know. Loving someone so much that you can't forgive them? Holding on to that anger for your whole life? She was younger than I am now when she came to America with me—a baby—in tow. She knew one person here, her mentor's niece, who I call Aunt Lana. All my mother had with her was a single suitcase with a Titian and a Rembrandt sketch hidden in the lining. A gift from her mentor, who had also given drawings to his niece when she emigrated. The two of them sold those drawings to start their business together and then to buy the building where they lived and worked. My mother never dwelled on what she had lost. She couldn't, she once told me, because the loss was as big as the ocean she'd crossed to come here. She felt that if she did, she'd drown in the memories. She said she stood on the deck of the boat the night before it docked in New York Harbor and looked up into the sky, at the moon, and threw every one of her memories into that black, black water. She wiped her mind clean of Russia and the horrible regime that had ruined her life and the life of everyone she loved. That's when she changed her name, and mine, and started over."

"What was your name before?"

"She never told me. All these secrets… Every time I discover another one, I feel like she's left me all over again," I say and choke back a sob. "I'm sorry. Would you believe I normally never cry? I don't know what's wrong with me."

"There's nothing wrong with you. Nothing at all." Jules takes me in his arms and holds me close to him. As soon as he does, I'm not thinking about my past anymore but about how strong his arms feel around me. About how much I love his scent, that mixture of the woods and leather. About how warm I am despite the temperature. And about how I don't want him to let go.

"I'm sure it was very hard for your mother. She obviously had her reasons for keeping so much from you, but that doesn't make it any easier for you to cope with now. If it helps at all, I won't leave. I'll stick it out with you until you figure all of this out. Okay?"

"It does help," I whisper into his coat. But in the back

of my mind, I think that it might be kindness that makes him want to help, or there could be some other reason. Ted had another reason, and I didn't see that either. I should keep that thought front and center. Focus on it. But how can I when I can smell him and feel his arms and all this from him and more?

"Isobelle Moon, sitting here right now, you look like the saddest girl in the world. And it's breaking my heart."

He leans down and kisses me. The first kiss is sweet and kind. The same way he kissed me back in New York. The second kiss is a little less sweet and a bit hungrier. But when we get to the third time, I kiss him back, and it changes the embrace. The hunger and the passion in his touch surprises me. The pure electricity that feels like it's replaced the blood in my veins surprises me. The kisses wipe out all other thoughts. I feel as if I've climbed out of a suffocating room and discovered an intoxicating landscape previously unknown to me.

This feels like something I have been waiting for—affirmation that it *can* be the way I always imagined. That there is someone out there who *can* touch me so deeply, to reach my core, and this time for all the right reasons.

Other times that I've been out on a date with a man, when the time came to kiss him, the intimacy would only heighten how much of a stranger he was to me. The very act of coming together has always made me feel more apart. Even with Ted, as much as I thought I liked and admired him, as flattered as I was by his attention, I never quite felt totally comfortable with him. Not like this. Part of me always stood just outside our embraces, watching.

But with Jules, even though I know I shouldn't trust him so fast, I'm right in it. Despite my track record, despite my worries, I feel an immediate rush of lust that surges through me, surprising me. And thrilling me. I want to be with him. Even if I'm wrong again. I want him to go on holding me like this, blocking out the rest of the world. I've disappeared into his kisses. It's not that I've stopped asking the questions, it's that I don't care what the answers are anymore. Even if this turns out badly, I wouldn't give it up.

"Can we go back to the hotel?" he asks in a hoarse voice. "I want to be with you."

"Yes," I whisper against his neck.

He takes my arm and holds it close to him, and we walk the few blocks back, not saying anything. The pressure of wanting him builds so that by the time the elevator doors open on his floor and we're alone in the hallway, I feel as if I might explode with anticipation. We don't even make it to his door before he pushes me up against the wall and kisses me again. I kiss him back, and when we break apart, only because we need to breathe, my lips feel swollen, bruised. He holds my hand and pulls me toward his room. After fumbling with the key, he pushes the door open, and we fall inside.

Jules unbuttons my coat, pulls it off, and drops it on the floor. He rips off his own coat and drops it as well. While he kisses me again, he shrugs off his suit jacket, and I step out of my shoes.

There are no lights on, but the window is open and the ambient streetlights illuminate the room enough for me to see his face, suffused with want. His eyes are half shut with lust. I know mine are the same.

At first, we are all heat and hurry. More clothes thrown off, dropped where they land. Us not making it to the bed but only to the couch. Our lips do not lose contact. Now his shirt is off, and my blouse is opened. I gasp at the feeling of bare skin touching. I reach back and unhook my brassiere. I need more of me to be naked against him. He gasps, reaches out, cups my breasts with his palms, and at the same time leans forward and kisses first one nipple and then the other.

Our first time is fast and urgent. I push him to finish when I realize that I can't stop myself from rising over the crest. I have only been with one other man, but I know that there is something special about how I am responding to Jules and he to me.

Our second time is on the bed, and the urgency is gone. I am not religious, but there is something almost sacred about the slow burning, blurring of lines of time and place and Jules and me. There is an intensity to our heat. A slow, building heat. And tender kisses everywhere. An exploration of who he is, by me. And who I am, by him. And then who we are together—because we are new together—from the moment he pulled me on top of him, from the way he cradles me afterwards, from the way our curves fit into each other—we are new together. Even my perfume mixes with his woodsy cologne to create a wholly new scent. Yes, everything about us is new, and yet how we touch and smell and taste is all just like I've dreamed, and it makes me feel as if I knew him all along or as if I was waiting to know him.

Chapter 20

Sofiya Petrovitch
Petrograd
October 1918

The restoration of the Renaissance painting was proving difficult. Sofiya straightened up and stretched. She wanted to solve the puzzle of what was underneath the repainting. According to the museum notes, the Tiepolo had last been worked on in the early 1800s. And badly, which was not unusual. Restoration was an evolving art, far more sophisticated now than it had been a hundred years ago.

"Do you want to take a break, Sofiya?" Filatov Roman Sokolov asked. His name derived from a falcon, sokol, and even though it wasn't exactly his name, everyone called him Professor Sokol—which made him smile. He was proud of his name and wore a pinky ring with a stylized falcon carved out of a carnelian. The bird was a symbol of success, victory, and rising above a situation which he liked to muse upon.

"Thank you, but I'm fine, Professor Sokol."

The seventy-six-year-old head of the restoration department deserved the title of professor. It was said that if you wanted a career as a restorer, you could waste your time at the Art Institute or you could work for Filatov Roman Sokolov. But they warned it was more difficult to have him take you on, even as an apprentice, than it was to compete in the program at the Institute. Sofiya's father had brought her to him when she was twelve years old and insisted she wanted to learn restoration.

"Let's sit and talk and have some tea," the professor had said to her and dismissed his friend and co-worker, her father.

The professor poured tea into two glasses that sat in very simple *podstakanniks* and brought them to the table where Sofiya sat staring ahead of her at a painting on an easel.

"I wish we had some sugar left," he said as he handed her the tea.

"It doesn't matter. Thank you for the tea."

"Sofiya, you are very young to know what you want to do," the professor had said. "How is it that you have made this decision?"

"Turning something ugly and broken into something beautiful again is like magic. I want to make magic."

He nodded as if he was satisfied with her answer. But he knew something was missing from her reasoning, and it would be a long time until she realized what it was. What she had said though was more than impressive for a twelve-year-old, and he took her on.

Sofiya stopped thinking about the past and resumed working on the Tiepolo that was giving her so much trouble.

About ten minutes later, the door burst open, and Carpathian ran in. She'd never seen him so distraught and disheveled. There were cuts and bruises on his hands and face. Dried blood on his chin and neck.

"I have to talk to you, Sofiya."

"Oh my God, are you all right? What happened?"

Of course, she knew before he answered that he wasn't all right. Who was *all right*? They were living in a world that had become unstable. From one minute to the next, they never knew what new rules would be put in place. Who would be robbed, or shot, or die of starvation. They said that the average citizen in St. Petersburg had lost fifteen percent of his or her body weight because of the food shortages. Before the war, over one and a half million people lived in their city. Now they were down to less than seven hundred and fifty thousand.

"They came today." He was out of breath. "Twelve soldiers. On orders of the provisional government. They took over the House of Fabergé."

"Sit down, sit down," the professor said as he pulled out a chair and practically pushed Carpathian into it. "I will get tea."

Returning to her role as nurse, Sofiya said she would get some gauze and bandages and clean up his face.

"That can wait, I have to tell you—"

"It can't wait, actually. I won't be long, we have everything I need here."

And they did. There was alcohol and gauze that they used in their work that would serve her well in cleaning and bandaging Carpathian's cuts and scratches.

She gathered what she needed and returned to his side.

"I worried that this would happen one day," he said. "It's happened to everyone else—Fabergé knew it would happen. Every one of the workmasters have feared it. And some of us have taken precautions but not enough. Never enough. Those monsters had us open the safes and they plundered—"

"Stop talking now. I need to clean this, and I don't want your head moving."

He obeyed.

Despite everything Carpathian had gone through, from losing part of his foot to not having a memory, to Sofiya refusing to see him, to his reaction to the tsar's abdication and all the other terrible things happening in Petrograd, Sofiya had never seen him the way he was now, and she was frightened.

Carpathian had always looked for the silver lining. Always tried to reframe the situation so he could find a way to right the wrong or solve the problem or change the outcome. He always had an idea, a plan. He designed jewelry like that, and he lived that way. You came up with an idea, a vision and then you planned how to execute it, and if you came up against a problem, you stopped and, applying logic, you reworked your solution.

"I couldn't do anything," he said now as she stepped away after bandaging the cut.

"Have some tea," the professor said. He had gotten to know Carpathian in the last few months. Often when Carpathian came to pick Sofiya up at the end of the day, he and the professor would play a game of chess. The professor kept a board in the studio for anyone who cared to come and take a break. He was a brilliant player and enjoyed nothing more than a game at the end of the day.

"Tell us what happened, slowly," the professor said.

"The Bolsheviks entered the store and lined up all of us employees at gunpoint. They then started to systematically empty the cabinets and worktables into sacks. When they came to my station, I pushed them away. I didn't think about it, didn't realize what would happen, didn't plan it. I just pushed the soldier away, and he grabbed me by the collar and shouted that I had no right to fight them.

"'We aren't interested in your bourgeois rights. We have the right now. To take this...' He picked up a necklace I was working on and threw it on the floor and stepped on it, grinding his heel and then tossed the smashed piece in with everything else."

As he described the scene, Carpathian's voice remained hushed. The professor and Sofiya had to lean forward to hear all of his words.

"Then the guard picked up a gold chain that wasn't yet assembled, pulled it apart and threw the links into his sack. 'Do you see?' he asked as he picked up one of my files. 'I have the right to do anything I want to your workplace, to these objects of the aristocracy, or to you...' And then he took the file and cut my neck."

"You were lucky. He missed your artery by millimeters," Sofiya said.

"Lucky?" Carpathian laughed sarcastically. "There's nothing left of the House of Fabergé, Sofiya. There's nothing left. They forced us to open the safe and took everything. We should have fought harder. We should have used our files and pliers and blowtorches. We should have burned down the building and melted all the gold rather than let these thugs take what they took."

"It would have turned even more violent if anyone had fought back," the professor said. "None of your tools could compete with the guns."

"Sofiya." Carpathian looked directly into her eyes with such anguish. In a sad whisper that she could barely make out, he said, "They have your tiara."

She sucked in her breath. There were worse things than this, she thought. Russia was starving. Well-heeled people had been thrown out of their homes that had been turned over to workers. Families were living three or four to a room. Everyone had to queue up for food, but what they got was inadequate and often spoiled or rancid. Yes, there was a black market, but not many could afford it. Fewer than that had anything of value left to sell in exchange for gray meat and mealy potatoes.

But Sofiya couldn't rationalize her loss. The tiara was all she had left from her dearest friend, who was now living in Siberia and suffering worse than all of them. Living a life they were in no way prepared for. A life that no one thought would be spared.

Carpathian stood up and knelt before her. He took her hand.

"I don't know how, but I swear I will make this up to you," he said and then he laid his head in her lap and for the first and last time in her life, she saw him weep.

Chapter 21

Isobelle Moon
New York City
December 1948

It has been a long time since I have woken up with a man, and never in a luxury hotel. Jules is still asleep beside me, curled on his side, his arm across my chest. For a while, I just lie here feeling the high-count Egyptian cotton sheets with my fingertips. Despite the circumstances, and the man lying beside me, and the sensuality of his arm heavy against my breasts, I cannot help but think about my mother's love of fine things.

She was a careful spender. Too careful, I often thought, given how successful the antiques store was. But having lived through such brutal years in Russia, she said she couldn't ever relax about having enough money. She told me how one of her mother's friends sold a whole set of sterling silver flatware for a ham. A gold bracelet for a week's worth of potato flour that was mealy at that. In America, my mother became an inveterate saver, and yet she indulged in certain things because she told me that beauty was important too. She learned that in Russia as well. How a ballet could make you forget for a few hours how terrible things were. How listening to a symphony could fuel your dreams for a week.

Beauty was my mother's only religion. And when I was growing up, she made sure we worshiped something lovely and magical every day, be it walking two blocks to visit a single painting in the Metropolitan Museum, examining a magnificent tree in Central Park, visiting Bergdorf Goodman to try a new perfume or stopping by the French bakery on Lexington Ave and 65th Street for a perfect Charlotte Russe. My mother was an odd combination of someone who was both haunted by the past and yet lived in the moment. An impossible incongruity, I always thought. But she said it was the haunting that made her live in the moment. The past was always there. Just a backwards glance was all it took. So, to save herself—and me—she had to stay focused and stay in the present.

We can never know our parents fully. We can't see their lives through an objective lens. We are of them in a way that we are not of anyone else, and with that bond comes blinders on our side and a distancing on theirs. They don't want to share their mistakes with us lest we follow in their footsteps. They don't want us to see their flaws lest we use them against them. They need to present an authority that prevents full disclosure. And no one hides their own secrets better than a parent whose life is filled with a tragedy they don't want to relive.

As the sun fills the hotel room with a cold winter early-morning light, I carefully move Jules' arm, get up, and visit the bathroom. I use the sundries the hotel provided. I brush my teeth and then take a shower, enjoying a shampoo so fragrant I can almost picture the garden where the flowers grew.

After I'm done, I wrap myself in one of the two terrycloth robes behind the door, go out, and find Jules sitting up in bed.

"I'm guessing you are as hungry as I am, so I've ordered room service."

And order he did. I laugh when the waiter arrives with the table. There are so many silver dome-covered dishes: scrambled eggs, waffles, silver dollar pancakes with butter and boysenberry syrup, toast with more butter and marmalade, bacon, sausages, orange juice, and coffee.

"Are you feeling okay?" Jules asks as he tucks into his second waffle and smears butter on it.

I nod and smile. "I am. Wonderful, really."

"Me too. I wanted to tell you that wasn't planned," he says. "I didn't set you up to stay over. But to be honest, I have been thinking about you this way for quite a while."

"I'm a little surprised."

"Why?"

"You…" I stumble.

"Isobelle? What is it? What aren't you saying?"

"You have such a glamorous life. You mix with actresses, models, and daughters of the richest men in the country. You've been written up in gossip columns since you graduated from high school. Restaurant maître d's know you and give you the best table in the house. Your shop is one of the most exclusive jewelry stores in the country. I don't exactly fit the mold. I'm not your type."

"How do you know what my type is? From the store? From who I have to do business with? That you aren't part of the social scene or a Hollywood star is exactly why I've been thinking about you. I haven't met anyone in a long time as authentic as you are. As sensitive and talented. I've had enough of the crowd that I socialize with and work with to last me a long time. They are my clients, Isobelle, that doesn't mean I would let them into my heart."

I get up and go over to him. As shy as I am, I also feel empowered and want to let him know how much his words mean to me. I lean down to kiss his cheek and thank him, but he turns his head so that the kiss winds up on his lips. I taste butter and maple syrup. He puts his arms around me, pulls me down onto his lap, and kisses me harder. Then he pushes away from the table, and the food is forgotten as we make our way back to the bed and nourish ourselves another way.

At nine o'clock, we are on the steps of the administration building when the doors open. Upstairs, Miss Rezot is waiting for us.

"I found the books you were looking for. It's the oddest thing. It seems that someone else was here yesterday looking at them. No one has requested them for years, and then twice in one day. So they were on the trolley, but here you go."

I wonder who else would have wanted to see these books. And why. From Jules' expression, I think he's wondering the same thing, and then he asks her directly.

"I'm sorry, but I wouldn't be able to share that information."

He nods, not happy but accepting her response.

We retire to a table with the previously missing Fersman books. Jules gives me volume one and he takes number two, and we start page by page, looking for anything that might be relevant.

That the People's Commissariat of Finances Moscow funded this work is obvious. At the top of every page are the words *Russian Treasure of Diamonds and Precious Stones*. Above that an embossed hammer. A protective piece of paper describing the item separates each photo.

There are blocks of texts describing the history of the collection going back to Peter the Great, as well as paragraphs of the kind of propaganda that my mother told me about on those infrequent occasions she was willing to talk about her homeland and the horrors of the war.

The history of the Diamond-Treasure reflects the history of the Romanovs during the first two centuries, with their exceeding lavishness in some cases, and their extreme avarice [in] others.

I'm halfway through the book when I find a photograph of a treasure table overflowing with jewels: crowns, brooches, necklaces, rings, earrings, bracelets, sceptres. Like all the other photographs in the book, the black and white photo is grainy and of questionable quality.

I peer at it carefully. It is difficult to see the details of any of the tiaras.

"This might be something but…I just can't get it in focus," I complain.

Jules pulls his loupe out of his briefcase and hands it to me. Opening it, I examine the photo again.

"Look, Jules, this one has a very similar shape to my mother's tiara." I hand him the loupe and push the book toward him.

"I think you're right. Now we need to find a photo of it on its own with an item number."

We each go through two of the catalogs, examining every individual photo, comparing every tiara to the one in the group shot. We find an individual photograph of every tiara on the treasure table along with a detailed description, except for the one that resembles my mother's. There is no separate photo of that one. But there is a description of it that I believe fits.

"Read this," I tell Jules.

He reads over my shoulder.

No. 2014. Diamond diadem with sapphires.

A beautiful piece, with large, dark sapphires and loosely hanging pendeloques. Its design is not very successful. The workmanship refers to the second half of the XIX~th century, and probably the stones were taken from the reserve.

Dimensions: length—42 cent.; height form 3-5 cent.

Sapphires: 9 beautiful old Ceylon stones weighing totally about 145 m. c.; among these – one large stone in the centre of 34.20 m. c. (w.) [metric carat weight?, seems redundant]

Diamonds: 28 pendeloques of ancient cutting, of average quality, weighing about 28 m. c.; 8 large diamonds, white, of good ancient cutting, total weight 12 m. c.; 320 small diamonds of good quality – 80 m.c.; 92 roses [rose cuts] – about 1 m. c.

Setting—gold

Not mentioned in the old inventories.

Inv. 1922—No. 4

"Okay, let's go back and see if we can find a corresponding picture for number 2014."

Neither of us find it in any of the four-volume catalogs.

"Why would it be in the picture on the table but not anywhere in the rest of the catalog?" I ask.

"I don't know," Jules says. He stares at the books on the table for a moment. "Unless there is another catalog that's marked differently. Let's look again through the cards for something—anything—dated Russia 1920-1930 with jewelry or imperial or Romanov in the description."

We go to work. After about forty-five minutes, Jules says he thinks he might have a match. "All it says is *Russian Jewel Album*, but that's good enough for me."

It takes only a few minutes to find the slim volume in the stacks. It has a worn maroon leather binding but no other identification. At the table, Jules opens it. The title page is hand-colored and signed by an artist whose name neither of us can make out. But we can read what is below that—a place and date—Moscow, 1922.

My mother told me so little about my father, but I do know that he lived in Moscow following his prison sentence and went back to work with Fabergé, evaluating and appraising their jewelry. That was where and when I was conceived.

I tell that to Jules. "It's possible this was what he was working on," I say.

He stares down at the cover and touches the elaborate jeweled motif with reverence. He points to the title spelled out in Cyrillic.

"I wish one of us could read this now, but at least we'll find someone who can translate it for us later." Jules removes a small Minox camera from his pocket. A few of the architects at SOM have these miniature cameras that were originally created for German spies in the 1920s. Tiny enough to carry in a jacket pocket, they're great for taking photos on-site without having to lug around a lot of equipment.

Jules snaps a few pictures of the cover of the album and

then opens it.

On the first page is a sceptre and orb that I recognize from the full catalog we'd pored over earlier. He turns to the next page. And then the next. There are fifty-one pages. Most have a single item, a few have two. Each item is one we saw in one of the four official volumes we've already inspected. Each item except for four.

There is a diamond and sapphire bracelet in this book that is not in any of the others.

There is also a sapphire and diamond brooch.

There is a gold and emerald necklace.

And there is a kokoshnik-style diamond and sapphire tiara. Without question, its design and size match the skeleton of the tiara I found in my mother's hiding place.

I reach for the first volume of the 1925 Fersman catalog. There in part one, plate one—on the page we'd bookmarked—is the wider shot of the table crammed full of all the jewels. Jules and I examine it, then look back at the shot we found in the maroon, untitled catalog.

"It is the same tiara, isn't it?"

Jules looks from one to the other again.

"Yes. Without a doubt. I'm not sure how it could be in that group photo but not anywhere else in the larger catalog. Maybe Miss Rezot knows."

Jules goes to get her, and she returns with him a few moments later. We explain what we've found, and she examines the red leather book.

"I've never seen this before," she says with some surprise. "I'm a little bit obsessed with Fersman and the work he did, but I don't know what this is." She goes through it again, trying to make sense of what she's looking at based on the facts she has. "We know the original inventory and pictures of the imperial jewels was made by

Fersman with the help of Fabergé from 1921 to 1922."

Jules looks at me. Neither of us knew that. It's a very important fact since it connects my father, who was working for Fabergé—who was working for Fersman—to the tiara.

"And it looks like that's when this red-covered album was printed during those two years," she continues. "But this red album only contains a fraction of the photos in the 1925 catalog. And the 1925 shows everything that is in the 1922 album except four objects. And to make it even more complicated, not all of those four items are in the group shot on the table, only two are." She points to the photo of the table. "I suppose...yes, it's entirely possible that this shot of the table was taken in 1922 and then Fersman used it in his 1925 catalog even though by then, four of those pieces had disappeared."

We both thank Miss Rezot, who leaves us with our discoveries.

"She said those four pieces had disappeared, but they might have been stolen," Jules says. "We have to get the Midas Society involved in this. If your tiara was in fact part of a cache stolen from the imperial family, it has to be returned, Isobelle."

I am suddenly wary of the turn this conversation has taken. "What do you mean? It was my mother's."

"But whose was it before it was hers? If it was stolen and not sold, we need to make that right. That's what we do, I explained that to you. Return precious objects to whom they belong."

It's as if I am sitting at the table with a stranger. He doesn't care about me or my quest or my confusion or my loss. This is my worst fear rising to the surface. Like a dead body in an Agatha Christie novel. It's been dumped in the lake, but it bobs to the surface—another man using me to get what he needs to earn his stripes.

"I trusted you," I say to Jules. "You can't just do what you want with the tiara."

"It's the right thing."

"No, it's how you are planning to make points with the society so you can get your promotion."

Chapter 22

Sofiya Petrovitch
Petrograd
November 1918

Carpathian went to work for Agathon Fabergé, who was running an illegal antique store only two blocks from his father's now state-owned jewelry emporium. According to the rules, such privately owned shops were not allowed, but they hoped the rules would soon change. After all, rules changed every day in Petrograd. Sometimes Sofiya still slipped and called it by its pre-revolutionary name, St. Petersburg. And every time her father heard her do it, he corrected her. He who had a strain of aristocratic blood in his veins had become Citizen Petrov, accepting the new government.

"For your sake, and your mother's, I have no choice. To do less would be foolish," he argued at dinner when the two of them criticized his acquiescence. "This is not the time for idealism. It won't put food on the table. It won't save our jobs. And that is my primary responsibility. My only responsibility. I will say or do anything I can to make sure the two of you are taken care of. Don't you understand how dire this is? How serious?"

"But we are artists—" Sofiya's mother started to argue as she ladled the soup into bowls.

"We have our apartment still, with no strangers living in our rooms, unlike the great majority of our friends. We still have jobs that give us greater rations so we can have soup like this and real bread for dinner. I will not fall on a philosophical sword and starve to death like Vladimir Morosofsy. He died. Do you both understand that? He starved to death because he fought the new provisional government so loudly, he was fired and now is of no use to anyone. No!" Sofiya's father banged his hand down on the table. "I will not do that."

As he spoke, Sofiya couldn't help but notice he was staring at a painting on the wall that her mother had done. A watercolor of the tsar with Olga and Tatiana and Sofiya sitting in the garden at the Alexander Palace the summer she turned thirteen. His eyes appeared glued to the portrait, even as they filled with tears for what had been.

Carpathian had been working at the shop for a month when he came to call one night after dinner. He had with him a small gift for Sofiya, a powder blue guilloche egg charm and a very unusual chain.

"I made this for you," he said as he showed it to her.

The gold chain that hung down between her breasts was made up of eight smaller chains, each connecting to the next with a springing catch. "You can clip an egg on each, this way, and then attach it back to the next bit of chain." He showed her how to attach the new egg to the chain. "And if you give me the white red cross egg your parents gave you, we can add that as well."

She pulled it out from under her blouse. Carpathian took the egg off of its chain and attached it to the new one.

"I will make you some more eggs," he said. "There is room for them. I just need to get some more supplies. I'll fill up your whole chain with beautiful eggs in every shade of blue to match your eyes."

"I love it," she said, putting it on. "I won't take it off."

He smiled. "You are such a romantic. You have to take it off. You can't sleep with it. The little eggs will press into you here." He pushed his finger lightly into her chest above her breast. "And they will hurt if you roll over." Then he hesitated. "Do you sleep on your stomach or your back? I don't know."

"I sleep on my back," she said and then whispered, "I so badly want to spend a whole night with you."

"And I with you, little one. But your parents would never allow it. You have your reputation to worry about."

"Seriously? The world is all upside down. My father is a member of the party, and my mother is teaching anyone who wants to be an artist regardless of their talent. The tsar and tsarina are prisoners in a barely heated house in Siberia without a garden to grow vegetables or the ability to go to church. I don't care about my reputation anymore. I just care about being with you."

She felt wanton but free. She never thought about the fact that he was still married anymore. Their very existence in this rancid, corrupt country was at risk every day. Watching everyone she loved suffering, barely recognizing her city, had changed her bourgeois priorities.

"And I want to be with you. But you know I don't have

an apartment of my own."

"But you still have a bedroom, don't you?"

"Yes, I still have a bedroom."

"With a door?"

"Yes, with a door."

"A bed and a door. That's all we need to pretend that we are in Paris or London or anywhere that there are no Bolsheviks, yes?"

"Yes."

"We can pretend we are in the little hotel in London I stayed when I visited for Mr. Fabergé. You would have loved it. It was on a tiny street and looked so unassuming from the outside, but inside there was a courtyard and the rooms all looked down on a little square of green plants with so many flowers their scent wafted up to the room."

"You went to London?"

He nodded. "Once, yes."

"I went with my parents several times. My mother still has family there. They live near Portobello Road. They owned a frame shop. The first time we visited I watched my uncle restore a painting. I watched him, mesmerized. My mother said for over an hour. He used gold leaf to repair a section of a medieval manuscript page. I still remember how magical it was for something that was ruined to be restored to all of its former glory in just an hour. We were supposed to go on to Bath for the rest of our holiday, but I refused to go. I was eight years old and demanded that my parents leave me with my uncle so I could watch him do more."

"What did they do?"

"They asked my uncle if he would let me stay. He said yes, of course. They left me with him for four days. Four days that changed my life. I was fascinated and intrigued. Something in what he did simply but profoundly spoke to me. When I watched him repair a tear in a canvas, my mind was made up. To see something that was ruined restored that way was more magical to me than even how my mother created a painting out of a box of paints and a brush. I've always wondered why that was. Isn't it more astonishing that you can take a blank canvas and in days have a whole garden or the ocean or a person captured forever?"

"You're a fixer, that's why you were such a good nurse," he said. "Fixing us all, be it with bandages or soup or reading to us the from novels until your gentle voice made us forget our wounds."

"Is that what I did?"

"Well, not exactly for me." He laughed. "I didn't need forgetting but remembering. And you helped me remember."

She shrugged. "And brought you back to a wife and a child who is not yours and destroyed all your dreams."

"Ah, no. You gave me back my past even if parts of it were a bit tarnished. You gave me back my work, my mentor, my friends. You gave me back my art. Who knows how long it would have taken, if ever, for me to wind my way back to the House of Fabergé?"

"And to the traitor Dimitry and the ransacking of the store and—"

He put his hand on her lips.

"Shh. No more bitterness on my behalf. I am thankful for Dimitry. Not angry. He showed me how fickle Irina was. How duplicitous. How unworthy. He freed me from the one thing standing between you and me. So don't damn him."

"What were you doing in London?" she asked.

"Carl Fabergé asked me to help him with something."

It was a vague answer. "Did you see the city?"

"A bit." Another vague answer.

There was something that Carpathian wasn't saying. It wasn't like him to be secretive, and it wasn't like her to push. Or to feel that she needed to.

"It's nothing we need to talk about now." Carpathian put an end to the questions.

She looked at him curiously.

"I haven't mentioned this, but my mother is a bit of a mystic. She's been having a premonition for years. I'm a rationalist, but she's been right about so many things before. Because of that, I think it best to move on to another subject."

"What is the premonition?"

"Not tonight, Sofiya. Tonight, let's just be together and not think about everything that is wrong with the world beyond these doors."

"You will have to tell me at some point."

"Yes, but only when I'm certain I won't be burdening you."

She wanted to know more, but she trusted him. So she smiled and rested her head against his chest, and they sat in her parents' parlor and he stroked her hair, and they planned the night they were soon going to spend together.

Chapter 23

Isobelle Moon
New York City
December 1948

There should be a lot to discuss on the train back from Washington to New York. We've solved one piece of the tiara puzzle, found more questions, and taken a step in our personal relationship. But as we speed toward New York without speaking to each other, I can't help but wonder if we've made a mistake. No, if I've made a mistake.

After a half hour has passed, Jules reading his book, me staring out the window, I shift in my seat, summon my courage, and say, "Maybe we should talk."

He shrugs. "Sure, let's talk."

Clearly, he's irritated. Maybe he hasn't been using me, but he's sorry we made love. He certainly didn't give me that impression either last night or this morning. But he could have just been stringing me along. Having gained my trust, maybe he assumed that if we found out the tiara was stolen,

I'd turn my treasure over to him. Then he'd have his fifth jewel in the crown—I cringe at my own pun—and he would be given full membership in the Midas Society. But I've made it clear I don't intend to turn the tiara over to his society. Is that why he seems so surly?

"What's wrong?" he asks.

I am on shaky ground and not sure how to address my concerns. My last—really my *only* romantic relationship—was a farce. I was too naïve to understand what was happening, and my mistake in trusting Ted still haunts me. I don't trust my instincts.

"I know you are disappointed that I won't turn over the tiara to you, but I can't. It's connected to my mother's past. I know she never would have stolen it. You didn't know her..."

"But clearly someone did steal it. Maybe it wasn't your mother. Perhaps whoever stole it gave it to her without her telling her about its provenance. But there is no question that at least in 1922 it was part of the treasure trove the Bolsheviks appropriated from the Romanovs, other royals and wealthy citizens. The family of whomever it belonged to deserves to have it returned. Or at least deserves us making an effort to find out."

This was all beside the point to me. I had a bigger question. A more important problem I needed to solve. I had to know if I'd gone ahead and made a second terrible mistake believing the best of someone who didn't deserve it.

"Was what we did last night...no...what I want to ask you is why did you..." I need to just come out and ask him. But I can't bring myself to say it. I try again. "Did you think I'd be more willing to go along with your plan if I...if we spent... If—"

He is frowning as he interrupts.

"Are you asking me if I had sex with you so that you'd be more willing to give me the tiara?" His face is twisted into fury. "Are you, Isobelle?"

"Yes, that's what I am asking."

Jules looks at me as if he's never seen me before. He doesn't answer. Instead, he opens his book and starts reading again. I look out of the window once more, thinking that I'm not any better off for having brought it up. If anything, I've made it worse, and I have no answers. What should I do or say or ask now? I feel that familiar sting of tears and force myself not to cry. I rest my head on the window. I am so tired and just so sad. I know more about the history of the tiara than I knew yesterday, but none of it helps me understand why my mother had it or why she hid it. And I've slept with a man who I thought I knew, who I thought I respected and was starting to really like, only to be left wondering if I have been played. Again.

After another half hour when the last call for lunch is announced, Jules gruffly asks me if I want to go to the dining room, but I decline. I don't want to sit opposite him in stony silence, having only been asked out of politeness.

He leaves, and I give in to my despair. I was so drawn to him. We'd been so passionate… I'm nothing but sick to my stomach at how much of a fool I am.

After lunch, Jules returns to his seat and goes to sleep. Which is its own kind of affront because every time I glance over at him, I am reminded of why he is so tired. And that makes me think of what we did. Of the passionate connection we made. A connection that has now been severed. I try to convince myself that I should at least be relieved to have discovered the deception now before I developed even more feelings toward Jules, but I can't. Jules already mattered to me more than I thought he did. The excitement, the possibility, the potential of us made me feel I'd finally found someone I'd always been looking for.

He wakes up a half hour before we finally arrive at Penn Station. We don't speak still until we are outside of the station and on the street.

Jules offers to get a taxi and take me home, but I say I can manage on my own. My words sound hollow when I thank him for taking me to Washington. "And if you'll tell me how much the rooms were, I'd like to reimburse you for both of them and the dinner. You didn't wind up getting what you came for, and there's no reason you should be out all that money. I'd prefer to pay for the research since I'm the one who hopefully will benefit from it, not you."

I feel more tears well up, but I refuse to let myself cry now. I've gotten this far, I can't give in to self-pity. I wrap my scarf tightly around my neck, turn, and walk away from Jules toward the line of people waiting to get a taxi.

As I stand in the bitter wind, I wonder for what seems like the hundredth time what is wrong with me that I missed the clues. Did I get fooled because Jules was so good at being empathetic? At figuring out the particulars of my life and playing to them? At acting as if he cared while hiding his true motives? And the sex. How stupid of me to assume that because he enjoyed it, it meant anything more to him. Just because I felt passion and tenderness, I should not have attributed those same feelings to him. He was a consummate lover. But wasn't Ted as well?

I shiver and move up in the queue. It takes another five minutes before I make it to the head of the line, get in my taxi, and give the driver my address. Thankfully, there isn't much traffic, and I'm home twenty minutes later. I make a cup of tea with my mother's favorite honey—flavored with a vanilla stick—and sip it slowly while perusing our bookshelves looking for something that will be as comforting as the hot drink. I pull out *Frenchman's Creek* by Daphne Du Maurier, which I read when I was in high school and only remember it as an absorbing adventure. But as it turns out, it is much more. It feels as if I'm reading it for the first time since as an adult, I see it is a paean to passion and the power of love. It's tragic, but totally perfect, and the ending gives me the excuse to finally give in and weep.

Wednesday morning, I get to the bus stop a little earlier than usual. It's freezing, and I'm relieved when a bus arrives promptly. Aboard, I deposit my token and take a seat. Just as the driver pulls out, I look out the window on my left and see the Russian man just arriving at the stop. As we drive off, I crane my neck to get a better view. I can tell that he sees me, and for a moment our eyes meet.

Once I get to the office, I don't have much time to think about him or anything else. Ted informs me that our Connecticut clients are expected on Friday and my "little holiday," as he calls it, has resulted in a backlog of plans that need to be drawn up. Being busy for the next few days suits me. It gives me less time to dwell on the tiara, on Jules, and the mystery of the man who appeared at the bus stop.

The only downside to my long hours is the tiresome effort I have to make to keep myself from turning around and automatically looking out the window. I don't want to see Jules.

By Saturday, I'm worn out. Between the arduous drafting at work, my concern about the Russian man, and my disappointment in myself over Jules, I'm ready for two days of hibernation. Over a breakfast of toast with butter and marmalade and coffee, I watch the snow swirl outside my kitchen window and decide that I'm going to read all day and do nothing. But no sooner do I open the new Agatha

Christie I just bought than I hear my mother's voice telling me to get back to renovation, which I've ignored for the last few weeks.

After a half hour of stripping, I have a pile of the faded cabbage rose print wallpaper lying in a heap at my feet. There's only one section left on the wall opposite the bed. Reaching up, I jerk it down. Mid-way, about at chest height, there's another niche nestled between two studs. Why hadn't it occurred to me there would be something else hidden away in this room? Inside of this one is a single envelope. The addressee is written in an elegant hand in Cyrillic. As is the address, except for the number 516. The triangular red and white stamp is also in Cyrillic. I turn the envelope over. The seal has already been broken. Reaching inside, I withdraw a sheet of writing paper so thin I'm afraid I'll tear it. One glance tells me I won't be able to read it since it's written in Russian. I realize there's something else inside the envelope and pull out a black and white photograph. Standing on a snowy street corner, three men pose for the camera. I turn it over. In the same color ink and handwriting are what I assume to be three names, also in Cyrillic. Beneath that are four numbers—a year—1922.

I shiver. I don't believe in ghosts. I don't believe in fate. Or psychic phenomena. Or powers beyond our control. Yet this is at least the third time that a seemingly impossible coincidence has occurred. The first was finding the tiara and bill of sale that led me across the street to Alford Reed Jewelers. The next was seeing the man from the bus stop in Jules' office. And now this? We'd gone to D.C. to research the tiara in a book published in 1925 but we'd stumbled on an album that had been published in 1922 that had deepened this whole mystery. Would this letter and a photo yield any more clues?

Still holding the letter and the photo, I take in the rest of the room. Has my mother surrounded herself with hidden memories? Are there still more? I shudder. Did she think of these treasures every time she came into her bedroom? When she got into bed? Were they like talismans that made her feel safe? Or cursed items she couldn't bear to see but couldn't bear to destroy either?

My mother was young when she arrived in America. About the age I am now. She left everything behind and came to a foreign country with a little baby only months old. She must have been so frightened, and yet in my whole life I never saw her show fear. When I was little and scared, she would take my hands into hers, press her forehead up against mine, and offer her remedy: "Let's play the *worst* game."

Now, still holding the letter, staring down at the photo, I play the game with my mother's ghost.

What is the worst that could happen during this hunt for the truth about the tiara? The one thing I know with all my heart is that if it was stolen, my mother didn't take it. I have no doubt about that. So the worst thing would be to prove it was stolen, and then not be able to keep it. Which wouldn't be so terrible since I never knew it even existed until a few weeks ago. Then what? The worst could be that I'd never solve the mystery my mother left me. Which isn't so terrible either. If I hadn't decided to renovate, I never would have learned of the tiara's existence.

No, the real worst thing has already happened. Jules showed his true colors, and now we won't ever see each other again. That isn't as easy *a worst* to dismiss. But I don't want to think about that now. Now I want to know about this letter and photo.

Taking them with me, I go upstairs to Aunt Lana's apartment and ring the bell. Uncle Paul answers and greets me warmly. Together, we go into the kitchen where my aunt is baking. She is, as always, pleased to see me. Just as I start to tell them that I've found something new, the phone rings, and Uncle Paul goes inside to answer it. Aunt Lana tells me to sit, insisting on making tea in her beautiful old samovar and presenting it in her *podstakanniks*.

"I love these glasses," I tell her as I take the tea. "I love knowing how far they came to be here. And how carefully you treat them."

"They remind me of people I loved. Of a time when the world seemed simpler, and we were all more innocent."

"I used to ask my mother why she never brought anything with her from Russia," I say as I take my first sip. "She used to say she brought me and that was enough. I never believed her."

She laughs. "I remember her saying that to you." She shakes her head. "Sophia was a terrible liar, wasn't she?"

I laugh. "She was."

"And it was a big problem when it came to dealing with our customers. We'd find a chest of drawers in a dump, bring it back here, restore it, and make it look good enough to have come out of a palace. Then a customer would come in, notice it, ask her where it came from, and your mother would tell them." She shakes her head and laughs, and I join in.

"So what did you find this time?" she asks.

I hand her the letter and photo. "I never knew why she was lying, but clearly she was, and here's proof. She brought more than a few things from the past with her and kept them. Well-hidden, maybe, but kept nonetheless."

Aunt Lana picks up the photo first and examines it.

"Do you know who these men are?" I ask. "Is one of them my father? Every time I asked Mama if I could see a picture of him, she said she had no pictures. But there's this…"

"I never met your father, so I don't know if he is one of these men. Let me read the letter and see if it explains anything."

As she reads, I stare at the photo, going from face to face, but the men are so hard to make out. Not just because the photo is cracked and yellowed. It's winter and the men are all wearing heavy coats and big hats. That and the shot is taken from too far away to allow really close scrutiny.

"The letter is from Carpathian," Aunt Lana says. "The only name I ever heard Sophia use for your father, though being Russian, he would have had at least three names. He writes that he misses her so much since she left the day before. That it is still so strange to be working in Moscow and that he still wakes up and can't believe he has gone from being in prison to living in a fine hotel and sorting through the treasures of the imperial family. Let me read this to you:

"'I feel as if I am defiling our very heritage. To judge the jewels by their value on the open market is to completely ignore their cultural significance. As someone who has spent his life creating objects that honor our heritage, this is not only a travesty, it is pure blasphemy. Is a diamond that sits in a sceptre not more than a rock that would look pretty around some socialite's neck? I abhor what we are doing and would prefer to quit and take my chances going underground. But then I think about you and the baby you are carrying and that makes the future worth securing.

"'I hope my plan, my darling Sofiya, ensures you and our child have what you need. If the worst happens, don't squander it trying to get me out of prison. I will do that from my side with my buttons.

"'You said you found it hard to believe I could work so

closely with Dimitry. You thought it would be hard—but not at all. I am actually thankful to him for seducing Irina. Marriage is sacred. I was too young to know that. She is too fickle to have ever understood it. And if not for Dimitry, my sense of responsibility when I got out of the hospital would have taken me in a very different direction. I will close now. Enclosed is what you asked for, the only photo I have of myself, along with Agathon Fabergé and Dimitry. I hope you can come to Moscow again soon. I yearn to put my head against your belly and feel our child's little kicks. You and the baby make everything bearable and worthwhile.

"'Take care of the tiara, my love. If the worst happens, it is the key to your future and our child's. If the worst does not happen and I survive, it is the key to where I will wait for you, no matter how long it takes you to come to me.

"'With all my love, Carpathian.'"

Aunt Lana wipes away a tear as she finishes. "The worst did happen. We know that. Given that he was already in prison before your mother left Petrograd, Carpathian must have been arrested very shortly after this letter was written."

"Wasn't it dangerous for him to reveal so much in a letter sent via post?" I ask.

"Yes, everyone knew officials scrutinized mail sent by government workers at that time. It would have also put your mother in danger to receive a letter like this. Carpathian never would have risked it. Maybe he had a friend who helped deliver their correspondence so that it wouldn't be read by government officials."

"Or maybe he wasn't as careful as he should have been and did send it by post and that's why he was caught and arrested. He criticizes the government in this letter and mentions the tiara… Maybe that's how he wound up in prison."

Aunt Lana re-folds the letter. "In that horrible prison where he died. Your mother never stopped loving him, though. Imagine how wonderful he was, how pure his heart must have been for her to remain faithful to his memory for the rest of her life and never look for another man."

I must have frowned without realizing it.

"What is it, Isobelle?"

"He might not have been such a saint. If you put all the pieces together, it's possible that he stole the tiara. In 1922, he was working in Moscow for Fabergé, who we know was working for Fersman. We also know what they were doing—appraising, photographing and cataloging the imperial jewels. The only photos we found of the tiara are dated 1922. My father went to prison in 1922, and there he died. What crime did he commit? Stealing a priceless tiara from the Bolsheviks? It's certainly possible. My mother came to America in 1922, and I found the tiara here in New York. But after all that, how much did any of it help my mother in the end? The sapphires weren't even real."

"From the letter, I doubt he knew about the sapphires."

"He was a jeweler, Aunt Lana. How could he not know? Mr. Reed told us that both before the revolution and after, people often replaced stones with paste in order to sell the originals or safeguard them. A jeweler who was appraising a piece would know to look for that exact thing."

"Let's say you are right that he stole it—even though I'm not convinced. Why would he steal a piece that had fake stones in it? Why give that tiara to your mother? If he was going to risk getting caught, why not steal something of serious value?"

I am so frustrated. At every turn, all I've found is just more dead ends. Or a betrayal. I want to rip up the letter. Tear the photograph to bits. Instead, I take a few sips of my tea and try to figure out the puzzle.

"You said my mother told you she sold some of her grandmother's jewelry to help raise money to buy this building?"

"Yes."

"Let's say that's not what she sold. Let's say she didn't want to tell you she had a stolen tiara. When she came back from selling the jewelry, did she seemed pleased by how much she made? Disappointed? Did she say anything about the effort?"

Aunt Lana plays with the handle of her tea glass. "Maybe she did… I didn't think much of this at the time, but I do remember her coming home with the check. And she was depressed. I asked her if she was upset that she'd had to sell her family heirlooms. Your mother was so pragmatic. She laughed at me and called me sentimental and said that wasn't what was bothering her. It was that she hadn't gotten nearly as much money as she'd hoped to add to the kitty we had. She said yes, that she'd thought they would be worth much more and that she was angry at Carpathian for throwing his life away over such a paltry sum."

"Did you ask her what my father had to do with my grandmother's jewelry?"

Aunt Lana shakes her head. "I'm sure I did, but I don't remember what she told me. Or if she even answered me. You have to remember, every conversation we had about the past was painful. It was still all so fresh, and we all had lost so much. We each kept Russia alive in us in our own way. Your mother locked her Russia away. I understood her reasons for doing so. We were in America. With our English-sounding names and our growing business and our children, how much good was there in shining too much light on those shrines? Your mother and I both struggled in our own ways. We missed our families, our homes, our friends. But where we were alike was our determination to make our lives here work.

"Sweetheart, I don't know who that tiara belonged to before it was your mother's. I don't know if your mother thought your father knew about the paste or that he had been the one to switch the stones. But whatever happened, when she came home that day, it was with several thousand dollars and with what we had saved and sold our drawings for, we had enough to buy this building and open our shop. She did good for you. She gave you everything any mother could have."

I nod, not sure I can speak. Knowing that, she reaches out and takes my hand. All this talk about my mother has made us both sad. She insists on making me something to eat, and I accept, not wanting to go downstairs quite yet anyway.

Finally, about a half hour later, I take the letter and the photograph and go back downstairs. I work on the bedroom walls for the next few hours, hoping but not finding another niche. At half past four, my back aching, I pour myself a glass of red wine. I pick up the newest Agatha Christie novel I have yet to start and stick the photo of the three Russian men—one of whom is my father—inside. Book and glass in hand, I go into the living room, where I sit in the chair by the window. It's started snowing again, and as I sip the wine, I stare out into swirling whiteness. It occurs to me I have continued buying my mother's favorite wine. I've never stopped to wonder if there is another I'd like better. I never rebelled against her choices for me, either. As much as I asked her about her refusal to talk about her past, I didn't fight her on it. I should have.

As what is left of the daylight disappears, as the snow continues and darkness falls, the French ormolu clock that my mother rescued from a garbage heap and restored chimes five times. It's the hour when I always feel my mother's presence strongest. She always made tea at five o'clock in the evening. Strong Earl Gray she'd steep to make it as black as she could and serve it in her mismatched Limoges china cups. One might be a rose pattern. Another a spring flower design. Unlike Aunt Lana, there was no samovar, no Russian fancy tea glass holders in our apartment. Her French china was yet one more snub to the past.

"Why did you wipe it all away?" I ask her now, out loud. Calling upon her ghost. Demanding she give me the answers she denied me all my life.

I hear her voice in my head the way I often have since her passing. Her sweet voice answering me. Is it my imagination? My need? An old answer she gave once before, now remembered? Or my mother's spirit so strong it comes and goes at will.

"It hurt too much to hold on," she says.

I nod, open the book, and take out the photo. But I haven't turned on the light to even try and read yet, and it is too dark in the room to make out the men's faces. Rising, I take the photo to the desk in the corner. I turn on the seashell lamp—another throwaway my mother rescued. The 1910 lampshade is constructed of shells fitted together like stained glass. The shells are thin enough to cast a warm yellow glow. Opening the top drawer, I root around for the magnifying glass and then, folding it over the photo, study the three men. Which was my father? Which was Agathon? Which was Dimitry, and what had he done that would make my mother think it was hard for my father to work with him?

Was the man in the center older than the other two? The men on either side of him appeared to be about the same age. I can't guess at their hair type or if it's light or dark with those hats on. And they are too far from the camera for me to make out their individual features. They are all about the same height, the one on the far right a bit taller than the other two.

I'm staring, willing something to stand out. Does one of them look slightly familiar? I focus on him, the man on the left. Yes, he does. Is there some kind of genetic bond that allows me to pick out my father? I smile at the thought. I doubt it's possible. But what do I really know about what's possible?

I've heard my mother speak to me from beyond the grave. I lived in a secret city inhabited by scientists who figured out how to blow up the universe by splitting one tiny single atom. I've read that Einstein and many others believe time is a continuum—that the present, past, and future all exist at once. If that is true, my mother, my father, my grandparents, and I are somehow all connected in this moment.

I return to my seat by the window. I see that my glass is empty and go to the kitchen to pour more wine. I've just topped off my glass when the doorbell rings. Had I left something with Aunt Lana? From the kitchen, I go to the foyer and open the door.

It's not Aunt Lana but a man. A man who I have seen before at my bus stop, at Jules' office, and the skating rink. A man who I am almost certain I have just been staring at in a twenty-five-year-old photograph.

Chapter 24

Sofiya Petrovitch
Petrograd
January 1919

Sofiya walked to the antiques store to bring Carpathian some pastries she'd made two days before. The door was locked, which was normal. But no one answered. After a few minutes of her continually banging on the door, a neighbor across the hall came out.

"They arrested them," the woman said.

"Arrested them?"

"Yes, the police came and arrested them for operating an illegal establishment. They shut it down. Confiscated the stock and hauled the two men off."

"Two men? Are you sure? Both of them?" She was holding her breath, hoping there was a chance the woman hadn't really seen two men taken into custody.

"I'm sorry, but yes, I'm sure."

Sofiya felt faint for the first time in her life. Jail? Carpathian?

"Do you know which jail? When was this? What time?"

The woman only knew what time it had been and nothing else.

Clutching the bag of pastries, Sofiya left. She walked out into the street. The wind had picked up, and snow had started falling and with each step, more of it landed in her hair and on her face.

Which way to go? What police station would they have been taken to? What was she to do? Hurrying to the Hermitage, she found her father in his office and told him what had happened.

"We have to help him," she insisted.

"We can't get involved."

There were four paintings in her father's office that afternoon. All leaning against the wall. They were stunning. By a French painter named George De La Tour. The quality of light he had been able to achieve on a flat surface took Sofiya's breath away.

She stared at the painting of a young Mary Magdalene reading by candlelight, the skin of her hands translucent. What could she say to her father to get him to change his mind?

"Please," she said. "He saved my life when I was being robbed that day. And now he is in prison somewhere. We can't leave him there, we have to help him."

"We cannot get involved, darling. It is far too dangerous. All of our jobs here are tenuous. One bad decision, and we can be ousted. What good would I be to you and your mother going to the store without a ration book?"

Sofiya walked out of his office and to the restoration studio, where the professor was bent over a canvas.

He looked up when she came in and instantly read her face and mood. "What is the matter?"

She relayed the story, this time, tears running down her cheeks.

The professor made tea and as he handed it to her, he said he could help her.

"But I don't want you to put yourself in danger."

"No worries. No danger. There's always someone who will do a little favor in exchange for a valuable painting."

"You'd steal a painting?"

"Now, child, would I do that? Haven't I taken an oath?"

She shook her head. "But then what do you mean?"

"It's time for me to tell you my secret. Come."

He led Sofiya to the end of the large supply closet at the far end of the studio. He opened the door, and she followed him inside. There were shelves on two of the walls. Leaning against the third wall were dozens and dozens of rolls of canvas from different eras that he had collected to match paintings damaged so seriously they needed to be patched. It was the least preferred method to restoring something, but occasionally it was inevitable.

"Help me move these to the other wall," the professor instructed.

They were three-quarters of the way done when Sofiya saw a door that had been concealed by the canvas rolls. Taking his keychain out of his smock pocket, he unlocked the door. "You should know about this anyway in case anything should happen to me."

The professor had to stoop to walk through the door, as did Sofiya.

He turned on the light, and the cavernous storage room

came alive with color. Paintings were lined against every wall. Dozens and dozens of them from every era in every style. Renaissance, baroque, impressionistic, portraits, landscapes, still lifes by so many great painters. They glowed luminous and perfect, a fortune of masterpieces hidden away and locked up.

"Why are these here? Why aren't they hanging on the walls?" she asked.

"These are insurance. I've been working on them for over seventeen years, since the first rumblings of revolution. You only have to read history to know that there are certain currencies that survive any regime. Gems of any kind, be they diamonds or Rubens or Rembrandts, will always have a value."

"You mean you've been stealing paintings for seventeen years?"

He burst out laughing. "Dear Sofiya, look at them. Closely."

She examined first one and then the next. She didn't know what she was looking for, but whatever it was, she didn't see it. They were simply one amazing painting after another, hidden away in a cubby hole deep inside the Hermitage.

"I give up, Professor. What am I looking for?"

"They are all copies."

"No!" She started around the room again, looking at each even more closely, carefully, trying to find just one clue that these were not originals.

"Are you sure?"

"Sure? Yes, I painted them. Each one has a tiny giveaway. Let me show you."

He pulled out a Rembrandt portrait of a very old woman, turned it upside down, and pointed to the flat edge of the stretcher. "On the bottom of each canvas you'll find a little green bit of color that appears to be a smear but if you study it under a magnifying glass, you'll see the abstracted form of a falcon."

She understood the reference immediately—it was a pictorial version of his name, a secret signature of sorts.

"These are perfect."

"To be a restorer means to excel at copying another artist's style, does it not?"

"Yes but…why?"

"Well, I can't sell one of my own paintings and make enough money for a loaf of bread. That's not my talent. This is."

"But the oath?"

At the end of the first year of Sofiya's apprenticeship, the professor had held a small graduation ceremony. Just the two of them, two shot glasses, and a bottle of vodka.

"You've completed a very hard year. Now it will get harder, but I am sure you are up to the task," he had said. "To your future." He held up his glass. She clinked hers to his, and they drank.

"Now you have to take an oath," he'd said.

"Really?"

"Yes. Please, repeat this after me. 'I solemnly swear never to use my talent to impersonate another artist for personal gain.'"

She was confused. "But our work is to do just that and get paid for it."

"We repair. We don't pretend. You must promise never to create fake masterpieces in order to sell them and fill your own pockets."

But hadn't the professor done just that? Wasn't she looking at proof that he'd broken the oath he'd had her take?

"All through the tsar's reign, there have been rumblings of the coming revolution. You know this. Your father and I have been discussing it at your family's dinner table for years. Many people closed their eyes and ears and pretended that there would never come a day of reckoning. But you can't starve people and treat them badly and leave them uneducated and not expect someone to come along and organize the peasants into revolt. The greatest threat to any regime is the uneducated poor in search of a crust of bread. One only has to look back at France not a little more than a hundred years ago to see the ramifications of the ruling class ignoring the signs. As I am sorry to say our tsar did. But you didn't ask for a history lesson. I didn't have gold coins to hide away like the tsar did, or diamonds to sew into my hems and corsets like the tsarina and her daughters did. What I have is a talent to mimic great painters. So this is my bank account. I decided that it would not be breaking my oath to scam the scammers. To lie to the liars. To cheat the cheaters. None of these things are a crime. It is perfectly all right to sell one of these on the black market to some fool who is greedy and corrupt in order to put food on my children's table or to get your Carpathian out of jail. So my dear Sofiya, which one should we choose?"

She was overcome with gratitude. She took her mentor's hand and kissed his liver-spotted skin. He smelled of linseed oil and turpentine and acetone, and she wondered if the tears that fell from her eyes diluted the scent at all. And then a wave of fear hit.

"You can't…what if you get caught? I could never survive knowing that you'd—"

The professor interrupted her with a laugh. "Caught? By whom? I'm not selling to the Louvre, child, but to some corrupt official in the provisional government who is trying to prove he has class. It's not saints who removed the imperial family. Despite what they claim, you know these men are not fairly distributing the wealth they are confiscating. They say cream rises to the top? Shit does too. Forgive me, I shouldn't speak so, but they infuriate me with their lofty words and filthy deeds."

He threw his hands up in the air. "Enough philosophy, Sofiya. Pick a painting."

Together they looked through the canvases. There were Rubens and Rembrandts and Canalettos. There were Dutch still lifes and landscapes. There were copies of Fragonard's romantic idylls. In the end, she chose a Delacroix of a white horse frightened by a storm. The horse was on its hind legs, its head at an awkward angle, its forelegs high in the air with a gray swirling sky over an angry sea in the background. A painting of conflict and trouble. It seemed fitting.

"I want you to come with me," the professor said. "See how it is done. If anything happens to me, the stockroom is yours. If nothing happens to me but you need more help, you can come to me anytime and take whatever you need. At the same time, I want you to start on a painting yourself so that you have your own nest egg if you ever need it."

The professor took the Delacroix off the stretcher and rolled it up. Back in the main part of the studio he put the roll against his back and tied it to his body with a cord. Then he put his coat on over it.

"Why are you hiding it?" she asked.

"Questions are to be avoided whenever one is able. If I just walked out with it, a guard doing his duty might very well stop me and ask why I was removing a painting from the Hermitage. Now what would I say? Where would I need to take it? What would a painting need that we cannot do for it in the most well respected and specialized restoration workshop in all of Russia? So I would have to lie. And say it wasn't a painting that belonged to the Hermitage but a copy a student of mine had dropped off for a critique. And then the guard would ask to see it and what if he thought it was too good? What if he called over another guard? What if he called your father out of his office and he thought it was an original and I would have to tell him? He's scared of the Bolsheviks. If he thought I was stealing from them, it would weigh on him. He wouldn't want to turn me in, but he'd be afraid not to. And on and on and on. So do you see? It's much easier to just roll up a canvas and keep it under my coat. That's why none of the paintings in the storeroom are very big. I'm not sure you noticed. But there's nothing that would be difficult to transport."

Once outside, they walked to the train station. Sofiya had not been to the black market herself. She knew many people who sold their goods there in order to get extra flour or meat or soap or tea… But since her father's job was a cultural necessity and her mother was being a good proletariat and teaching art at the university, along with Sofiya's rations they all had enough to get by. Certainly, there was no abundance, but neither were they suffering. The uprisings had been going on for over a year by then. Most people had lost at least ten percent of their weight if not more. Sofiya had friends from secondary school who had resisted the Bolsheviks and fought back. Some had been imprisoned. Others had lost their jobs and were dying of starvation or typhoid. Her dear friend Grand Duchess Olga and her sisters and parents and brothers, her other family who she would never see again, had been hungry in their exile. For what seemed like the millionth time, Sofiya wondered where they were now. No one had any idea where the tsarina and the duchesses had been taken after the tsar had been shot. The one tutor who had gone with them into exile had been the last one to see them. He had come to dinner upon his return to Petrograd and told Sofiya and her parents that he was afraid they, along with the tsarevich, had been killed as well. Why wouldn't the monsters kill them? What use were they to anyone anymore?

Sofiya and Professor Sokolov walked through the black market. She was surprised at all the activity going on out in the open, given that it was all illegal. She saw a man selling a chandelier, silver candlesticks, several ball gowns, and pairs of shoes. A woman had a makeshift table set up with bottles of perfume and feathers. Some sold furniture fine chairs and tables. Others offered household goods: samovars, linens, and rugs. One could decorate a palace with all that was on offer, Sofiya considered with astonishment.

As they walked through the crowd, she overheard some of the transactions.

"They are selling their things for nothing," Sofiya said to him. "A man just sold a gold pocket watch for the price of a pound of flour."

"Yes, yes, that is what we have been reduced to. There is no luxury anymore in Russia. There is only survival. For us all."

They went down an alley. There was less activity now. The atmosphere was different. Sofiya felt a shiver of fear as she followed the professor into a building, through an entryway and up a flight of steps.

He knocked on a door which was opened after a moment by a middle-aged man who had dark eyes and dirty hair and who smelled of onions.

"So the collector is back to see me." The man clapped his hands. "It has been a while."

The professor nodded. "I've been lucky that I haven't

had to visit, haven't I?"

The man laughed. One of his front teeth was missing.

"But here you are. I told you you'd be back."

"Well, I wanted to introduce you to my niece. In case she ever has to visit you, I wanted you to know her. I might have to send her without me at some point. If it is necessary."

The man nodded, turned and looked Sofiya over, much like he would if he was inspecting a canvas.

"Pleased to make your acquaintance. You may call me Ivan."

She offered her hand. The professor had warned her before not to give her real name. "Natasha," she said.

"Now," the man said to the professor, "was the introduction the only reason for your visit?"

"Not at all," the professor said as he unbuttoned his overcoat. Pulling out the painting, he unrolled it. "Here we have a Delacroix."

Ivan took the canvas and laid it out on a table. He grabbed a magnifying glass and inspected the painting's surface. He spent quite a while doing that. Then he turned it over. Sofiya was struck with the gentle care that this gruff and dirty man used in examining the artwork.

"This is a fine, fine painting. How much are you hoping to get?"

"Enough to bribe a guard to let a man out of prison."

"I don't think that will be a problem at all. French paintings are especially easy to move. How about I give you enough rubles for that now. And then split whatever I get over that with you 60/40."

"With you getting the larger share as usual," the professor said.

"With me taking the lion's share of the danger as well."

"What of the danger I put myself in coming here?"

"There is danger everywhere. No matter what I still am in more danger than you. Do you want your money or not?"

"I do," the professor said.

Sofiya felt something inside of her give. The professor was going through all this to help her. Had come to this filthy place and was dealing with this despicable man to help her.

"How can I ever repay you?" she asked once they were on the street and heading back down the alley.

"There is nothing to repay. What have I done? You saw, I have dozens of these. This is only the second one I have had to sell. I'll never use them up. I'm not even doing you a favor. You are so miserable it is affecting your work, and that affects my studio. And then I am unhappy. So consider this a totally selfish act."

She smiled and took his arm in hers, and they walked back to the museum, the professor asking her questions about Carpathian and telling her how he was going to try and buy her lover's way out of prison.

Chapter 25

Isobelle Moon
New York City
December 1948

My mother and I never had a telepathic bond when she was alive. I never thought about her and had the phone ring at exactly that minute with her on the other end. She never called me when I didn't feel well, saying she had sensed I was sick. She didn't wait for me to come home, worried because she'd had a premonition that something bad had happened to me at school.

But several times since her death, I swore I heard her giving me advice or making suggestions. And since I've returned from Washington D.C., I've had at least three dreams in which she's trying to get to me, to tell me something that's important, but I wake up before hearing it.

That, plus all the recent coincidences, have unnerved me. I am hard-pressed to explain any of this. Especially this latest occurrence.

"I'm sorry, I don't understand," I say.

"You don't speak Russian?" he asks in accented English.

The question about my linguistic skills centers me in the reality of the moment. I shake my head and answer. "No. I don't. My mother never spoke Russian to me."

I still haven't opened the door all the way. I'm nervous. I don't know who this man is exactly. There are too many disparate pieces. He was at the bus stop...at the skating rink...he visited Mr. Reed and then Jules looking for the tiara...he was in an old photo my mother hid away.

"Ah, I see. I am so sorry. And sorry if I've frightened you."

"Yes?" I say, continuing to keep the door partially closed.

"Please let me introduce myself. My name is Sergei Zorin," he says and waits expectantly in a way that suggests I will react.

"Yes, Mr. Zorin, what is it you want?"

"You don't know who I am?"

"I'm not sure, no. I know you are acquainted with my friend, Jules Reed. And I believe I've seen you in an old photograph but——"

"A photo from Russia?" he asks excitedly.

"Yes. My mother kept a photo with three men in it, and you do look like one of them, but none of them were named Sergei. There was my father, Carpathian, a man named Dimitry, and another named Agathon, who I believe was Agathon Fabergé."

"Was it taken on a Moscow street?"

I nod.

"I am in that photo. It's me with Dimitry and Agathon. I am your father," he says.

I feel like I'm stumbling, except I'm not moving.

"My father?"

"Yes, your father," he says gently.

I have the absurd desire to laugh at the impossibility of what he is suggesting. I know what happened to my father and explain it to the man standing on the welcome mat in our hallway.

"That's not possible. My father's name was Carpathian. And he died in prison in 1922." I feel a sudden and overwhelming sadness. My whole life I've wished that wasn't what happened. Except it had. "So I'm sorry, but I can't be your daughter."

"Carpathian, yes, of course. I see the problem." He smiles broadly, and it confuses me. "Isobelle," he continues, "that name, Carpathian, it was your mother's name for me."

"What do you mean?"

"Can I come in?" he asks.

Even though he clearly knows things about me and my mother that a stranger couldn't know, it seems like such a big decision to let him past the door. While I am still deliberating, he continues speaking.

"I understand how confusing this must be. Let me try to explain. Isobelle, your mother made up a name for me. Carpathian wasn't my birth name. Didn't she ever tell you that?"

"No, she only said your name was Carpathian and that our last name was a complicated Russian name she shortened to Moon."

He shakes his head.

"Zorin is not so complicated. Sergei Zorin. That's my

name. That's your father's name."

"She would have told me if my father had another name."

"She *should* have told you."

I suddenly feel unmoored.

"Why wouldn't my mother tell me the truth?"

He looks pained. As if he too is struggling for an answer.

Waiting for his response, I feel myself hoping that he will have one that will make sense of everything.

"I don't know why. What *did* she tell you about me?"

"That you'd been hurt and were in the hospital where she was a nurse. That you were a jeweler. How much she loved you."

He's looking at my hand, and I follow his glance. My fingers are white with the sustained strain of holding on to the door. I relax my grip.

"You're in shock," he says. "I'm sorry. You should sit down. Let me come in. I can get you some water if you tell me where the kitchen is."

"Yes, all right…" I stammer and hold the door open for him. I watch this man walk over the threshold. I watch him walk into the foyer and then into the living room. He is in the apartment where my mother and I lived for over twenty years. In the apartment where I questioned her relentlessly about the man who was my father, who she missed so much she could barely speak of him for a few minutes without emotions overwhelming her. I can't stop staring at him, at his physical characteristics: the shape of his nose, his brow, the color of his eyes. Do I recognize him? Or just think I do from having looked at the old photograph. If he is my father shouldn't I feel our connection?

"Let me take your coat and hat," I say, the manners my

mother drummed into me taking over despite my dazed state.

He shrugs out of the coat, unwraps the scarf from around his neck, takes off his hat, and then hands me all three items. I hang them up on the wrought iron hall tree, where I have been hanging my own coat, hat, and scarf since I can remember. Where my mother hung hers. I stare at the clothing thinking that if this man is really my father, his outer garments are here in our apartment...that *he* is here in our apartment where he existed as a memory only.

"Please, have a seat." I'm speaking the right words but not sure how I am managing to form them. I know I am staring at him again, trying to understand what seems impossible. And then by rote, without having to even think about it, I offer him refreshments. Tea, coffee? I remember I was drinking wine when the doorbell rang and offer that as well.

"I think if you have brandy, we could probably both use some."

I am thankful for the time it takes for me to remove crystal snifters from the cabinet, unscrew the brandy bottle, and pour out the amber liquid.

I walk back over to the couch, where he's taken a seat. I hand him one of the snifters. He smiles at me as he takes the proffered glass, and for a moment I revel in that smile and let it settle down on me like an embrace.

I sit opposite him in the chair that is catty-corner to the sofa and think that I might be sitting here with a man I never allowed myself to dream I would ever meet.

"Let me try to make sense of this for you. You are Sofiya Petrovitch's daughter, yes?"

I remember hearing that name before. Hadn't Alford Reed told me that the man looking for the owner of the tiara had said her name was Petrovitch?

"Our name was Moon."

"And before that, it was Petrovitch."

"But you said your name was Zorin. Wouldn't that be my mother's last name?"

"Actually no, we never married. But I am your father."

"Well then there is a mistake. My parents were married. My mother wore a wedding ring. I have it, I can show you—" I start to get up, but Sergei Zorin puts his hand out.

"No, that's all right, I believe you, and I can explain that too. But first," he says and raises his glass, "a toast, to finding my daughter at last." His voice breaks a little, and he looks away for a second as if overwhelmed by the emotion of the moment.

Before I can move my glass to meet his, he leans forward and clinks my glass with his. Too hard. The sound is jarring. I can't stop studying his face. His features are strong. His nose is prominent, his jaw square. He has a beard that is the same dark brown color as his hair, which is cropped short. He's not an elegant man but a powerful one. He doesn't look like my imaginary father. The one who has been a phantom in my daydreams for as long as I can remember. Yes, he has that same typical Russian coloring I have. But he's not distinctive-looking, and that's how my mother had always described him. Not just handsome but distinctive. And his eyes…my mother always said she saw him in my eyes…that we both had the same eyes…the eyes of a dreamer. Yes, the shade of blue is right, but do I recognize myself in this man's eyes?

"I've been trying to find you and your mother for years," the man says. He's still *the man*—I can't allow myself to think of him as my father yet. He's the man from the street still. The man from Jules' office.

"How did you…?" I break off. "I don't even know what I want to ask first."

"I can understand that. Take another sip of the brandy. It's very restorative. Agathon always had a bottle of brandy on hand even during those years when a pound of potato flour was more precious than gold."

Agathon, I remember that name. From the photo. I take a sip of the drink and notice my hand is shaking.

"Before I tell you any more, I want to say that I am more grateful than I can describe to finally be here with you. I had begun to fear I'd never find you. So many times, I almost gave up. But now here we are, and my heart is bursting." He puts his hand on his chest and smiles at me so tenderly that I suddenly worry about how he will feel if I'm not his daughter but the child of another couple.

He takes another sip of his brandy and looks around the room. Noticing the dozens of framed pictures on the piano, he stands, goes over to them, and inspects them. Immediately, he picks up one of my mother from about five years ago. He holds it gingerly, as if he might bruise it. "Yes, Sofiya Petrovitch…your mother was so lovely."

He recognized her right away. He called her by the other name. Is it possible after all? Sofiya Petrovitch—that was my mother's name before she became Sophia Moon?

He replaces the frame on the piano top and picks up another then says, "Are there no pictures from Russia other than this one when she was a child? Or are there more she kept put away?" He is holding the picture of my grandparents and my mother when she was about ten years old, all three of them bundled up and in a troika, smiling at the photographer.

"There are others from when she was a child in an album."

"But none of us?" He sounds both surprised and disappointed. "None of your mother and me together?"

I shake my head.

"She never showed you a photo of your father?"

"No. None. She said that during the revolution it wasn't so easy to get ahold of film…" And then I remember. "There was just the one I mentioned before, the one I just found…"

I walk over to the desk, tripping on the chair leg beside it.

"Be careful," he calls out with real concern and worry.

In all the years of growing up, my mother had told me to be careful thousands of times. Hearing this man say it with so much emotion unsettles me. Sitting at the desk, I try to catch my breath. My heart is racing due to the almost mishap. No, that's not the only reason. I simply do not know how to process anything that is happening.

I pick up the photo I'd found earlier. Take a breath. I stand and walk over to where Sergei Zorin is at the piano and hand it to him.

"My mother had this hidden way."

He examines the photo. "Such a long time ago this was." He shakes his head in disbelief. "No other photos but this." He sounds so sad.

He leans the photo against the edge of a bronze bust of Beethoven and continues to peruse the other framed images. Leaning in, he examines a silver-framed photo of my mother and me seated at the table one Easter Sunday when I was about six. Both of us wearing Easter bonnets.

He looks back at me, smiling. "You both look so happy. Where is this one taken?"

"Every year, my mother, my Aunt Lana, Uncle Paul, their son, and I would all dress up and walk up Fifth Avenue in the parade and afterwards go to the Waldorf Astoria for lunch."

"I'm attempting to learn about your whole life in five minutes," he says as he picks up another photo, this one of my mother and me when I was about eleven, taken at Jones Beach on a hot summer day. My mother is wearing a sundress and a big floppy hat. I'm in a bathing suit.

"Your mother was a wonderful woman," he says wistfully.

"Yes."

"You must miss her terribly."

I nod. Swallow. Try to think of what to say. Do I ask him if he misses her? Did he find someone else? Does he have other children? I'm flooded with questions, but I don't ask a single one of them.

"Missing is one of the true tragedies in life," he says. "That ache that nothing soothes. I thought time would soften it. It's supposed to, isn't it? But all these years later, I still long for what I had. What we all had. What is no more."

He points to a photo of me in a school play. "How old were you here?"

"About eight."

He nods. "How much time I've lost." He sighs.

Now he's looking at a shot of me in cap and gown at my graduation from Cooper Union, then one of my mother and Aunt Lana in front of the shop, then one of my mother and me riding horses in Central Park when I was fourteen.

I'm staring at a stranger who says he is my father, standing here in our home, looking at our photos. I'm trying to feel something other than shock and confusion. Maybe if my mother was here, if they were standing together, if she was smiling at him, or crying with joy to be with him again...if there was a single memory I could connect to, it would be easier. But there isn't.

"We thought you had died," I say again, not realizing until the words are out of my mouth that I am repeating myself.

"So many of us did die. The prisons in Siberia were..." He stops. Shakes his head. "There's time another day for the details of that hell. They were terrible years, that's all I want to say about them now. But after six years in that frozen tundra, I was finally able to escape and managed to get to Finland. Fabergé had originally emigrated there. He had died by the time I arrived, but two jewelers from the workshop had followed him and set up shop, and they helped me. I was ill for a long time. But once I was strong enough, I began searching for you and your mother. I wrote letters to people we had known in Petrograd. Either they said they didn't know anything other than that she had left but they didn't know where she'd gone, or I didn't get any response at all. So many years had passed. Many of the people I'd once known had died. Or left. Since your mother was a world-class restorer for the Hermitage, I assumed that she would have settled somewhere she could get work at another museum. So I started contacting museums all over the world. No one had ever heard of her. Next, I checked auction houses and private collectors. I contacted art schools that taught restoration. All to no avail."

"She went to work for herself. She and Aunt Lana opened a shop."

He nods. "And not as Sofiya Petrovitch, making the search all the more difficult."

"So then you decided to search for her via the tiara?"

"Yes. There was always the chance that she might need to sell it in order to make a new start. The search for the tiara was more complicated than writing to museums and auction houses and asking if they knew Sofiya Petrovitch. I had to go in person for this mission. I started traveling to all the major cities with large Russian emigre populations and visiting the important jewelers there, asking if they'd seen her or the piece. I went to London and Paris and Madrid and Geneva. I knew your mother would be smart enough to take it to someone who would understand its value, so I didn't waste my time with pawn shops. I came up empty at every turn. Until I got to New York and after meeting with a dozen jewelers found Mr. Reed. At first, he acted as if he had no idea what I was talking about. But something in his demeanor suggested he'd at least seen the tiara. I threw myself on his mercy, telling him about my trials and years in prison and begging him to tell me what he knew."

"But he wouldn't?"

"Not then."

I remember what Jules had mentioned, about a break-in, and want to ask if in fact Sergei Zorin had been the one to bribe the cleaning crew so he could check the files, but I can't bring myself to. If he's my father, my dead father brought back to life as if by magic, I don't want him to be the man behind that nefarious effort.

"Not then," I repeat. "But when *I* brought him the tiara a few weeks ago, he did contact you and told you that he had seen it again?"

"Yes. And I went to see him. But there was a mix-up. It seems the message he left for me was not recorded properly, and he wasn't in fact at his place of work. I met with his grandson."

"Yes, I saw you there."

"You did?"

"Through the window. I actually work across the street from Jules. I saw you in his office. I'd seen you at the bus station too. I was actually frightened by the coincidence. I thought you were following me."

"Well, I was, but I didn't mean to frighten you. I just didn't know how to do this…" He lifts his hands and lets them fall back to his side. I look at them. My mother had told me about how talented my father was. About the enamel eggs he'd made for her. About how graceful and beautiful his hands were. Were this man's hands graceful? I decide that perhaps they are, and that reassures me.

He continues explaining: "I wanted to approach you without scaring you, which I have gone and done anyway."

I take a sip of my brandy. The burn is good. I take another sip. This is real, this stinging in my throat. I watch Sergei Zorin and realize I am starting to believe that he is not a stranger but is, in fact, my father. And that fact astounds me. I'm swirling in a vortex of emotions all powerful, all overwhelming. We are sitting across the coffee table from each other. Separated by more than the glass. There is an ocean of memory, of experiences, of lives lived and losses endured, and moments and celebrations and anniversaries not shared. How does he take his tea? And does he like to read? What music does he like? What does he think is funny? Does he like his steak rare or well done? Does he enjoy opera? Did he ice skate as well as my mother did?

"Thank goodness for the tiara," he says. "Or I wouldn't have found you at all."

"I didn't even know it existed until this past Thanksgiving."

"Your mother didn't tell you about it?"

"No. Not a word. I found it while I was… I am in the process of doing some renovations."

"You, yourself?" he asks.

"Yes. I'm an architect."

"That is amazing. A real accomplishment."

His praise is so welcome. My father is proud of me, I think.

"I'd like to see some of your work," he adds.

"I'd love to show it to you. Mostly it's just drawings. I haven't done any projects on my own."

He nods. "You will. You come from a long line of talented men and women. And you know what else I'd like to see? The tiara," he says. "It once brought your mother back to me and now it has brought me to you."

"All that's left of it is its frame. She sold the stones. For very little, actually. The diamonds were small. The sapphires weren't real. But you must have known that."

He frowns. "No. The sapphires were real. They were, in fact, worth a fortune."

"Maybe at one point there were real sapphires in it, but what my mother took to Mr. Reed was a silver over gold tiara with about three thousand dollars' worth of diamonds and eight blue glass simulated sapphires. It's what the receipt says as well."

"And you have it?"

"The receipt?"

"No, the tiara."

"Actually, I don't. Jules... Mr. Reed's grandson has it in his vault. I really need to pick it up from him."

He puts his glass to his lips and drains what is left of the brandy. "Yes, you probably should."

Sometimes he shows his emotions. Others, like now, he's somewhat inscrutable. I wonder if prison does that to you. If you need to hide your emotions there. Does that make being incarcerated easier? I have only met one other person who was imprisoned—Mr. Reed—but his situation seems as far as one could be from a Bolshevik-run institution in Siberia.

"Where do you live?" I ask. Then wonder why I'm asking. There are a million things about him I don't know. Why do I care where he lives?

"Still in Finland. I am staying with friends in Brooklyn now."

I'm staring at his face. Watching him form words, answer questions that don't matter while I wait to feel that ineffable something that connects us, that links me to him, him to my mother other than words.

"And the people in the picture—Dimitry and Agathon—were they your friends as well?"

"The man in the center is Agathon Fabergé. I worked for him. And the other man, Dimitry Zorin, was my cousin and one of my closest friends. He worked for Agathon as well. Before the revolution, we both worked for Carl Fabergé, Agathon's father. Dimitry was Henrik's assistant when the tiara was made, before it became your mother's."

"What happened to Dimitry?"

"After we were arrested in 1922, we were sent to different prisons. I later found out he didn't survive." He raises his hands again in a gesture that is becoming familiar to me. When he is overcome with a memory, he dismisses it this way.

"My mother had hidden this photo of you. Can you think of a reason she wouldn't have wanted me to see it?"

"No. But you said she didn't like to talk much about the past?"

"She said if she didn't keep the past buried, the memories would bury her alive. As if remembering would be a burden, and she wasn't strong enough to bear its weight."

"Bury the memories or become one of the walking dead," he says, shaking his head mournfully. "Those were the choices we were given. Your mother had you to live for. To smile for. To embrace the present for."

"And you?" I ask.

"I had a dream."

I wonder if this is what I've been waiting for, if it's the dream that connects us—mine for a father and his for a daughter.

Chapter 26

Sofiya Petrovitch
Petrograd
September 1920

Despite Sofiya's overly generous bribes to prison officials, it appeared her efforts to buy Carpathian's release had failed. Spring ended, summer passed, and fall settled on Petrograd with an early frost in mid-September.

On September 19, she finished late at the Hermitage and trudged home, tired, dirty, and discouraged. The talk was all about the coming winter and the fear that the food and clothing and sundry shortages would only get worse.

She stopped at the food store on the way home—her mother had asked her to pick up the flour and meat for the week, but the flour was moldy, and the meat was gray gristle.

She should have stopped in early that morning, but instead she'd gone to Comrade Vladimir Rostocovitz's office to see if he had any information at all about Carpathian's release. He kept her waiting, as usual. And then also as usual, took the envelope she handed over. When she told him that she had no more funds, that this was the last of it, he ushered her out without any words of hope.

Twilight had fallen. Sofiya walked slowly. The violet and gray sky reminded her of a painting by El Greco that hung in the museum. Thinking about art was sometimes the only thing that kept her sane. As she rounded the corner of the block where she lived, she noticed a man leaning against her building, smoking a cigarette. He was tall and skinny— everyone was by now. Normally she would pick up her pace, not make contact, and pass him by as quickly as she could. One never knew who was simply loitering, or who was waiting for a target to rip off.

But she couldn't pass him by. He was too close to the front door. Key in hand, she approached cautiously, annoyed that she was going to have to ask him to move. She was about thirty steps away when he looked up at the sky and blew out smoke from his cigarette.

Was it possible? She had never given up hope, but at the same time she had stopped expecting that he would ever return.

She ran.

He heard her footsteps and turned to her.

Sofiya flew into Carpathian's arms, and he pulled her as close to him as he could. Squeezing her so hard she thought he was going to bruise her. But she didn't care.

For a few minutes, they said nothing. Just stood on the street, holding on to each other.

"Come upstairs," she finally said.

"I thought you'd never ask," he laughed. To hear him tease her was such a relief after so long, she started to cry. He pulled her to him again and then arm in arm they went inside.

Upstairs, she dropped her parcels and brought him into the sitting room. Her parents weren't home yet. She took out a bottle of vodka and two glasses and put them in front of him.

"Can you put on some music?" he asked. "I haven't heard any music for so long."

"Any preference?" she asked.

"Yes, *Pictures at an Exhibition*, please. I would lie in bed—if you could call it that—at night and play it in my head and make up paintings for each of the sections. Sometimes a phrase would elude me, and I'd try and try to hear it. I would want to scream for the frustration of not being able to. I'd imagine we were at the museum, together you and I, walking down the grand halls and examining the paintings. And in my mind, I'd paint them."

She put on the recording and sat beside him on the settee. He put his arm around her and pulled her so that her head was on his shoulder. He reached out and touched her hair, tentatively at first.

"This is real, isn't it, my little Scheherazade? I imagined it so many times."

"I thought I'd never see you again."

"Never ever will I let that happen. I will always find you. I promise."

She wished she could believe him. In their terrible crazy world she knew he couldn't make promises like that. All they could do was try to keep hold of each other, that was all.

"When did you get out?"

"Five days ago. I wanted to come sooner, but I was too

weak. And too dirty."

She wanted to chide him, but she knew him well enough to know he couldn't have let her see him like that. For a moment she thought about Comrade Vladimir Rostocovitz taking her money even though he knew Carpathian had been released. Well, what did it matter in the end? Let him have it.

"Where are you staying?" she asked.

"Agathon has moved in with his children's nurse, Maria Borzhova. And I have been staying there. Her daughter was living with her, but she got married, and the authorities have not yet realized there is an empty room."

"You mean no one has reported her yet?"

"Well, to be precise, the landlord who would have reported her was paid off. Fabergé made sure of that."

"I wish you could move in here with us. Maybe if I ask my father—"

"Don't stir that hornet's nest again. Your father is protecting you and your mother. He works for the government. I am considered an ex-convict now as well as a radical speculator. It's a nice room at Maria Borzhova's apartment. And she's a warm, motherly woman. You can come and be with me there. Oh, how I have missed you."

He kissed her.

"What is wrong?" he asked.

She shook her head.

"Something is wrong, I can tell."

"I don't know. It was so difficult not knowing what was happening to you. Not knowing if you were going to be all right. And now you're back as if nothing happened. Living with Agathon. He's the reason you went to prison. If you are going to work with him again…"

The very last thing she'd imagined upon their reunion was arguing.

"What are you suggesting I do?"

"Anything else."

Carpathian shook his head. "There is more to this than you know."

"Then tell me."

"We have a plan. An escape plan. It will take a while but…"

"It's a dream. You can't escape. You can only apply for a visa. To leave another way but the legal way is to risk being killed, you know that."

"They will never allow me to leave. They will never allow Agathon to leave. Not unless we can bribe them."

"And that is what you are planning?"

"There are ways to get a large sum, yes…"

Sofiya pushed him away and stood.

"So you are going back to criminal activity?"

Part of her was proud that he was not broken like so many men and women were. She wanted him to fight. To hold on to what he believed. But she was more afraid than she was proud. She wanted him with her more than she wanted him to remain an idealist.

She took his hands. "Please, don't. My father and I have talked about this, that when you got out of prison. he would help you apply for a job at the museum and—"

"I appreciate it, Sofiya. But I want to give you more than a ration card. I want to take you out of Russia. To London, where we can start over. I know jewelers there who will hire me, and we can live there well."

She sighed. "No more dreams, Carpathian. No more dreams." She paced. She wanted to go to him and hold him. And at the same time, she wanted to throw him out because she knew with everything in her being that if he went back to the life he had been living before, there would be no good end. No one outsmarted the Cheka. The secret police were everywhere, and no one escaped them for long. If he was arrested again it would be the end. You didn't get a second chance. You were sent to Siberia, and so few ever returned from that frozen tundra.

"We can't live without dreams," he said.

"I'm not. I have my dream. To sit with you in the Winter Palace garden and smell the wisteria. To find enough rations at the cooperative to make you a cake. To hold your hand and skate on the Neva when it freezes."

He shook his head at that. "I'm afraid that might be beyond me."

"I can give that one up." She tried to laugh, but it sounded more like a sob. "I can live with the simplest of dreams coming true. To look at the moon with you next to me…instead of so far away. Did you look at the moon when you were in prison?"

"I suppose so, why?"

"While you were gone, I went up to the roof every night before I went to sleep and looked up at the moon and imagined you were looking at the moon as well. The same moon, no matter where we were, no matter how far apart. I would imagine that my thoughts were rising up to the moon and that yours were there too and we were together in that way. For a few moments every night. Looking up at the moon."

"My little romantic. I love you for that. But not for the size of your dreams."

"Having any bigger dreams is foolish now. Why open the door to disappointment? Why invite dissatisfaction? If you shrink your world down to elements you have some control over, if you want things that are possible, you don't get destroyed."

"I can't bear to see you like this."

"Like what?"

"You're giving up."

"I am being realistic."

"Oh no, Sofiya. I won't let you do that."

And despite her protests and pleas, he explained why she wouldn't have to.

As it turned out, it wasn't the money Sofiya had used to bribe Comrade Vladimir Rostocovitz that had procured Carpathian's release from prison.

Fabergé had also been arrested May 30th, 1919. While still in prison, in August of 1920, he negotiated a deal with the provisional government. A deal that would change everything for all of them.

Lenin had created *The State Administration for the Formation of the State Fund of Precious Metals and Precious Stones of the Russian Federation.* More conveniently known as the *GoKhran.* Run by the Ministry of Finance in Moscow, its job was the storage, dispensing and use of precious metals and precious stones. Its goal was to sell Russia's treasures abroad in order to pay for the farming machinery and other vital products that the starving country desperately needed.

The job of cataloging and appraising the jewels was overseen by Alexander Yevgenyevich Fersman, a prominent geochemist and mineralogist, and a member of the Soviet Academy of Sciences.

Almost immediately Fersman noticed that there was major theft occurring from within. The employees were stealing from the organization. In total, more than two dozen people were sentenced to death and another thirty-five were sent to prison.

This created a dearth of appraisers in the department. And finding new ones proved more difficult than Fersman could have imagined. With a reputation for executing and imprisoning its employees, no one wanted to work for GoKhran.

No one, that is, but people who needed something in return. Fersman knew Agathon Fabergé. He was, after all, the son of Carl Fabergé and one of the five best trained gemologists in Petrograd, perhaps in Russia. Fersman went to visit him in prison and offered him a deal. If Fabergé agreed to help him assess and catalog the imperial jewels, he would be given his six-room apartment back with its antique furniture, gem and stamp collections intact. Fabergé said he couldn't do the job alone and insisted on having his two assistants—also imprisoned—released as well. Fabergé also managed to get a two-hundred-ruble salary for himself, and fifty each for his two assistants.

Carpathian was finally released in April, 1921. All the work needed to be finished by January 1, 1922.

"I'll have to spend some months in Moscow, but I will be free. Able to see you. And working with a man I trust," Carpathian explained.

Sofiya was mollified. Carpathian would be working for the government. He would be safe. They spent as much time as they could for the next few weeks, and then Carpathian moved to Moscow.

In his first letter, delivered by one of Fabergé's cousins who was able to go back and forth between Moscow and Petrograd since he was also working for Fersman, Carpathian told her all about their lodgings at the National Hotel across from the Kremlin, where they were treated extremely well. He marveled at his luck, going from prison to a luxury hotel. But more than that, he was happy to be back in his milieu, handling precious gems and jewelry. He described his first day to her.

We arrived at the armory building and were shown to a large office the three of us will share. Trunks lined the wall. Soldiers with rifles guarded the trunks. Dimitry and I watched Agathon open the first one. We all stared at the glitter and shine. And then Agathon took out a sceptre. And then a necklace. And then a crown.

We were staring at the Romanov coronation jewels.

Sofiya, we have all worked with jewelry all of our lives, but here at our feet was all of the magnificence of centuries of royal jewels. And that was just one trunk! Over the next months, our job will be to evaluate, catalog, repair and put prices on these priceless treasures that once belonged to our dead tsar and his missing family and a government that no longer exists.

She cried reading Carpathian's letter describing this moment. She missed Olga and wished so desperately to know what had happened to her. Everyone whispered the family was dead, but she didn't want to believe it. No one knew for sure, she told herself, and held on to that shred of hope.

Twice Sofiya tried to go and visit Carpathian. The train ride between Moscow and Petrograd took over six hours if it ran smoothly. Which it almost never did. They'd had an efficient railway system before 1917, but ever since, like everything else, there was nothing you could count on.

Both times she'd tried, ticket in hand, she'd waited for the train at the station for an entire day. Every time she asked the station master when it was expected he would shrug. The same way the shopkeepers shrugged when you asked when they would have millet without mold. Or butter again. Or if they had any rye flour. The same way you saw people in the street shrug when you asked how they were, or if they had coal or if spring would come.

Each winter from 1918 to when Sofiya finally left Russia in 1922, she always doubted that spring would actually arrive. It was hard to believe in nature when nothing else was dependable. When neighbors stole from neighbors, fathers from sons, sons from mothers. When thugs pulled packages from the hands of people in the streets.

She finally managed to make it to Moscow on her third try.

Staying in the hotel with Carpathian was like being on a honeymoon. He had requested a day off—the most they would give him—but they wrung every second out of their time together. She had arrived in the afternoon. Carpathian was still at the armory but had written her and told her to get a sledge at the station to take her to the hotel and that he would leave a note with the manager to let her up to his room.

All went smoothly. The manager was most solicitous and took Sofiya's suitcase and led her to Carpathian's small room that servants of wealthy aristocrats were given when they had stayed there in pre-revolution days. But it was in the corner and had windows facing both east and south, and the view was glorious. Somehow Carpathian had managed to have flowers in the room for her with a note, and a bottle of French wine which she hadn't tasted for almost four years.

In his letters, Carpathian had written that the hotel was an anomaly, a moment out of time. Since dignitaries from other countries still visited Russia, the government understood the need to allow the hotel to continue as it had been. The linens were spotless, the bathroom down the hall—which had to be shared—was clean and outfitted with fine milled soaps and thick towels.

As well off as the Petrovitch family was, her father didn't want them selling their treasures for luxury. You never knew when something more valuable than a half bottle of perfume would be needed. Better to live with coarse soap, her father said, than deplete the valuables they had unless they were desperate. So the enamel eggs Sofiya wore on a chain, her mother's diamond collette, her father's cufflinks, and their silver service remained theirs, unlike the prized possessions of so many of their friends and neighbors.

After the terrible train ride, the first thing Sofiya did was take a bath. A long bath in the most lovely-smelling bath salts. Since it was still late afternoon, the other people who had rooms on this part of the floor were at work. And no one disturbed her.

Back in Carpathian's room, she toweled her hair, put on her dressing gown, and sat down in a comfortable chair by the window to examine the view.

She fell asleep and woke up to hear her name being whispered. Evening had arrived and with it, Carpathian had returned.

"My little Scheherazade, here at last. Welcome to my new prison."

"It's very luxurious."

"Isn't it? And all I have to do is sell my soul every day."

"Is it terrible work?"

"There's time for me to tell you all about that. But not tonight. Tonight is just for us. I have made a reservation in the dining room downstairs. This hotel is quite magnificent, and I've made friends over the last few months with many of the staff. They've conspired to treat us like guests tonight. But first…"

He took her hand.

"We have some time before our 8:30 reservation. We're dining late, as is the custom in the National."

"And what do you want to do before dinner?"

Instead of telling her, he showed her, gently leading her over to the bed and untying the knot on her dressing gown very slowly. When he'd pushed it down over her shoulders, he held her at arm's length.

"It's cold, can't we get under the covers?" she asked.

"Give me a minute. Just a minute. I imagine you here like this every night. And now you really are here. I want to look at you. To sear this picture into my mind for all the times I am going to have to remember it again. When I only have you in my imagination."

Chapter 27

Isobelle Moon
New York City
December 1948

Sergei Zorin and I talked for another hour. I put out cold cuts and salad and some bread and then we continued talking while we ate the makeshift dinner.

Over coffee and some cookies I found in the cabinet, he asked to see my designs, and I showed him a few that I had at home. As he examined them carefully and praised them proudly, I felt a deep sense of satisfaction. He wanted to know what I was working on now, and I told him about the Connecticut project. When we were done eating, he suggested we spend the day together tomorrow to continue getting to know each other and making up for lost time, so we made plans. Then at the door, right before he left, he asked me to retrieve the tiara from Reed's so he could see it again, then apologized.

"I am sorry if I am being a sentimental old man. But I miss your mother so much still," he said. "And it was a connection between us."

I told him I would arrange it. Which is why I am sitting here at 10:00 p.m. staring at the phone trying to get up the nerve to call Jules. I don't want to hear his voice and remember how it sounded whispering to me in the Hay Adams hotel during that long, precious night.

Even though I'm alone in my apartment and no one can hear me, I laugh. Isn't that just perfectly ironic? Understanding comes when you are not looking for it. I am so much my mother's daughter. Here I am confronted with a memory, a wonderful but bittersweet memory, and I'd rather hide from it than embrace it. I'd rather pretend it never happened and get no joy from it at all than risk remembering the bit of pain attached to it as well.

Jules sounds glad to hear from me. I tell him about my shocking visitor. He asks me far more questions than I can answer, and when I've said 'I don't know' about a dozen times, he chuckles.

"But you are the queen of questions," he says.

Something inside me warms that he knows me so well. Then hurts that I can't trust him.

"I was too shocked to even think of half of the things you just asked," I tell him, trying to keep my voice light and not give in to how I'm feeling, not to say what I really want to. "We did talk about the tiara, though. He confirmed it absolutely belonged to my mother before she met him. Which all leads me to this call. He asked me if he could see it, as a sentimental gesture. I told him that I'd get it back from you so he could."

"About that, I was going to telephone you tomorrow,"

he says.

"Yes?"

"I called my mother…"

I don't have any idea where this is going.

"She gave me permission to tell you something because without doing so this won't make any sense."

"Okay."

I'm looking out the window. A pigeon lands on the three inches of snow sitting on the ledge and cocks his head at me. I feel sorry for him outside in the storm. I want to open the window and let it in, but I know better.

"My mother is the head of the Midas Society."

Out of all the shocks I've had in the last twenty-four hours, this is one too many, and it takes me a moment to recover. I try to recollect what he'd told me about the society and its rules. And then it hits me why he talked to her.

"No. I told you—"

"Isobelle, please," he interrupts. "Please just listen to me for a minute, can you just give me that?"

"Okay." I can hear the uncertainty in my voice. I wonder if he knows me well enough to hear it as well.

"I don't want to take the tiara from you. Neither does my mother. We're both more than willing to give you the benefit of the doubt that your mother was not a thief. But how did she come to have it? We think it's important to find out the truth rather than ignore it. There is a member of the society who is a Russian jeweler and an expert on imperial jewels and pieces created before the revolution. If you give my mother permission, she will call him and see what he thinks."

"I don't know."

"What's the worst that can happen?" Jules asks.

I cringe. I'm in no mood to play that game now.

"Look, if it turns out that it does belong to someone else, my mother feels that you'll be allowed to keep it. The only value it has is sentimental. It's just important historically, to know."

Reluctantly, I agree.

"I miss you," Jules says.

His voice is soft and kind, and there's a hint of lust in it. Even coming over the wires, it thrills me.

Do I dare respond in kind? Don't I know better? The response might just be insurance on his part to make sure I don't change my mind. I don't answer.

"You really don't trust me."

"I really don't trust anyone."

"Can I come over now? And talk? Just talk. I want to try to convince you that—"

"No, I'm too distracted. Too confused about what happened today."

"I can understand that," he says. "A visit from a ghost would do that to me too. Especially such an important one. How about tomorrow?"

"My father—God, it feels so strange to say those words—my father wants to see me. It's awkward between us. Two strangers trying to be family. But I said yes."

"How about I meet you and him for lunch then? Maybe this would be easier for you with some emotional support."

For the first time in hours I take a deep breath and let go of some of my anxiety.

"He wants to see some of my life in New York. Some of what he missed."

"I'll meet you both at the skating rink for lunch. Like your mother, he must have been quite a skater. Then after lunch we can show him your office and take him up to mine to show him the tiara."

"All right. Yes, thank you. Goodnight, Jules."

"Isobelle, when you get into bed tonight instead of thinking about tomorrow and worrying…"

He really does know me.

"Pretend that I'm there with you, helping you relax, not letting you do any thinking at all."

I can feel the blush rising up to my cheeks, and before I figure out what to answer he says, "Goodnight, darling Isobelle," and hangs up.

In the morning, I wake up relieved to have slept through the night and not dreamt at all. My nerves come back as I get dressed for the day. I'm wearing gray flannel trousers and a white sweater set. I put on my mother's egg necklace over the sweater. I'm not sure I want to confront my father with such a potent reminder of his past on a day when he's asked to learn about mine, but I still want my mother's spirit with me during this strange meeting.

He arrives at 11:00, and I invite him in and offer him a cup of the coffee I've just made.

"So have you planned what you will show me from your childhood? The places a father and daughter would have gone? The things we would have done?"

I want to answer without rancor, but I'm suddenly angry. At him. At my mother. At my circumstances. I grew up without having had a father in my life. At times that was difficult. I felt left out, deprived of the kind of family life most of my friends had. My mother's reluctance to form a strong bond with any other man made it even more difficult. I knew she was lonely, and I suffered for her. I spent more time at home when I was a teenager. Hesitated to accept invitations to friends' houses too often.

"I've invited a friend to join us for lunch. You've already met him, actually. Jules Reed is coming. He's meeting us at the restaurant, and if you want to see the tiara, he's offered to open up the office so you can go and see it afterwards."

"Am I being too sentimental, Isobelle?"

"No, not at all."

"It's just that I gave it to your mother the last time I saw her. I've spent the last twenty-five years without her..." He shrugs. "I've upset you, I'm sorry."

"It's not about the tiara, no. It's just...I know you didn't choose to abandon us. But there was just so little I knew about you it was difficult for me. And now, sometimes it's not easy to hear about the past."

He nods, thinking. "I understand. And I am sorry. You are right. Let's just spend the day together and get to know each other now. How about every hour I'll answer three of your questions, and you can answer three of mine?"

It sounds silly, almost juvenile. But I don't want to make fun of his suggestion. I don't know this man, but my mother loved him for nearly her entire life. Even though, if I am honest, I don't find myself warming to him, it's clear I matter to him a great deal, and don't I owe it to my mother to give my father a chance?

"All right," I say.

"Good. I'll go first with my questions," he says.

I nod.

"What was your favorite subject in grade school?" he asks.

I didn't have to think. "English, because I loved reading so much."

"How did you wind up becoming an architect?"

"Uncle Paul, that's Aunt Lana's husband, is an architect who works for the firm that built the Empire State Building. When I was a little girl, my mother and Aunt Lana would bring me and their son Michael down to the construction site so we could see New York City's tallest building going up. We were all fascinated. It was magical. It still is, whenever I go there."

"Can we go visit there as well? Of course, I've seen it from a distance, but I'd love my daughter to take me there."

I smile despite myself. I never dreamed that one day I'd be taking my father to the Empire State Building.

"Yes," I say.

"About Jules meeting us for lunch, is he your boyfriend?"

What are Jules and I? I thought I'd never see him again after Washington. Now I've agreed to lend him the tiara to show the Midas Society. I don't know what he is.

I shrug. "I thought he might be. I'm not sure now."

"Do you want him to be?"

"That's your fourth question." I'm relieved I don't have to answer.

"Well, that's perfect. I can grill him a little over lunch and find out what his intentions are."

I must look horrified.

"I'm just kidding. But I am glad he's coming. I only wish your mother was joining us as well."

I feel a lump in my throat. I want to tell him that she is always with me. Even since she has died. I want to tell my father about the dreams. And yet, at the same time, I feel that it's too soon for that. I don't know him well enough to know how he'll react, and I'm not sure I can handle his incredulity, or worse, ridicule.

"It's my turn for questions," I say.

He nods.

"What do you remember the most about my mother?"

My father closes his eyes for a moment. "How beautiful

she was. I remember once, I was working in the shop and she came to see me. She'd just come in from the cold and her cheeks were rosy and her eyes glittered more than any diamond I'd ever set. Her face was so expressive."

I nod. It was so true. There were so many times that my mother didn't have to say a word, just look at me, and I'd know what she was thinking.

"Why do you think she was so reluctant to talk to me about you?" I ask as my second question. It's not quite about him, but it's what I want to know.

"I believe it's what you said yesterday. The memories hurt too much. It must have been very painful to think about me dying in prison, believing she hadn't been able to prevent it."

"Why did you go to prison?" My third question.

"I stole the tiara from the hoard of treasures the Bolsheviks were planning on selling."

"You stole it?" I immediately think of Jules and his mission. "I thought it was my mother's?"

"It was. I stole it back for her, Isobelle. Your mother brought it to the shop in 1917 with a loose stone and asked me to repair it. I took it in to fix, and it was in our safe at Fabergé's when the store was nationalized. The tiara was confiscated along with everything else. When it turned up again in Moscow years later, I stole it back and returned it to your mother. It was very valuable. I wanted it to be an insurance policy for her. For you. My theft was discovered, and I was sent to Siberia."

"Where did she get it in the first place?" I ask.

"That I don't know. How she got it…that was always a mystery." His eyes are looking out the window, but something about his glance suggests he's looking way past Madison Avenue and at another world a lifetime ago.

We leave to go meet Jules. It's a mild winter day, and when I suggest walking, he agrees.

When we reach 57th Street, I point out where I work, and he says he's excited to see my office later. As we pass Tiffany and Company, he stops and stares up at the building wistfully.

"Tiffany was a rival of sorts of Fabergé, but they were comrades as well. Carl Fabergé knew Tiffany's head gemologist, George Kunz, and was very impressed with him. And Agathon Fabergé, who I worked with for years in Petrograd and then in Moscow, knew Mr. Kunz even better."

I know all these names. All the threads are connecting. Weaving together. I nod, not interrupting.

"Mr. Kunz was interested in new gemstones being discovered in the Russian mines. He came to visit the workshop several times before the revolution."

"I'd like to know more about the time you spent in Moscow helping to catalog the imperial jewels."

"Did your mother tell you about those days?"

"Not very much, no. But I know she visited you there. Did she come often?"

We are still standing in front of Tiffany's. He points to a display of men and women's watches in the window. "I can't buy you any of the time that we've lost not knowing each other but I'd like to come back here with you when the store is open and buy you one of those watches. Which one do you like?"

I am honestly touched. I point to a rectangular watch with a white face and gold letters on a thin gold bracelet. There are no stones on this one like some of the others.

"But it's the plainest one there," he says. "You are the daughter of a jeweler. Wouldn't you like the one framed in ruby baguettes?"

"I'm sorry, but I like the styling of the simpler one better."

He smiles. "No need to apologize. We'll come back and you can try it on and make sure."

"That would be a lovely gift, thank you."

We continue walking.

"Did your mother leave you any jewelry?" he asks as we wait for the light to turn green at the next corner.

"Her wedding ring, which I know was also my grandmother's ring, right?"

He nods.

"And a necklace with enamel eggs." I finger it inside my coat.

He nods again and smiles. "All those eggs. Sometimes I see them in my dreams."

"She loved them. All the more, she told me, because you made them for her."

"In another lifetime," he says with a now familiar sadness.

I want to say something that will give him some solace, but I'm not sure anything can, and while I'm trying to fashion the right words, the light changes.

Jules is waiting for us at Rockefeller Center and suggests we skate before our 1:00 p.m. lunch reservation. My father is, as we'd guessed, an excellent skater. I try to imagine my mother skating with him. Picturing them in a romantic dance as their silver blades sprayed ice. But the image won't come clear. It's like a frozen frame of a black and white movie of two actors. She's facing me, and I can make out her features, but he's turned away at just that moment. And I'm reminded of a dream I had two nights before. My mother so sharply in focus. The man beside her, still a blur. The way he has been all my life. Even now that I know his face.

When we are done, we return to the benches to remove our skates before our lunch. I'm sitting to the left of Jules, who is to the left of my father, so I don't see it when my father takes off his skate, but I hear what he says.

"Ach. It's wet." He sounds disgusted.

I look over, around Jules, surprised by my father's vehemence. "What is wet?"

"I stepped in some melting ice," he says. "In the war"— he rips off his sock—"we lived in trenches, and our feet were always wet. I couldn't stand it. I still can't."

"But it will be so uncomfortable to go barefoot in your shoe."

"During lunch? No, I'll be fine."

Once we're all back in our shoes, we proceed to the restaurant, are seated, and given menus. As the drinks arrive, Jules asks my father the first in a series of questions about the Fabergé studio and what it was like to work there. He begins opening up about his past with less hesitancy than when I tried to get him to give me the details I am so hungry for.

I watch these two men, one whom I have so many feelings for, who touches me and moves me even though I worry about trusting him, and this other man for whom I have no feelings yet, only curiosity. I only hope that one day he will come into focus and not remain the blur that he's been in my life and in my dreams.

Chapter 28

Sofiya Petrovitch
Petrograd
January 1922

Sofiya returned home from Moscow sad, lonely, and tired. She didn't unpack her things but went straight to bed. In the morning, she went to work, and so it wasn't until the following evening that she finally unpacked her clothes. At the bottom of her suitcase was a leather box that she felt before she saw it. Lifting it out, she let out a shout. She knew it by the royal blue leather and the shape. She started to cry as she opened it and saw the precious tiara that Olga had given her, that had brought her back to Carpathian. She touched the sapphires and set them swaying and watched the play of light.

What had Carpathian done? How had he retrieved it? There was a note inside the box. She opened it.

Dearest Scheherazade,

It's my fault that you were separated from your treasure in the first place. Now you have it back. Keep it close by. It is worth even more now than it was before. But I'll tell you more about its true value when next I see you. Know that I would give you all the stars and the moon if I could, but for now, this is all I can manage.

Carpathian

Sofiya held it and wondered how he had managed to get it back. She knew that when the Bolsheviks had nationalized Fabergé's shop, the tiara had been in the vault along with so many other precious jewels. Over the weekend, Carpathian had told her how strange it was to be evaluating jewels that he and his fellow workers at the shop had made. But he hadn't even hinted that he'd recovered her tiara.

She wondered why.

She never found out.

That night, she called Carpathian at the National to thank him. It was difficult to get through since he didn't have a telephone in his room—the hotel had not installed lines in the servants' rooms. But in the past, whenever she'd left a message with the front desk, they had someone go upstairs to let Carpathian know. He'd come directly downstairs and phone her back within minutes. It was never ideal speaking to him while he was standing in the hotel lobby, but those calls and their letters were all they had.

All they had…a phrase that could have been the theme of those years. There were so many times Sofiya's mother or father or the professor would shrug and say, "It's all we have," whether it was food or coal or oil or an old coat that had become threadbare or a bit of news that things were going to change. One tried not complaining, but when you made the mistake of saying, *I wish there was some butter for this bread instead of lard*, you'd hear the refrain: *It's all we have.* What wasn't said but implied was: *And we should be grateful.* Because they were at least alive.

Carpathian didn't call her back that evening. Which didn't worry her that much. There had been other instances he had not called until the next night. But he didn't call her back the next evening either. And that did worry her. That was the first time he hadn't returned a call within twenty-four hours. She worried that he might be ill.

On Wednesday night, she called the National again.

The manager said that Sergei Zorin had picked up the message on Monday night, of that he was certain.

Sofiya asked if he might send another message up. "I'm worried he might be ill. If he does happen to be there and is unwell, can you call me? I could try to come back to care for him."

An hour later, the manager did call back. "Sergei Zorin is not in his room. I wanted you to know because you sounded so worried. Our boy did leave a note with your message in case he comes back without checking at the desk first."

There was something in the manager's voice that made her ask if the boy had noticed anything unusual.

"Well, yes. Perhaps. I was going to handle it and then let you know."

"Tell me now, please."

"Sergei Zorin has equipment in his room to make coffee. Each morning, room service drops off a fresh cup and a flask of fresh milk, along with a roll and a piece of fruit. After Comrade Zorin eats his breakfast, he always rinses out the cup, the flask, and his plate and puts it all back on the tray and leaves it outside the room, on the floor where the housekeepers retrieve it on their daily rounds."

"Yes?"

"Well, there were plates still on the table. Unwashed. That in itself would not be that unusual if it were anyone else, but Comrade Zorin has been staying with us for over six months now. And he's very regular in his habits."

She smiled despite her growing concern.

The manager continued. "I was concerned enough to contact housekeeping and they said that both Tuesday's tray and today's were never taken in. They picked them up with the milk and fruit and roll untouched."

"Something is wrong," she blurted out.

"Yes, I agree. I will be checking with Agathon Fabergé when he returns tonight. Either he or I will call you back."

"That would be most helpful, thank you."

Sofiya went through the motions of helping her mother to prepare dinner and then sat at the table with her parents and participated in the conversation as best she could.

There had been a crisis at the Hermitage and her father was relaying the story. Sofiya nodded and made what she hoped were appropriate comments now and then, but the fact was, she was barely listening. She wasn't hungry and couldn't think straight for fear of what had happened to Carpathian.

It wasn't at all unusual for people to suddenly disappear. Just look at the grand duchesses and the tsarina. It had been three years since anyone had known of their whereabouts. Everyone suspected but no one wanted to believe the worst. You heard stories all the time about the Cheka arriving on doorsteps or offices or factories or universities and taking someone away for some infringement or another. Their crimes could be as inconsequential as lying about how many people were living in an apartment, or as serious as planning counterrevolutionary efforts.

It was after nine o'clock when the phone rang. Sofiya ran to answer it.

"Hello?"

"Is this the jeweler's friend?" a man asked.

"Yes, this is—"

"This is his boss," he interrupted.

She understood immediately. Everyone knew to be wary about the phones lest they were spied upon. Agathon Fabergé was on the other end of the phone, and he had interrupted to stop her from using her name. That suggested the news involved danger. If Carpathian was ill, there would be no need for secrecy.

Sofiya felt as if time stopped. As if the world had stopped moving on its axis. The wait was interminable until he spoke again.

"I'm so sorry, but he was arrested on Monday morning."

"For what?"

"Stealing from the government."

"Stealing what?"

"I am not at liberty to discuss," he interrupted again.

Agathon Fabergé continued. "If there is anyone who knows anything, they may be in danger as well."

She understood exactly what he was telling her. "Where was he taken?" she asked.

"That is something I do not yet know. The authorities have questioned me repeatedly, but I wasn't at all aware of what was being planned or why. As soon as I find out where he is being held, I or someone else will be in touch."

"Please, please do let me know."

She held on to the phone even after the line cut out. Several minutes passed before her mother came into the room and found her sitting on the floor still cradling the handset. When she tried to take it away from her daughter, Sofiya held on, tightly. It was all she had connecting her to Carpathian, and she didn't want to sever that faint tie.

"You have to let go, darling," Fedora whispered as she uncurled her daughter's fingers and hung up the telephone. Then she took Sofiya by both hands and helped her to stand. Leading her to the parlor, she sat her on the couch and wrapped an arm around her and listened to her sob out what Agathon Fabergé had told her.

"We will speak to your father about this. We will make a plan."

"But the last time…" She was crying and trying to talk at the same time. "Last time he hadn't even done anything…and we couldn't get him out. Not even…with all that money from the painting."

"That was last time, and most likely a different prison. It's easier now to bribe people."

"Are you sure, Mama?"

"Of course, you hear about it all the time. I promise we will do something." She held Sofiya tightly until she stopped sobbing. "Let me get us some tea with brandy."

As Sofiya sat on the couch, anger began to replace the tears. Why had Carpathian done something so rash? Yes, she cared about the tiara, but not that much. She missed it because Olga had given it to her. But not enough for him to risk his life. Why, oh why, had he done something so dangerous?

For the rest of her life, his action would remain a mystery to her. To die for a romantic gesture just made no sense.

Chapter 29

Isobelle Moon
New York City
December 1948

Jules telephones me late Monday morning with news.

"My mother called to tell me she has a client who is a Russian jewelry expert. According to him, if the tiara is in fact the same one as what we saw in the catalog, there may be much more to this mystery than we think. What that means is anyone's guess because he refused to say more without knowing if it is the same piece. So my mother is suggesting that I bring you, with the tiara, to meet with her at the society headquarters in France later this week."

"To France?"

"Yes, that's where the society headquarters are. Near Cannes on the Cote d'Azur. Do you think you can get a few days off?"

"I dread the thought of asking…"

I don't want to say anything more. I'm in the office

here, alone, but anyone might walk in and overhear me.

"You can't be scared of him, Isobelle. He's the one who should be scared of you telling Mr. Bunshaft what's been going on. Right?"

While I appreciate the sentiment, it's a typical male response. Nothing I could ever say would scare Ted. He is one of Skidmore's stars. I am an assistant. A female assistant at that. Nevertheless, I summon my courage, and with the end goal in mind, march myself into his office.

Ted is sitting at his desk, reading over some plans. I recognize them as plans I drafted the week before. Ted is handsome in his navy suit, white shirt, and navy-striped tie. He looks every inch the successful young architect with a bright and shining future ahead of him. But the slick veneer wore thin for me a long time ago. I know that he takes advantage of people to get ahead. I know he is capable of selling someone out to advance his career. I know when faced with his duplicity and cruelty, he just smiles. I see that smile now and shiver as he looks up at me. His dark eyes glitter. I have tried to forget about our time at Oak Ridge. His flattering seduction. The excitement of the sexual episodes and then the betrayal. What I thought was intimacy was nothing but him being clever. I was and remain nothing more to him than an accessory to his lusty ambition.

I should have suspected. I should have been more protective of my talent. I should have been a better friend. I should have been smarter. I should never have fallen for his sweet talk. But I didn't do any of those things. That I have still not managed to get away from this man is my fault. My weakness. And I hate myself for it.

"How can I help you?" Ted asks.

I tell him about the trip.

He complains about the workload. The recent holidays.

Mentions my illness—which was when I stayed over in Washington. "But I'll make a deal with you, Isobelle," he says.

He hands me a thick pile of drawings. "All the problems are marked. I know you'll figure out the solutions in no time. If you can get these resolved, redrawn, and back on my desk by Wednesday morning, you can take off Thursday and Friday. But you better be back here on Monday."

I should hurl the plans in his face. Or take them and knock on Mr. Bunshaft's door. But I don't do any of those things. I don't say a word. I don't meet his eye. I try not to notice his smirk. With sudden clarity, I realize my need to discover the truth behind the tiara is greater than my desire to go head-to-head with this scoundrel and reveal his true colors. I'm so lost inside the mystery at this point, I'm not even sure why any of it matters anymore. My mother is gone. Yes, my father has appeared in my life, but the tiara won't help me process my feelings for him. So why do I feel such a strong wind at my back to go to Cannes with Jules? Whatever we learn there won't make any difference to me now. Yet somehow, I know it will.

It's my lunch hour, and without really allowing myself to think about it, I step out of Ted's office and head to the ladies' break room. I put on my coat and galoshes and cross the street. Before I know it, I am in the outer room of Alford Reed Jewelers.

Jules comes out to greet me, and as soon as I see him, I feel the threat of tears.

"What is it?" he asks.

"I've gotten used to telling you things. And considering your opinions. And taking your advice. I had felt alone for a long time before I met you and now suddenly don't feel so alone anymore. And I don't want to give all that up."

"You don't have to." He smiles as he takes my arm and brings me into his office.

"I think I do. I shouldn't trust you."

"Why? Because the asshole you work for used you? And is doing it still? Has every man you've been with since him had to pay for that?"

"I haven't been with anyone else since him but you."

His face registers a pleasant surprise. "Well, then am I going to have to pay for it even if I've done nothing to deserve it? Do I have to prove myself because of Ted? Am I on probation until I make some innocent slip that you'll twist into a betrayal? Because that's what you're waiting for, isn't it? For me to somehow convince you that I'm just like him. Well I'm not. In fact, I'm insulted, Isobelle. I haven't done anything but try to help. But I like you. I like you a lot…"

I don't say anything. I know I should apologize, but I'm silent.

"Can you admit you are wrong to suspect me because of him?"

I still don't say anything.

"Seriously? You can't admit that you are wrong?" he asks.

"It's not so much that I can't be wrong," I answer. "I just have a hard time admitting when someone else is right."

He laughs. "Yeah, I can see that. But you *are* wrong here. So get over it. I'm never going to hurt you, Isobelle. Will you please not shut down again? Promise me you'll always tell me what's bothering you when it's bothering you. The worst that will happen is we'll have a fight about it and then get over it."

"The worst that will happen…" I think about my mother and the game. "But I hate to fight."

"No one likes to fight. But I've seen what happens when you don't argue things out. My ex-wife couldn't fight. She'd do anything to avoid confrontation. Nothing good ever came of it."

"What did happen between you? Is that okay to ask? You never told me."

Jules turns and looks out the window for a moment and then back at me. "Let's go get a bite to eat. I'll tell you over a champagne cocktail, all right?"

"Drinking at lunch?"

"Every man in the city does it, so can you."

Outside he hails a taxi, and once we're inside he gives the driver the address of the Metropolitan Museum of Art.

"I thought we were going for lunch," I say.

"I have to pick up a pair of Egyptian earrings from the jewelry department that one of my clients wanted to donate and asked me to handle for her. Unfortunately, the museum has ascertained they aren't authentic. But they have a lovely dining room. Two birds. One stone."

It is indeed a lovely dining room. My mother and I frequented it often. Decorated in apple green and shades of coral and lemon yellow, the tables are well-appointed. The Chippendale chairs are covered in leather. There's always music, and when we enter a recording of Chopin's *Nocturnes* is playing. Jules leads me to the section at the north end that offers more formal service and a maître d' shows us to a table.

As soon as we are seated, Jules orders us champagne cocktails.

I begin to protest. "I really don't think I should."

"You'll eat and soak it up," Jules says. "Besides, you need some fortification. You're dealing with a lot."

The waiter arrives with our cocktails and then takes our

orders. I order the special, poached filet of sole Marguery, and Jules orders the same.

When he leaves, Jules lifts his glass to me. I raise mine.

"To fighting," he says.

I laugh and touch his glass with mine.

We both take a sip. It's cold and delicious, the bubbles bursting in my mouth. I take another sip.

"Maybe we should have toasted to your finding your father," he says.

"I suppose."

"I'd think you'd be elated about your father showing up," Jules says. "Why do you seem so tentative?"

"It's too much to take in. No. That's not really it. He just doesn't feel like my father. I know that's ridiculous. What would my father feel like? But he's a stranger to me. And I had a dream last night that I can't stop thinking about. My mother was sitting on the edge of my bed here in New York. And then she took my hand and, poof, we were in Russia, in a garden in St. Petersburg. She was telling me that my father had been sent to prison and how hard she was trying to get him out. She was holding my hand and wearing the egg necklace. She was fingering the charms. *Your father was so proud of his work at Fabergé, it was his legacy.* But it was the way she said *your father.* As if there was a message in the emphasis. And then I woke up."

"What do you think it means?"

I shake my head.

"I just don't know."

"I think dreams hold validity. Maybe even have the power to portend the future. Certainly help us locate answers to problems our conscious minds haven't yet processed. I've read a lot about what Freud and Jung think about them. So indulge me. Try telling me the first thing that comes to your mind about your father or about your father and the eggs. Don't overthink it."

"Okay. When he first came to the apartment on Saturday night and then the next evening, when he came back with me after skating to meet Aunt Lana and Uncle Paul—that whole time I was wearing the necklace. I saw him glance at the eggs, but he never reacted the way I would have expected."

"How would you have expected?"

"He gave them to my mother…they were his work. Sentimental symbols of his affection. Shouldn't he have reacted more proudly? Or at least made some comment?"

"You might assume that. But it also could have been too difficult for him to look at them. He was already dealing with the emotions of finding his daughter. Talking about your mother and his gifts to her could have been too hard."

"I suppose." I hesitate.

"Do you believe in ghosts?" Jules asks.

"I don't know really. I've never been much for the supernatural except in movies. Do you?"

"I believe in our need to sometimes summon a recreation of a loved one when we want them to tell us what to do or force us to see the truth."

"That would suggest that everything our ghosts do and says is already known to us. That because the ghost comes from inside of me, for instance, everything she says is something that I know."

"That your unconscious mind knows, yes," Jules says.

I take another sip of my cocktail, thinking over what Jules has said.

"What did you think of him?" I ask Jules.

"Your father?"

I nod.

"Well-spoken. Very interesting. Charming. Serious."

The waiter arrives with our meals, and once he puts the plates down, Jules waits for me to take a first bite.

We move on to discussing plans for the trip. I tell him I got the okay to take off from work but don't offer any further explanation. I'm relieved when Jules doesn't press for one.

Once we are finished eating, the waiter offers us the menus for dessert. I decline, but Jules orders a piece of apple pie à la mode. We both ask for coffee.

"You were going to tell me about your ex-wife," I say. "About what happened."

"I was away, in Europe during the war, and she started to drink. When she was good and drunk, she'd write me letters and tell me how she really felt about me. About everything she claimed to have endured when we were married that she never said anything about."

"Did she have legitimate gripes?"

"Of course. I'm only human. A vacation we were supposed to go on that I had to cancel to fly to Los Angeles and bring a suite of jewelry to a big star. A surprise party that she threw for me that I was angry about. That she hadn't gotten pregnant. But I was overseas. Fighting a miserable war. I couldn't fly home and commiserate with her."

"Tough spot to be in."

He nods. "Yes. I'll give her that she had a right to all that anger. But not to what she did about it."

"What did she do?"

"When we got married, we moved into a lovely place on Park Avenue, and she had free rein to decorate it. I brought over my library and my collection of paintings and lithographs. Some of which my grandfather had bought for me over the years. Some my mother had given me. Other pieces I'd collected myself. And then one day, my grandfather saw two of the paintings he'd given me up for auction at Parke Benet. Through friends, he found out she had put them up. He tried to get in touch with her, and when she didn't return any of his calls, he went to see her. The doorman told him that Mrs. Reed had moved out over six months before. He wrote me, and when I told him I didn't know anything about it, he hired a private investigator who found her living with her sister in Florida. Lots of money in the bank. It turns out that while I was gone, she sold the apartment and everything in it, including my books and every painting, drawing and print. She spent six weeks in Reno and divorced me. There was nothing I could do about it. We were married. What was mine was hers."

"You could have probably taken her to court since you had all those things before the marriage."

"I could have, but what good would it have done? It was all sold, Isobelle. I couldn't get it back. I learned a lot about myself in the process. The whole marriage, I'm ashamed to admit, was more of a rebellion than anything else. My mother was dead set against me getting married before I went off to war. She often complained I was too impetuous. A trait she said I inherited from my father."

"I'm so sorry."

He shakes his head. "Don't be. I'm being far too maudlin. I'm fine. So I lost my beloved library and some valuable artwork. And my pride, which was probably the hardest part. But as you saw in my apartment, I've rebuilt some of my collection already."

After lunch, I accompany Jules upstairs to the jewelry department, where he picks up the earrings. On the way down, I tell him that I want to show him something.

We detour through the European painting wing and

stop in front of a Rubens.

"This was in the Hermitage. My mother restored it," I say.

Jules examines it. "That's amazing." He's impressed.

"Yes"—I lower my voice—"but according to her, it's a fake."

"Seriously?"

I nod. "My mother said she worked on it with her mentor, Filatov Roman Sokolov, and he was positive."

"How did it wind up here?"

"The same way some of those imperial jewels did. The Soviets started off by selling off what they stole from the noble and wealthy to finance the industrialization of the country. They also ransacked churches for icons to sell. Finally, there was nothing left but the artwork that they'd held on to. Their cultural treasures. My grandfather, who had worked at the Hermitage his whole career, was one of the heads of the agency set up to oversee those sales—the Antiquariat, created by the People's Commissariat of Enlightenment. My grandfather was charged with choosing two hundred and fifty works that could be sold for at least five thousand rubles each in order to raise two million rubles.

"With the help of Filatov Roman Sokolov, he picked all the paintings they believed to be fakes or that had been so heavily restored that if it were to come to light their value would be diminished. It was their little joke on a government they despised. At first, the sales were all done in secret. But in 1933, the *New York Times* started reporting on them. By 1938, the Soviets were shamed into not raiding any more of their national treasures, but it was too late. A good percentage of the museum's paintings were gone. Some came here. Some went to the British Museum. Others were sold to private investors. In 1937, Andrew Mellon, who had bought almost two dozen of them, donated his to the U.S. government to start the National Gallery of Art.

"My mother used to bring me here all the time. She especially loved visiting the paintings she'd worked on. We'd stand in the gallery and watch people's reactions."

"Did she miss restoring paintings?"

"She didn't totally stop. She and Aunt Lana scoured flea markets and antique fairs and bought artwork as well as furniture which they restored and resold. She also took in the pieces from private collections."

"She had worked in the Hermitage. Surely, she was qualified to get a job in a museum. Even here in the Met."

"Too many memories, she said. My mother's life was all about erasing memories. All about being an American in America, not trying to recreate being a Russian American as so many emigres did. She told me how terrible those last years were, about the poverty, the rations, the roundups, and what it was like to live in fear. She said she never taught me Russian because she never wanted to hear it spoken again. That's why all this with my father now is so strange and difficult."

"Do you want to bring your father to Cannes with us?" Jules asks. "Maybe it will help if you can share something in the present."

I lean over and kiss his cheek. He pulls me into the hallway, away from the guard and the paintings.

"Not a good idea to tempt me like that, Isobelle. Even in public." And then he pulls me close to him and kisses me in a wholly different way, and for the moment I forget about all the things weighing on my mind.

Chapter 30

Sofiya Petrovitch
Petrograd
January 1922

Sofiya took the train to Moscow with money in hand to try and find someone who could help—who had seen or heard anything about Carpathian. She questioned Agathon and Dimitry, as well as the entire staff at the hotel. At night, she slept in his room, which had yet to be emptied thanks to the kind hotel manager, who had taken pity on her.

She remained in Moscow for over five weeks. And it was there, in Carpathian's room, that she first felt the baby growing inside her move. She sat on his bed and wept and swore that somehow, at least when their child was born, she'd make sure he knew whether he had a son or a daughter.

Moving from government office to government office,

she made a nuisance of herself. Because she was a woman, and because she had gold that the professor had gotten for her by selling another painting, she eventually gained access to some low-ranking officials.

Back at the hotel each evening, she would eat whatever the kitchen sent up—not because she was hungry but for the baby. At night, when she couldn't sleep for worry, she'd force herself to fantasize a scenario of Carpathian escaping. He had diamonds—he had shown them to her. They were hidden. Carpathian always wore one specific wool vest that had a dozen cloth-covered buttons going up the front. Beneath the simple fabric covering on each fastener was a brilliant round diamond. Carpathian believed in insurance policies, he had told Sofiya so many times. And those diamonds were his policy. Since the vest was not among his things, she assumed he had been wearing it when he was arrested. She wanted to believe he would be able to use them and get out. She willed herself to adopt Carpathian's hopeful attitude. Until, finally, she was told by an official to whom she'd given the last of her cache of gold that Carpathian had been sent to the Gulag in Siberia. She didn't know if he had enough diamonds to help him there. And so, a deeper level of fear set in. The stories that came back about what it was like there for the prisoners were really stories about how they died. Prisoners worked fourteen-hour workdays regardless of the extreme weather. Those that didn't die of exhaustion or starvation died from disease or execution.

There was no reason to stay in Moscow now that she knew where Carpathian was. She returned home after six weeks. If there was a way to buy Carpathian out of the Gulag, she could do it from Petrograd as well as she could from Moscow.

As soon as she stepped over the threshold of her

parents' apartment, she knew something was wrong. Her father was sitting alone at the kitchen table, an unopened newspaper in front of him, along with a bowl of untouched soup and a heel of stale bread.

He had aged ten years in the weeks she had been gone.

"What is it?" she asked.

"Your mother," he said in a low, sad voice.

"What?"

"She made me promise not to tell you while you were in Moscow. But she's not well..."

Sofiya ran to their bedroom. Her mother wasn't there. Nor in Sofiya's bedroom. Nor the sitting room. She ran back into the kitchen.

"Where is she?"

"I was able to get her into a sanatorium in the Crimea. They aren't sure if we caught it in time."

"Caught what?" Sofiya shouted.

"Your mother has tuberculosis."

What little there was left of her hope flew. It was as if all the lights in the Hermitage had been turned off at once. Where there were once gold-framed paintings of luminous landscapes, vibrant portraits, and still lifes of brilliant flowers, there was now darkness. All the beauty had gone out of the world.

Sofiya could see that her father was trying to be brave for her sake, but she knew too much about the disease. They all did. They had seen too many of their friends and co-workers felled by it.

She didn't sleep that night. The next day, instead of going back to work, she decided to visit her mother. The Lesnoye Sanatorium was 1800 kilometers away in the middle of a large pine forest on the shores of the Volga River. Sofiya's father had described it as a paradise compared to

Petrograd. Her mother's cure involved rest, fresh air, and good nutrition, including their special drink, Kumis, which was made from fermented mare's milk.

For three days, Sofiya waited at the station for the train, only to go home each night after the station master announced that all were still delayed.

On the fourth evening, her father was waiting for her when she returned, having been unsuccessful once more. He was sitting in the parlor with his head in his hands. For the rest of her life, whenever she felt sad, she would see the image of her father that night. She didn't have to ask what was wrong.

She sat down at his feet. He put his hands on her shoulders and she leaned against his legs. And then for the first time since Carpathian had been arrested, she wept. She cried for her beautiful mother who had lost her battle with her illness. She cried for Carpathian, who seemed as lost to her now as her mother. She cried for her father, who she knew would be lost without his wife of thirty years. She hated his love in that moment. No one should ever feel that level of emotion for another person. Because if you love that hard, you have to break that hard. If you care that much about another human being, those very feelings can destroy you. Sofiya never wanted to love anyone again. Ever. She never wanted to worry about anyone. Or fear for anyone. Or panic over anyone being ill or missing or dead or dying. The grief wasn't a small price to pay for the love—it was the greatest price. The pain was too gripping, too painful, too all-encompassing. She never wanted to feel any of it. Except she knew as she sat there on the hard floor, listening to her father's quiet sobs, that there was one love she was yet to know that would be even greater than all the others and that she was powerless to do anything to stop it from overwhelming her life.

Fedora's funeral was crowded with students who she had taught over the years. They came with drawings and paintings of flowers that they laid at the feet of her coffin. Roses and tulips and irises and peonies...endless pictures laid like a carpet of flowers at her feet.

At home after the burial, Sofiya's father went into the bedroom he had shared with her mother since before Sofiya was born, and he did not come out that evening. She knocked around dinner time, but he didn't answer. She thought about opening the door, but she wanted him to take whatever time he needed.

She sat in her own room with the book of Pushkin she had taken from Carpathian's room. The only thing she'd taken. He'd read her those poems when they lay in his bed. And now she held the book to her chest as if it could give her some solace—she'd lost her mother and her lover—both gone in a matter of weeks.

The following morning, her father was waiting for her at the breakfast table with strong tea and some stale bread he'd toasted over the flame. They ate and drank in silence.

"I'm going to have a baby," Sofiya finally told him after they'd finished eating.

She had decided to tell him, hoping that the idea of a grandchild on the way might fill some tiny bit of the large hole left in his heart.

"Yes, I know. Your mother knew. We talked about it."

"She knew?"

"She said she could see it in your body."

Tears filled Sofiya's eyes. She wished her mother had told her that she knew. Wished they had talked about it. Wished her mother had given her some advice, had told her what it was like to be pregnant and what it was like to have a child.

"Yes, she knew, and we talked. We decided, Sofiya, that you would not have your child here. Not in Petrograd. Not in Russia. All she wanted for you, all I want for you, is to get away from here and where you can get nutritious food and live in a clean, safe place and bring up our grandchild in a country where he or she will have a chance at a good life."

"But you are here," she said.

"I am. But that doesn't matter. We won't be separated for long. This siege is winding down. There are rumors in the paper every day that the sanctions will be lifted soon. I will join you soon. In the meantime, I have arranged for you to leave—"

"How?" It was so difficult for anyone to leave Russia. The paperwork and requests took months to work their way through the government, and if you had any counter revolutionary history or consorted with those who did, or if you were connected to the aristocracy, or worse yet, the imperial family, there was no chance of emigration. Because of Sofiya's mother having taught the grand duchesses, there was a mark against her. But as it turned out, in the last two years as teacher at the free art institute, she also had schooled the children of the man who was now the head of the provisional government. Like everyone, he could be bought.

"You have Rembrandt and Rubens and Velasquez to thank for these papers by way of our dear friend Sokolov," Sofiya's father said as he put a passport on the table.

Sofiya protested that she couldn't leave Russia. She couldn't leave her mother's grave. She couldn't leave her father. She couldn't leave Carpathian in a prison cell even though she knew that she had reached an impasse there. Once you had been sent to the Gulag there was no extradition. Not for diamonds, not for gold. Not for paintings that no one knew were forgeries.

Sofiya's father had her emigration all worked out. A ship to Malta. Then another to New York City, where the professor's niece, who was also a restorer, would be waiting for her. Sofiya wouldn't be alone.

In the end, it wasn't her father's insistence. It wasn't that it was her mother's last wish. It wasn't that leaving was probably what Carpathian would want for her if he were there to advise her. It was the baby who was starting to grow inside of her. She thought about Carpathian's last letter to her. It had been delivered while she was in Moscow and waiting for her upon her return. His words about the tiara being an insurance policy for hers and the baby's survival made Sofiya think her father could be right about her fleeing, though fleeing was the last thing she wanted to do. Didn't she owe it to her child to give him, or her, a chance?

Chapter 31

Isobelle Moon
Paris
January 1949

We flew from New York to Paris, stayed overnight at the Lutecia Hotel, then the next morning took the train to Cannes. We arrive in the port city in the afternoon, where a car is waiting to drive us to Jules' mother's villa. Our luggage is placed in the trunk except for Jules' carry-on that holds the tiara in its leather case. The silver over gold skeleton isn't worth more than a few hundred dollars in materials, but to me and my father, it is too precious an object to entrust to baggage.

As we wind our way through a narrow, twisting road nestled in lush green hills high above the city, it's the light I can't get over—buttery against the serene cerulean blue skies. The very air shimmers. I don't wonder why Picasso and Matisse preferred living here in the South to anywhere else. The air's luminosity, even now in winter, is unlike anything I've ever seen.

Jules tells my father and me how this area first became popular during the Victorian times when the wealthy British began to winter here. And while it's now a popular summer destination, in part thanks to Hemingway and Fitzgerald, I can understand why it drew crowds this time of year as well.

Jules' mother's villa is called *Le Paradis* and for good reason. The early nineteenth-century building sits on a perfect site overlooking the city and beyond it the Mediterranean—the sapphire water flecked with golden highlights from the afternoon sun.

A majordomo greets Jules and shows us all to our respective rooms. Jules has already told us his mother is spending the evening at the society dormitory off the coast, where she will meet us in the morning. He suggests we all retire for a few hours and meet up again for dinner.

I'm grateful for the reprieve. My room is lovely, a peach and green confection with its own patio overlooking the water. The lace canopy bed calls to me. Kicking off my shoes and dropping my coat on a chaise, I lie down and sink into the feather duvet and pillows. I'm not used to international travel. This is the first time I've been out of the United States—and I have never dealt with a time difference before.

Before I know it, I open my eyes to see a maid unpacking my suitcase and putting away my clothes. I'd packed my usual outfit of trousers and blouses, but I'd also packed two dinner dresses—a black and a pale green—and several pastel scarves. I glance at the ormolu clock on the mantle and see it is already seven at night. Sensing that I'm awake, she welcomes me and informs me in charmingly accented English that cocktails will be served downstairs in a half hour.

Groggy, I force myself to get up, wash and change into one of the dresses and at 7:30 join Jules and my father in the living room. Once we all have aperitifs in hand, Jules takes us on a tour of the house, which he tells us once belonged to a member of the Rothschild family, who, he says, still own significant property in Cannes, Cap Ferrat, and other choice spots on the Riviera.

I'm in awe of the villa. Everything, from the moldings to the drapery to the artwork on the walls, is of the very best quality and taste. There are vases of cut flowers in every room and the scents of jasmine and orange blossom follow me everywhere.

At dinner, Jules tells us stories about the villa's history up to when his mother bought it from an elderly widow a dozen years ago.

My father asks a lot of questions and is, as usual, quite charming. I'm a little surprised by how well he's fit in here. He seems to have brought all the appropriate dinner attire— a navy blazer with gold buttons and gray slacks. Every time I've seen him, he's been well-dressed if not a bit elegant. He has a jeweler's attention to detail, the same kind of attention I've noticed in Jules.

When dinner ends, my father excuses himself to retire. Jules suggests he and I take a walk in the gardens. Even though it's a little chilly, I agree.

He's quiet as we stroll down an allée of trees toward a fountain that is carefully lit by fairy lights. We circle it, and he takes me to a glass-enclosed folly that's even higher on the property than the house. Inside are wicker couches with deep cushions, a bar, and an easel and paints. He admits they are his, but that he only dabbles and isn't very good. I insist on him showing me some of his work. Shyly, he pulls out a canvas of the bay at night with mountains in the distance. I look out at the same scene he painted. His impressionistic interpretation is impressive.

"You're very good," I offer.

He shrugs. "Just a hobby." Then he takes my hand. "Come, sit."

He leads me to the couch.

"You seem uncomfortable," he says.

"Now?"

"Since we left New York."

I nod. "I guess I am. It's just getting used to having a father."

"I like him," Jules says.

"So do I, but..." I hesitate, not sure how to put my feelings into words. "I certainly didn't have any expectations about him. I had no idea he was alive. But I just can't quite connect to him."

Jules puts his arm around me and pulls me toward him.

"I know, but it's early days still." He takes my hand and holds it tightly. "I can't actually imagine what you are going through."

"It's not terrible, it's just odd."

"Can I ask you something else?"

"Sure."

"I hate what happened to us after Washington. That you could think I would betray you. You believe me now, don't you? That I'm on your side. That I want to help you solve your mystery. That I'm not trying to use the tiara to gain my admission into full-fledged membership in the society. Because if you don't, I'll do whatever I have to in order to prove it to you."

"I believe you. At least I want to. I just…it's just…" I take a deep breath. "I don't know how to tell if someone is being honest with me or not. I had no idea Ted was using me. It never occurred to me. How do I know you're not?"

He leans forward and kisses me. It's a different kiss than we've shared before. Gentle. Ernest. Simple, if that makes sense.

"If it turns out that the tiara was stolen before your mother owned it, if we solve the mystery of where it came from, if it is in fact my fifth trial and they offer me full membership, I am going to turn it down and wait for the next puzzle that comes my way. I won't use this one as a steppingstone. No matter what."

I'm stunned. "I don't want you to give up something so important for me."

"Maybe I'm giving it up for something more important—you."

Jules traces my jawline with his forefinger and trails it down my neck and to the top buttons of my blouse and works the first one loose. Then he bends down and kisses the swell of my breast. Feeling his lips soft against my skin, I arch up to him. He unbuttons another button and then another and then opens my blouse. The air is colder than I expected, and I shiver, partly because of the temperature and partly because Jules has reached behind me and unclasped my bra and pulled it down, exposing my breasts to the night and his mouth.

When I don't think I can take any more of his gentle licking and kissing, he asks me if I want to go up to my room or stay here.

In answer, I fumble for his belt buckle and start to undress him. I can tell he's hard already, and I'm aching to feel him again. Excited and nervous and shy to be so hungry for him, to be grabbing for him, to be burying my head in his neck and inhaling his scent as if it is oxygen. And maybe it is.

Jules and I undress in a hurry. I'm lying on the couch now in nothing but my panties. He reaches down between my legs, presses down with the palm of his hand, and I gasp.

"I want to watch how this makes you feel. I want to give this to you."

I've never had anyone ask anything like this of me. I'm not sure I can do it. I feel so exposed. But as he slips two fingers under the elastic and strokes me, up and down and then in circles, as he smiles, feeling my response, I suddenly want to show him. Want him to watch. Want him to look at me with his heavy-lidded, lust-filled eyes. I want him to want me but wait. To give me this gift. I want him to see it all. Nothing hidden. Nothing unsaid.

"Tell me, Isobelle," he whispers. "Have you imagined this since our night in Washington?"

He wants me to talk. I've never done that before either. I don't think I can. I'll be too embarrassed.

"Tell me," he insists.

As I start to whisper the words that yes, yes, I imagined this every night since then... That, yes, I want this—and more... That I want him to fill me up... As I say these words, I break open. I don't know where I am or what time it is or how I am even breathing, but I know that something in me that has always been locked away is now freed. That with Jules, I can be all the things I only imagined being in secret. I can show him my want and my need and not be judged. Not be thought of as too forward and aggressive. Not be too wanton. I have never been myself with a man...until now. Until this minute. And when the orgasm takes over, sending me crashing into its pleasure, I feel as if all of me is going to pour out. That I'm going to burst with the pure joy of it, with the physical release, with the ecstasy, that I am broken and that I don't mind. At all.

In the morning, Jules and my father and I are driven by speedboat across the harbor to Ile Saint-Honorat. It is a fifteen-minute boat ride, and on the short trip, Jules tells us about the little island.

"There has been a working monastery, the Cistercian Congregation of the Immaculate Conception, here since the tenth century. There is an abbey and seven chapels. For over nine hundred years there have been monks living here and making wine and liqueurs along with honey and various other edibles. It's a small congregation. Usually there are no more than twenty to twenty-five monks in residence to handle every stage of their efforts, from pruning, disbudding and harvesting the grapes all by hand. There are also some ruins, including a cannonball furnace from Napoleonic days. Visitors who ferry over are welcome to wander, have lunch, swim in the coves, or walk the olive and pine-tree-lined paths."

"And the society?" I ask.

He smiles enigmatically. An expression I have come to love. I saw it several times last night, and the thought of that now makes me blush. It seems inappropriate to remember our tryst, here with my father, on our way to try and discover the true history of my mother's legacy.

"You'll see," is all he says.

Our boat bypasses the large dock, which Jules says is where the ferry from Cannes drops off and picks up passengers and instead drives around to the other side of the island which looks even more wild and uninhabited. We pull into a small dock, and Jules jumps off to help the captain tie up and then help my father and me disembark.

It's a short walk down a path lined with olive and pine

trees to the ruins of an ancient chapel.

"Is this one of the seven chapels you mentioned?" my father asks.

"No, this one isn't counted as there's nothing left of it but this shell," he says. "Or so it appears, yes?"

We both agree.

Jules walks us inside the stone edifice, three walls open to the elements. There's nothing here but weeds and fallen stones and a partial circular staircase leading up to nowhere.

But also, it turns out, leading down. Because once we've stepped inside the little enclosure, what appears to be a solid stone enclosure begins to move. It's an elevator disguised to look like part of the ruin, and it takes us down and opens into a stone lobby filled with cool pine-scented air.

We walk down a short hallway. Ahead are glass doors, the kind I'd expect to see in an office building in New York. Here they are incongruous.

"Welcome to the Midas Society," Jules says as he opens them, and we step into a modern reception room.

A middle-aged woman in a chic black suit greets Jules, in French, by name. He returns the greeting and speaks to her for a few moments. She hands him some sheets of paper and two pens. He ushers us to a couch at the end of the room.

"I'll need you to fill these out. They are simple agreements that you won't divulge our location, or anything you discuss or see here. We keep our operation as secret as possible."

"But can't anyone just come here?" my father asks. "The entrance was concealed but not completely."

"No one sees the staircase you saw unless we are expecting them."

"How does that work?" my father asks.

"It's raised from down here by the receptionist," Jules explains.

"How does she know to raise it?"

"Mademoiselle Verlaine has an appointment book and a telescope-like device set up to view both the dock and the ruin above us. As I told Isobelle, while our existence and mission aren't widely publicized, it's not totally a secret. Our members and methods are, however. So back to these agreements," he says and hands each of us a waiver and a pen.

After we both sign, he collects them, gives them back to the receptionist, says a few words to her, and then escorts us down a long hallway. The ceiling is stone and arched, clearly built hundreds of years ago. The walls are smooth and plaster, built in the last five to ten years.

"How did people get in down here before you built such a well-hidden modern convenience?" my father asks.

"We have another entrance through the stone door in the reception area," Jules says. "It leads to a tunnel that goes all the way from here to the main ferry. It floods often and wasn't very efficient, so the society stopped using it when they built the hydraulic elevator."

We are walking past drawings. Some are pen and ink, some watercolors, some pencil or gouache sketches, some blueprints that I'm more familiar with. Each is of a single *objet d'art*, a piece of jewelry, a coin or a stamp. Some look as if they've been done more recently, some are on very old paper or parchment and look ancient. Each has a small plaque beneath it. We're moving too fast for me to stop and read them all, but I guess at what they are.

"Are all these objects the society has recovered?"

"Yes," Jules says. "It's a rich history of items all stolen or lost. All returned."

I'm fascinated by the drawings but more so by the combination of ancient cellar and present-day office. The architect who worked on it very creatively kept as many of the old structural elements as possible, and the overall sensation is that you're caught between times. Ancient and modern all mixed together.

We enter a vaulted room which clearly dates back to the Middle Ages based on the ceiling construction, but here too, the thick pile carpet and leather upholstered chairs set up around a stainless steel and glass table don't look more than a decade old.

There are four settings prepared for us. At each is a thermos and china cup. In the middle of the table is a tray with a silver coffee pot, creamer, sugar, and tongs, along with a basket of croissants and pain au chocolate so fresh I can smell the butter.

There's also a slide projector and a reel-to-reel tape recorder on the table.

Moments after Jules offers us seats, the door opens, and a woman enters.

"*Bonjour*," she says and introduces herself as Genevieve Tavel. Even if I hadn't seen a photo of her in Jules' apartment, I would know her. She has the same green eyes ringed with amber as her son. The same patrician bone structure. And while she's not as tall as Jules, she towers over me. Her rich auburn hair tumbles to her shoulders in waves, like his does. When she shakes my hand, she covers it in both of hers, and I catch a whiff of an evocative scent of vanilla mixed with amber.

After welcoming my father, Madame Tavel embraces her son and invites us all to sit down, which we do, and to partake of the beverage and bread basket. After a few minutes of pleasant banter, Jules asks me if it's all right to show her the tiara. I nod, and he takes the leather box that has been in the Reed vault for the past several weeks and hands it to her. I turn and see my father's eyes riveted to the case. I wonder what he's feeling. He hasn't seen the tiara for more than twenty-six years.

"Would you mind if I take this over there?" Madame Tavel points to a side table I hadn't noticed before. On it is an array of tools, a camera, and a microscope. A lamp hangs above it.

"Of course," I tell her.

Madame Tavel turns on the lamp and does a thorough examination of first the case and then the tiara. At some point my father gets up and goes over to watch her more closely.

When she's done, she puts the tiara back in the case and carries it back and puts it in the middle of the table.

"I have a presentation for you from our client in London. He described the tiara and told me what marks to look for. He instructed me that if I in fact found the right markings, I should feel free to show you this slide show and play you his tape, which might help explain what you appear to have. Then I have some questions as well that might further our mutual desire to figure out the story behind this object. Does that sound amenable to you?" she asks me.

"Of course."

Madame Tavel walks over to the door and dims the light, throwing the room into darkness. Returning to the table, she turns on the projector, and a drawing of the tiara appears, projected onto the wall. We all twist our chairs to face front. I am closest to her on her right. Jules is opposite me. My father is behind me.

Madame turns on the tape machine. A man's voice with a familiar Russian accent begins to speak.

"We call this the Last Tiara because it was in fact the last tiara the House of Fabergé made for the imperial family. Specifically made for the tsar to give to his eldest daughter on the occasion of her birthday. We have all the original paperwork."

Madame clicks the projector, and another drawing appears of the tiara from a different angle. Much like the blueprints we do, this one is very precise, with measurements written on the side.

The voice continues. "The tiara included diamonds and sapphires all of unusual quality. But that is not what made the piece so precious. The tsar knew there were troubles coming to his country, and he was desperate to provide for his children and protect their futures. He had five objects made, one for each child. Each was a secret map to where he had hidden a treasure outside of Russia. There have been rumors of these jeweled maps for years. But only the tsar and the children and Fabergé himself, who made them, knew what they were. The whereabouts of all five pieces are unknown to this day. We were not aware of any of them having survived the revolution and subsequent upheaval in Russia. The sapphire tiara was last seen in 1922 when it was photographed as part of the collection of imperial jewels that the Bolsheviks were trying to sell."

The slide changes, and up comes the photo that Jules and I saw in the Fersman catalog of the table of treasures.

"This photo appears in a 1925 catalog of those jewels. The photo was taken in 1922, shortly before the tiara was stolen and returned to the woman whom Grand Duchess Olga had gifted it to in 1917. We don't know if that woman knew it was more than a jeweled headpiece of exquisite workmanship but was in fact a map to a cemetery where one of the tsar's treasures had been hidden the year before. For a long time, no one other than the tsar and Carl Fabergé himself knew that the tiara was also a map to that crypt. We only became aware of it when it was brought back to the shop in 1917 for repairs. The duchess, indeed the whole royal family, had already disappeared. As we now know, they had in fact been murdered. But at that point, their whereabouts were still unknown. As distraught as Carl Fabergé was at the state of our government and the fate of his friend the tsar, he was elated to see the tiara had somehow made it back to us. We were a country torn apart, broken, and bankrupt. We feared each day that we were going to come under the new government's auspices.

"Mr. Fabergé was so nervous those last days, so frantic at what was to come of his company, his family, his country, that seeing the tiara, he decided to confide in me in case the worst happened…he wanted to insure someone else knew what secret the tiara held. First, he removed all the stones. Then he showed me how to place a paper map of the city of London behind the tiara's ornamental crown. The empty oval where the largest sapphire would sit circled the exact spot on the map where a tomb was located in one of London's main cemeteries. He also showed me how a removable key was cleverly built into the tiara's band. When you pulled out the last two-inch section, you saw it was a small key which opened a mausoleum that had not been opened, except to place the tsar's treasure inside, since the mid-1880s."

I have been listening to the recording with every ounce of my attention. Not believing the things I am hearing about the tiara my mother had in her possession for all of her adult life.

"In 1922, the tiara was stolen back from the Bolsheviks and returned to its rightful owner. Unfortunately, the

Bolsheviks realized that it had been stolen. I was one of the men blamed and imprisoned. I spent seven years in the Gulag before escaping. Like most of us jewelers, I had hidden away my own cache in case I ever needed it. I had bought ten rather sizable diamonds from our stock at Fabergé and had a seamstress turn them into cloth-covered buttons. I replaced the wooden buttons on a favorite vest, sewing them with thread made of steel. I wore the vest throughout my first incarceration and would have used one or more of the buttons to escape, but ironically those guards were so frightened of their superiors they could not be bribed. They were probably the only guards in all of Russia who were so conscientious."

Here the man laughs and then continues. "During my second incarceration in Siberia, I learned the guards themselves were so badly punished if a prisoner escaped that bribery was nearly impossible. It took me several long years until I finally made contact with a warden who was as anxious to get out of that miserable frozen tundra as I was. It cost me all of my buttons, but I escaped to Finland like so many of us did as it was the easiest country to get to—if you could survive the journey. Assuming the woman who owned the tiara didn't know its secret, I tried to find her. I made every effort to learn her whereabouts. I assumed she changed her name, as so many Russians did, but without any clue as to what name she took, I had no luck in finding her. So I left and came to London in the hopes that she would somehow figure out what she had in her possession and come here to take possession of the treasure. Alas, that has not come to pass. So I am submitting my case to the Midas Society for consideration to help me find the tiara and the woman who owns it."

The recording ends. Madame Tavel shuts off the tape

machine and the slide projector. We are still sitting in darkness for a moment, and the lights go on.

The chair behind me is empty.

"I didn't hear him leave," Jules says as he wastes no time reaching across the table to the middle where the leather case sits.

"Neither did I," his mother adds.

I watch Jules, knowing what he is going to find even as I hold out one thin shred of hope that somehow, somehow, I'm wrong.

Madame Tavel has gotten up and walked over to Jules' seat, watching over his shoulder. I too have stood and moved over to watch as Jules opens the box.

I'm looking down at the inside of the case, seeing nothing but pale cream-colored silk lining indented into a depression where the tiara once lay. It is now gone, along with the man claiming to be my father.

Chapter 32

Sofiya Petrovitch
Petrograd
March 1922

Leaving Petrograd was leaving the hope of being reunited with Carpathian. It meant accepting grief and loneliness. Sofiya traveled with very few things. They all knew there would be thieves along the way. She carried one suitcase so she would never have to let go of it. In it were two rolled-up faked drawings from the secret closet in the Hermitage, some family photos, the tiara in its royal blue leather box, her mother's watercolor set, Carpathian's copy of Pushkin, and two changes of clothes. Her father promised that as soon as it was possible and things settled down, he would come visit, but when he put her on the train, he pressed a letter into her hand that told her the truth of what he expected.

My darling Sofiya,

Who knows when and if the situation here will change and you and I will meet again? I will do everything on heaven and earth to get to you. Keep me informed always about your whereabouts once you get to America. I will miss you more than life itself, but there is no hope for your baby here in the hell that this city and this country has become. We've been lucky, me, you, your mother, to have lived the way we have since 1917. And we have a lifetime of memories to keep us company. I will be lonely but satisfied that I accomplished what your mother and I wanted for you — safe passage to a safe place where you can start over and build a new family.

I know what it is to love deeply – your mother and I were very devoted to each other — but what you don't know — what I never told you — is that I had a young wife before your mother. The reason I tell you now is to give you hope. I loved her so much that when she died only a year after our marriage, I thought that I too was going to die of a broken heart. She was pregnant with our first child. And they both died in childbirth — child death — I always think of it. I wanted to take my own life as well. I walked by the frozen Neva night after night thinking about giving myself to the ice and the frigid waters. When I remember my despair now, and I do remember it, what surprises me still is that I survived it. That is the mystery of our lives. That we do survive the unthinkable. We overcome the unimaginable.

I didn't believe I would ever love anyone again. And for more than two years I lived in despair and depression. And then one day, I walked into the Renaissance room at the museum— yes, I know the significance of which room it was — the very word means rebirth and renewal — and there was your mother sketching in front of a Raphael. It wasn't her beauty that drew me to her — though you and I both know how beautiful she was. It wasn't the sweep of her hair or the curve of her waist or the rose perfume I could smell in the air — it was the intensity of her attention to her task and the passion with which she *loved what she was doing. I watched her for a long time that day without her ever noticing me. And the longer I watched and the longer she didn't notice me the more amazed I was. You know the story. I smile thinking of it now. She put down her pencil and turned to me and asked me if I'd enjoyed the show. She knew the whole time that I was there. And she laughed, and I was reborn in that laugh.*

You will never find a man with whom you feel exactly the same as how you feel for Carpathian. But you have to open yourself to the hope that there is another man waiting for you on the opposite shore who will make you happy… Make you laugh… Give you more children.

Promise me, darling child, that you will at least entertain that hope.

When I think of everything that I hate about our world, the worst is that it has robbed you of hope. You were a child who believed in magic. Who looked at a bird and thought you could paint it healed. But these last years I've seen the bitterness and sadness replace that irrepressible spirit that was once yours. Look for it again when you arrive on the shores of your new country.

Until we meet again soon — and for as long as I have breath, I will try to ensure we do —

Your loving papa

Sofiya arrived in New York City, at Ellis Island, a month after leaving Petrograd. When it was her turn to give her name, she hesitated. And then gave the man waiting a brand-new name. *Sophia Moon.* In honor of Carpathian. If she could not be his wife in name, she would be in spirit. Their child would have a name that belonged to them. And Sophia would teach her, or him, to look up into the night sky and think of the man who she had loved and who had loved her back so much he'd sacrificed his own life so that she and their child could have a future.

True to his word, the professor had arranged for his

niece to meet Sophia. Svetlana took her in, and together they built a life. Two young women trained in art restoration at the most prestigious museum in the world opened an antique restoration shop in New York City and worked on tables and chairs and inexpensive studio paintings and made a modest living while they raised their children.

The Depression came, and with it terrible memories of Petrograd and the revolution. But Sophia had her treasure and thought it would see her through.

When the building they rented became available, Sophia and Lana sold the paintings they'd smuggled out of Russia, but it wasn't quite enough. So Sophia took the tiara to a jeweler on Fifth Avenue. It was time to sell it and ensure their future. Yes, she'd gotten a little money for the diamonds. And it helped her and Lana buy this building and set up their own shop. But she hadn't gotten the kind of money that she'd expected, that Carpathian had suggested the tiara was worth—that was another dream. The jeweler said the sapphires were paste. Had Carpathian known? Had he switched them for the real stones? Would he have done that? Why? Or had he just assumed when he'd repaired the tiara that the stones were authentic and never focused on them? Or had the stones been switched by someone else during the time between when they had been confiscated and when Carpathian had stolen the tiara back?

She sold the stones but wouldn't sell the frame even though the jeweler wanted it. The silver skeleton, a necklace with enamel eggs, a letter and a photo, along with a battered copy of Pushkin was all she had left of Carpathian. A meager inheritance. But enough memories to last a lifetime.

Sophia never stopped wondering what had happened to Carpathian. And she never met a man to spend her life with. She never got the official date of Carpathian's death. Over three hundred thousand men died in the purges. And the Soviets cared nothing for preserving their names for their families.

And then one day, in the winter of 1947, after so many years, she was crossing the street, and saw the past waiting for her. She was suddenly so close to a time so far away.

Sophia saw Dimitry on the other side of the street. And knew exactly who he was—the man who had slept with Carpathian's wife. The man who had survived when Carpathian had not. Sophia always had wondered, because of the letters exchanged between her and Carpathian—and because she had possession of an imperial jewel, if Dimitry would come to claim it. She'd wondered for years if he was the assailant back on that day in Petrograd who had come up behind her and tried to grab the tiara away from her. She wanted to finally confront Dimitry. Accuse him. She wanted to watch him deny it so she would know once and for all what had happened. So she stepped out to cross the street, and that's when the car hit her. She heard the screech and then felt the thud. A sudden jolt and pressure. And pain. And then everything was dark, cold and quiet.

Chapter 33

Isobelle Moon
London
January 1949

Jules and I fly to London in a private plane his mother arranged. It is the most turbulent flight I've ever endured. If I wasn't anxious enough before, I'm quite a mess of nerves now.

From the moment we discovered the missing tiara in the conference room at the society, we have been moving fast, trying to keep pace with the man claiming to be my father and to make sense of each new discovery along the way. We have no idea when during the presentation he might have fled. So, depending on what point in the recording that he left the room, he could have been on his way back to Cannes by the time we realized he was missing.

Jules and his mother acted quickly, and within minutes,

they were able to piece together Zorin's escape from various people he encountered—two of whom he hurt badly on his way off the island.

The Midas Society receptionist told us that Sergei Zorin had come out of the conference room, claimed he was having a claustrophobic reaction to being underground, and asked if he could go up to the ground level to get some fresh air.

Of course, she sent the elevator up for him.

We were then able to track Zorin's passage once he made it to ground level. He approached the guard who had earlier seen him come in with Madame Tavel and was unprepared for Zorin's attack. After stunning that guard, Zorin did the same to the next guard. Then apparently, he bypassed the private dock and made his way to the general dock, where he boarded a waiting ferry.

Using as detailed a description as we all could give her, Madame Tavel was able to describe Sergei Zorin to the dock master that she learned he had hired one of the taxis always waiting at the ferry station. More phone calls led to Madame learning he'd found his way to the small Cannes airport. From there, he was able to find a private plane with a pilot who had some time on his hands and could use the extra cash and fly him to London.

As our plane heads to our destination, Jules and I wonder if Zorin's head start will give him enough time to find the right size map. Because on our way to the airport, Jules realized that was the missing piece of this puzzle. Finding the correct location depends on having the one particular map that lines up correctly with the tiara. And the jeweler didn't mention that on the tape. Just knowing the treasure is in an unnamed cemetery won't help Zorin much. There are dozens of cemeteries in London.

Jules' mother stayed behind in Cannes in order to contact her Russian client. Not only to alert him that Zorin was on his way but to find out where the tomb was because I want to be there if he shows up.

There are a million chances this will all go wrong. That Madame Tavel won't reach her client, and that Sergei Zorin will find the right size map and steal the treasure and be long gone before anyone can stop him.

On the ride into the city, I'm obsessed with re-writing history. If only I could turn back the clock and not answer the door that day when he came to meet me. Or if I refused to talk to him. Or go back further and never start to renovate my mother's bedroom. Or even further and force her to tell me about her past, to show me the tiara. To get to the bottom of what it was.

When we land at the airport at three that afternoon, we're met by an airport official Madame Tavel had contacted. He immediately ushers us to a private office so Jules can call his mother and find out if she's been able to reach her client.

Jules listens to his mother for a moment, then asks the official for some paper and a pen. He takes down some information and then Jules hurries off the call.

"My mother's ordered a car and driver to be at our disposal and take us to our final destination. He should be just outside," Jules says as he folds up the piece of paper, then takes my hand and leads me out of the airport.

"What did you find out?" I ask.

"Let's get in the car first," he says. "We have at least a forty-minute drive ahead of us. I'll explain once we are on our way."

Inside the Mercedes, Jules gives the driver the address his mother gave him after contacting her London client.

"North Lodge, Old Brompton Road in West Brompton."

"Right you are, mate," the driver says, and we're off.

Within minutes, we've hit highway traffic.

"Where is this place we're going? Is the client going to meet us there? Is he already there waiting for Zorin? With the police? What's going to happen?"

Jules stares at me for a moment as if he's not sure where to start. Then gives me one of his half-smiles. "Yes, right. A million questions. Now for some answers, but not necessarily in that order. My mother got in touch with her client. He gave her the location where we're going. Apparently, there is a map of London that fits behind the tiara hidden under the silk lining in the tiara's leather case. If we had known that all this would be—"

I can't help thinking that we had everything we needed all along, but don't say it now. "But we didn't know it. How does the client know where the tomb is if we had the tiara all the time?"

"Maybe from when Fabergé showed him how to use the tiara, but I don't know for sure. My mother didn't explain that. Only that he's about as far from the destination as we are. He could get there before us or not—it all depends on traffic. As for Zorin, we have no idea how long it will take him to hit on a map that's the right size and lines up over a cemetery. If he's lucky he could get there before all of us."

Jules leans forward a little toward the driver.

"Do you know anything about where we're going?"

"A bit, sir. Brompton Cemetery is the only one in London designated as a Crown cemetery..."

I look at Jules, and we exchange a glance.

"A Crown cemetery?" Jules asks.

The driver nods. "It means the cemetery is owned by

the Crown and managed by the Royal Parks. Brompton dates back to 1840 when it was consecrated by Charles James Blomfield, Bishop of London. It is one of the most highly regarded of the seven garden cemeteries in our city. If I remember correctly, it has over a hundred and fifty thousand resting places. But it's the gardens themselves that make it as much of a tourist destination as a place to go and pay your respects to the dead. That's why I know so much about it... I'm a bit of an amateur gardener myself. Brompton is a sixteen-hectare haven for nature lovers. There are dozens of species of trees, wooded areas and meadows, filled with snowdrops and bluebells, wild lupin, and broad-leaf pea, depending on the season. Once the land was used for market gardens, and you can still find wild cabbages, asparagus, and garlic growing. Some people come to bird watch and others to study the butterflies."

Jules and I exchange another glance. This is far more information than we expected.

"So what kind of tomb are we looking for once we get there?" I ask Jules.

He shifts his eyes to the driver. "I'll know it when I see it based on what my mother said."

"And what if Zorin gets there first? What if he's already gotten in and is gone?"

"If luck is on our side, he won't have. That's all we can hope for. And that our client called ahead and the cemetery guards are positioned at the gates waiting for him."

I'm nodding. Taking it all in. The traffic is brutal. We are barely moving. And my frustration is overwhelming.

"Jules?"

"Yes?"

"Is there any possibility that Zorin is my father? That my mother knew he wasn't dead but given what kind of man he was, she was protecting us from him ever finding us? Maybe she knew he was going to try to steal what was hers, what the duchess wanted her to have and that's why she changed her name and hid the tiara away."

"I think you're stretching here," Jules says as he leans toward me and takes me in his arms. I bury my face in his neck and smell his wonderful, familiar scent. He smooths down my hair and holds me.

"Maybe he was different before the Revolution and then when he changed—"

"Isobelle"—he rubs my back—"anything is possible, but…"

I can hear the doubt in his voice, but part of me isn't ready to give up that one shred of hope.

"Did your mother tell you what your father was like when they met? Do you even know how they met?" Jules asks.

"Yes. My mother was a nurse during the First World War. The hospitals were so desperate for help, most girls, including the grand duchesses, became nurses, even if they had no previous training. They learned on the job. My mother had developed a crush on a patient in a coma and used to read to him every morning and evening before she left for the day. My father was also a patient there. His cot was in the row behind the man in the coma and he'd listen to her reading. One night the man in the coma died. The next morning, when my mother arrived and discovered her patient's passing, she was disconsolate. My father tried to comfort her. He told her he had come to relish listening to her reading and asked her to continue. To read to him instead. And she did. He called her his 'little Scheherazade.'"

"What was he in the hospital for?"

"I'm not sure she ever told me that," I say. Then I

remember. "Yes, she did. My mother did tell me. He was in the hospital because he'd gotten frostbite and had two toes on his right foot amputated."

"Two toes?" Jules asks.

"Yes."

"You said his right foot?"

"Yes, my mother told me he used to make a joke that his right foot had become his wrong foot."

"Isobelle, at the skating rink. I saw it was his right sock that got soaked. I saw him take it off. If he was missing toes…" The expression on Jules' face is grave, and I know it's time to let go of the single shred of hope I was holding on to.

Chapter 34

Isobelle Moon
London
January 1949

The traffic finally opens up, and we speed through the streets until we reach the cemetery gates where a young man appears to be waiting for us beside a guardhouse. He's wearing gardener's clothes.

"Are you Jules Reed?" he asks.

Jules nods.

"Right then, why don't you come this way."

He looks to the gatehouse, where a uniformed guard is on duty. "Radio me if he shows up," he says, and we start to follow him.

"The name is Harry Riley. Head gardener here. I've got instructions to bring you to the Monument."

"What monument is that?" Jules asks.

We're on a twisting path through a wooded area lined with lovely old pine trees. It's cold, but there's no snow on the ground. I hear birdsong up above our heads. It's late afternoon and dusk is falling, the sky a milky lavender already. Every sound makes me turn. A twig breaking. A rock rolling. A dog's bark in the distance.

"It's called The Monument for Hannah Courtoy, an unmarried mother of two daughters. It's all very mysterious. There is a keyhole on the monument but no key. We don't think anyone has opened the door in almost a hundred years, but we can't be sure. All we know for certain is Miss Courtoy died in 1848, but the construction of the tomb wasn't completed for another five years. They say that Mr. Samuel Warner, who was an inventor, and Mr. Joseph Bonomi, who was an architect and Egyptologist, built the tomb to be a time machine."

"A what?" I don't think I've understood him correctly.

"Yes, a time machine. The two of them were quite serious about it. They studied time travel and what they called teleportation. There are five more plinths like this one in other cemeteries in London and one in Paris, France. Warner's papers say that if used correctly these monuments will allow you to travel through time. Both men made sure that they were laid to rest nearby. Warner is buried near to the Courtoy plinth. And Bonomi's tombstone, which is just sixty feet away, has very similar hieroglyphics on it. There's a story that Warner was murdered to prevent him from implementing his designs for the teleportation device."

We walk down a slight incline. Twilight has not yet descended, and there's more than enough light to make out the monument. I recall my studies of Egyptian architecture and identify this as a temple-pylon made of polished granite, at least twenty feet high with deeply engraved bands of hieroglyphics encircling its circumference.

A man, who Harry Riley acknowledges with a call out, stands to the side of the monument. "No sign of anyone else. But if Bobby does spot your man, he's going to radio me. And I'll come up with some of the boys. You sure you don't want to call the police in on this?"

"I'm certain. Thank you, Harry," the man says in a deep-throated voice that is heavy with a Russian accent.

As he steps forward toward me, the first thing I notice is his accentuated limp. He looks at me, studies me, his eyes traveling over my face. He takes one more step closer and reaches out for both my hands just as Harry's radio crackles to life.

We can all hear the voice on the other end.

"Someone has just come through the gate. Heading your way. And we're right behind him."

The Russian gestures to Jules, Harry, and me to come with him and leads us behind the monument into deep shadows. I can smell the cold now, along with pine and the smell, impossibly of roses, the perfume that my mother always wore.

"We watch. Be quiet," the Russian whispers. "When Zorin arrives, you let me go to him but be ready"—he looks at Jules and Harry—"in case he has a weapon. Harry, give Mr. Reed one of your shovels."

I want to laugh at the absurdity of the arsenal of garden tools stacked up on the backside of the Egyptian plinth. There are four heavy-looking metal shovels, a rake, and a hose, coiled.

After the Russian finishes giving orders, we wait in silence. I can hear my own heartbeat. A crow caws somewhere deeper in the cemetery. Thanks to the late hour, the shadows offer us cover. Finally, we hear footsteps sound.

Far away. Then closer. And then closer.

The man who I thought was my father is standing in front of the plinth. Staring at it. He is holding the tiara and pulling apart the head band.

I don't mean to, but I gasp audibly seeing the piece released. Sergei Zorin, if that is even his name, looks around, trying to place the sound.

The Russian steps out in front of our hiding place.

"Dimitry Zorin?" he says.

Dimitry? Wasn't that the name of the man in the photo I found in my mother's bedroom?

The man who said he was my father, who had called himself Sergei Zorin, turns. "You," he spits out. "I knew it was your voice on the tape. But you were supposed to have died in Siberia."

"Okay then, I died. So now I am a ghost come to haunt you for what you have done and what you are attempting to do. For pretending to be me so you could steal something else that didn't belong to me. Like my wife, eh?"

Before the man whose name we now know is Dimitry can respond, the guard and head gardener come up behind him and grab hold of his arms, twisting them behind his back. The tiara and the silver over gold key fall to the ground. Dimitry struggles to break free, but the men have him in their grip. He's not giving up easily, trying to kick them, to no avail.

Harry pulls out a rope and starts to tie Dimitry Zorin's right wrist and then his left.

The Russian client reaches down and picks up first the tiara and then the key. I notice how he holds them both so reverently, almost caressing them with his long graceful fingers, with his jeweler's hands, hands that someone could describe as beautiful, I think remembering how my mother had once described them to me.

"I'll take these," the Russian says to Dimitry Zorin. "We're going to turn you over to the French police for your antics at the Midas Society. You'll be charged with petty larceny and assault only. But believe me, we will not hesitate to make sure you are charged with far more serious offenses and put away for much longer if you ever try to contact me or my daughter again. Is that clear?"

Chapter 35

Isobelle Moon
London
January 1949

We are in a cozy living room in the Notting Hill section of London. Jules and I are seated on a couch. The Russian, whose name is in fact Sergei Zorin, sits opposite me. The man who is my father. Who has, in the last thirty minutes, learned about me, about my quest, and that the woman he has loved for all of his life lost hers. There have been tears. And smiles. And finally, like the Russian he is, he's made us tea, the Russian way, and also brought out vodka and shot glasses and a plate of savory biscuits. The tiara is on the same table as the food and drink, its silver skeleton gleaming in the light.

"I have a question," I say.

"How unusual," Jules teases.

Sergei Zorin looks confused.

"You'll soon learn that Isobelle is never wanting for questions. She has an endless supply."

"I look forward to getting to know that about you, and more," he says. "It makes it just a little bit easier to accept that my Sofiya is gone… I have lost her but found you. So what did you want to ask?"

"Do you know what happened to the sapphires?"

"What do you mean?" Sergei Zorin asks.

"When my mother went to sell the stones in the tiara to help her and my aunt buy the building they wanted for their shop and home, she discovered the diamonds were real— but not worth much because of their size. And the sapphires, which should have brought in a lot because they were so large, were paste."

Sergei Zorin shakes his head. "The sapphires in the tiara were real when I took it from the Bolshevik vault in 1922 and gave it back to your mother. I am certain of that."

"Well, when she took them to Mr. Reed, they were paste."

Jules makes a small sound halfway between a cough and a sigh.

I turn. "What is it?"

"You never asked. I never told you. It never came up. But the reason my grandfather is incarcerated is for stealing stones out of jewelry he was repairing or appraising and replacing them with paste. I'm sorry…" Jules runs his hand over his eyes. "I'm so, so sorry Isobelle, it never occurred to me to ask him."

"I'm not sure I understand," I say.

"I certainly don't know for sure, but based on what you are saying"—he nods to Sergei Zorin—"the stones were real when Mrs. Moon left Europe. The next person who had anything to do with the tiara was my grandfather, who declared the sapphires fake but bought them anyway along with the diamonds."

"But he's such a warm man—" I'm at a loss.

"Who has done some very illegal things. His charm is one of the reasons it took so long for his deeds to catch up to him. I'm sorry, Isobelle. I promise I'll make it up to you."

I shake my head. "You're not responsible."

"Not directly, but it is my shop now, and it has prospered to the degree it has because of many such thefts."

We're both quiet for a few moments.

"Your grandfather is an amazingly innovative jeweler, Jules. I've been aware of his work for years, and I hope that he can go back to doing his life's work," Sergei Zorin says.

I know I need to start thinking of Sergei Zorin as my father, but until this morning—was it really only this morning?—I thought another man was my father.

"I do too," Jules says. "So does he. He certainly seems to want to make amends. Turning over the business to me was the first one. When he gets out of prison, he won't return to being an owner at Reed's, he will come back as head designer. I just hope he's reformed."

"Sometimes people do. Sometimes, though..." Sergei Zorin shrugs.

"Are you thinking of Dimitry?" I ask.

He nods. "He was my cousin. We grew up together. I didn't even know he was still alive. So many didn't make it..." He shakes his head. "My own cousin, and he betrayed me in every way possible...right up to today." He shakes his head again. "But..." There's a light in his eyes. Hope, where in most men there would only be anger. "Tomorrow," he says, "we will go back and open the tomb and reclaim a much greater treasure."

"So you know what is inside?" I ask.

"Ah, yes. Mr. Fabergé sent me to place it here on behalf of the tsar in 1914."

"What is it?" Jules asks.

"A wonderful Fabergé egg called The Tiara Egg. It has never been seen. We made it expressly to put away for the future. The egg is dark red enamel decorated with gold trim and ropes of rose-cut diamonds. It opens like a jewel case with a gold clasp to reveal a tiara sitting on a cushion. There is value in the style, design, and materials, of course. But the real value is in the cushion that the tiny tiara sits on… it's a forty-carat diamond cut like a pillow. Worth a fortune. A legacy from the tsar to his daughter so that no matter what happened, she would always have something to sell if necessary."

"A forty-carat diamond?" Jules' eyes shine. "I want to see that."

"And so you shall."

He smiles at Jules, then at me. "The two of you? Are together?"

I hold my breath. I don't want to assume anything. I can only guess how Jules will answer.

"We are. At least I hope…" Jules looks at me.

I nod.

"Well, that diamond is too big for an engagement ring, but if I remember correctly, the miniature tiara sitting on the cushion is actually a ring with a ruby center stone that is of some value in its own right."

I turn and look at Jules. He takes my hand and gives me his wonderful half-smile.

"As beautiful as that sounds," I say, "I can't keep any part of the egg." I turn to Jules. "I'd like you to take the egg to the Midas Society. I'd like you to learn who it belongs to and return the treasure to them. It will be your fifth case."

The half-smile becomes a full one, and he squeezes my hand.

"That won't be necessary," Sergei Zorin says. "You are the rightful owner, Isobelle. The duchess gifted your mother the tiara, knowing full well, I suspect, what it was. She must have feared the worst was coming for her, her sisters, brother, and parents and wanted someone with a chance at surviving to be its caretaker. To see to at least this part of the royal family's legacy."

Jules nods. "If the duchess gave the tiara to Sophia Moon, then yes, both the tiara and the treasure in the tomb belong to Sophia's heir."

"I could never accept a Fabergé egg. I know how valuable they are. It needs to be in a museum," I insist.

"We can figure all that out afterwards," Sergei Zorin says. "First, we must retrieve the egg from inside the tomb. We can do that tomorrow. Tonight," he says, "I will tell you the tale of how I met your mother and how the story has its ending here. A sad and happy ending at the same time."

I'm looking at him, and because of how the light in the room has shifted or because of everything he's said, this time I see the man in the old black and white photograph I found behind the wallpaper. I see the man my mother fell in love with. And most astonishing of all, I see myself in my father's face.

"When Sofiya Petrovitch was nineteen years old, she volunteered—along with her friends the Grand Duchesses Olga and Tatiana—to be nurses…"

Afterword

"Isobelle, can you hear me?"

Sophia watches her daughter, asleep in her childhood bed. She has returned to New York from London with Jules and her father, who even now is sleeping in the half-renovated bedroom next door. Yes, Carpathian is sleeping in Sophia's bed, and she is astonished with the amazement of that.

Sophia smooths her daughter's ebony curls, sees her stir and smile, but not wake. Not yet. Sophia feels her daughter's peace, and so at last, her own. She thinks that this is probably the last time she will reach out to Isobelle in this way, but she wants to sing her a final lullaby so Isobelle can have its comfort to hold on to. Not just for now but for the future when she is married to Jules, for when they have their own daughter. Because Sophia knows, without knowing how, that they will have a daughter, and that Isobelle will go on to build magnificent buildings, and Jules will make beautiful jewelry. And while their life will not always be easy, it will be filled with enough joys to mitigate its pains.

Isobelle turns on her side, her right hand coming out from under the coverlet, and oh so carefully, Sophia takes it and holds it in her own. Does her daughter feel her touch, Sophia wonders?

Outside, the first tangerine colors of dawn tease the edges of the drapes. Sophia knows it is time for her to go now, and so she speaks her last.

"That December night, after I stepped out into the street, after the car hit me, as I lay there, all I could think about was how sorry I was that I hadn't told you my story and that you might never learn it. If I had thought your father was still alive, I would not have kept it to myself. But I was wrong. You deserved to know, you curious darling, you determined soul. I am so glad you found my meager clue and it led you to the answers to your endless questions that I brushed off with a wave of my hand and a curt caution that: we can never go back, so why do you need to know?

"But now that you have found your father, you have found your story. Our story. You and your Jules have solved the mystery. You have the map to my secret city—which is finally yours to walk through and discover. Now you can go forward with Jules—planning your future together with your father and Jules' mother and his grandfather by your side.

"And I? I will finally be able to rest. Please tell your father that I still miss him deeply. That I never ceased loving him or thinking about him. Tell him that I never stopped looking up at the moon. And now when you both look up, into that vast black velvet sky full of sparkling diamond stars and spheres, know I will be there looking down and our family, in our way, will be together again for all time."

Acknowledgements

To Liz Berry. For a million reasons, what would I do without you? As a business partner, brainstormer, beta reader, and trusted and beloved friend. When I came to this crossroad and didn't know what to do, you did, and I will forever be grateful.

To Rose Tozer, the senior librarian at the Gemological Institute of America for her tireless help and enthusiasm for this project. You gave me so much of your time during both the research and writing phases. From looking up what sapphires might have cost in 1948 to photographing the 1922 and 1925 Fersman Catalogs, I truly would have been lost without you.

To my dear friend Jillian Stein, who has joined our little cabal at Evil Eye Corp. and whose talents show off my books better than I could have imagined anyone could.

To Sarah Branham, the very best editor. If this book shines, it is because of your insights, advice and yes, tough love. As well as Kasi Alexander and Chelle Olsen who went over and beyond and made so much of a difference.

To Alan Dingman for all of my beautiful covers, especially this one.

To Ann-Marie Nevis and Jennifer Watson, PR experts par excellence, your efforts and integrity are legion. I am so lucky to have you both on my team.

To Steve Berry who helped me figure out the most complicated aspect of the plot and to Doug Scofield who helped me figure out the physical mystery of the tiara itself.

To my agent Dan Conaway for your support through the easy times and the tough. And to everyone at Writers House for all your hard work.

To Natalie White who is my right hand and my left hand at AuthorBuzz.com—without you I wouldn't have the sanity or the time to write.

To all the amazing jewelry experts who have shared their wisdom (some of whom I am now lucky enough to count as friends): Marion Fasel (and Hunter), Daniel Morris, Hilary and Ben Macklowe, Simon Teakle, Warren Lagerloef and the team at Gemx Club for providing so much entertainment and inspiration.

To Randy Susan Meyers, Alyson Richman, Jess Bird, Lucinda Riley, Linda Francis Lee and C.W. Gortner who all listened to me panic over this book and even though I already knew it, proved again what wonderful friends you are.

About M.J. Rose

New York Times bestseller M.J. Rose (www.mjrose.com) grew up in New York City mostly in the labyrinthine galleries of the Metropolitan Museum, the dark tunnels and lush gardens of Central Park and reading her mother's favorite books before she was allowed. She believes mystery and magic are all around us but we are too often too busy to notice... books that exaggerate mystery and magic draw attention to it and remind us to look for it and revel in it.

Rose's work has appeared in many magazines including *Oprah* magazine and she has been featured in the *New York Times, Newsweek, Wall Street Journal, Time, USA Today* and on the Today Show, and NPR radio. Rose graduated from Syracuse University, spent the '80s in advertising, has a commercial in the Museum of Modern Art in New York City and since 2005 has run the first marketing company for authors - Authorbuzz.com. She is also the co-founder of Evil Eye Corp.

Rose lives in Connecticut with her husband, the musician and composer Doug Scofield.